the FIRE SERMON

the FIRE SERMON

FRANCESCA HAIG

HARPER
Voyager

HarperCollins*Publishers*
1 London Bridge Street
London SE1 9GF

www.harpercollins.co.uk

Published by Harper*Voyager*
An imprint of HarperCollins*Publishers* 2015
1

A catalogue record for this book
is available from the British Library

HB ISBN: 978 00 0 756305 0
TPB ISBN: 978 00 0 811767 2

Set in Janson Text
Typeset by Palimpsest Book Production Ltd, Falkirk, Stirlingshire

Printed and bound in Great Britain by
Clays Ltd, St Ives plc

This book is dedicated, with love and admiration, to my brother, Peter, and my sister, Clara. Knowing how much they mean to me, it should come as no surprise that my first novel is about siblings.

CHAPTER 1

I'd always thought they would come for me at night, but it was the hottest part of the day when the six men rode onto the plain. It was harvest time; the whole settlement had been up early, and would be working late. Decent harvests were never guaranteed on the blighted land permitted to Omegas. Last season, heavy rains had released deeply buried blast-ash in the earth. The root vegetables had come up tiny, or not at all. A whole field of potatoes grew downwards - we found them, blind-eyed and shrunken, five feet under the mucky surface. A boy drowned digging for them. The pit was only a few yards deep but the clay wall gave way and he never came up. I'd thought of moving on, but all the valleys were rain-clogged, and no settlement welcomed strangers in a hungry season.

So I'd stayed through the bleak year. The others swapped stories about the drought, when the crops had failed three years in a row. I'd only been a child, then, but even I remembered seeing the carcasses of starved cattle, sailing the dust-fields on rafts of their own bones. But that was more than a decade ago. *This won't be as bad as the drought years*, we said to one another, as if repetition would make it true. The next spring, we watched the stalks in the wheat fields carefully. The early crops came up strong, and the long, engorged carrots we dug that year were the source of much giggling amongst the younger teenagers. From my own small plot I harvested a fat sack of garlic which I carried to market in my arms like a baby. All spring I watched the wheat in the shared fields growing sturdy and tall. The lavender behind my cottage was giddy with bees and, inside, my shelves were loaded with food.

It was mid-harvest when they came. I felt it first. Had been feeling it, if I were honest with myself, for months. But now I sensed it clearly, a sudden alertness that I could never explain to anybody who wasn't a seer. It was a feeling of something shifting: like a cloud moving across the sun, or the wind changing direction. I straightened, scythe in hand, and looked south. By the time the shouts came, from the far end of the settlement, I was already running. As the cry went up and the six mounted men galloped into sight, the others ran too – it wasn't uncommon for Alphas to raid Omega settlements, stealing anything of value. But I knew what they were after. I knew, too, that there was little point in running. That I was six months too late to heed my mother's warning. Even as I ducked the fence and sprinted toward the boulder-strewn edge of the settlement, I knew they would get me.

They barely slowed to grab me. One simply scooped me up as I ran, snatching the earth from under my feet. He knocked the scythe from my hand with a blow to my wrist and threw me face-down across the front of the saddle. When I kicked out, it only seemed to spur the horse to greater speed. The jarring, as I bounced on my ribs and guts, was more painful than the blow had been. A strong hand was on my back, and I could feel the man's body over mine as he leaned forward, pressing the horse onwards. I opened my eyes, but shut them again swiftly when I was greeted by the upside-down view of the hoof-whipped ground bolting by.

Just when we seemed to be slowing and I dared to open my eyes again, I felt the insistent tip of a blade at my back.

'We're under orders not to kill you,' he said. 'Not even to knock you out, your twin said. But anything short of that, we won't hesitate, if you give us any trouble. I'll start by slicing a finger off, and you'd better believe I wouldn't even stop riding to do it. Understand, Cassandra?'

I tried to say yes, managed a breathless grunt.

We rode on. From the endless jolting and the hanging upside down, I was sick twice – the second time on his leather boot, I noted with some satisfaction. Cursing, he stopped his mount and hauled me upright, looping a rope around my body so that my arms were bound at my sides. Sitting in front of him, the pressure in my head was eased as the blood flowed back down to my body. The rope cut into my arms but at least it held me steady, grasped firmly by the man at my back. We travelled that way for the rest of the day. At nightfall, when the dark was slipping over the horizon like a noose, we stopped briefly and dismounted to eat. Another of the men offered me bread but I could manage only a few sips from the water flask, the water warm and musty. Then I was again hoisted up, in front of a different man now, his black beard prickling the back of my neck. He pulled a sack over my head, but in the darkness it made little difference.

I sensed the city in the distance, long before the clang of hoofs beneath us indicated that we'd reached paved roads. Through the sacking covering my face, glints of light began to show. I could feel the presence of people all about me – more even than at Haven on market day. Thousands of them, I guessed. The road steepened as we rode on, slowly now, the hoofs noisy on cobbles. Then we halted, and I was passed, almost tossed, down to another man, who dragged me, stumbling, for several minutes, pausing often while doors were unlocked. Each time we moved on, I heard the doors being locked again behind us. Each scrape of a bolt sliding back was like another blow.

Finally, I was pushed down onto a soft surface. I heard a rasp of metal behind me, a knife sliding from a sheath. Before I had time to cry out, the rope around my body fell away, slit. Hands fumbled at my neck, and the sack was ripped from my head, the rough hessian grazing my nose. I was on a low bed, in a small room. A cell. There was no window. The man who'd untied me was already locking the metal door behind him.

Slumped on the bed, the taste of mud and vomit in my mouth, I finally allowed myself to cry. Partly for myself, and partly for my twin; for what he'd become.

CHAPTER 2

The next morning, as usual, I woke from dreams of fire.

As the months passed, the moments after such dreams were the only times I was grateful to wake to the confines of the cell. The room's greyness, the familiarity of its implacable walls, were the opposite of the vast and savage excess of the blast I dreamed of nightly.

There were no written tales or pictures of the blast. What was the point of writing it, or drawing it, when it was etched on every surface? Even now, more than four hundred years after it had destroyed everything, it was still visible in every tumbled cliff, scorched plain, and ash-clogged river. Every face. It had become the only story the earth could tell, so who else would record it? A history written in ashes, in bones. Before the blast, they say there'd been sermons about fire, about the end of the world. The fire itself gave the last sermon; after that there were no more.

Most who survived were deafened and blinded. Many others found themselves alone – if they told their stories, it was only to the wind. And even if they had companions, no survivor could ever properly describe the moment it happened: the new colour of the sky, the roar of sound that ended everything. Struggling to describe it, the survivors would have found themselves, like me, stranded in that space where words ran out and sound began.

The blast shattered time. In an instant, it cleaved time irrevocably into Before and After. Now, hundreds of years later, in the After, no survivors remained, no testimonies. Only seers like me could glimpse it, momentarily, in the instant before waking, or when it ambushed us in the half-second of a blink: the flash, the horizon burning up like paper.

The only tales of the blast were sung by the bards. When I was a child, the bard who passed through the village each autumn sang of other nations, across the sea, sending the flame down from the sky, and of the radiation and the Long Winter that had followed. I must have been eight or nine when, at Haven market, Zach and I heard an older bard with frost-grey hair singing the same tune but with different words. The chorus about the Long Winter was the same, but she made no mention of other nations. Each verse she sang just described the fire, and how it had consumed everything.

When I'd pulled our father's hand and asked him, he'd shrugged. There were lots of versions of the song, he said. What difference did it make? If there'd once been other lands, across the sea, there were no longer, as far as any sailor had lived to tell. The occasional rumours of Elsewhere, countries over the sea, were only rumours – no more to be believed than the rumours about an island where Omegas lived free of Alpha oppression. To be overheard speculating about such things was to invite public flogging, or to end up in the stocks, like the Omega we'd once seen outside Haven, pinned under the scathing sun until his tongue was a scaled blue lizard protruding from his mouth, while two bored Council soldiers kept watch, kicking him from time to time to ensure he was still alive.

Don't ask questions, our father said; not about the Before, not about Elsewhere, not about the island. People in the Before asked too many questions, probed too far, and look what that got them. This is the world now, or all we'll ever know of it: bounded by the sea to the north, west, and south; the deadlands to the east. And it made no difference where the blast came from. All that mattered was that it came. It was all so long ago, as unknowable as the Before that it had destroyed, and from which only rumours and ruins remained.

*

In my first months in the cell, I was granted the occasional gift of sky. Every few weeks, in the company of other imprisoned Omegas, I was escorted on to the ramparts for some exercise and a few moments of fresh air. We were taken in groups of three, with at least as many guards. They watched us carefully, keeping us not only apart but also well away from the crenellations that overlooked the city below. The first outing, I'd learned not to try to approach the other prisoners, let alone to speak. As the guards escorted us up from the cells, one of them had grumbled about the slow pace of the pale-haired prisoner, hopping on one leg. 'I'd be quicker if you hadn't taken away my cane,' she'd pointed out. They didn't respond, and she'd rolled her eyes at me. It wasn't even a smile, but it was the first hint of warmth I'd seen since entering the Keeping Rooms. When we reached the ramparts, I'd tried to sidle close enough to her to attempt a whisper. I was still ten feet from her when the guards tackled me against the wall so hard that my shoulder-blades were bruised against the stone. As they hustled me back down to the cell one of them spat at me. 'Don't talk to the others,' he said. 'Don't even look at them, do you hear?' With my arms held behind my back, I couldn't wipe his spittle from my cheek. Its warmth was a foul intimacy. I never saw the woman again.

A month or more later was my third outing to the ramparts, and the last for any of us. I was standing by the door, letting my eyes accustom to the glint of sun on polished stone. Two guards stood to my right, chatting quietly. Twenty feet to my left, another guard leaned against the wall, watching a male Omega. He'd been in the Keeping Rooms longer than me, I guessed. His skin, which must once have been dark, was now a dirty grey. More telling were the twitchy motions of his hands, and the way he kept moving his lips, as if they didn't fit over his gums. The whole time we'd been up there, he had walked backwards and forth on the same small patch of stones, dragging his twisted right leg. Despite the interdiction on speaking to one another, I could periodically hear his muttered counting: *Two hundred and forty-seven. Two hundred and forty-eight.*

Everyone knew that many seers went mad – that over years the visions burned our minds away. The visions were flame, and we were the wick. This man wasn't a seer, but it didn't surprise me that anyone held for long enough in the Keeping Rooms would go mad. What chance, then, for me, contending with the visions at the same time as the unrelenting walls of my cell? In a year or two, I thought, that might be me, counting out my footsteps as if the neatness of numbers could impose some order on a broken mind.

Between me and the pacing man was another prisoner,

perhaps a few years older than me, a one-armed woman with dark hair and a cheerful face. It was the second time we'd been taken to the ramparts together. I walked as close to the edge of the ramparts as the guards would allow, and stared beyond the sandstone crenellations as I tried to contrive some way that I might speak or signal to her. I couldn't get close enough to the edge to get a proper look at the city that unfolded beneath the mountainside fort. The horizon was curtailed by the ramparts, beyond which I could see only the hills, painted grey with distance.

I realised the counting had stopped. By the time I'd turned around to see what had changed, the older Omega had already rushed at the woman and gripped her neck between his hands. With only one arm she couldn't fight hard enough or cry out quickly enough. The guards reached them while I was still yards away, and in seconds they'd pulled him off her, but it was too late.

I'd closed my eyes to block the sight of her body, face down on the flagstones, head turned sideways at an impossible angle. But for a seer there's no refuge behind closed eyelids. In my shuddering mind I saw what else happened at precisely the moment that she died: a hundred feet above us, inside the fort, a glass of wine dropped, sharding red over a marble floor. A man in a velvet jacket fell backwards, scrambled for a second to his knees, and died, his hands to his neck.

After that, there were no more trips to the ramparts. Sometimes I thought I could hear the mad Omega shouting and thrashing the walls, but it was only a dull thud, a throb in the night. I never knew whether I was really hearing it, or just sensing it.

Inside my cell, it was almost never dark. A glass ball suspended in the ceiling gave off a pale light. It was lit constantly, and emitted off a slight buzz, so low that I some-times wondered whether it was just a ringing in my own ears. For the first few days I watched it nervously, waiting for it to burn out and leave me in total darkness. But this was no candle, not even an oil lamp. The light it gave off was different: cooler, and unwavering. Its sterile light only faltered every few weeks, when it would flicker for several seconds and disappear, leaving me in a formless black world. But it never lasted more than one or two minutes. Each time the light would return, blinking a couple of times, like somebody waking from sleep, before resuming its vigil. I came to welcome these intermittent breakdowns. They were the only interruptions from the light's ceaseless glare.

This must be the Electric, I supposed. I'd heard the stories: it was like a kind of magic, the key to most of the technology from the Before. Whatever it had been, though, it was supposed to be gone now. Any machines not already destroyed in the blast had been done away with in the purges that followed, when the survivors had destroyed all traces of the technology that had brought the world to ash. All remnants of the Before were taboo, but none more than the machines. And while the penalties for breaking the taboo were brutal, the law was mainly policed by fear alone. The danger was inscribed on the surface of our scorched world, and on the twisted bodies of the Omegas. We needed no reminders.

But here was a machine, a piece of the Electric, hanging from the ceiling of my cell. Not anything terrifying or powerful, like the things people whispered about. Not a weapon, or a bomb, or even a carriage that could move without a horse. Just this glass bulb, the size of my fist, blaring light at the top of my cell. I couldn't stop staring at it, the knot of extreme brightness at its core, sharply white, as though a spark from the blast itself were captured there. I stared at it for so long that when I closed my eyes the bright shape of it was etched on my eyelids' darkness. I was fascinated, and appalled, wincing beneath the light in those first days as though it might explode.

When I watched the light, it wasn't only the taboo that scared me – it was what this act of witness meant for me. If word got out that the Council was breaking the taboo, there'd be another purge. The terror of the blast, and the machines that had wrought it, was still too real, too visceral, for people to tolerate. I knew the light was a life sentence: now I'd seen it, I'd never be allowed out.

More than anything else, I missed the sky. A narrow vent, just below the ceiling, let in fresh air from somewhere, but never even a glimpse of sunlight. I calculated time's passage by the arrival of food trays twice a day through the slot in the base of the door. As the months since that last visit to the ramparts receded, I found I could recall the sky in the abstract, but couldn't properly picture it. I thought of the stories of the Long Winter, after the blast, when the air had been so thick with ash that nobody saw the sky for years and years. They say there were children born in that time who never saw the sky at all. I wondered whether they'd believed in it; whether imagining the sky had become an act of faith for them, as it now was for me.

Counting days was the only way I could cling to any sense of time, but as the tally grew it became its own torture. I wasn't counting down towards any prospect of release: the numbers only climbed, and with them the sense of suspension, of floating in an indefinite world of darkness and isolation. After the visits to the ramparts were stopped, the only regular milestone was The Confessor coming each fortnight to interrogate me about my visions. She told me that the other Omegas saw no one. Thinking of The Confessor, I didn't know if I should envy or pity them.

*

They say the twins started to appear in the second and third generations of the After. In the Long Winter there were no twins – barely any births at all, and fewer who survived. They were the years of melted bodies and failed, unrecognisable infants. So few lived, and fewer still could breed, so that it seemed unlikely humans would carry on at all.

At first, in the struggle to repopulate, the onslaught of twins must have been greeted with joy. So many babies, and so many of them normal. There was always one boy and one girl, with one from each pair perfect. Not just well formed, but strong, robust. But soon the fatal symmetry became evident; the price to be paid for each perfect baby was its twin. They came in many different forms: limbs missing, or atrophied, or occasionally multiplied. Absent eyes, extra eyes, or eyes sealed shut. These were the Omegas, the shadow counterparts to the Alphas. The Alphas called them mutants, said they were the poison that Alphas cast out, even in the womb. The stain of the blast that, while it couldn't be removed, had at least been displaced onto the lesser twin. The Omegas carried the burden of the mutations, leaving the Alphas unencumbered.

Not entirely unencumbered, though. While the difference between twins was visible, the link between them was not. But it nonetheless asserted itself, every time, in the most unanswerable way. It made no difference that nobody could understand how it worked. At first, they might have dismissed it as coincidence. But gradually, disbelief was overruled by fact, by the evidence of bodies. The twins came in pairs, and they died in pairs. Wherever they were, and no matter how far apart, whenever someone died, their twin died too.

Extreme pain, too, or serious illness, would affect both twins. A high fever in one twin would soon peak in the other; if one twin was knocked out, the other would lose consciousness as well, wherever he or she was. Minor injuries or sickness didn't seem to bridge the divide, but severe pain would see one twin wake, screaming, from the other twin's wound.

When it became clear that Omegas were infertile, it was assumed for a while that they would die out. That they were only a temporary blight, a readjustment after the blast. But each generation since then was the same: all twins, always one Alpha and one Omega. Only Alphas could produce children, but each child they produced came with its Omega twin.

When Zach and I were born, a perfect match, our parents must have counted and recounted: limbs, fingers, toes. The complete set. They would have been disbelieving, though; nobody dodged the split between Alpha and Omega. Nobody. It wasn't unheard of for an Omega to have a deformation that only became apparent later: one leg that refused to grow in tandem with the other; deafness that passed unnoticed in infancy; an arm that turned out to be stunted or weak. But there were also rumours, all over, about those few whose difference never showed itself physically: the boy who seemed normal until he screamed and ran from the cottage minutes before the roof-beam's sudden collapse; the girl who wept over the shepherd's dog a week before the cart from the next village ran it down. These were the Omegas whose mutation was invisible: the seers.

They were rare – only one in every few thousand, if that. Everybody knew of the seer who came to the market each month at Haven, the big town downstream. Although Omegas weren't permitted at the Alpha market, he'd been tolerated for years, lurking at the back of the stalls, behind the stacked crates and the mounds of spoiled vegetables. By the time I first went to the market he was old, but still plying his trade, charging a bronze coin in exchange for predicting next season's weather to farmers, or telling a merchant's daughter whom she'd end up marrying. But he was always odd: he muttered to himself steadily, an unending incantation. Once, when Zach and I walked past with Dad, the seer shouted, 'Fire. Forever fire.' The stall-holders nearby didn't even flinch – evidently such outbursts were common. That was the fate of most seers: the blast burned its way through their minds, as they were forced to relive it.

I don't know when I first realised my own difference, but I was old enough to know that it had to be hidden. In the early years, I was as oblivious as my parents. What child doesn't wake, screaming, from a bad dream? It took a long time for me to understand that there was something different about my dreams. The consistency of my dreams of the blast. The way that I'd dream of a storm that wouldn't arrive until the following night. How the details and scenes in my dreams extended far beyond my own experience of the village, its forty or so stone houses clustered around the central green with its stone-rimmed well. All I had ever known was this shallow valley, the houses and the wooden barns grouped a hundred feet from the river, high enough up to avoid the floods that drenched the fields with rich silt each winter. But my dreams thronged with unfamiliar landscapes and strange faces. Forts that loomed ten times the height of our own small house with its rough-sanded floors and low, beamed ceilings. Cities with streets wider than the river itself, and swollen with crowds.

By the time I was old enough to wonder at this, I was old enough to know that Zach was sleeping through each night, undisturbed. In the cot that we shared, I taught myself to lie in silence, to calm my frenzied breathing. When the visions came in the daytime, especially the roaring flash of the blast, I learned not to cry out. The first time Dad took us downstream to Haven, I recognised the jostling market square from my dreams, but when I saw Zach hang back and grip Dad's hand, I imitated my brother's dumbfounded stare.

So our parents waited. Like all parents, they'd made only a single cot for us, expecting to send one child away as soon as we'd been split and weaned. When, at three, we remained stubbornly unsplit, our father built a pair of larger beds. Although our neighbour, Mick, was known throughout the valley for his skill at carpentry, this time Dad didn't ask for his help. He built the beds himself, almost furtively, in the small walled yard outside the kitchen window. In the years that followed, whenever my lopsided, ill-made bed creaked I remembered the expression on Dad's face when he'd dragged the beds into the room, setting them as far apart as the narrow walls would allow.

Mum and Dad hardly spoke to us, anymore. Those were the drought years, when everything was rationed, and it seemed to me that even words had become scarce. In our valley, where the low-lying fields were usually flooded every winter, the river thinned to an apathetic trickle, the exposed riverbed on each side cracked like old pottery. Even in our well-off village, there was nothing to spare. Our harvests were poor the first two years, and in the third year without rain the crops failed altogether, and we lived off hoarded coins. The dried-up fields were scoured by dust. Some of the livestock died – there was no animal feed to buy, even for those with coins. There were stories of people starving, further east. The Council sent patrols through all the villages, to protect against Omega raids. That was the summer they erected the wall around Haven, and most of the larger Alpha towns. But the only Omegas I glimpsed in those years, passing our village on the way to the refuges, looked too thin and weary to threaten anyone.

Even when the drought had broken, the Council patrols continued. Mum and Dad's vigilance didn't change, either. The slightest difference between me and Zach was anticipated, seized on, and dissected. When we both came down with the winter fever, I overheard my parents' long discussion about who had sickened first. I must have been six or seven. Through the floor of our bedroom I could hear, from the kitchen below, my father's loud insistence that I'd looked flushed the night before, a good ten hours before both Zach and I had woken with our fevers peaking in perfect unison.

That was when I realised that Dad's wariness around us was distrust, not habitual gruffness; that Mum's constant watchfulness was something other than maternal devotion. Zach used to follow Dad around all day, from the well to the field to the barn. As we grew older, and Dad became prickly and wary with us, he began to shoo Zach away, shouting at him to get back to the house. Still Zach would find excuses to tail him when he could. If Dad was gathering fallen wood from the copse upstream, Zach would drag me there too, to search for mushrooms. If Dad was harvesting in the maize field, Zach would find a sudden enthusiasm for fixing the broken gate to the next paddock. He kept a safe distance, but trailed our father like an oddly misplaced shadow.

At night I clenched my eyes shut when Mum and Dad would talk about us, as if that would block out the voices that seeped through the floorboards. In the bed against the opposite wall I could hear Zach shift slightly, and the unhurried rhythm of his breathing. I didn't know if he was asleep, or just pretending.

*

'You've seen something new.'

I scanned the cell's grey ceiling to avoid The Confessor's eyes. Her questions were always like this: phrased blankly, as statements, as if she already knew everything. Of course, I could never be sure that she didn't. I knew, myself, what it was to catch glimpses of other people's thoughts, or to be woken by memories that weren't my own. But The Confessor wasn't just a seer; she used her power knowingly. Each time she came to the cell, I could feel her mind circling mine. I'd always refused to talk to her, but I was never sure how much I succeeded in concealing.

'Just the blast. The same.'

She unclasped and reclasped her hands. 'Tell me something you haven't told me twenty times before.'

'There's nothing. Just the blast.'

I searched her face, but it revealed nothing of what she knew. I'm out of practice, I thought. Too long in the cell, cut off from people. And anyway, The Confessor was inscrutable. I tried to concentrate. Her face was nearly as pale as mine had become over the long months in the cell. The brand was somehow more conspicuous on her face than on others', because the rest of her features were so imperturbable. Her skin as smooth as a polished river pebble, except for the tight redness of the brand, puckering at the centre of her forehead. It was hard to tell her age. If you just glanced at her, you might think her the same age as me and Zach. To me, however, she seemed decades older: it was the intensity of her stare, the powers that it barely concealed.

'Zach wants you to help me.'

'Then tell him to come himself. Tell him to see me.'

The Confessor laughed. 'The guards told me you screamed his name for the first few weeks. Even now, after three months in here, you really think he's going to come?'

'He'll come,' I said. 'He'll come eventually.'

'You seem certain of that,' she said. She cocked her head slightly. 'Are you certain that you want him to?'

I would never explain to her that it wasn't a matter of wanting, any more than a river wants to move downstream. How could I explain to her that he needed me, even though I was the one in the cell?

I tried to change the subject.

'I don't even know what you want,' I said. 'What you think I can do.'

She rolled her eyes. 'You're like me, Cass. Which means I know what you're capable of, even if you won't admit it.'

I tried a strategic concession. 'It's been more frequent. The blast.'

'Unfortunately I doubt that you can have much valuable information to give us about something that happened four hundred years ago.'

I could feel her mind probing at the edges of mine. It was like unfamiliar hands on my body. I tried to emulate her inscrutability, to close my mind.

The Confessor sat back. 'Tell me about the island.'

She'd spoken quietly, but I had to hide my shock that I

had been infiltrated so easily. I'd only begun to see the island in the last few weeks, since the final trip to the ramparts. The first few times I dreamed of it, I'd doubted myself, wondered if those glimpses of sea and sky were a fantasy rather than a vision. Just a daydream of open space, to counteract the contraction of my daily reality into those four grey walls, the narrow bed, the single chair. But the visions came too regularly, and were too detailed and consistent. I knew that what I had seen was real, just as I knew that I could never speak of it. Now, in the overbearing silence of the room, my own breathing sounded loud.

'I've seen it too, you know,' she said. 'You will tell me.'

When her mind probed mine, I was laid bare. It was like watching Dad skin a rabbit: the moment when he'd peel back the skin, leaving all the inner workings exposed.

I tried to seal my mind around images of the island: the city concealed in its caldera, houses clambering on one another up the steep sides. The water, merciless grey, stretching in all directions, pocked by outcrops of sharp stone. I could see it all, as I'd seen it many nights in dreams. I tried to think of myself as holding its secret inside my mouth, the same way the island nursed the secret city, nestled in the crater.

Standing, I said, 'There is no island.'

The Confessor stood too. 'You'd better hope not.'

*

As we grew older the scrutiny of our parents was matched only by that of Zach himself. To him, every day we weren't split was another day he was branded by the suspicion of being an Omega, another day he was prevented from assuming his rightful place in Alpha society. So, unsplit, the two of us lingered at the margins of village life. When other children went to school, we studied together at the kitchen table. When other children played together by the river, we played only with each other, or followed the others at a distance, copying their games. Keeping far enough away to avoid the other children shouting or throwing stones at us, Zach and I could only hear fragments of the rhymes they sang. Later, at home, we would try to echo them, filling in the gaps with our own invented words and lines. We existed in our own small orbit of suspicion. To the rest of the village, we were objects of curiosity and, later, outright hostility. After a while, the whispers of the neighbours ceased being whispers, and became shouts: '*Poison. Freak. Imposter.*' They didn't know which one of us was dangerous, so they despised us equally. Each time another set of twins was born in the village, and then split, our unsplit state became more conspicuous. Our neighbours' Omega son, Oscar, whose left leg ended at the knee, was sent away at nine months old to be cared for by Omega relatives. We often passed the remaining twin, little Meg, playing alone in the fenced yard of their house.

'She must miss her twin,' I said to Zach as we walked by, watching Meg chewing listlessly on the head of a small wooden horse.

'Sure,' he said. 'I bet she's devastated that she doesn't have to share her life with a freak anymore.'

'He must miss his family too.'

'Omegas don't have family,' he said, repeating the familiar line from one of the Council posters. 'Anyway, you know what happens to parents who try to hang on to their Omega kids.'

I'd heard the stories. The Council showed no mercy to the occasional parent who resisted the split and tried to keep both twins. It was the same for those rare Alphas who were found to be in a relationship with an Omega. There were rumours of public floggings, and worse. But most parents relinquished their Omega babies readily, eager to be rid of their deformed offspring. The Council taught that prolonged proximity to Omegas was dangerous. The neighbours' hisses of *poison* revealed both disdain and fear. Omegas needed to be cast out of Alpha society, just as the poison was cast out of the Alpha twin in the womb. Was that the one thing Omegas are spared, I wondered? Since we can't have children, at least we'd never have to experience sending a child away.

I knew my time to be sent away was coming, and that my secrecy was only deferring the inevitable. I'd even begun to wonder whether my current existence – the perpetual scrutiny of my parents and the rest of the village – was any better than the exile that was bound to follow. Zach was the one person who understood my odd, liminal life, because he shared it. But I felt his dark, calm eyes on me all the time.

In search of less watchful company, I'd caught three of the red beetles that always flocked by the well. I kept them in a jar on the windowsill, had enjoyed seeing them crawl about, and hearing the muted clatter of their wings against the glass. A week later I found the largest one pinned to the wooden sill, one wing gone, making an endless circle on the pivot of its guts.

'It was an experiment,' said Zach. 'I wanted to test how long it could live like that.'

I told our parents. 'He's just bored,' my mother said. 'It's driving him crazy, the two of you not being in school like you should be.' But the unspoken truth continued to circle, like the beetle stuck on the pin: only one of us would ever be allowed to go to school.

I squashed the beetle myself, with the heel of my shoe,

to put an end to its circular torment. That night, I took the jar and the two remaining beetles with me to the well. When I removed the lid and tipped the jar on its side, they were reluctant to venture out. I coaxed them out with a blade of grass, transferring them carefully to the stone rim on which I sat. One attempted a short flight, landing on my bare leg. I let it sit there for a while before blowing it gently back into flight.

Zach saw the empty jar that night, beside my bed. Neither of us said anything.

*

About a year later, gathering firewood by the river on a still afternoon, I made my mistake. I was walking just behind Zach when I sensed something: a part-glimpse of a vision, intruding between the real world and my sight. I dashed to catch up with him, knocked him out of the way before the branch had even begun to fall. It was an instinctive response, the kind I'd grown used to repressing. Later I would wonder whether it was fear for his safety that led to my lapse, or just exhaustion under the constant scrutiny. Either way, he was safe, sprawled beneath me on the path, by the time the massive bough creaked and fell, snagging and tearing off other branches on the way down, to land finally where Zach had stood earlier.

When his eyes met mine I was amazed at the relief in them.

'It wouldn't have done much damage,' I said.

'I know.' He helped me up, brushed some leaves off the side of my dress.

'I saw it.' I was speaking too quickly. 'Saw it starting to fall, I mean.'

'You don't need to explain,' he said. 'And I should thank you, for getting me out of the way.' For the first time in years, he was smiling at me in the unguarded, wide-mouthed way that I remembered from our early childhood. I knew him too well to be glad.

He insisted on adding my own bundle of firewood to his, carrying the whole load all the way back to the village. 'I owe you,' he said.

In the weeks that followed we passed most of the time together, the same as always, but he was less rough in our games. He waited for me on the walk to the well. When we took the shortcut across the field, he called behind to warn me when he came across a patch of stinging nettles. My hair went unpulled, my possessions undisturbed.

Zach's new knowledge allowed me some respite from his daily cruelties, but it wasn't enough to declare us split. For that, he needed proof – years of impassioned but futile assertions on his part had taught him that. He waited a while for me to slip up again and reveal myself, but for nearly a whole year more I managed to hold my secret. The visions had grown stronger, but I'd trained myself not to react, not to cry out at the flashes of flame that punctuated my nights, or at the images of distant places that drifted into my waking thoughts. I spent more time alone, venturing far upstream, even as far as the deep gorge leading away from the river, where the abandoned silos were hidden. Zach no longer followed me when I went off by myself.

I never entered the silos, of course. All such remnants were taboo. Our broken world was scattered with these ruins, but it was against the law to enter them, just as it was forbidden to own any relics. I'd heard rumours that some desperate Omegas had been known to raid the wreckage, searching out usable fragments. But what would be left to salvage after all these centuries? The blast had levelled most cities. And even if there were anything salvageable in the taboo towns now, centuries later, who would dare to take it, knowing the penalty? More frightening than the law were the rumours of what those remnants could hold. The radiation, said to shelter like a nest of wasps in such relics. The contaminating presence of the past. If the Before was mentioned at all, it was in hushed voices, with a mixture of awe and disgust.

Zach and I used to dare each other to get close to the silos. Always braver than me, once he ran right up to the closest one and placed a hand on the curved concrete wall before running back to me, giddy with pride and fear. But these days I was always alone, and would sit for hours under a tree that overlooked the silos. The three huge, tubular buildings were more intact than many such ruins – they'd been shielded by the gorge that surrounded them, and by the fourth silo, which must have taken the brunt of the blast. It had collapsed entirely, leaving only its circular base. Twisted metal spars rose out of the dust like the grasping fingers of a world buried alive. But I was grateful for the silos, despite their ugliness – they guaranteed that nobody else would go near the place, so I could at least count on solitude. And unlike the walls of Haven, or the larger of the villages nearby, there were no Council posters flapping at the wind: *Vigilance against Contamination from Omegas. Alpha Unity: Support Increased Tithes for Omegas.* Since the drought years, everything seemed scarcer except for new Council posters.

I wondered, sometimes, whether I was drawn to the ruins because I recognised myself in them. We Omegas, in our brokenness, were like those taboo ruins: dangerous. Contaminating. Reminders of the blast and what it had wrought.

Although Zach no longer came with me to the silos, or on my other wanderings, I knew he was still observing me more intently than ever. When I came back from the silos, tired from the long walk, he'd smile at me in his watchful way, ask politely about my day. He knew where I'd been, but never told our parents, although they would have been furious. But he left me alone. He was like a snake, drawing back before the strike.

The first time he tried to expose me, he took my favourite doll, Scarlett, the one in the red dress that Mum had sewn. When Zach and I had first been given separate beds, I'd hung on to that doll for comfort at night. Even at twelve, I always slept with Scarlett under one arm, the coarse, plaited wool of her hair reassuringly scratchy against my skin. Then one morning she was gone.

When I asked about Scarlett at breakfast, Zach was buoyant with triumph. 'It's hidden, outside the village. I took it while Cass was asleep.' He turned to our parents. 'If she finds where I buried it, she has to be a seer. It'll be proof.' Our mother chided him, and put a hand on my shoulder, but all day I saw how my parents watched me even more carefully than usual.

I cried, as I had planned. Seeing the hopeful alertness of my parents made it easy. How keen they were to solve the riddle that Zach and I had become, even if it meant being rid of me. In the evening, I pulled from the small toybox an unfamiliar-looking doll with awkwardly chopped short hair and a simple white smock. That night, tucked under my left arm, Scarlett was returned from the toybox exile that I'd imposed on her a week before, when I'd swapped her red dress onto an unfavoured doll, and hacked off her long hair.

From then on Scarlett remained secret, in full view, on my bed. I never bothered to go to the lightning-charred willow downstream and dig up the doll in the red dress that Zach had buried there.

CHAPTER 3

Downstairs, Mum and Dad were fighting again, the sound of their argument drifting up through the floorboards, insidious as smoke.

'It's more of a problem every day,' Dad said.

Mum's voice was quieter. 'They're not "a problem" – they're our children.'

'One of them is,' he replied. A pot clattered loudly on the table. 'The other one's dangerous. Poison. We just don't know which one.'

Zach hated to let me see him cry, but the dregs of the candle threw out enough light for me to see the slight shuddering of his back under the blanket. I slipped out from under my quilt. The floorboards creaked slightly as I took the two steps to the edge of Zach's bed.

'He doesn't mean it,' I whispered, putting a hand on his back. 'He doesn't mean to hurt you when he says things like that.'

He sat up, shrugging off my hand. I was surprised to see he didn't even try to wipe away the tears. 'I'm not hurt by him,' he said. 'What he says, it's all true. You want to pat me on the back, comfort me, act like you're the caring one? It's not them hurting me. Not even the other kids, the ones who throw stones. See all of this?' The sweep of his hand took in the sounds from the kitchen below, as well as his own tear-streaked face. 'It's all your fault. You're the problem, Cass, not them. You're the reason we're stuck in this limbo.'

I was suddenly aware of the cold boards underfoot, and the night air on my bare arms.

'You want to show you really care about me?' he said. 'Then tell them the truth. You could end it right away.'

'Do you really want me sent away? It's me. I'm not some strange creature. Forget what the Council says about contamination. It's just me. You know me.'

'You keep saying that. Why should I think I know you? You've never been honest with me. You never told me the truth. You made me figure it out for myself.'

'I couldn't tell you,' I said. Even admitting as much to him, alone in our room, was risky.

'Because you didn't trust me. You want to make out that we're so close. But you're the one who's lied this whole time. You never trusted me enough to tell me the truth. All these years, you left me to wonder. To fear that it might be me who was the freak. And now you think I should trust you?'

I retreated to my bed. He was still staring at me. Could things ever have been different, if I'd trusted him with the truth? Could we have found a way to share the secret, to make our way together? Had he caught his distrust from me? Maybe that was the poison I'd been carrying – not the contamination of the blast that all Omegas bore, but the secret.

A tear had settled on the top of his upper lip. It glinted gold in the candlelight.

I didn't want him to see the matching tear on my face. I reached out to the table and snuffed the flame.

'It's got to end,' he whispered into the darkness. It was half a plea, half a threat.

*

His impatience to expose me grew with our father's illness. Dad fell sick when we'd just turned thirteen. As with the previous year, there was no mention of our birthday – our age had become an increasingly shameful reminder of our unsplit state. That night, Zach had whispered across the bedroom: 'You know what day it was today?'

'Of course,' I said.

'Happy birthday,' he said. It was only a whisper, so it was hard to tell whether he was being sarcastic.

Two days later, Dad collapsed. Dad, who had always seemed as robust and solid as the huge oak cross-beam that ran the length of the kitchen ceiling. He hauled buckets of water up the well faster than anyone else in the village, and when Zach and I were smaller he could carry us both at once. He still could, I thought, except that he rarely touched us now. Then, in the middle of the paddock on a hot day, he stumbled to his knees. From where I sat, shelling peas on the stone wall at the front of our yard, I heard the shouts of the others working near him in the field.

That night, after the neighbours had carried him back to the cottage, our mother sent for Dad's twin, Alice, from the Omega settlement up on the plain. Zach himself went with Mick in the bullock cart to fetch her, returning the next day with our aunt lying in the hay on the back of the cart. We'd never met her before, and looking at her, the only similarity I could see between her and Dad was the fever that currently slickened their flesh. She was thin, with long hair, darker than Dad's. The coarse, brown fabric of her dress had been mended many times and was now flecked with hay. Beneath the strands of hair that stuck to her sweaty forehead we could make out the brand: Omega.

We cared for her as much as we could, but it was clear from the start that she hadn't long. We couldn't allow her in the house, of course, but even her presence in the shed was enough to enrage Zach. On the second day his fury climaxed. 'It's disgusting,' he shouted. 'She's disgusting. How can she be here, with us running around after her like servants? She's killing him. And it's dangerous for all of us, having her so close.'

Mum didn't bother to hush him, but said calmly, 'She'd be killing him more quickly if we'd left her in her own filthy hut.'

This silenced Zach. He wanted Alice gone, but not at the expense of admitting to Mum what he had told me in bed the night before: what he'd seen at the settlement when he collected Alice. Her small, tidy cottage; the whitewashed walls; the posies of dried herbs hanging above the hearth, just as they hung above ours.

Mum continued, 'If we save her, we save him.'

It was only at night, when the candle was out and no voices could be heard from Mum and Dad's room, that Zach would tell me about what he'd seen at the settlement. He told me that other Omegas at the settlement had tried to stop them from taking Alice away – that they'd wanted to keep caring for her there. But no Omega would dare to argue with an Alpha, and Mick had brandished his whip until they backed away.

'Isn't it cruel, though, to take her from her family?' I whispered.

'Omegas don't have family,' Zach recited.

'Not children, obviously, but people she loves. Friends, or maybe a husband.'

'A husband?' He let the word hang. Officially Omegas weren't allowed to marry, but everyone knew that they still did, although the Council wouldn't recognise any such unions.

'You know what I mean.'

'She didn't live with anyone,' he said. 'It was just a few other freaks from her settlement, claiming they knew what was best for her.'

We'd barely seen Omegas before, let alone spent time in close quarters with one. Little Oscar next door had been sent away as soon as he was branded and weaned. The few Omegas who passed through the area rarely stayed more than a night, camping just downstream of the village. They were itinerants, on the way to try their luck at one of the larger Omega settlements in the south. Or, in years when the harvest had been poor, there'd be Omegas who'd given up on farming the half-blighted land they were permitted to settle on, and were heading to one of the refuges near Wyndham. The refuges were the Council's concession to the fatal bond between twins. Omegas couldn't be allowed to starve to death and take their twins with them, so there were refuges near all large towns, where Omegas would be taken in, and fed and housed by the Council. Few Omegas went willingly, though – it was a place of last resort, for the starving or sick. The refuges were workhouses, and those who sought their help had to repay the Council's generosity with labour, working on the farms within the refuge complex until the Council judged the debt repaid. Few Omegas were willing to trade their freedom for the safety of three meals a day.

I'd gone out with Mum, once, to give some food-scraps to one group on their way to the refuge near Wyndham. It was dark, and the man who stepped away from the fire and accepted the bundle from Mum had done so in silence, gesturing at his throat to indicate that he was mute. I tried not to stare at the brand on his forehead. He was so thin that the knuckles were the widest part of each finger, his knees the widest part of each leg. His very skin seemed insufficient, stretched miserly over his bones. I thought perhaps that we might join the travellers at the fire for a few minutes, but the guardedness in Mum's eyes was more than matched by that in the Omega man's. Behind him, I could see the group gathered around a thriving blaze. It was hard to distinguish between the strange shapes thrown by the firelight and the actual deformities of the Omegas. I could make out one man who leaned forward and poked at the fire with a stick, held between the two stumps of his arms.

Looking at the group, their huddled stance, their thin and cowed bodies, it was hard to believe the occasional whispers of an Omega resistance, or of the island where it was supposed to be brewing. How could they dream of challenging the Council, with its thousands of soldiers? The Omegas I'd seen were all too poor, too crippled. And, like the rest of us, they must know the stories of what had happened, a century ago or more, when there'd been an Omega uprising in the east. Of course, the Council couldn't kill them without killing their Alpha counterparts, but what they did to the rebels, they say, was worse. Torture so terrible that their Alpha twins, even those hundreds of miles away, fell screaming to the ground. As for the rebel Omegas, they were never seen again, but apparently their Alpha twins continued to suffer unexplained pain for years.

After they'd crushed the uprising, the Council set the east ablaze. They burned all the settlements out there, even those that had never been involved in the uprising. The soldiers torched all the crops and houses, even though the east was already a bleak zone on the brink of the deadlands, a place so dire no Alphas would live there. They left nothing standing, until it was as if the deadlands themselves had crept further west.

I thought of those stories as I watched the group of Omegas, their unfamiliar bodies bending over the bundle of scraps my mother had given them. When she took my hand and led me quickly back to the village, I was ashamed at my own relief. The image of the mute Omega, his eyes avoiding ours as he took the food, stayed with me for weeks.

My father's twin was not mute. For three days Alice groaned, shouted and cursed. The sweet, milky stench of her breath pervaded the shed first, and then the house as Dad grew sicker. All the herbs Mum threw on the fire could not quell it. While our mother took care of Dad inside, Zach and I were to take turns sitting with Alice. By unspoken contract we sat together most of the time, rather than taking turns alone.

One morning, when Alice's cursing had subsided into coughs, Zach asked her quietly, 'What's wrong with you?'

She met his eyes clearly. 'It's the fever. I have the fever – your father too, now.'

He scowled. 'But before that – what's wrong with you?'

Alice burst out laughing, then coughing, then laughing again. Beckoning us closer, she drew aside the sweaty sheet that covered her. Her nightgown reached just below her knees. We looked at her legs, our distaste battling with our curiosity. At first I could see no difference at all: her legs were thin but strong. Her feet were just feet. I'd heard a story once about an Omega with nails grown like scales, all over his flesh, but Alice's toenails were not only in place, but neatly clipped and clean.

Zach was impatient. 'What? What is it?'

'Don't they teach you to count at your school?'

I said what Zach would not. 'We don't go to school. We can't – we've not been split.'

He interrupted quickly: 'But we can count. We learn at home – numbers, writing, all sorts of things.' His eyes, like mine, went quickly back to her feet. On the left foot: five toes; on the right foot: seven.

'That's my problem, sweetheart,' said Alice. 'My toes don't add up.' She looked at Zach's deflated face, and stopped her grinning. 'I suppose there's more,' she said, almost kindly. 'You've not seen me walk, only stagger to and from your cart, but I've always limped – my right leg's shorter than the other, and weaker. And you know I can't have children: a *dead-end*, as the Alphas like to call us. But the toes are the main problem: I never had a nice round number.' She went back to laughing, then looked straight at Zach, raised an eyebrow. 'If we were all so drastically different from Alphas, darling, why would they need to brand us?' He didn't answer. She went on: 'And if Omegas are all so helpless, why do you think the Council's so afraid of the island?'

Zach threw a glance over his shoulder, hushed her so urgently that I felt his spittle on my arm. 'There is no island. Everyone knows. It's just a rumour, a lie.'

'Then why do you look so scared?'

I answered this time. 'On the road to Haven, last time we went, there was a burnt-down hut. Dad said it belonged to a couple of Omegas who spread rumours of the island.'

'He said Council soldiers took them away in the night,' Zach added, looking at the door again.

'And people say there's a square in Wyndham,' I said, 'where they whip Omegas who've been heard just talking about the island. They whip them in public, for everyone to see.'

Alice shrugged. 'Seems like a lot of trouble for the Council to go to, if it's just a rumour. Just a lie.'

'It is – is a lie, I mean,' hissed Zach. 'You need to shut up – you're mad, and you'll get us in trouble. There could never be a place like that, just for Omegas. They'd never manage it. And the Council would find it.'

'They haven't found it yet.'

'Because it doesn't exist,' he said. 'It's just an idea.'

'Maybe that's enough,' she said, grinning. She was still grinning several minutes later when the fever tipped her back into unconsciousness.

He stood. 'I'm going to check on Dad.'

I nodded, pressed the cool flannel again to my aunt's head. 'Dad'll be just the same – unconscious, I mean,' I said. Zach left anyway, letting the shed door bang loudly behind him.

With the cloth resting there, over the brand in the centre of Alice's forehead, I thought I could begin to recognise some of my father's features in her face. I pictured Dad, thirty feet away in the cottage. Each time I passed the cloth across her forehead, grimacing with every gust of the sickened breath, I imagined that I was soothing him. After a minute I reached out and placed my own small hand over Alice's, a gesture of closeness my father had not allowed for years. I wondered if it was wrong, to feel this closeness to this stranger who had brought my father's illness to the house like an unwelcome gift.

*

Alice had fallen asleep, her breath gurgling slightly in the back of her throat. When I stepped out of the shed, Zach was sitting cross-legged on the ground, in the slant of afternoon sun.

I joined him. He was fiddling with a piece of hay, exploring the spaces between his teeth.

After a while, he said, 'I saw him fall, you know.'

I should have realised, knowing how Zach still followed Dad around whenever he could.

'I was looking for birds' eggs in the trees by the top paddock,' he went on. 'I saw it. One moment he was standing. Then, just like that: he fell.' Zach spat out a splinter of hay. 'He staggered a bit, like he'd drunk too much, and sort of propped himself up with his pitchfork. Then he fell again, face first, so I couldn't see him for the wheat.'

'I'm sorry. It must have been scary.'

'Why are you sorry? It's her that should be sorry.' He gestured at the shed behind us, from where we could hear Alice, her sodden lungs doing battle with the air.

'He's going to die, isn't he?'

There was no point lying to him, so I just nodded.

'Can't you do anything?' he said. He grabbed my hand. Amongst everything that had happened over those last few days – Dad's collapse, and Alice's arrival – the strangest of all was Zach reaching out for my hand, something he'd not done since we were tiny.

When we were younger, Zach had found a fossil in the riverbed: a small black stone imprinted with the curlicue of an ancient snail. The snail had become stone, and the stone had become snail. Zach and I were like that, I often thought. We were embedded in each other. First by twinship, then by the years spent together. It wasn't a matter of choice, any more than the stone or the snail had chosen.

I squeezed his hand. 'What could I do?'

'Anything. I don't know. Something. It's not fair – she's killing him.'

'It's not like that. She's not doing it to spite him. It'd be the same for her if he'd fallen sick first.'

'It's not fair,' he said again.

'Sickness isn't fair, not to anyone. It just happens.'

'It doesn't, though. Not to Alphas – we hardly ever get sick. It's always Omegas. They're weak, sickly. It's the poison in them, from the blast. She's the weak one, the contaminated one. And she's going to drag Dad down with her.'

I couldn't argue with him about the illness – it was true that Omegas were more susceptible. 'It's not her fault,' I offered. 'And if he fell down a well, or got gored by a bullock, he'd take her with him.'

He dropped my hand. 'You don't care about him, because you're not one of us.'

'Of course I care.'

'Then do something,' he said. He wiped angrily at a tear that emerged from the corner of his eye.

'There's nothing I can do,' I said. I knew that seers were rumoured to have different strengths: a knack for predicting weather, or finding springs in arid land, or telling if somebody spoke the truth. But I'd never heard of any with a talent for healing. We couldn't change the world – only perceive it in crooked ways.

'I wouldn't tell anyone,' he whispered. 'If you could do something to help him, I'd not say a word. Not to anyone.'

It made no difference whether I believed him. 'There's nothing I can do,' I repeated.

'What's the point of you being a freak if you can't even do anything useful with it?'

I reached once more for his hand. 'He's my dad too.'

'Omegas don't have family,' he said, snatching his hand away.

*

Alice and Dad lasted two more days. It must have been well past midnight, and Zach and I were in the shed, asleep, Alice's jagged breath grating on our dreams. I woke suddenly. I shook Zach and said, without thinking of hiding my vision, 'Go to Dad. Go now.' He was gone before he could even accuse me of anything, his footsteps racing on the gravel path to the cottage. I stood to go too: nearby, my father was dying. But Alice opened her eyes, briefly at first, and then for longer. I didn't want her to be alone, in the cramped darkness of an unfamiliar shed. So I stayed.

They were buried together the next day, though the gravestone bore only his name. Mum had burned Alice's nightdress, along with the sheets from both fever-sweated beds. The sole tangible proof that Alice had existed was hanging on a piece of twine around my neck, under my dress: a large brass key. The night she died, when Alice had woken briefly and seen that she was alone with me, she'd taken the key from her neck and passed it to me.

'Behind my cottage, buried under the lavender, there's a chest. Things that will help you when you go there.' She entered another coughing fit.

I handed it back, loath to receive another uninvited gift from this woman. 'How do you know it will be me?'

She coughed again. 'I don't, Cass. I just hope it is.'

'Why?' I, more than Zach, had cared for this woman, this reeking stranger. Why would she now wish this upon me?

She pressed the key again into my resisting hand. 'Because your brother, he's so full of fear – he'll never cope if it's him.'

'He's not afraid of things – and he's strong.' I wasn't sure if I was coming to his defence, or my own. 'He's just angry, I suppose.'

Alice laughed, a rasp that differed only slightly from her usual coughing. 'Oh, he's angry all right. But it's all the same thing.' She waved my hand away impatiently as I tried to pass back the key.

In the end, I took it. I kept the key hidden, but it still felt like an admission, if only to myself. Looking at Zach's face as we stood in the graveyard, squinting in the relentless sun, I knew it wouldn't be long. Since Dad's death, I'd felt something shift in Zach's mind. The change in his thoughts felt like a rusted lock that finally gives way: the same decisiveness, the same satisfaction.

With Dad gone, our house was filled with waiting. I began to dream about the brand. In my dream that first night, I placed my hand again on Alice's head, and felt her scar burning into the flesh of my own palm.

*

Only a month after the burial, I came home to find the local Councilman there. It was late summer, the hay freshly cut and sharp underfoot as I walked across the fields. On the path up from the river I saw the blurring of the sky above our cottage, and wondered why the fire was lit on such a hot day.

They were waiting for me inside. The moment I saw the black iron handle sticking out of the fire, I heard again the hiss of branded flesh that had sounded in my recent dreams, and I turned to run. It was my mother who grabbed me, hard, by the arm.

'You know the Councilman, Cass, from downstream.'

I didn't struggle, but kept my eyes fixed on the brand in the fire. The shape at its end, glowing in the coals, was smaller than I'd pictured it in my dreams. It occurred to me that it was made for use on infants.

'Thirteen years now, Cassandra, we've waited for you and your brother to be split,' said the Councilman. He reminded me of my father; his big hands. 'It's too long. One of you where you shouldn't be, and one missing out on school. We can't have an Omega here, contaminating the village. It's dangerous, especially for the other twin. You each need to take your proper place.'

'This is our proper place: here. This is our home.' I was shouting, but Mum interrupted me quickly.

'Zach told us, Cass.'

The Councilman took over. 'Your twin came to see me.'

Zach had been standing behind the Councilman, head slightly bowed. Now he looked up at me. I don't know what I'd expected to see in his eyes: triumph, I suppose. Perhaps contrition. Instead he looked as he so often did: wary, watchful. Afraid, even, but my own fear dragged my eyes back to the brand, from its long black handle down to the shape at the end, a serpentine curve in the coals.

'How do you know he's not lying?' I asked the Councilman.

He laughed. 'Why would he lie about this? Zach's shown courage.' He stepped up to the fireplace and lifted the brand. Methodically, he knocked it twice against the iron grill to shake loose the ash that clung to it.

'Courage?' I threw off my mother's grasp.

The Councilman stepped back from the fire, the brand held high. To my surprise, Mum didn't grab me again, or make any move to stop me as I backed away. It was the Councilman who moved, quicker than I would have imagined, given his size. He grabbed Zach by the neck and pressed him against the wall beside the hearth. In the Councilman's other hand, raised above Zach's face, the brand was smoking slightly.

I shook my head, as if trying to shake the world into some sort of sense. My eyes met Zach's. Even with the brand so close to his face that its shadow fell across his eyes, I could now see the smirk of triumph. And I admired him, as I always had: my twin; my brave, clever twin. He'd managed to surprise me after all. Could I bring myself to surprise him? Call his bluff and play along, let him be branded and exiled?

I almost could have brought myself to do it, if I hadn't detected, beneath his triumph, that splinter of terror, insistent as the brand itself. My own face was screwed up against the sizzling heat that I could sense in front of his.

'He lied. It's me. I'm the seer.' I forced my voice into calmness. 'He knew I'd tell you the truth.'

The Councilman pulled back the brand, but didn't release Zach.

'Why not tell us, if you knew it was her?'

'I tried, for years. Nobody believed me,' Zach said, his voice half-crushed by the Councilman's hand at his throat. 'I couldn't prove it. I could never catch her out.'

'And how do we know we can believe her now?'

In the end it was a relief for me to tell it all: how the flashes of vision came to me at night, at first, and later even when I was awake. How the blast tore open my sleep with its roar of light. How I sometimes knew things before they happened: the falling branch, the doll, the brand itself. My mother and the Councilman listened carefully. Only Zach, knowing it already, was impatient.

Finally the Councilman spoke. 'You've given us all quite the runaround, girl. If it wasn't for your brother, you might have kept on playing us for fools.' He plunged the brand back into the coals with such force that it sparked against the metal grating. 'Did you think you were different from the rest of the filthy Omegas?' He hadn't let go of the handle of the brand. 'Better than them, just because you're a seer?' He pulled the brand again from the fire. 'See this?' He had me now by the throat. The brand, only inches away, singed a few strands of my hair. The smell and the heat forced my eyes shut. 'See this?' he said again, waving the brand before my clenched eyes. 'This is what you are.'

I didn't cry out when he pressed it to my forehead, though I heard Zach give a grunt of pain. My hand was at my chest, clutching the key that hung there. I squeezed it so tightly that later, upstairs, I saw that it had left its imprint on my flesh.

CHAPTER 4

They let me stay for four days, until the burn had begun to heal. It was Zach who rubbed balm on my forehead. He winced as he did it, whether from pain or disgust I didn't know.

'Hold still.' His tongue emerged from the corner of his mouth as he peered close to clean the wound. He'd always done that when he concentrated. I was extra aware of these small things, now, knowing that I wouldn't see them anymore.

He dabbed again. He was very gentle, but I couldn't help but flinch as he touched the raw skin.

'Sorry,' he said.

Not sorry for exposing me – sorry only for the blistered flesh.

'It'll get better in a few weeks. But I'll be gone by then. You're not sorry about that.'

He put down the cloth and looked out the window. 'It couldn't stay the same. It couldn't be the two of us, any longer. It's not right.'

'You realise you're going to be by yourself, now.'

He shook his head. 'You kept me by myself. I can go to school now. I'll have the others.'

'The ones who throw rocks at us when we pass by the school? It was me who cleaned up the wound when Nick landed that rock right above your eye. Who's going to mop up your blood once they've sent me away?'

'You don't get it, do you?' He smiled at me. For the first time I could remember, he was perfectly serene. 'They only threw rocks because of you. Because you made us both into a freak show. Nobody's going to be throwing rocks at me now. Not ever again.'

It was refreshing, in a way, to be able to speak openly after all the subterfuge. For those few days before I left, we were more comfortable together than we had been for years.

'You didn't see it coming?' he asked, on my last night, when he'd blown out the candle on the table between our beds.

'I saw the brand. I felt it burning.'

'But you didn't know how I'd do it? That I'd declare myself the Omega?'

'I guess I only got a glimpse of what would happen in the end. That it would be me.'

'But it might have been me. If you hadn't said.'

'Maybe.' I shifted again. The only bearable way to lie was on my back, so that the burn didn't touch the pillow. 'In my dreams, it was always me branded.' Did that mean that staying silent had never been an option? Had he known so surely that I would speak up? And what if I hadn't?

I left at dawn the next day. Zach's happiness was barely disguised, and didn't surprise me, though I was saddened to see how my mother rushed the farewell. She avoided looking at my face, as she had ever since the branding. I'd seen it only once myself, sneaking into Mum's room to meet my new face in the small mirror there. The burn was still raised and blistered, but despite the inflammation surrounding it, the mark was clear. I remembered the Councilman's words, and repeated them to myself: 'This is what I am.' Holding my finger just above the scorched flesh I traced the shape: the incomplete circle, like an inverted horseshoe, with a short horizontal line spreading out at each end. 'This is what I am,' I said again.

What surprised me, when I left, was my own relief. Although the pain of my brand was still sharp, and although Mum pushed a parcel of food into my arms when I tried to embrace her, there was something liberating about leaving behind those years of hiding. When Zach said, 'Take care of yourself,' I nearly laughed out loud.

'You mean: take care of *you*.'

He looked straight at me, not averting his eyes from my brand the way our mother did. 'Yes.'

I thought that maybe, for the first time in years, we were being honest with each other.

Of course, I cried. I was thirteen years old and I had never been parted from my family before. The furthest I'd ever been from Zach was the day he journeyed to collect Alice. I wondered if it would have been easier if I'd been branded as a child. I would have been raised in an Omega settlement, never known what it was to be with my family, with my twin. I might even have had friends, though never having experienced any closeness apart from with Zach, I didn't really know what that might mean. At least, I thought, I don't have to hide who I am anymore.

I was wrong. I was hardly even out of the village when I passed a group of children my own age. Although Zach and I had not been able to attend the school, we knew all the local children, had even played with them in the early years, before our strange togetherness became a public problem. Zach had always carried himself with confidence, and insisted he would fight anyone who said he wasn't an Alpha. But as the years passed, parents began to warn their children away from the unsplit twins, so we'd relied more and more on each other for company, even as Zach's resentment at our isolation grew. During the last few years the other children had not just avoided us, but had openly taunted us, hurling rocks and insults if our parents were out of sight.

The four children, three boys and a girl, had been riding on a pair of old donkeys, taking turns to race each other on their comically awkward mounts. I heard them from a distance, and saw them shortly afterwards. I kept my head down and kept to the side of the narrow road, but word of our split had spread quickly, and when they grew close enough to see my brand they were filled with the excitement of seeing the news confirmed.

They surrounded me. Nick, the tallest of the boys, spoke first, while the others looked with undisguised disgust at my brand.

'Looks like Zach can finally come to school.'

Nick hadn't spoken to either of us for years, other than to shout slurs, but it seemed my branding had immediately returned Zach to favour.

Another of the boys spoke: 'Your kind don't belong here.'

'I'm leaving,' I said, and tried to break away, but Nick blocked my way and shoved me back towards the others, who shoved me again. I dropped my parcel and instinctively shielded the wound on my head as the boys' blows sent me stumbling from side to side within the tiny ring they had formed. A taunt accompanied each shove: 'freak'; 'dead-end'; 'poison'.

My hands still over my face, I turned to Ruth, a dark-haired girl who lived only a few houses from us. I whispered, 'Stop them. Please.'

Ruth reached forward, and for a second I thought she was going to take my arm. Instead she bent down, grabbed my flask, and emptied my water slowly on to the ground, where one of the donkeys made a futile attempt to slurp at it as it sank into the sandy soil. 'That's our water,' Ruth said. 'From the Alpha well. You've been contaminating it long enough, freak.'

They left me without looking back. I waited until they were out of sight before gathering my things and making my way down to the river. Emptying the flask had been a harmless act: the river water, though brackish and warm, was perfectly safe to drink. But even as I crouched at the river's edge to fill the flask again, I knew the significance of Ruth's gesture. To the Alphas, perhaps even my own mother, my life up to now had been a lie, my place in the village kept through deceit.

For the rest of the day I avoided the road, instead scrambling along the banks of the river. I fastened my shawl over my head, flinching when it touched my burn. The one time I passed a farmer, an Alpha woman bringing her goats down to the river's edge to drink, I scuttled past in silence, head down. I didn't stop when I reached the gorge leading west to the silos, but pushed onwards, further south than I'd ever been.

It had taken Zach more than half a day in the cart to reach the Omega settlement when he collected Alice. For me, on foot, avoiding the roads, my footsteps never quite keeping time with the throbbing of my head, it took nearly three days. Several times a day I stopped to bathe my forehead in the river, and to tear off some bread from the parcel Mum had given me. I slept on the riverbank, glad of the midsummer warmth. On the second morning I re-joined the road, where it curved away from the river to climb up the valley. Although I was still afraid of encountering people, it was for a different reason. I was in Omega country now.

The landscape itself was different. The Alphas had always claimed the best land for their own. The valley where I'd been raised was good farming country, the soil plush with river-silt. Up here there was no valley to shield the land from the harsh light, which glared from the rocky soil. The grass, where it grew at all, was brittle and pale, and the roadside was covered with brambles. Their barbed leaves glistened with spiderwebs, a thick mist that did not lift. There was some other strangeness, too, that I couldn't work out until I looked about to refill my flask, and realised that, for the first time in my life, I couldn't hear the river. Its noise had been the backdrop to my entire life, and I knew it intimately: the surge of the high water in flood season, the heavy buzz of insects that drifted over the still pools in summer. The river had always provided the spine of my mental map of the area: upstream from the village was south, past the gorge and the silos that Zach and I used to dare each other to approach. Further upstream lay Wyndham, the biggest city and the Council's base. I'd never been that far, but had heard stories of its size and wealth. Even the refuge outside Wyndham, Mum had told me, was bigger than any town I'd seen. Downstream led north, through the fields, larger villages. A day's walk downriver was Haven, the market-town where Dad used to take us when we were smaller. Beyond Haven, the shallow rapids took the river beyond my knowledge.

Now, in Omega country, I was still confident that I could find my way – I could usually sense the landscape, just as

I could sense emotions and events. But without the river, I felt cut loose, turning about on this unfamiliar plain. There was only one road and I followed it as my mother had told me. I left it only once, following some tell-tale birds to a small spring that bubbled from a crack in the rock, from which I drank quickly before scrambling back to the barren road.

By the time I saw the settlement, night was lowering on the plain, and the first lamps had been lit in the windows. The cluster of houses was smaller than my village, but substantial enough that there could be no doubt. A huddle of low buildings, surrounded by a spread of fields, where the recently harvested crops were bald in patches and inter-rupted by large boulders. I pulled back the shawl that covered my head, waving away the flies that made busy with the still-seeping burn. *This is what I am*, I reminded myself, one hand on the key that hung at my neck. But as I approached, a small figure on the wide and broken road, I wished that Zach were by my side. A stupid thought, I reprimanded myself. Nonetheless, he had been like the sound of the river to me: always there.

CHAPTER 5

In the years that followed, I was grateful at least for Alice's cottage, and the stash of bronze coins that I'd found in the buried chest beneath the lavender. After six years at the settlement there were few coins left, but the money had allowed me to eke out the leanest months of the bad season, to pay the Council's tithe collectors (who came without fail, regardless of the success or failure of crops), and to help some of those who might otherwise have gone hungry. Little Oscar, from my parents' village, was there, being raised by his relatives in a cottage near my own. He'd been sent away much too young to remember me, but whenever I saw him it felt like a link with the village, and with those that I'd left behind. But although the others at the settlement still referred to the cottage as 'Alice's place', I gradually began to feel established there.

The other Omegas had grown used to me, too, though they tended to keep their distance. I understood their wariness: arriving there, newly branded at thirteen, meant that I would never quite be seen as one of them. That was compounded by the fact that I was a seer. Once or twice I

overheard mutterings about my absence of any visible mutation. *Easy enough for her*, I heard my neighbour Claire say
to her wife, Nessa, when I offered to help them with the
rethatching of their roof. *It's not like she's had to struggle like
the rest of us.* Another time, at work in my garden, I heard
Nessa warning Claire to steer clear of me. *I don't want her
sitting in my kitchen. We've got enough troubles without a
neighbour who can read your mind.* There was no point trying
to explain to her that it didn't work like that – that being
a seer was a series of impressions, not a neat narrative, and
that I was more likely to catch a glimpse of a town ten
miles east, or of the blast itself, than to be privy to Nessa's
thoughts. I kept silent, went on picking the snails from my
broad-bean stems, and pretended I'd heard nothing. I'd
learned, by then, that if Omegas were seen as dangerous,
seers were doubly so. I found myself spending more time
alone than I had at the village, where I'd had Zach's
company, however grudging.

I'd been surprised to find books at Alice's cottage. Omegas
weren't allowed to go to school, so most couldn't read. But
in the buried chest, along with the coins, were two note-
books of handwritten recipes, and one of songs, some of
which I'd heard bards sing in our village. For me and Zach,
forbidden entry to school in our unsplit state, reading had
been a furtive and therefore somehow intimate act. The
two of us, under our mother's tutelage or, more often, alone
together, scratching out the shapes of letters in the clay
banks of the river, or in the dust of the yard behind the
house. Later, there were books, but only a few. A reading
primer with pictures that our father had kept from his own
childhood. The Village Book, held in the Village Hall and
laboriously inscribed with histories of the area, of the local
Councilmen, and of the laws they oversaw. Even in our

relatively well-off village, books were a rarity: reading was for making out instructions on a seed packet bought at market, or reading in the Village Book the names of the two travelling Omegas who had been fined and whipped for stealing a sheep. In the settlement, where few could read and fewer would admit to it, books were an indulgence we couldn't afford.

I didn't tell anyone about Alice's books, but I read and re-read them so many times that the pages began to come away from the spines as I turned them, as if the books existed in a perpetual autumn. In the evenings, when we'd all finished working in the fields and I went home to the cottage, I'd spend hours in Alice's kitchen, following her compact, scrawled guidance for adding rosemary to a loaf of bread, or the easiest way to peel a clove of garlic. When I first followed her instructions, and learned to crush the garlic with the flat of my knife so that the clove slipped from its dry husk like a sweet from its wrapper, I felt closer to Alice than to any of the others in the settlement.

In those quiet evenings, I thought often of my mother, and of Zach. At first, Mum wrote to me a few times a year, her letters carried by Alpha traders who wouldn't even dismount at the settlement to drop them, instead tossing them from their saddle bags. Two years after I arrived at the settlement, she wrote that Zach had an apprenticeship at the Council, at Wyndham. Over the next year or so, more news filtered through: that Zach provided good service. That he grew in power. Then, after five years in the settlement, Mum wrote that Zach's master had died, and Zach had taken over his post. We were only eighteen, but most Councillors started young. They died young too – the rivalries and factions within the Council were legendary. The Judge, who'd been in charge as long as I could remember, was a rare exception, as old as my parents. Most of the others were young. Stories reached us, even in the settlement, of the rise and fall of various Councillors. In the brutal world of the Council fort at Wyndham, it seemed, ruthlessness and ambition counted for more than experience. It didn't surprise me that Zach had been drawn to it, or that he should have done well. I tried to picture him in the splendour of the Council chambers. I thought of his smile of triumph when he'd exposed me, and what he'd said afterwards: *Nobody's going to be throwing rocks at me now. Not ever again.* And while I feared for him, I didn't envy him, even in the year the harvest failed and we went hungry in the settlement.

By that stage Mum's letters were rare – a year or more between them – and for news of the rest of the world I had to rely on the gossip picked up at the Omega market to the west, or shared by the itinerants who passed through our settlement. Along with their small bundles of possessions, they carried with them stories. Those heading west were seeking better land to farm, as the bleak land closer to the deadlands in the east barely produced enough to pay the Council tithes, let alone to live on. But those coming from the west spoke of Council crack-downs: Omegas forced out of long-held settlements, where the land was now deemed too good for them; Alpha raiders who stole and destroyed crops. More and more people forced to seek out the refuges. Rumours of harsher treatment of Omegas came steadily. Even in our settlement, which had decent land compared to many, we were feeling the impact of the ever-higher tithes demanded by the Council collectors. Twice, too, Alpha raiders had attacked us. The first time they came, they'd beaten Ben, whose cottage was at the edge of the settlement. They'd taken everything they could carry, including the coins he'd put aside for the next month's tithes. The second time they came was after the failed harvest; not finding anything to steal, they'd contented themselves with setting fire to the barn. When I suggested to my neighbours that we should report it to the Council, they rolled their eyes.

'So they can send some soldiers out to burn down the rest of the settlement?' said Claire.

'You lived too long in that Alpha village, Cass,' added Nessa. 'You still haven't got it.'

I was learning, though, with each story of brutality that found its way to the settlement. There were other rumours, too, though these were rare, and were shared more furtively: murmurings about Omega resistance, and whispers about the island. But watching my neighbours' resignation as we rebuilt the barn, these ideas seemed far-fetched. The Council had ruled for hundreds of years; the idea that there could be any place free of their control was nothing but wishful thinking.

And why bother with the resistance, anyway? The fatal bond between twins was our safety net. Ever since the drought years there'd been more and more restrictions on Omegas, but at the same time as we griped about tithes, or the limitation of settlements to ever poorer land, we knew that the Council would ultimately protect us. That was what the refuges were for – and after the failed harvest, more and more Omegas considered them. That winter had left my bones straining towards the outside of my skin. It had worn us all down to bones and teeth, and finally one couple from our settlement left for the refuge near Wyndham. We couldn't persuade them to stay, to gamble on the promise of new crops in spring. They'd had enough. So the whole settlement stood together in the dawn light, watching them lock up their cottage, before trudging off down the rock-strewn road.

'Don't know why they're bothering to lock up,' said Nessa. 'They won't be coming back.'

'At least they'll be fed,' Claire replied. 'Only fair that they should have to work for it.'

'For a while, sure. But these days they're saying that once you're in, you're in for good.'

She shrugged. 'It's their choice to go.' I looked again at the retreating figures. The meagre packs they carried looked bigger on their wasted bodies. What choice did they really have?

'Anyway,' she continued. 'You can't tell me you'd rather there were no refuges. At least we know the Council wouldn't let us starve.'

'Not *wouldn't*.' Ben, the oldest at the settlement, joined in. 'They *would* if they could get away with it. But *could* not. There's a difference.'

*

In spring, when the new crops had come in and the hunger was receding, my mother arrived in a bullock cart. When Ben showed her to my cottage, I didn't quite know how to greet her. She looked the same, which only made me more aware of how much I must have changed. Not just the inevitable growth of six years, but the fact that I'd lived as an Omega for that time. That had changed me more than the hunger ever could. I'd encountered a few Alphas since coming to the settlement – the Council's tithe-collectors; the shady merchants who sometimes came to the Omega market. Even amongst Alphas there were the outcast and the poor, passing through the Omega settlements in search of something better. All of them looked at us with contempt, if they met our eyes at all. I'd heard the names they called us: *freak*, *dead-end*. More hurtful than the words was their manner, the small movements that revealed their contempt, and their fear of Omega contamination. Even the most ragged of the Alpha merchants, those who stooped to trade with Omegas, would wince at the touch of an Omega hand when passing a coin.

Although I'd been branded an Omega when I left the village, I hadn't really known what it meant. I remembered how hurt I'd been when my mother hadn't hugged me goodbye. Now, as she stood awkwardly in my small kitchen, I knew better even than to reach out to her.

We sat opposite each other at my kitchen table.

'I just came to give you this,' she said, passing me a gold coin. Zach, she said, had sent her six of them, each one worth half a year's harvest.

The coin warmed quickly in my hand as I turned it over, then back again. 'Why give this to me?'

'You're going to need it.'

I gestured at the cottage around us, at the vines, heavy with figs, visible through the small window. 'I don't need it. I'm doing fine. And you've never cared, before.'

She leaned forward, spoke quietly. 'You can't stay here.'

I dropped the coin on the table. It spun noisily for a few seconds, settled with a clunk on the scratched wood. 'What do you mean? Wasn't it enough for you to drive me out of the village?'

Mum shook her head. 'I didn't want to have to do this. Maybe I shouldn't have. But you have to take the money and go. Soon. It's Zach.'

I sighed. 'It's always Zach.'

'He's powerful, now. That means he has enemies. People

57

are talking – about him, about what he's done at the Council.'

'What he's done? We're nineteen. He's only been on the Council for a year.'

'You've heard of The General?'

'Everyone's heard of The General.' Omegas in particular. Each time a new anti-Omega policy was rumoured, it was her name people were whispering at the market. When the tithe-collectors had demanded higher rates from us over the last two years, it was always based on The General's latest 'reforms'.

'She's only a year older than you and Zach, if that. People make enemies on the Council, Cass. Most Councillors don't live long.' Nor did their twins, though she didn't need to state it. 'You know what Zach's like. Driven. Ambitious. He's going by the name The Reformer now. He has followers, works with important people. It won't be long before somebody tries to get to you.'

'No.' I shoved the coin across the table to her. 'I won't leave. And even if he has enemies, he wouldn't let them get to me. He'd keep me safe.'

She reached across the table, as if to take my hand, but stopped herself. How long had it been, I wondered, since anyone had touched me with tenderness?

'That's what I'm afraid of.'

I looked blankly at her. 'What do you mean?'

'You've heard of the Keeping Rooms.'

This was one of the many stories that had blown through the settlement, like the tumbleweeds that snagged and rolled across the plain. Whispers that somewhere beneath the Council chambers at Wyndham was a secret prison where Councillors would keep their Omega twins. It was called the Keeping Rooms: an underground complex where Omegas were locked indefinitely, so that their powerful counterparts wouldn't be vulnerable to any attack on their Omega twins.

'That? It's just a rumour. And even if it were true, Zach would never do it. He wouldn't. I know him best.'

'No. You're closest to him. It's not the same thing. He'll come for you, Cass. He'll lock you away, to protect himself.'

I shook my head. 'He wouldn't do it.'

Was I trying to convince her, or myself? Either way, she didn't argue with me. We both knew that I wouldn't leave.

Before going, Mum reached down from the cart and pressed the coin into my hand again. I felt it in my palm as the cart receded into the distance. And I didn't spend it; not to run, or even to buy food. I kept it with me, as I'd once kept the key from Alice, and I thought of Zach whenever I held it.

It was Zach who'd taught me to repress my visions, as a child. His need to expose me had made me vigilant about not acknowledging or revealing anything of what I knew. Now I was doing it again, and again it was for him. I refused to countenance the scenes that came to me, just before waking, or during the moments in the field when I paused to splash water from my flask onto my face. I placed my trust in him, rather than in my visions. He wouldn't do it, I repeated to myself. I thought of how gently he'd bathed my wound, after the branding. I remembered the days, months and years that the two of us, viewed with suspicion by the rest of the village, had spent together. And while I clearly recalled his hostility, his many cruelties, I knew also that he had depended on me as closely as I had depended on him.

So I worked, harder than ever before. When the harvest came, always the busiest time of year, my hands were calloused by the scythe, and the wheat chaff worked its way under my fingernails until they bled. I tried to concentrate on the immediate sounds: the rasp of the scythe, the thuds of the bundled wheat being tossed down, the shouts of the other workers. Every day I worked late, until the reluctant night finally arrived, and I made my way back to the cottage in the dark.

And it worked. I'd almost convinced myself that they weren't coming at all, until they arrived and I realised that the approach of the armed riders was as familiar as the scythe in my hand or the path between the fields that led to the cottage.

As the rider hoisted me upwards, I caught a hint of gold below. The coin had fallen from my pocket to the ground, and was quickly lost in the hoof-churned mud.

CHAPTER 6

By the time Zach came to my cell, I'd counted one hundred and eighteen days. Two hundred and thirty-six meal trays. Eight visits from The Confessor.

His footsteps were as unmistakable to me as the sound of his voice, or the particular rhythm of his breath while sleeping. In the moments it took him to open the lock, it felt as if all the years without him were unspooling again. I'd sprung up at the sound of his footsteps, but by the time he'd opened the door I'd forced myself to resume my seat on the bed.

He stood for a while in the doorway. When I looked at him, I saw double: the man in front of me, and the boy he evoked. He was tall, now, and he wore his dark hair longer, swept behind his ears. His face had filled out, softening the sharp angles of his cheekbones and chin. I'd remembered that in summer he used to have freckles – a scattering of them across his nose, like the first handful of dust thrown on to a coffin. There was no sign of them now, his skin only a few degrees less pale than my own cell-blanched flesh.

He stepped in and locked the door behind him, slipping the keys into his pocket.

'Aren't you going to say anything?' he said.

I didn't dare to speak, not wanting my voice to betray how much I'd hated him, or how much I'd missed him.

Zach went on. 'Don't you want me to tell you why I had to do it?'

'I know why you've done it.'

He gave a half-laugh. 'I'd almost forgotten how hard you can be to talk to.'

'It's not my job to make this easy for you.'

He began to pace. His voice stayed calm, his words coming with the same measured rate as his footsteps. 'You can't let me have anything, can you? Not even the explanation. I knew what I wanted to say to you. I'd practised it. But here you are, the same as always, claiming to know everything.'

'I can't let you have anything?' I echoed. 'You got everything. You got to stay. You got Mum.' My voice cracked on her name.

'It was too late,' he said, halting his pacing. 'Alice had already killed Dad. And you'd already poisoned everything. It was like you'd contaminated me – all those years of being unsplit. The others never accepted me. Not properly. It should have been the life I'd wanted.' He held his empty hands out, fingers splayed. 'But you'd already ruined everything.'

'I had nothing,' I said. 'There were days in the settlement when we were all going hungry. But you couldn't even let me have that. You've got me locked away here, and you still think you're hard done by?'

'I don't have a choice, Cass.'

'Why are you trying to convince me? You want me to absolve you? Tell you I understand?'

'You said you did understand.'

'I said I know why you've done it. I know what your reasoning was. You've made enemies, now that you're a big player in the Council. You think they could use me to get at you. That doesn't make it right to lock me away.'

'What would you have done?'

'Since when have you cared what I want or think?'

He was angry now. 'Everything's always depended on you. My whole life was on hold – it couldn't start until you were gone.'

'It had started. We had a life.' I thought, as I so often did, of those years we spent together, the two of us existing at the margins of the village. 'You just wanted a different one.'

'No. I wanted my life. Mine. You made it impossible. And now I'm on my way to achieving something big. I can't let you get in the way.'

'So you're ruining my life, to protect yours.'

'There's only one life between us – that's what you don't realise. You've always acted as if we can both have what we want. That's not how the world works.'

'So change it. You said you want to be a big, important person and change the world. It didn't occur to you that we were changing the world, every day we weren't split?'

He fell quiet. After a few minutes he came and sat beside me, sighing slightly as he slumped back. When he drew his knees up in front of him, they were much higher than mine. The hair on his arms was thicker and darker than I remembered, not tinged blond from the sun as it used to be. Our bodies had changed so much in the years since I'd seen him, but these new bodies slipped automatically back into the same old symmetry: sitting side by side on the bed, backs against the wall, just as we used to sit on my bed in the village.

I whispered to him, like we used to do back then, when our parents were arguing downstairs. 'You don't have to be this person, Zach.'

He stood up, taking the bunch of keys from his pocket. 'I wouldn't have to be, if it weren't for you. If you hadn't made everything so hard right from the start.'

In the months of waiting for him to come to the cell, I'd thought carefully about what I would say, and I'd promised myself I'd stay calm. But as he moved toward the door, my intentions abandoned me. The prospect of being left alone again in the cell loomed in front of me, and I felt too full of blood, until my whole body was a pulse, racing. I ran at him, grabbed at the keys he held.

He was half a head taller than me; stronger, too, after my six lean years in the settlement and the months of stagnation in the cell. With one arm stretched out, hand splayed about my neck, he kept me away from him with barely a struggle. I knew, even as I clawed and kicked at him, that it was pointless. If I were to succeed in knocking him out, or breaking his arm, I'd only find myself as incapacitated as him. But in my mind I wasn't fighting him; I was fighting the very walls of the cell, and the concrete floor, and the indifference of the hours that came and went while I festered in that room. I threw my whole weight against him, until the bones of his hand were rasping against my jawbone as he held me at arm's length. Still he didn't relent, even when I felt the flesh of his forearm snag and rip under my nails.

He leaned forward so that I could hear his whisper over my own frantic breath.

'I should almost be grateful to you. The others on the Council, they might talk about the risk posed by Omegas. The threat of contamination. But they haven't lived it, not like I have. They don't know how dangerous you can be.'

I was aware of my own shaking; it was only when he let his arm fall that I saw that he was shaking too. We stood like that for a long time. The space between us was quaking with our panted breaths, noisy as the night before a summer storm, when the air broils and the cicadas hiss and the whole world rattles and waits.

'Please. Don't do this, Zach.' As I begged, I remembered how he'd begged me to reveal myself as the Omega, that night in the bedroom when we were children. Was this how he'd felt then?

He said nothing, just turned away. As he left, and locked the door behind him, I looked down at my still-juddering fists and saw his blood, bleeding from under the nails of my right hand.

*

The Confessor had taken to bringing a map with her. Dispensing with any preliminaries, she would lock the door behind her, spread the map out on my bed, and then look up at me. 'Show me where the island is.' Sometimes she'd circle particular areas with a finger. 'We know it's off the west or south-west coasts. We're getting closer – we will find them.'

'Then what do you need me for?'

'Because your brother isn't known for his patience.'

I tried to laugh. 'What are you going to do? Torture me? Threaten to kill me? Any serious pain and you're torturing Zach.'

The Confessor leaned in. 'You think there's nothing worse than what we've already done to you? You have no idea how lucky you are. And you're only going to keep being lucky if you make yourself useful to us.' She thrust the map forwards again. The intensity of her gaze felt physical. It was as searing as the branding iron on my forehead all those years ago.

'Like you make yourself useful, working for them? A performing freak for your Alpha masters?'

She leaned forward, ever so slowly, until her face was so close to mine that I could see the tiny hairs on her cheeks, fine and pale as corn-silk. Her nostrils flared slightly as she took a deep, slow breath, and then another.

'Are you so sure that they're in charge of me?' she whispered.

She groped more deeply into my mind. When we were children, Zach and I had levered up a large, flat stone. It had revealed all the worms and grubs underneath, ripped from darkness into light, squirming white in their fleshy nakedness. Now, under The Confessor's gaze, I was no more than those grubs. There was nothing of me that she couldn't see, couldn't take.

I'd learned, after the initial shock, to clench my mind closed, like an eye. Like a fist. To block her out as I struggled to preserve anything of myself. I knew I had to keep the island safe from her. But, selfishly, I found myself just as worried about protecting those few personal memories that I treasured.

The autumn afternoon when Zach and I were practising our writing in the yard behind the house. While the chickens pecked and scuffled around us, we had squatted, sticks in hand, and scratched our clumsy letters in the dust. He wrote my name, and I wrote his.

The long days by the river, when the other children were in school, and Zach and I would pass each other the treasures we turned up in our aimless wanderings. He showed me the stone with the snail fossil etched into it. I brought to him an opened river-oyster shell, its inside like the blinded milky eye of an Omega beggar I'd seen on the road to Haven.

And the memory of all those nights, when we would pass stories and whispers between the beds, just as we swapped those riverside treasures during the day. Lying in the dark, hearing the rain's muted spatter on the thatch, Zach offered me the story of how the bullocks in the neighbour's field had charged at him when he took the shortcut to the well, and how he'd had to climb a tree to escape being trampled. I told him how I'd seen the other children rigging up a new swing from the oak in the schoolyard, when I'd peered over the wall we were never allowed to cross.

'We have our own swing,' he'd said.

It was true, though it wasn't a proper swing – just a spot we'd found, upstream, where a willow grew so close to the water that you could grasp the low draped branches and swing out above the river. On hot days, we'd compete to see who could swing furthest out, dropping triumphant into the river below.

There were more recent memories, too, from the settlement. The evenings when I'd sit in front of my small fire and read Alice's book of recipes, or her collection of songs, and picture her sitting in the same spot, years earlier, and writing them.

And later, the warmth on the coin from my mother's hand, when she'd passed it to me in her attempt to warn me about Zach. It was a small thing to treasure: not even a touch – just the second-hand warmth of a coin that she'd held. But it was all I had of her, from those last few years, and it was mine.

All these things were now exposed to The Confessor's

dispassionate gaze. To her, they were no more than clutter in a drawer that she was rifling through, in search of something more valuable. Each time she moved on, she left me scrabbling to reassemble the disarranged mess of my mind.

When The Confessor stood and left, taking the map with her, I knew I should have been pleased that I'd managed to keep her from the island. But in concentrating on concealing those, I was forced to leave so much else exposed. These memories, these scraps of the life I'd lived before the cell, she just picked up, turned over, and cast aside. And although they were insignificant to her, nothing she'd touched was untarnished. After each visit, I felt I had fewer memories for her to peruse.

*

The next day, Zach came. His visits were rarer these days, and when he did come, he usually avoided my eyes, fidgeting with his keys instead. He hardly spoke, responding with shrugs to most of my questions. But every few weeks I'd hear the key in the lock, the door scrape along the floor, and in he'd come, my twin, my jailer, to sit at the far end of my bed. I didn't know why he came, any more than I knew why I was always glad when I heard his footsteps in the corridor.

'You need to talk to her,' he said. 'Just tell her what you see. Or let her in.'

'Into my mind, you mean?'

He shrugged. 'Don't sound so horrified. You're like her, after all.'

I shook my head. 'I don't do what she does. I don't poke around in other people's minds. And she can stay the hell out of mine – it's the only thing I've got here.' I didn't know how to express to him what it was like when she tried to probe my mind. How it left me feeling sullied, unsafe even in my own head.

He gave a sigh that turned into a laugh. 'I'd be impressed that you've held her out this long, except that I already knew how stubborn you are.'

'Then you should know it's not going to change. I won't help you.'

'You need to, Cass.' He leaned close to me. For a moment I thought he might take my hand, as he had all those years ago when our father was dying and he'd begged for my help. His pupils flared and contracted in their own uneven pulse. When he was this close to me, I could see the bloodied flakes of skin on his lower lip. I remembered how he used to chew his lip when Mum and Dad were fighting downstairs, or when the other children in the village were taunting us.

'What are you scared of?' I whispered. 'Are you afraid of The Confessor?'

He stood. 'There are worse things we could do to you than this cell, you know.' He slapped at the wall. His open palm left a mark on the dusty concrete. 'Worse things happening to some of the Omegas kept here. It's only because you're a seer that you get to live like this.' Stretching his neck backwards, he dragged his hands down his face, took a few breaths with his eyes closed. 'I told her you'd be useful.'

'You want me to be grateful? For this?' I gestured at the cell around us. The walls had become a vice around my life, everything crushed down to these few square yards of greyness. And my mind, too, had started to feel cell-like: enclosed and murky. Worst of all was the grim indifference of time, which kept passing, while I was stuck here in this endless half-life of meal trays and relentless light.

'You don't know the care I take of you. Everything you eat –' he gestured to the tray on the floor '– I have somebody taste it first. Every jug of water. Everything.'

'I'm touched by your concern for me,' I said. 'But as I recall, when I was living my own life, in the settlement, I didn't even have to worry about people trying to poison me.'

'Your own life? You weren't so keen on "your own life" all those years that you were trying to claim mine.'

'I wasn't trying to claim anything. I just didn't want to be sent away, any more than you did.' Silence. 'If you'd just let me on the ramparts occasionally, like when I was first here. Or to talk to some of the other prisoners. Just to be able to talk to someone else.'

He shook his head. 'You know I can't. You saw what happened on the ramparts that time. It could have been you who that madman attacked.' He looked at me with what could have been tenderness. 'The whole point of having you here is to keep you safe.'

'If we were allowed to talk to one another, that wouldn't have happened. He wouldn't have gone mad. Why would the other Omegas here ever hurt me? They're in the same situation as I am. Why deny us company?'

'Because of who their twins are.'

'Their twins are your friends, your Council cronies.'

'You're so naïve, Cass. They're the people I work with, work for – not my friends. You think some of them wouldn't like to get their own twins to finish you off, to get at me?'

'Then where does it end? By your logic, we should all spend our lives in padded cells, Alphas and Omegas alike.'

'It's not just me,' he said. 'It's always happened: using those who are close to people to manipulate them. Even in the Before. If they needed to control somebody, they could kidnap their husband, child, lover. The only difference in the After is that, now, it's more direct. In the Before, you had to watch your back. Now, we all have two backs to watch. It's that simple.'

'It's only simple because you reduce having a twin to a liability. You're paranoid.'

'And you're wilfully naïve.'

'Is that why you come down here?' I asked him as he stood and unlocked the door. 'Because you can't trust anybody else up there, in the Council?'

'That would imply I could trust you,' he said, pulling the door shut behind him. I heard the key turn.

*

I calculated that it must have been at least a year since I'd seen the sky. In the artificially lit world of the Keeping Rooms, even my dreams changed; my day-time visions too. When I'd first started to have visions of the island, I'd wondered if they were just a fantasy to alleviate the horror of my confinement. Now that new, darker visions began to intrude, for a long time I thought they might just be morbid imaginings, that the horror of my long isolation had seeped into my dreams. As my tally of days in the Keeping Rooms crept upwards, I was growing distrustful of my own mind. But what I saw was too alien, and too consistent, for me to believe that I'd come up with it myself. The details, too, were so vivid that I was convinced I couldn't have created them: the glass tanks, real right down to the dust on the rubber seals at the base. The wires and panels above the tanks, each panel speckled by tiny lights, red or green. The tubes, flesh-coloured and rubbery, emerging from the top of each tank.

How could I have invented such a sight, when I couldn't even decipher what it was? All that I knew for sure was that it was taboo, like the glass ball of light in my cell. The tubes and wires that I saw surrounding the tanks matched the stories of the Before, and all its Electric alchemy. The lights, too, were the same unnatural spark as the light in my cell. Each light, unwavering, was a dot of pure colour, without heat. This was a machine – but a machine for what? It was both messier and more awesome than the whispers about the Before had led me to believe. The tangle of wires and tubes looked disordered, improvised. But the whole, the pulsating mass of connections, lights, and tanks, was so huge and so complex that it couldn't help be impressive, despite the shudder it provoked in me.

At first, the tanks were all that the visions showed me. Then, floating within the tanks, I saw the bodies, suspended in a viscous liquid that seemed to slow everything until even the waving of their hair was lethargic. From each drooping mouth, a tube. But the eyes were the worst. Most had their eyes closed, but even those few with open eyes wore entirely blank expressions, their eyes utterly empty. These were the ruins of people. I thought of Zach's words, when I'd complained about the cell: *There are worse things we could do to you than this cell, you know.*

I sensed the tanks most acutely when Zach came, though he did this rarely now. The tank room was like a smell that clung to him. Even as I heard his key in the lock I could feel the faces looming into sight. After he left, they crowded me for hours with their closed eyes and open mouths. They were all Omegas, all suspended in the timelessness of those glass vats. As the months passed, even as Zach's visits grew rarer, my awareness of the tank room became near-constant. Far from being abstract, it felt not only real but close. It became so pressing a physical presence that I felt as if I could navigate by it: the sure pull of that room, perhaps only hundreds of feet away, had become my compass point. Just as the river had once been the basis of my mental map of the valley where I grew up, now my imagination's map of the fort was oriented by two locations: the cell, and the tank room. Beneath it all, the river was still there. I could sense it running deep underfoot, its ceaseless movement taunting me with my own stagnation.

*

One day The Confessor unlocked the door, but didn't step inside the cell.

'Get up,' she said, holding the door open.

I hadn't been out of the cell for more than a year. I wondered if she was taunting me. In the last few months, I'd sometimes begun to fear I was going mad. Looking through the open door, I distrusted even the strip of corridor I could make out. To my space-starved eyes, the concrete passageway seemed as far-fetched as a mountain vista under sunlight.

'Hurry up. I'm going to show you something. We don't have long.'

Even with three armed soldiers standing by, and The Confessor watching me impatiently, I couldn't hide my excitement as we stepped through the door.

She refused to tell me where she was taking me, or to respond at all to any of my questions. She walked briskly, a few steps ahead of me, the guards following closely behind.

As it turned out, it wasn't far: just to the end of the corridor, through another locked door, then down a flight of stairs to another row of doors.

'We're not going outside?' I asked, facing the row of cell doors that mimicked my own: the grey steel; the narrow slot for meal trays near the base; the observation hatch at eye-level, which could be opened only from the corridor, not within.

'This isn't a picnic excursion,' she said. 'There's something you need to see.'

She walked to the third door and slid open the hatch. Like the one in my cell, it clearly hadn't been opened often – it slid awkwardly, shrieking with rust.

The Confessor stepped back. 'Go on,' she said, gesturing at the hatch.

I stepped towards the door, leaned closer to the opening. It was darker inside the cell, the single Electric light no match for the rows of them in the corridor. But even as my eyes were adjusting, I could see that the cell was just like mine. The same narrow bed, the same grey walls.

'Look closer,' said The Confessor, her breath warm on the back of my ear.

That's when I saw the man. He was standing against the wall, in the darkest corner of the cell, watching the door warily.

'Who are you?' he said, stepping forward, eyes narrowing to see me more clearly. His voice was as rusty as the observation hatch, grating with disuse.

'Don't talk to him,' said The Confessor. 'Just watch.'

'Who are you?' he said, louder this time. He was perhaps ten years older than me. I hadn't seen him before, on any of those early visits to the ramparts, but his long beard and his pale skin showed that he wasn't new to the Keeping Rooms.

'I'm Cass,' I said.

'There's no point talking to him,' said The Confessor. She sounded almost bored. 'Just watch. It'll happen soon. I've been feeling it coming for days.'

The man stepped forward again, only feet from the door now, so close that I could have reached out to him through the small opening. He was missing one hand, and his brand was visible through his matted hair.

'Is there someone else there with you?' he said. 'I haven't seen anyone for months. Not since they brought me here.' He stepped closer, his hand raised.

Then he buckled. It was as sudden as that, his legs giving way like a sand embankment in heavy rain. His hands went to his stomach, and twice his whole body contracted. He made no noise; the only thing to emerge from his mouth was a stream of blood, black in the candlelight. He didn't move again.

I had no chance to speak, or to respond at all, other than to jump back from the hatch when he fell. Before I could look in again, The Confessor had grabbed my arm, turned me to face her.

'See? You think you're safe here?' She pushed me back against the door, the steel cold against my bare arms. 'That man's twin thought she was safe, because she had him locked up down here. But she made enough enemies on the Council that even the Keeping Rooms couldn't protect her. They couldn't get at him, so they had to take her out directly. They still managed it.'

I already knew. The horror of the man's death was doubled for me. I'd seen it the moment the man fell: a woman lying on her stomach in a bed, her dark hair neatly plaited, and a knife in her back.

'Did Zach do this?'

She shook her head dismissively. 'Not this time. And that's not important – what you need to realise is that even he can't protect you, not necessarily. He's in favour at the moment, sure, but his plans are ambitious. If the Council turns on him, they'll find a way to get to one of you.'

Her face was so close to mine that I could see the individual eyelashes, and the vein that pulsed on her forehead, just to the left of her brand. I closed my eyes, but the darkness only filled with memories of the man on the floor behind me, the false tongue of blood hanging from his mouth. I couldn't breathe.

She spoke very slowly. 'You need to start helping Zach, and helping me. If he fails, if the other Councillors turn on him, they'll get to one of you.'

'I won't help you,' I said. I thought of the tank rooms, what Zach had done to those floating people. But those horrors seemed distant compared to the bleeding body on the floor behind me, and The Confessor's implacable face close to mine.

'I can't,' I said. 'I have nothing to tell you.'

I was wondering how much longer I could keep from crying in front of her, but she suddenly turned.

'Put her back in her cell,' she called over her shoulder to the guards as she walked away.

*

My world was reduced to the cell, the walls, the roof, the floor. The mercilessness of the door. I tried to picture the outside world: the morning sun throwing sharp shadows over the stubble of freshly cut wheat; the night sky infinitely wide above the river. But these had become concepts, rather than realities. They were as lost to me as the smell of rain, the feel of river-sand underfoot, the sound of birds announcing the dawn. All those things were less real, now, than the visions of the tank room, and of those bodies, sodden-fleshed and silent, floating amongst the tubes. The visions of the island had become rare, too. Those glimpses of open sea could no longer penetrate the cell. The tally of my days in the Keeping Rooms was growing until I felt the cell was crammed with them. It was as though the cell were slowly filling with water. I could barely breathe for the weight of lost weeks, months, and now years. Is this how it begins, I wondered, the madness that so often stalks seers? If it were going to happen, then the years of imprisonment could only accelerate the process. I'd heard my father describe the seer at Haven market as *out of his mind*. Now that turn of phrase felt like a literal description. The Confessor's probing, and the visions of the tanks, were so all-consuming that there was no room left in my own mind for anything else, least of all myself.

Zach came to see me so rarely now – sometimes months passed between visits. When he did come, I could hardly speak to him. I noticed, though, how much his face had changed over my years in the Keeping Rooms. He was thinner, so his lips were now the only part of his face with any softness. I wondered if I'd changed too, and whether he would notice if I had.

'You know it can't go on like this,' he said.

I nodded, but I felt as though I was underwater, his words muffled and distant. My cell's cramped walls and low ceiling conspired to create echoes, doubling every noise so that any sounds were always just a little unsteady. Now the echo had started to feel like part of a broader blurring – everything was slipping out of focus.

'If it were up to me,' he went on, 'I'd keep you here. But

I've started something, and I need to finish it. I thought maybe I could keep you out of it, if you made yourself useful. But you won't give her anything.'

He didn't need to specify who 'her' was.

'She won't put up with it any longer.' He spoke so low that I could barely hear him, as if he could hardly bear to hear his own admission of fear. He leaned forward so our faces were close. 'If it were up to me, I'd keep you here,' he said, louder now. I didn't know why it mattered so much to him to convince me of this. I turned my head to the wall.

*

At first I didn't know why the dreams of the empty tank terrified me so. I'd been seeing the tanks for three years now. They always sickened me, but they'd become familiar – my body no longer flinched in surprise when I saw them in a dream. I'd grown used to them, the same way I'd grown used to the brand on my own face. Why, then, when I dreamed of the empty tank, did I wake tangled in sheets wet with sudden-sprung sweat? The tank was empty – it should have been less horrifying than the occupied ones that normally plagued my nights. It just sat there, a glass belly waiting to be filled.

For the fourth night in a row, I dreamed of the same tank again. It sat in the same dull light; the wires and pipes clustered above it as they always had. The curve of the glass was the same, but something was acutely wrong. This time the glass curved not away from me, but around me. I could feel a tube in my own mouth, its rubbery intrusion into my windpipe, and the pain at the corner of my mouth where, protruding, the tube had eroded my skin. I couldn't close my mouth, or keep out the liquid that now filled the tank, foully sweet. My eyes, too, couldn't close. The viscous fluid blurred my vision, everything wavering and softened, as if seen through one of the heat-waves that hovered above the settlement's fields on midsummer days.

When I woke, I screamed until my throat was gravelled and my voice couldn't stick on any note, juddering and jerking between them. I screamed Zach's name, until that single syllable took on strange shapes, became unrecognis-able. In my first weeks in the Keeping Rooms I'd learned that screaming achieved nothing, brought nobody to the cell door, but I screamed nonetheless.

For six more nights I felt the tank fill around me, unable to move as the fluid took possession of my flesh, closing finally over my head, around the tubes that threaded into me at the throat and wrists. Each night, until I woke myself, screaming, I was suspended from the throat tube like a fish on a line.

I couldn't eat. Each attempt to swallow reminded me of the tube down my throat, and I gagged and retched. I did what I could to avoid sleep, when the visions came most easily. At night, I paced the cell, counting footsteps until the numbers blurred. I took to pinching my arms and pulling hairs from my head, one at a time, trying to use the pain not just to keep myself awake, but to locate myself in my real body, and to keep at bay the tanked self of my dreams. Nothing worked. It was all unravelling: my body; my mind. Time itself was jumpy and fragmented now. Some days I slipped through hours like someone skidding, out of control, down a scree-slope. Other times I could have sworn that time stopped, and a single breath seemed to last a year. I thought of the mad seer at Haven market, and the mad

Omega on the ramparts. This is how it happens, I thought. This is how my own mind deserts me.

In the end, I scratched a note into the meal tray with the edge of my blunted spoon. *Zach: urgent – important vision. Will tell you (only you) in exchange for ten minutes outside, on the ramparts.*

He sent The Confessor, as I'd known he would.

She sat in her usual chair, back to the door. The previous days must have left me looking ragged, but she made no comment on it. I wondered whether she even saw it, or whether her mental acuity meant she had no need for external observations. 'Normally, you're not so keen to share your visions. Quite the opposite. Which makes us curious, you see.'

'If Zach's so curious, send him. I won't tell you.'

I'd known this would be the hardest part. I could feel The Confessor probing my mind, the way our mother used to pry open the shells of river-mussels, circling the seam, testing with the knife for the one weak spot from which to lever open the shell.

'Closing your eyes won't stop me, you know.'

I hadn't even noticed I'd closed them until The Confessor spoke. I realised that my teeth, too, were clenched tight. I forced myself to look straight at her. 'You'll get nothing.'

'Perhaps. Maybe you're getting better at this. Or maybe there's nothing there – no special vision, no helpful insight.'

'Oh, so it's a trap? What am I going to do? Shimmy down the walls on a rope made of bedsheets? Come on.' I paused. It was hard to talk and brace my mind against The Confessor at the same time. 'I just want to see the sky. If I'm going to tell you what I know, why shouldn't I trade it for that?'

'It's not a trade if you've got nothing to offer us.'

'It's about the island,' I blurted. I'd hoped not to give away even this much, but the terror of the tanks made me reckless.

'I see. The island that you've insisted for the last four years doesn't exist.'

I nodded, mute. While her expression didn't change, I felt her mind, eager now, like the hands of an unwelcome suitor. I concentrated harder than ever, trying to open my mind without allowing her full access. I focused on giving away only a glimpse, just a fraction of a glimpse, enough to confirm the value of my visions without revealing anything that would be disastrous for the island, or for my own plans. I fixed my mind on a single image, the way a lone shaft of light would fall between the curtains of my kitchen at the settlement, illuminating only a fragment of the opposite wall. Just the town on the island, just one of its busy, steep streets. Close-up, no identifying features of the landscape. Just the town, its market-hub, the houses stacked on the rising ground. Just the town.

I heard The Confessor's intake of breath.

'Enough,' I said. 'Tell Zach what he has to do, and I'll tell him everything.'

But it wasn't enough. The probing continued, almost frenzied now. Once, at the settlement, I'd woken to find a raven had picked its way through a gap in the thatch and become trapped in my tiny bedroom, dashing from wall to wall in a cacophony of feathers until it found the open window. The Confessor's presence in my head felt like that now: the same mixture of desperation and aggression.

I didn't speak. Instead, for the first time, I tried to match The Confessor in her probing. I pictured my mother's hands above the mussel-bowl. I tried to make my mind the knife. I'd always resisted doing this: visions had always been something I'd suffered, rather than used. The violation I'd felt in my sessions with The Confessor had made me even more unwilling to use my own mind that way. So I was surprised at how easily it came to me: like peeling back a curtain. And what I saw were just fragments, just like my dreams, but it was enough. I saw a place I hadn't seen before. A huge, round chamber. There were no tanks this time. Only wires, like those in my visions of the tank room, but infinitely multiplied. They climbed the curved walls, which were stacked with metal boxes.

I felt The Confessor recoil. She stood so quickly the chair was knocked backwards, and she leaned over me. 'Don't try to play me at my own game.'

I tried to hide my shaking hands as I met her gaze. 'Send me my twin.'

*

When he finally came, the next afternoon, he looked shocked at the state of me.

'Are you sick? Has someone done something to you?' He rushed to where I stood, grabbing my elbow and guiding me to the chair. 'How did they do this? Nobody else can get in here, except The Confessor.'

'Nobody has. It's this place itself.' I gestured at the cell. 'You can't seriously expect me to be blooming with health and joy. Anyway,' I said, 'you don't look so great yourself.' I still hadn't got used to this new Zach, his face stripped back to bone, with dark circles spreading like stains from beneath his eyes.

'Probably because I've been up most of the night trying to work out what you're playing at.'

'Why does it have to be complicated? I need to get outside, Zach. Just for a few moments. I'm going mad in here.' It was no ploy to say this, even if I couldn't let Zach know the true source of my terror. I was genuinely at the limit of my endurance, as my shattered appearance attested.

'It's too dangerous. You know that. You know I don't keep you in here for fun.'

I shook my head. 'Just think about how dangerous it is for you if I go mad. I could do anything.'

He just laughed. 'Trust me – you're not in a position to threaten me.'

'I'm not threatening you. I'm offering you something – something that could really help you.'

'And since when have you ever been interested in helping me?'

'Since I started losing my mind in here. I need this. Just ten minutes in the light. To see the sky. It's not a lot to ask, especially given what I can tell you.'

He shook his head. 'I'd believe you if you'd ever given us anything useful before. The Confessor says you sit there like a wax doll in her sessions with you. You've never even admitted the island exists, and now you're telling us you know something useful about it. So why trust you now?'

I sighed. 'Fine. I lied to her about the island.' He stood, walked quickly to the door. I spoke to his back. 'I knew that's what it would take to get you here. But I'm not lying about having something useful to tell you. I couldn't tell her.'

'Why? That's her job, collecting information.'

'Because it's about her.'

He paused, hand still on the door, his other hand holding the hefty bunch of keys that he always carried.

'That's why it had to be you I told. It's about her – what she's planning to do to you.'

'I'm not going to believe this crap,' he spat. 'She's the one person here I can trust. More than you.'

I shrugged. 'You don't have to believe it. I'll just tell you what I know, and it's up to you whether you believe it or not.'

He stared at me for a few moments. I watched as he turned, inserted the key, opened the door. He still didn't speak. Finally he stepped outside, leaving the door open behind him. 'Ten minutes,' he called back as he headed down the corridor. 'Then we come back here, and you tell me everything.'

CHAPTER 7

Later, when I tried to remember the moment of stepping outside the cell, I couldn't. I'd just chased after Zach, blindly following him through the long corridor, through another locked door, and then up a flight of stairs. It was only at the top of the stairs, where three high windows let in the light, that I felt the enormity of it. I was at once shielding my wincing eyes and gaping at the window for more. Already the fog of the last few weeks was dispersing; my mind felt clearer than it had for months. It was as if the fort above the cells had been a physical weight, bearing down on me. As we made our way out of the depths of the fort, I was shedding the burden.

Ignoring me, Zach led me along another long corridor, unlocked a larger door, then paused. 'I don't know if you're stupid enough to try anything, but don't bother.' I tried to disregard the light and fresh air streaming in from the partly opened door, and to concentrate on his words. 'You know you can't fight me. The other doors leading to the ramparts are locked. And stay close to me.'

He pushed the door fully open. Despite the pain from

my glare-struck eyes, the fresh air itself was intoxicating. I took heaving breaths as I stepped out.

The long, narrow rampart was unchanged since those escorted visits four years ago, in the first months of my imprisonment. It was a terrace, perhaps sixty feet long, protruding halfway up the sheer face of the fort. In front of us, crenellations toothed the wall that overlooked the drop below. Behind us, the wall of the fort continued vertically, carved straight into the side of the mountain. I heard Zach locking the door from which we'd just emerged, in the centre of the rampart. At each end of the terrace, either side of us, identical doors were set in the wall, their solid wood criss-crossed by metal spars.

For a few moments I just stood there, head tilted slightly back, sun on my face. When I approached the battlements, Zach shifted to block my way.

I laughed. 'Relax. You can't blame me for wanting to see. My view's been fairly limited for the last four years.'

He nodded, but stayed close to me as I reached the edge and leaned over the waist-high wall to see the city below.

'I've never seen the city properly before,' I said. 'It was night when they brought me from the settlement, and I had something over my head. And when they used to let us up here, we were never allowed near the edge.'

From this height, Wyndham was like a jumble of buildings tossed down the slope. It was too chaotic to be beautiful, but its size alone was impressive. The city clambered up the mountainside, as high as the base of the fort, but also spread out into the flat of the plain, where roads faded into the hills and the blurred horizon. The river meandered into view from the south, curving around the base of the city before disappearing into the deep caverns of the mountain itself. Even from this high I could see movement: carts on the roads; washing draped from windows, patiently flapping in the breeze. So many people, so close to where I'd been, alone, for all those indistinguishable days and nights.

Zach had turned away from the city. I did the same, leaning back next to him against the low wall. On either side of us, merlons rose to above head-height.

'You said before that you don't trust anyone here, except The Confessor.'

He didn't respond, looked down at his hands.

'So why choose to live this way?' I asked. 'I'm here because I can't leave. But you could; you could just walk away.'

'Was this part of your bargain? That we have a little heart-to-heart? Because I didn't agree to that.' He turned around again, looking over Wyndham. 'Anyway, it's not that straightforward. There are things I need to do.' In the clear light I could see how prominent the bones had become in his face. He exhaled. 'I've started things here. They're my projects. I have to finish them. It's complicated.'

'It doesn't have to be.'

'You've always been such an idealist. Things are simple for you.' His voice matched the tiredness of his eyes.

'It could be simple for you too. You could just leave – go back to the village, work the land with Mum.'

Before he'd even turned, I knew I'd said the wrong thing. 'Work the land?' he hissed. 'Do you have any idea who I am, now? What I've achieved? And the village is the last place I'd ever go. Even after the split, I was never treated like the other Alphas. I thought it would get better, but it didn't.' His pointing finger jabbed towards me. 'You did that, all those years you dodged the split. I can never go back there.' He'd stepped away from me, stood halfway between me and the door.

Both hands on the wall behind me, I pushed upwards as I jumped, springing backwards to sit on the ledge and then scrambling to my feet. The movement was so quick that only by throwing my hands out to the merlons on either side was I able to catch myself from toppling back.

He lunged towards me, but hesitated as he saw how close I was to the edge. He raised both hands in front of him, helpless as a puppet. 'That's crazy. Get down, now. That's crazy.' His voice was high and strident.

I shook my head. 'One more word and I jump. Shout for a guard, and I jump.'

He inhaled, put a finger to his lips. I wasn't sure if he was hushing himself or me. 'OK,' he murmured. 'OK.' Again, I couldn't tell who he was trying to reassure. 'OK. But you wouldn't do it. You'd never survive it.'

'I know. And don't pretend it's me you're worried about.'

'Fine. Fair enough. But you couldn't do it to me. You wouldn't.'

'You called my bluff once already, at the split. I protected you that time. I can't do it again.'

He took a step forward; I edged back. Only my toes and the balls of my feet were on the wall now; my heels tremored over the emptiness below.

'I'll do it. There's no reason for me to go on living, in that cell.'

'I let you out – you're out here now, aren't you?'

I dared a glance over my shoulder, then turned back quickly, hoping my eyes didn't reveal too much of my terror.

'Here's what's going to happen.' The stones on each side were warm and rough under my outstretched hands. I wondered if it was the last texture I'd feel. 'Walk back, all the way to the door.' He nodded, kept nodding as he walked slowly backwards, hands still raised.

One arm still on the stone merlon to my right, I lifted my shirt and jumper with my other hand to reveal the makeshift rope I'd wrapped around my waist at dawn. I smiled at the thought of my comment to The Confessor the day before. All day the knotted strips of sheet had been digging into my stomach, but I hadn't dared to loosen it, already worried that the bulk beneath my clothes might be visible.

Unwinding the rope was a delicate task. At first I tried to keep one hand on the stone, but it was too difficult, the unwound loops dropping around my legs and threatening to tangle me. Finally I relented and used both hands. I'd edged forwards a little, but my heels were an inch, at most, from the brink. I kept my eyes on Zach. The white rope, slowly unfurling, trailed its way down the outer wall behind me.

I don't know whether I saw him tense, or just sensed his intention, but before he'd taken a single rushed step forward I raised a hand.

'Run at me and I jump, or we'll both end up going over. It amounts to the same thing.'

He stopped. His breathing was harsh, heavy. 'You'd seriously do it.'

It was a statement now, not a question. At least it spared me from giving an answer that I didn't have. I just looked at him, and he retreated again to the far wall.

The whole rope was unwound now. The base of the merlon was far too thick for me to pass the rope around, but at the top it narrowed to a single stone's thickness. To loop the rope around this, I had to turn sideways, my cheek pressed against the stone so that I could keep watching Zach while I reached upwards. To pass the rope from one hand to the other I had to wrap both arms around the merlon's breadth in an awkward embrace. When it was done, I was reluctant to relinquish the tight hold on the stone.

'You must be insane,' called Zach. 'The rope'll never hold. You'll fall and kill us both. And even if you do get down there alive, there're guards all along the outer perimeter. It's pointless.'

I looked at the rope. He had a point: to transform my sheet into any kind of length, I'd had to tear it into strips only two fingers thick. The knots looked shoddy, even to me. I knew I was light these days, but the rope was still uninspiring. And what Zach couldn't see was that the rope hung only part of the way down the face of the fort beneath me; from its frayed end, there was still a drop of at least twenty feet to the stone terrace below.

'Listen carefully,' I told him. 'You're going to go out that same door. You're going to lock it behind you. If I hear you shout for guards, I jump. If I hear you starting to unlock the door again, I jump. Even if I'm half-way down the rope and I see you peering down at me, I jump. You get behind that door and you count to one hundred before you even think about opening it, or making a sound. Got it?'

He bobbed his head. 'You've changed,' he said quietly.

'Four years in a cell will do that.' I wondered if this was the last time I'd see him. 'You could change too, you know.'

'No,' he said.

'It's your choice,' I said. 'Remember that. Now lock that door.'

Still facing me, his hand groped along the wall behind him and found the door handle. He had to turn to unlock it, but spun back to face me as he pulled it open. He was still staring as he stepped backwards into shadow and pulled the door closed. I heard the key rummaging for the lock, then the heavy tumbler sliding across.

I counted too, picturing him pressed against the door, making his way through the numbers in unison with me. *Forty-nine, fifty.* I realised I was crying, but whether from fear or sadness I didn't know. *Seventy-six, seventy-seven.* He'll be rushing, I thought, with his habitual impatience, but then making himself slow down, not wanting to burst out too soon and force my hand. And already, I knew, he'd be planning: where to position the guards, how to seal the city. He'd come after me, like I'd always known he would.

Ninety-nine. The lock moved slowly, but its age gave it away with a rusted squeal.

The Confessor would have seen through my plan, of course. But Zach sprinted straight to the point from which the rope hung. Half of his body was hanging over the edge, peering down at the prop rope, when I slipped out from behind the door, ran inside, and locked it behind me.

CHAPTER 8

I felt strangely calm. Behind me, through the heavy door, I could hear Zach's shouts. He was kicking the door too, but it was solidly braced in its frame and emitted only dulled thuds.

At first, as I ran, I was just tracing the route along which Zach had led me. Then, at a point that I couldn't quite pin down, I was guided by a different kind of memory. My body was a compass needle, faithfully seeking the tank room, which I could feel more strongly than ever. It was my greatest fear, but it was also my destination. I had to see it, to witness it in the flesh if I were ever to help those people, or even to spread the word. It was also the last place he would search for me. It was in the depths of the fort, far below any of the exits that a fugitive might be expected to seek. More importantly, if Zach had any suspicion that I knew about it, his most closely guarded secret, I'd have been tanked long ago.

Zach's heavy bundle of keys, which I'd snatched from the rampart door after locking it, jangled as I ran. At each locked door I closed my eyes and let instinct lead me to the right key. Locking each door behind me, I was heading down again, but into a different wing from the Keeping Rooms. Even so, I hated to feel the fort closing above me once more, to feel the distance between me and that momentary taste of sky and light.

There was a long corridor, narrower than the grander corridors above. It was made narrower still by the network of pipes that ran along its sides. From the low roof hung glass balls, emitting the same sterile, pale light that had illuminated my cell. At the corridor's end, down a short flight of steps, was the final door. My mind was so attuned to this place that I didn't even have to hesitate to choose the key.

In my visions the tank room had been silent. Entering it now I was disarmed by the noise: the constant whirring of the machinery, and the sounds that water makes in the dark. Beneath it all, underfoot, the thrum of the river. I'd sensed the river throughout my years in the cell, but here it was audible, insistent.

Despite the eeriness of the place, its familiarity was weirdly comforting: apart from the noise, it was just as I'd seen it. Along the long wall of the chamber, the tanks stood. From each emerged a number of tubes, tracing to control panels above. When I pressed my palm against the glass of the nearest tank, I was surprised by its warmth. In the half-light I strained to make out a shape inside the viscous fluid. Something within was moving in time with the machine's pulse. I knew what it would be, but squinted to see, hoping to be wrong.

As my eyes adjusted to the darkness, the shapes began to materialise, not just in this tank but along the whole row of tanks nearest to me. A young woman floated with her back to me, her three arms all raised as if reaching for the top of the liquid. A man curled in a foetal position near the base of his tank, his handless arms crossed over his knees. An old woman floated at a strange angle, her single eye closed beneath her brand. All of them were naked, and each body pulsed, barely perceptibly, in time with the machine's rhythm. The chamber was so long that the door at the far end was indistinct. The tanks went on and on, the horror endlessly repeated down the row.

I didn't know where the machine ended and the Electric began, or whether they were one and the same, but I knew that this alien sight was technology, and taboo. What sinister magic was in it, that permitted it to trap these people in this underwater sleep? The taboo might be a law, but it began in the gut: the nauseous recoil that churned my stomach when I looked at this web of wires and metal. The machines had ended the world. And as a seer, I'd seen the blast more directly than anyone: the pure destruction of that shear of hot light. Even spending the last four years beneath the Electric light of my cell hadn't done away with my instinctive terror at the sight of these wires, tubes and panels. I became aware of the sweat on my body, the shaking in my legs. This rumbling, many-parted machine was like a slumbering beast.

My hands were shaking, too. I'd thought the tanks had been vivid in my visions, but seeing them like this was worse. The tubes that violated the bodies, emerging at the mouth and the wrist. Tubes like puppet strings, suspending the bodies from the top of the tanks. If I could get out, if I could spread the word, surely even most Alphas would be horrified at this? And if I could indeed count on my visions, then somewhere outside was the island, where I might find those who would believe me, even help me.

Making the horror all the more uncanny was the weird

orderliness of the scene: the neatly laid-out rows of tanks; the perfect accord of the chests rising and falling to the machine's perpetual lullaby. Despite the variety of deformations on display in the tanks, there was a ghastly uniformity about their comatose state. I walked along the row, paused, leant my face against the glass of a tank, letting myself be calmed by the pulsing semi-darkness.

A shudder ran through the glass, shocking me back into alertness. I opened my eyes and was confronted by a face, pressed against the glass on which I was leaning. The boy who had drifted to the front of his tank had eerily pale skin, his veins clearly outlined. His light brown hair floated up from his head, and his mouth was partly open around the tube. Only one thing disturbed the near-stillness of the tableau: his eyes, wide open and alert.

I jumped back, my small cry lost almost immediately in the thick dampness and rhythmic hum of the room. Averting my eyes from the boy's stare, I looked down, but seeing that, like the others, he was naked, I fixed my eyes determinedly on his face. Despite his brand, his thin face reminded me of Zach. Later, I wondered whether that was why the boy had seemed so familiar.

I grasped at the thought that his open eyes must be empty, that they couldn't possibly signify consciousness. Some of the other tanked figures had open eyes, but they were no less absent for it. I stepped slightly to the side. If his eyes hadn't followed me I might have continued, all the way back to the door at the far end of the room, and beyond. Part of me was disappointed when I saw his dark eyes track my progress. At the same time, I knew that having witnessed that small movement of his eyes was a promise that I couldn't break.

The tank's lid seemed to be its only entry point, at least

three feet above my head. At that level a platform ran around the wall, reached by a ladder at the far corner of the room. I took several steps towards it, then looked frantically behind me to try to reassure the boy that I wasn't leaving. In the gloom it was already too late – he'd become a blur in the tank. I ran, counting tanks as I went, and trying not to think about their occupants, or about the empty tank that I passed at the end of the row. Climbing the ladder, I cringed at the sound my footsteps unleashed on the metal steps. On the ledge I counted my way back along the tanks. At the twelfth tank I reached over for the metal handle and found that the lid lifted to the side without resistance.

From above I could barely make out his drifting hair, now two feet below me. As I leaned down over the tank, the fluid smelled repulsively sweet. With my face turned up, away from the saccharine stench, I reached into the warm liquid, groped around, grasped something solid and gave a tentative tug. There was a slight resistance before what I was grasping came away in my hand. For an awful instant I imagined his fluid-soaked body somehow falling apart in my hands, but when I looked down I was both relieved and horrified to find that I was holding a pliable rubber tube. When I sought out his face I saw that the tube was now stripped from his mouth.

I plunged my hand back into the fluid and flinched when it was grasped, firmly, by his. Gripping the ledge's rail tightly with my other hand, I braced for his pull. At first he was light, the fluid taking his weight. As his head and chest breached the surface, however, he took on a tangible weight and I couldn't lift him further. His wrist, below the hand that I held, was pierced by another of the tubes. I reached out for his other arm but could see, now that his torso had emerged, that the left arm wasn't there. Without the thick warp of the tank's glass between us, he looked older: perhaps my own age, though in his wasted state it was hard to tell.

For a moment we stayed like that, hand in hand. Then he turned his head and bared his teeth and for an instant I thought he was going to bite me. Just as I was about to snatch my hand away, he grasped the tube in his wrist with his teeth and, with one jerk of his head, ripped it free.

Blood flared briefly, mixing with the fluid that coated his arm. He looked up at me and we pulled in unison. Small as I was, my strength was more than his, and the liquid coated our grasp with a slick film. For perhaps twenty seconds he hung, half out of the water, before our hands slipped apart and he slumped back into the tank. He opened his mouth again as if to speak, but only a pink bubble of bloodied water appeared. He reached up for my hand again, but as he raised his eyes to meet mine, I let go, turned and ran. When I glanced back at him, he'd already sunk beneath the surface.

It took me only a few seconds to run back along the platform and down to where I'd seen the wrench, near the bottom of the ladder. Back on the main floor now, I counted along the tanks until I reached his. He was no longer moving. From his open mouth and wrist, where the tubes had entered him, there were staccato bursts of blood. The released tubes were tangled, tentacle-like, around him, and his eyes were now closed.

It seemed that there was no sound at all when I swung the wrench into the glass. For a second nothing happened. Then, as if it had been holding its breath, the tank exhaled everything in a roar, a glass deluge that swept me backwards and off my feet.

The boy landed on me at the moment I hit the floor, and the impact drove me sharply down onto the glass fragments.

Together we skidded back across the darkness, colliding with the opposite wall in a tangle of limbs and glass.

The noise continued for longer than I'd believed possible, as the final huge panels of glass wrenched themselves free and the liquid heaved the broken pieces, shrieking, along the floor. The relief of quiet when the noise finally settled was short-lived; almost immediately an alarm sounded and the room was lit up. Strips in the ceiling gave off the same white glow as the light in my cell, but glaring many times brighter.

It was the presence of the naked boy lying against me, as much as the lights and the siren, that made me clamber up. He stood too, shakily, then fell back against the wall. I grabbed at his arm, pulling him upright. Even with the sound of footsteps pounding closer from the far end of the chamber, I noticed how strange it was to feel the flesh of another person, after the years in the Keeping Rooms.

I was facing the door through which I'd entered, but it was from the other end of the chamber, behind a larger set of doors, that I heard the footsteps coming. Between the unyielding shrieks of the alarm I could hear them, and shouting voices. I turned to the boy but he was on all fours, taking small, sputtering breaths between coughs. I couldn't concentrate – there was too much noise: the alarm, the machinery's hum, the approaching men. And underneath it all, the river. I tried to focus on the tug of the river on my mind. It pulled at me the same way that the currents had pulled at my body when I swam in the river as a child. I scanned the network of pipes that ran along the chamber, above the row of tanks. The smashed tank stood out like a missing tooth. At the far end of the row, some of the tanks were empty. Empty: not just of bodies but of liquid. There had to be some way of draining the tanks. Half leading, half dragging the boy back to the jagged crown of glass that ringed the base of the shattered tank, I saw that much of the base was a plug, a sealed pipe nearly as wide as the tank itself, sunk into the floor.

I stepped over the vertical glass remnants to stand in the shallow puddle of liquid that remained. The boy had recoiled when I pulled him after me, but I ignored his resistance, yanking him hard so that we were crouched together in the centre of what had been the tank. There were only two levers at the front of the tank, and when I stretched out over the sharp glass, I could reach the first of them. When I pulled it, a torrent of the sticky liquid was unleashed from a pipe suspended high above us, spraying down onto where we huddled. I closed my mouth tightly and tried to shield my eyes. The boy was on hands and knees now, knocked down by the inundation. I reached for the second lever, felt the glass scrape my arm. Through the glaze of liquid I could see the doors at the far end of the chamber begin to open. I felt the lever resist, resist, then give way, and then the world dropped away beneath us as we were flushed from the light.

CHAPTER 9

Afterwards, I thought about all the things that could have gone wrong. If there'd been a grate. If the drainage system hadn't led back to the river. If the airless pipe had continued any longer than it did, or if the final drop to the river had been from a greater height. It was always hard to distinguish between luck and intuition, and I was never certain if I'd sensed the escape route or simply stumbled upon it.

In the pipe I measured time only by the urgency of breath. In the first few moments I was exhilarated by the speed with which we dropped, dragged downward by the unhesitating liquid. Then the longing for air overtook every other consideration, even the fear of that closed space, or the sharp ridges of the pipe's joints jolting me at each curve. Then, suddenly, a different kind of darkness, and our falling was no longer contained but in the open air. It must have been more than twenty feet from the pipe's abrupt end down to the deep pool in which we landed, but even as I was falling, the bliss of air was greater than any fear. Landing, there was the double jolt of pain and relief to feel my body pummel into the boy's. When I surfaced, I could see the silhouette of his head, just a few feet away. His whole body jerked with each frantic stroke of his arm, but he was managing to keep his face above the surface.

It was light enough to see, but only just. I could make out the huge cavern around us, distantly lit by a large opening in the domed roof. High in the rock face on one side, several large pipes protruded, including the one from which we had burst. Some flowed loudly, others dripping intermittently into the deep pool below, where the boy and I trod water. Upstream the river was quickly concealed by increasing darkness, but fifty feet downstream the cavern opened up and the river flowed out to the daylight.

'Will they come after us?' He spoke for the first time. Despite his breathlessness, I was taken aback at how normal his voice sounded. It didn't seem to match the figure I'd seen floating in the tank, or the tube I'd pulled from his mouth so recently. He continued: 'If they saw us, will they risk it?'

I nodded, then realised he could scarcely see me. 'They'll know we lived, or me at least. Because of my twin.'

'They have him too?'

'Something like that.' I looked back up at the drooling mouths of the pipes above. 'They'll be coming – if not by the pipes, then by another route. They know this place; they built those pipes.'

He was already swimming awkwardly towards the bank of the pool, towards the cave mouth and the light. 'Stop,' I said. 'They'll be too fast, and they'll be looking for us downstream.'

'So we'll head away from the river – come on.'

'No – there's too many of them, and they're too fast. They'll be here in minutes.'

He was in the shallows already. He stood up, water to his waist, looking back at me. His thin torso was glowing pale in the cavern's dark. 'I'm not going back. I won't stay with you to be caught.'

'I know. But there's another way.'

He stopped. 'You know this place?'

'Yes.' I couldn't explain to him the kind of knowing that it was: the way that the river's shape was present in my mind, or how I felt the tug of its currents and divergences. Here in this cavern, where our voices echoed back at us, strangely distorted, I wondered if my seer mind worked in the same way: bouncing some silent signal off the world around me, sensing out its paths and crannies.

'They'll expect us to leave the cave, head downstream,' I said. 'But if we go upstream, there's another way – caves leading through the mountain, and another branch of the river.'

He looked doubtfully upstream where, away from the light, the river seemed to emerge from nowhere, deep in the black, cracked walls of the cavern.

'You're sure?'

I took a slow breath, closed my eyes, wondered how to convince him of something that felt so nebulous, even to me. The sound of a splash startled my eyes open, to find that he'd pushed off from the shallows towards me already.

'You've got me this far,' he said.

I trod water while I waited for him to reach me, and gazed up at the fissure in the roof, and the narrow shaft of light that it cast down, illuminating the water in front of me. That's when I saw the bones, in that one brightened strip in the murky water. I could see the bottom of the pool, and the collection of bones that littered it. One skull stared back at me from a single central eye socket; the bones of a hand reached up to us like a deathly beggar. Another skull lay upside down, a jawless container partly filled with sand. It was tiny – half the size of the other one. A baby's skull.

The boy heard my strangled yelp, followed my gaze. For a moment I thought he might be sick.

'Hell,' he said. 'We're not the first people to be flushed out of those tanks.'

'No. Just the first living ones.' I was struggling to tread water while keeping my legs drawn up as high as possible, recoiling from what lurked below us. As soon as he reached me we swam upstream; he nearly kept up, though his one-armed swimming was lurching and breathless. As we reached the top of the cavern the river surface was churning where the river surged through some fissure deep below. The darkness at this end of the cavern was less total than it had seemed at first, and we could discern a muted glow of light some feet beneath the surface. I looked at him. 'You can swim well enough?'

He looked back at the deep pool into which we had dropped. 'Now you ask me?'

Here, the current was strong enough that we had to hold fast to a jutting rock to stay in place. Over the water's sound other noises could now be heard: a clanging in the pipes above, and from the cavern's opening downstream, the clatter of hooves on shale. I hated the idea of diving under, closer to the bones. But at the moment the distant shapes of men on horseback appeared in the lightened opening, the boy and I took our deep breaths and committed ourselves once again to the water.

Whereas in the pipe we'd been propelled by the force of water, here we had to fight against it. The gap through which the river surged was several feet down, and when I first encountered the full force of the current surging through I was forced back with it. It took a hysteria of kicking and thrashing to enter the narrow tunnel that led towards the light. The opposing current forced me upwards against the tunnel's roof so that as I thrashed my way upstream I was scraped mercilessly by the jagged rock above. I had to drag my eyes open against the onslaught of water. Then the rock roof above me was gone, I had burst into a pool of light, and a few kicks took me to the surface.

He wasn't there. Looking down, I could make out nothing in the dark from which I'd emerged. I cursed myself as I turned from side to side, treading water, scanning the small cavern. How could I have thought he would get through in his weakened state, with his flailing, ungainly swimming? I'd concentrated so hard on my intangible senses, the instincts that led me to this second cavern, that I'd failed to use my eyes. I hadn't taken in how frail he was, reborn pale and wasted from the tank, with his single emaciated arm. I waited, treading water. This grotto was similar to the first, but whereas that cavern had an opening, a cave mouth leading to the world beyond, this one was enclosed on all sides. The only light glanced in from a slanted opening some sixty feet above. Punctuating the silence, heavy drops fell into the pool from the stalactites above. The drips kept count of the passing seconds as I waited. Surely he couldn't have held his breath this long? Surely that bony chest couldn't contain enough air to last all this time?

He scared me when he surfaced, so sudden and urgently, barely three feet from me. As he devoured the air in noisy gasps, I caught in his face the same desperation I'd seen through the glass of the tank. He was still coughing and cursing as we dragged ourselves up onto the rock ledge that ran around one side of the cave. It was littered with sharp stones, but it was a blessing to be free of the current's constant tow. I hadn't realised how cold the water was until I finally hauled myself clear of it. He'd managed to clamber out, though awkwardly, and as we slumped next to each other on the stones I noticed that his panting body, like mine, bore many marks of our journey. He caught me noting the grazes and cuts on his back and shoulders. I was reminded of his nakedness and turned quickly away.

As we lay there, each gazing up at the light beaming in through the cave's domed roof, I was acutely aware not of his body, but my own. After four years in the Keeping Rooms, I'd lost track of my body as an object, a thing visible to others. When I was captured, I'd been nineteen. Four years later, were these breasts the same? My face, which I'd not seen in all that time? My pale skin felt, suddenly, a strange costume. He was the naked one, but I felt oddly exposed.

I didn't have time to indulge these musings. He'd closed his eyes, but I shook his shoulder gently. 'They don't know about this place,' I said, 'and they'll be searching downstream at first. But they could find it. We have to move.' I pulled off my shoes, drained them of water before putting them on again.

'Please tell me your escape route doesn't involve any more stunts like that last one?'

I smiled, shook my head. 'No more swimming. For now, anyway.' I was up. 'But I hope you don't mind caves.'

In fact, it was he who led the way. Although he moved unsteadily, his eyes were better than mine in the darkness. I'd found the cave, groping along the ledge until it was reduced to a bare foothold, then scrabbling up a few feet to where the entrance was concealed by a jutting flake of rock. Before I entered I closed my eyes, rested my forehead momentarily against the damp stone, groping down the passage with my mind.

'You can't have been here before?'

I opened my eyes, looked back at him, shook my head.

'But you know where to go.' It wasn't a question, but I nodded anyway.

'I thought you must be a seer. Because you look perfect.' There was a pause. 'I mean, not perfect, but – I meant, you're branded, but I couldn't see anything wrong with you.'

I stepped quickly into the dark of the cave, sparing us both. Although I could feel the pull of the tunnel's general direction, in the absolute dark I had to feel my way along, crouching forwards, and bumping my head often on outcrops of stone. After I swore loudly at one such collision, he went in front, and we made better speed, with him calling out to warn me where the ceiling lowered. The darkness wasn't always total – at several points the tunnel branched upwards to tiny inlets of light, in ante-chambers off the main passage. After what felt like an hour or more, we stopped by one of these and sat leaning against one side of the narrow passage. By the pale gleam of light we could see the rough tool marks that pocked the walls.

'We might be the first people to come through here ever. I mean, since the Before.' I ran a hand over the pitted walls.

'This is from then? From the Before?'

I shook my head. 'Older, even.'

'What do you mean?'

'I mean, old even for the Before.'

The dark was incomplete, but the silence wasn't. The absence of noise in the tunnel was heavier than any silence I could remember.

'I should have said this earlier,' he said eventually, 'but thank you. You didn't have to get me out of that tank.'

'Yes I did.'

'I'm glad you think so. I can't imagine everyone would want a naked stranger slowing down their getaway.'

I laughed, disarmed. 'We should do something about that.' Taking off the sodden woollen jumper I wore over my shirt and trousers, I passed it to him, then turned away pointlessly while he put it on. When I turned back he'd managed to pull the wide neck down to his waist and wear it as a kind of skirt, the sleeves hanging empty.

'We should get moving,' I said, standing up. I waited for him to go first, and had to press against the wall as he squeezed past. 'I don't even know your name,' I called after him.

'The same goes for me, actually.'

'It's Cass.'

'No – I meant my name. I don't know it either.' He was several feet in front of me now, moving into the narrow passage ahead. I followed him, and the conversation felt somehow easier in the cloaking darkness.

'Are you serious?'

'I'm not being secretive. I'd tell you my name if I knew it. Not much point hiding stuff from a seer anyway.'

'It's not like that. I don't read minds. I just – feel things, sometimes, sometimes about places, sometimes about people. But it's not straightforward.'

'That's a shame.'

'Most people aren't that keen about me sensing stuff about them.'

'I thought maybe you could tell stuff about me – stuff I can't remember.'

'And you really can't remember anything?'

'Nothing before the tank.'

I stopped. 'Not even your twin?'

'Nothing.'

CHAPTER 10

In the tunnels we lost all sense of time. I knew only that it had been a long while since we'd last passed one of the light-shafts, and far longer since I'd eaten or drunk. I tried to ignore the hunger and thirst, to focus on feeling my way, and on dodging the low roof and narrow walls that regularly scraped the wounds on my back and arms. After years in my cell, even walking exhausted me. My breath was tight, my chest as cramped as the tunnels. The exhaustion was even worse for the boy, who stumbled regularly. The route, at least, was mainly uncomplicated, and the few times we encountered a junction I had to hesitate only briefly before choosing the path. We'd been heading slightly uphill for what felt like hours, and when the floor evened out slightly I suggested that we stop.

'I could use a sleep,' he agreed.

'But not for too long.'

'I don't think there's much chance of us sleeping for hours in blissful comfort,' he said, brushing some stones from the ground beneath him. 'Are you cold?'

'Not too much,' I lied. It had grown steadily colder as we made our way deeper into the tunnel.

We were lying close but not touching.

'What about scared?'

I thought for a minute. 'Yes. Scared of them catching us, or of getting lost, stuck in here. But that wouldn't be much worse than before.'

'You weren't in one of those things, though? Not in a tank?'

'No. Just a room.' I pictured the tanks again. My years in the cell – the madness I had felt encroaching, the claustrophobia and the hopelessness – seemed small compared to what he had endured.

It was quiet for a while. 'What about you?' I said. 'Are you scared?'

'I can't say I relish this cave business, but I don't feel scared like I probably should. It feels so – new, I suppose. Just to be out.'

'But what do we do next? When we get out of here?'

'I've no idea. But that feels OK too, somehow. There's a kind of symmetry to it, for me at least – I don't know what happened before, I don't know what's going to happen now.'

'They won't stop looking for us.'

He sighed, rolled on to his side. 'They can't be more curious about me than I am myself.'

We slept for perhaps an hour. I woke him and made him walk, but he was struggling against exhaustion. I couldn't imagine what it had done to him – his time in the tank, and his sudden release. His body was unused to itself; at first, he moved like a drunkard. 'Let's sleep' became his refrain, every few hours, and in the weird timelessness of the tunnel the whole journey began to feel like a dream or delirium: wake, walk, sleep briefly, wake, walk, sleep. When I finally saw the light ahead, it was only the pain in my eyes that convinced me I wasn't dreaming. The tunnel's narrow mouth was shielded by thick scrub, but enough sun crept through to show it was high daylight, though what day I didn't know.

We emerged, wincing at the light, on a steep embankment leading down to a river running wide and fast below us. I cursed at the thorned bush we had to clamber through at the cave's entrance, but was quickly mollified by the indecently fat berries that grew on its stems. Ignoring the thorns, I picked the fruit so greedily that I couldn't distinguish between the blood on my hands and the leaking berry-juice. He ate too, then turned back, his arm against the rock face, and vomited.

'Too fast?' I asked.

He wiped his mouth. 'Sorry. I think it's been a while. I mean – I know it's been a while since you ate, too, but I had that tube –'

I nodded. 'You don't know how long you were in there for?'

He looked down at himself. He was thin, but not starved – I'd seen worse amongst some of the Omegas at the settlement the year the crops failed. His light brown hair reached his shoulders, and under the bright sun his skin was the colour of bone. I could trace the structure of his bones under the network of tendons and faded muscles.

'Long enough to lose my tan,' he said. 'If I ever had one.'

We stayed at the cave mouth just time enough for him to eat again, more slowly, and this time he kept down some berries. Then the thirst demanded our attention, and we made our precarious way down the embankment, the thorns

111

snagging our clothes and skin. At least it was warmer, here – hot, even, in the sun.

At the river's edge he was more cautious, cupping mouthfuls in his hand to drink slowly, while I hunched on all fours to drink straight from the river.

'Have we ended up downstream from where the tunnel started? Won't they look this way?'

I shook my head. 'It's a different river. It branches off the other, upstream from Wyndham, and goes down the other side of the mountain. We cut through the mountain, more or less.'

'So is that how being a seer works, for you? Not that I'm not grateful for it. It just seems odd. I was thinking you'd be able to read my mind, but it seems that geography's more your thing.'

I grinned with him, but shook my head. 'Sorry to disappoint you. But it's not just places. Places are easiest for me, but I can usually get a feel for emotions, and things that are going to happen, too. There's not really a difference – I feel what's there. I could see that if we came upstream there'd be the cavern, then the cave. It existed, so I could feel it.'

'But things that are going to happen – they don't exist yet. It's not the same as a river that's been there forever.'

'I know. With events, they don't exist yet. But they will, so I can sense them. It's not like visions. It's more like – like memories. As if I'm out of kilter with time. I can remember things that haven't happened yet. But it's not consistent – sometimes I can predict little things, and miss the really big things. Sometimes it's the other way round.'

'And can you remember what happens next, for us?' he asked, sitting back and letting his feet dangle in the river.

'Not exactly. It's not always like that. And sometimes I

can't tell if something's just logic, just a good idea, or if it's a seer thing. Like now – I think we should go via the river, float downstream. But that just seems to make sense – because it's hard to move through this.' I gestured to the thick, high scrub that extended up both sides of the river-bank. 'And because we won't get lost, and they won't be able to hunt for us with dogs.'

He sighed. 'I thought when you got me out of that tank that I'd be done with floating in water for a while.'

'Sorry.'

'And I don't suppose there's time for a sleep first?'

I laughed, getting to my feet. 'Our neighbour, in the village where I grew up, had an old sheepdog that used to sleep all day on their doorstep. It was called Kip. That's what I'm going to call you: Kip. And no, we can't risk a sleep yet. We've already waited here too long.'

Unlike the river beneath Wyndham, here the water was a rich red-brown, soaked with peat. We stepped in together. At the shallower edges it was warmer, but as we moved towards the middle we flinched at the chill of the quick, deep water.

'What do you think?'

He raised an eyebrow. 'I'd settle for a bit warmer, ideally.'

'No – about the name.'

He grinned at me, turned to face upstream, lowered himself backwards into the river's flow. As he drifted down-stream he called back to me: 'After getting me out of that tank, you can call me whatever you like.'

I'd envisaged a gentle float downstream, but the river was not so generous. At points it ran too shallow and we had to scramble, sore-footed, over low rapids and slippery shale. At other points the rapids were too fast and deep, so we crawled out and climbed our way down the steep embankments, re-joining the river where it calmed. Twice Kip fell, skidding down the bank before he managed to grab a root or rock to pull up short of the river's clutches. At some points, where the river's banks were flat and grassy, we left the water to walk beside it, but I made sure we alternated between the river's sides so we left no clear trail on either. The thorned berry-bushes grew at several points on the banks, and Kip spotted some mushrooms on the underside of a log that hung over the river's edge. We were so hungry by that stage that even the rank taste didn't deter us.

It was late afternoon when he suggested we stop. 'If we get out now, at least our clothes will have a chance to dry while it's still sunny.'

I looked at his face, his jaw muscles tensed to suppress his shivering. 'Good idea.' I'd been starting to feel exposed in the river, as the landscape around it had become sparser, the thick scrub at the top of the embankment giving way to grass plains interrupted only by the occasional tree.

I led the way up the embankment. At several points I had to haul myself up by the roots of the trees that clung to the near-vertical slope. Beneath me I could hear Kip scrambling and cursing, but he kept up. It was Kip who spotted the path, lightly trodden but distinct, running along the top of the embankment. Silent now, we clambered back down a few feet to a ledge, overhung by tree roots, where we couldn't be seen from the path above. In our ragged state, we'd draw attention from anyone, not just our pursuers.

Looking at Kip, I saw that the day's sun had already reddened his back, which was also trellised with cuts and scratches.

He caught me looking at his raw shoulders. 'It's not as

if you got off scot-free either, you know,' he said, pointing at the bruises and scratches on my own burned shoulders. 'We're neither of us a picture at the moment.'

'You should stay out of the sun.'

'My complexion is the least of my worries at the moment. Capture, imprisonment, torture: absolutely. Sunburn: not so much.'

'You sound pretty cheerful for somebody with those sorts of things on your mind. Aren't you afraid?'

He smiled. 'Of going back? No.' He was still smiling, but he glanced down at the gorge below us, the river scouring its depths. 'Because I wouldn't. Even if they find us – I'd jump first.'

*

Although we were huddled close on the narrow ledge, the dark as it settled brought with it a sense of anonymity, made it easier to talk. I found myself telling Kip about the years in the Keeping Rooms, and even before: the six years at the settlement, and my childhood at the village too.

'Sorry – I've probably talked too much.'

I could feel his shrug where our shoulders touched. 'It's not as though I'm full of stories to share.'

Indeed, in the absence of his own past, he seemed almost hungry for the details of mine, prompting me, asking questions, particularly about Zach.

'That must be the oddest thing, for you, I suppose,' I said. 'I mean, it's all odd, obviously, but of all the things to forget, it must be strangest to not know about your twin.'

'I know. The rest – well, of course it's important. But I feel like I have some residual sense of who I am, and not knowing where I lived, or what I've done, doesn't affect that so much. But not knowing who my twin is – it's such a gap, makes me feel I can't really know myself. Not properly.'

'I can't imagine it. Like you're only half a person. Like losing a limb.' There was silence. 'Sorry. I didn't mean – obviously.'

He laughed. 'I know what you mean. But you shouldn't feel too sorry for me. Your twin hasn't exactly been a blessing.'

'I know. But I can't imagine anything else. And if he were someone else, I wouldn't be the same. I can't wish it were different, any more than you could wish for two arms. I can't even imagine not having Zach.'

'I suppose not. And with my twin, even though my mind's forgotten, my body can't have. If she gets hit by a cart tomorrow, it won't make a bit of difference that I don't know who, or where, she is. My body will remember pretty damn quick.'

We sat without talking for a while. 'Do you think she's like your twin?' he said. 'Do you think she put me in that tank?'

Forgetting the darkness, I shook my head. 'I don't know. It could be like that – somebody powerful, wanting you put away. But those tanks – they had to test them first, right? It could be that you're just unlucky, just somebody they got hold of.'

'And you weren't in the tanks. Maybe that means my twin isn't powerful, isn't important.'

'Would you prefer that?'

'I don't know. I guess it would mean that my twin didn't choose to do it to me. That it was like what you just said – just bad luck.'

'I know what you mean. But I think the reason I wasn't

in the tanks was because they wanted to use me – to find out what I saw.'

'If you weren't a seer, then, do you think Zach would've put you in the tanks?'

'He was going to anyway,' I said with a shudder, remembering the dreams that had tortured my last days in the cell. 'Soon.' I thought for a while. 'But if I weren't a seer, then everything would be different. We would have been split at the start, and he wouldn't have had to fight so hard against me all the time, to prove himself the Alpha. Things wouldn't have turned out the way they did. He wouldn't have turned out the way he did.'

'So it's all your fault? For being a seer?'

'That's not what I meant. But it's complicated.' I rolled away from him. 'We should get to sleep.'

*

I dreamed of The Confessor and woke with a shout. In the darkness, it took me a few moments to realise where I was. Kip, lying behind me, was trying to quiet me. Below us the river echoed his shushing sound.

'Sorry. Bad dream.'

'It's OK. You're OK.'

I nodded into the darkness, my breath slowing.

He continued: 'I mean, you're on the run from your twin, and doubtless an army of his followers, and you're halfway up a cliff with a semi-naked stranger with amnesia. But apart from that, no problems.'

I laughed. 'Thanks for the reassurance.'

'Any time,' he said, rolling on to his back.

I rolled onto my back too. Above us I could see the tree roots that made up our roof, and the sky beyond, a lighter shade of dark, pierced by stars. Above it all, I could sense The Confessor's searching, her mind seeking me. The night sky itself seemed to press down on me with the weight of her scrutiny.

'I keep dreaming about The Confessor,' I told him. 'Ever since we got away. I used to think about her, in the Keeping Rooms, and dread seeing her, but now I feel her all the time.'

'You think she's looking for you?'

'I know it. I can feel her – an awareness, seeking us out.'

Kip raised himself on his elbow. 'How aware, exactly? Does she know where we are?'

'No, I don't think so. Not yet. But she's looking. It's just – a presence, all the time.'

I thought again of the chamber I'd caught sight of, when I'd turned The Confessor's scrutiny back on her during that final interrogation. That chamber, thick with wires, had been hidden by her – the same way I had consciously concealed the island in my own mind. Her flaring anger when I saw the chamber in her thoughts had attested to its significance. But what was it, and why was she shielding it so fiercely?

I felt him settle back down beside me. 'I'm grateful for your seer stuff, don't get me wrong, but I don't envy you.'

Nobody would envy seers. The Alphas despised us, and other Omegas resented us. The visions were the hardest thing, though. I was always contending with the shards of past and future that punctured my days and nights, making me distrust my own place in time. Who would envy us our broken minds? I thought again of the mad seer at Haven market and his endless muttering.

'And you?' I asked him. 'Did you dream in the tanks?'

'The whole time I was in the tank, the bits I can

remember, I used to wish it was a dream, wish I'd wake up from it. A lot of the time I'd slip in and out of consciousness. But when I was asleep, I'd dream of the tank, and when I'd come to, it was still there.' He paused. 'Now, when I sleep, it's wonderful – there's nothing at all.'

'Why do you think you were the only one awake? In the tanks, I mean.'

'I don't know. Like I said, I wasn't awake all the time. And when I was, it wasn't like being awake properly. I couldn't move, or barely. I couldn't even see anything, really – it was dark most of the time. Sometimes, if I'd drifted close to the glass, I could just make out other tanks; sometimes even the other people, floating.' Somewhere nearby, a pigeon cooed. 'You scared me, when you woke up screaming like that,' he said eventually. 'I guess that's the downside to being a seer – the visions aren't exactly optional.'

'You scared me too, when I saw you the first time. I mean, the whole set-up was terrifying, but when you opened your eyes I nearly screamed.'

'It wouldn't have mattered. I think you made enough noise when you smashed the tank.'

I smiled, turned on my side to face him. Above the cliff opposite, dawn was beginning to declare itself, the darkness fading at the edges.

'Go back to sleep,' he said, reaching over and sweeping my hair back from where it had fallen over my eye, before rolling to his side, his back to me. I closed my eyes. After the isolation of the cell, it was nice to hear his breathing, slightly out of sync with my own.

CHAPTER 11

For two more days we stuck to the path that followed the river downstream. On the first day we heard people approaching, though I could never be sure what came first: my sense of unease or the distant thrum of hooves. We scrambled from the path and down the embankment. It was steep, and the river below it was rock-studded and fast, but we had no time for caution. We clung to the cliffside, concealed by an uprooted tree lodged above us. The percussion of the passing hooves dislodged clumps of loose dirt and leaves. We stayed there long after the sound had gone, then emerged quietly, brushing the mulch from our hair.

When we heard horses again, the next day, there was no cliff to shelter us. The steep bluffs had subsided into grassed banks leading gently to the river, which ran wide and slow here. There was less shelter, but at least the quiet river allowed us to hear the hooves coming. They were close, probably less than a few hundred yards away, and we were sheltered only by the river's bend. There was no time for words – we turned away from the river, sprinting so hard that the long, wiry marram grass sliced at our calves. The only cover within sight was a small cluster of bushes, and we dived behind them just as the first horse rounded the bend in the path. Half-submerged in leaves, we squinted through the scrub and watched the three riders slow to a walk as they neared the river. Kip's grip on my arm became rigid; I could feel the slight tremors of my body against his. The men were so close that, when they dismounted, I could feel the thud as each man landed lightly by his horse. They were Council soldiers, their long red tunics emblazoned with the Alpha insignia. One wore a sword, long enough that it brushed the top of the tall grass as he walked. The other two had bows slung across their backs.

We watched as they led the horses down to the river to drink. Even with my pulse loud in my ears, and my body thrumming with repressed shaking, I was fascinated by the horses. My only close encounter with them had been at my abduction from the settlement. I'd seen a few horses before, of course, ridden by travellers, or at the market in Haven, but they were rare. There were none in our village when I was a child, though there'd been sheep, cattle and donkeys. Later, at the settlement, there were no animals, of course – Omegas were forbidden not only to own animals, but even to buy or eat meat. In the settlement, the only horses we saw were ridden by passing Alpha traders, tithe collectors, or the Alpha raiders. We Omegas would exchange envious tales of the decadence of Wyndham: a horse for every soldier. Dogs not trained to guard, but even kept as pets. Meat eaten every week.

They say there were more animals in the Before – that they were common, and came in different types, more than we can even imagine. Once, when Zach had been to the market at Haven with Dad, he came back full of talk of a picture he'd seen. A travelling merchant had been hawking it on the sly, in one of the alleys off the market. He claimed it was a drawing from the Before. It showed hundreds of different types of birds. Not just the birds we knew of: the pale chickens or the stumpy grey pigeons, or even the gulls that sometimes came inland from the sea out west. Zach said that the picture had shown birds smaller than a chicken's egg, and others with a wingspan wider than our kitchen table. But he could describe it to me only in whispers, when we were in our room and the candle was out. He was already in trouble, he said, since Dad had hauled him away from the small crowd that had gathered around the merchant's stall. Such relics of the Before were taboo, and Dad in particular was impatient with any speculations about the past.

Whatever animals had existed in the Before, few survived the blast, and fewer still had survived the hungry decades of the Long Winter that followed. Unable to adapt like humans, most animals had died out. Even amongst the surviving species, there was a high rate of deformities – it wasn't unusual to see a three-legged pigeon, for example, or a whole flock of eyeless sheep, following their shepherd by the sound of a bell on a staff. Only that morning Kip and I had passed a two-headed snake stretched on a rock by the river's edge, observing us with both sets of eyes. I supposed deformations sometimes happened to horses too, though I'd never seen it. I'd never even known that horses came in different colours – the few I'd seen had all been brown. These three, now about thirty feet away and drinking noisily at the river's edge, were grey, their manes and tails a yellowing white. Their very size unnerved me, and the sound of their slurping and whinnying.

The men led the horses back toward us, away from the

river. The man with the sword bent to adjust a stirrup and for a moment his head was at our level, not ten feet away. I scrunched my eyes shut, as if that would hide me. But when I dared to open them again I saw something that terrified me far more than his sword. In a patch of dirt on the grassy path, right beside his horse's front legs, was the print of a bare foot. It wasn't even complete – just the indentation of Kip's toes and the ball of his foot. But once I'd seen it, the print seemed glaring, unmistakable. When the man bent down, my whole body braced to run. What hope did we have, though, against three armed soldiers, with horses? My breath was the frantic flutter of a moth. The man stepped back, and for a moment I thought he might have missed it. But then he bent again, lower this time. I closed my eyes again and gripped Kip's arm. It was over. Already I could feel the tank closing around me. Around us both.

When I opened my eyes again, the soldier was still bent low, busily inspecting his horse's hooves, one by one. He flicked a pebble from one hoof, straightened, and spat on the ground.

They left as quickly as they'd come, throwing themselves up into their saddles with a casual elegance.

From then on we avoided the path. Kip was subdued all afternoon. Whereas I'd been sensing The Confessor's avid scrutiny from the moment we'd escaped, seeing the soldiers had made the pursuit more real to him.

'They're not going to stop coming after us, are they,' he said that night. It wasn't a question, so I didn't answer. 'And where can we run to? I've only been thinking, so far, about getting as far away from Wyndham as possible. But *away* isn't really a destination.'

'We're not just running away,' I said. 'We're going to the

island.' I hadn't realised that, until I said it out loud. Nor had I realised that Kip was coming with me. But when I wasn't dreaming of The Confessor, I'd been dreaming of the island, its single peak rising from the broken sea. And ever since we left Wyndham we'd been heading roughly south-west, towards the distant coast. I wasn't sure whether that was chance, or whether I'd been steering us that way the whole time.

Kip had heard about the island already – it was becoming clear that his knowledge of general life was solid enough; the tank had left him with a frustratingly specific void that kept from him solely the details of his own life, his own identity. So he was aware of the island, but only in the way that I had been, before it had intruded on my visions. So, like me, he'd assumed it was a myth, a rumour – a furtive murmuring about a haven for Omegas, as vague and unlikely as the rumours about Elsewhere, other lands across the sea, lost to us since the blast. But when I told him that my visions had shown me the island, I was touched that he didn't doubt its reality.

'So the Council's really looking for it?' he asked. 'And has been for a while?'

I nodded, remembering The Confessor's interrogations on the subject. My jaw tightened at the thought of her eyes fixed on mine, her mind tightening around my own like a snare around a rabbit's neck.

'And given that they're looking for us already, you think it's a good idea to head for the one place we know they're also searching for?'

I wrinkled my nose. 'I know – it does seem like a bit of a perfect storm. But they wouldn't be looking for it if it weren't important. If we want to find out what the Council's doing with the tanks, or to try to piece together what's happened to you, I think the people who can help us are on the island.'

That night, The Confessor stepped into my dream. She was suddenly there, as real as the fallen tree under which Kip and I were huddled. From the mossy bank above us, she looked down with the expression of absolute indifference that I remembered so well from the Keeping Rooms. The only blemish on her perfect skin was the brand on her forehead. And she was here, standing over us, her face lit by the zealous full moon. There was no point in running, and no point screaming either. Her presence was total, as though she'd always been here, only we were too stupid to realise it. When her eyes met mine, my blood felt too thick, as if half frozen, dragging its granular way along my veins.

The pain in my hands woke me, not Kip's grip on my shoulder, or his voice, calling my name. I was scrabbling in the dirt, clawing into the ground and into the rotted base of the log by which we slept. By the time I was properly awake, I'd scraped a hole six inches deep, and those fingernails I hadn't broken off were thickly packed with dirt and splintered wood. I was crying out, too, an animal wail of terror that sounded strange to my own ears as I surfaced from the dream.

Kip was bent over me, still holding my shoulder. He leaned in, pulling me close, half to comfort me and half to silence me. I exhaled slowly, forcing my body to stillness, and pressed my forehead against his lowered head to quell my shaking. I felt the match of our brands, the scars mirroring each other as his forehead rested against mine.

'It's all right, shhhh, it's all right,' he murmured.

'It was her. She was here, in my dream. Right here.'

'And you were going to dig to safety?'

Now, in the light of his wry gaze, it seemed absurd. But although I mustered a laugh, my body was still shaking.

'It was only a dream,' he said.

'It's never *only* a dream,' I pointed out. 'Not for me.'

The reality was both better and worse than the dream. Better, because the bank above us was empty, the moss and fallen leaves undisturbed. And worse because her physical absence meant little: here or not, there was no escaping her scrutiny. Not by running, nor hiding, let alone by my foolish scrabbling in the dirt. She was seeking us, and I couldn't shake her off. She made the whole night sky a searching eye, and beneath it I was helpless, skewered by her gaze just as Zach had skewered my pet beetle on the pin.

We moved with a new urgency the next day. My awareness of her was physical, like a chronic pain. I carried her with me, and every place we passed through was tarnished by her presence. The Omegas were the vessels of contamination from the blast, as the Alphas never tired of telling us. But I felt as if The Confessor was the poison I carried now, the taint of her souring my very blood, and seeping out into the landscape that Kip and I were crossing.

At least, since our conversation about the island, Kip and I had a sense of purpose: I knew the island was hundreds of miles away, but having spoken the destination out loud made it seem somehow closer. Heading more sharply westward, we left the path, and the river. We drank greedily first, not knowing how long it would be before we found water again. The hunger was the main thing, though. Most days we managed to find some berries or mushrooms, though we were more wary of the latter since a cluster of black mushrooms on the second day had made us both cruelly sick. In a small pool, the first day after we left the river, Kip had caught a handful of tiny fish, using my jumper as a net. The fish were tiny shreds of silver, no bigger than my smallest fingernail. We ate them raw, our hunger overcoming our squeamishness. I knew we couldn't go on like this much longer.

Kip was coping better than I'd feared. In the first days out of the tanks, his body had a formlessness, everything softened by disuse. Even his skin had been dilated and puffy from his submersion in the tanks. Now, despite the scaffolding of his bones that became clearer each day, I could see him taking shape in front of me, his muscles lean and strained beneath his skin, which was now darkened by days of sun and dirt. At first his skin had been tender, easily damaged, the base of each bare foot a network of blisters, and we'd had to stop often. He still moved clumsily, rediscovering his body after the tank. There was a hesitation about his movements that never quite faded. But he stumbled less often now, and had taken to running ahead, scrambling up to vantage points. At times I wanted to tell him to take it easy, to save his energy, but I couldn't bring myself to suppress his delight in his body, newly his own again. But as the hunger grew, even he had fallen more and more quiet. As for my own body, it felt heavy, though I knew I was growing lighter each day. At night, when we burrowed into ditches, or the hollows beneath logs, I was kept awake by thoughts of food, and by the insistent sharpness of my bones digging into the earth. Even at my hungriest, though, I could never summon any nostalgia for the regular food trays of the Keeping Rooms.

Three days after leaving the river, we came upon the first village. It looked similar to the village where Zach and I had grown up, though this one was smaller. Not more than fifteen houses were gathered around a central well, with fields and an orchard spreading about them. Close to the large barn we could see figures at work. It must have been past midsummer, as the fields were freshly shorn, but the orchard provided enough cover for us to approach unseen. Occasional apples lay buried in the grass; they were shrunken and brown, skins puckered with age. We ate three each, in silence except for the staccato spitting out of pips.

'Alpha or Omega?' Kip asked, peering through the trees to the village beyond.

I gestured around us to the fields, the rows of apple trees. 'The land's good. Alpha's my guess.'

'And look – at the back of the big house.' He pointed at a long, narrow barn, divided into sections, each with a half-door.

'What about it?'

'It's a stable, for horses.'

'How can you recognise a stable but not know your own name?'

He shrugged, irritated. 'The same way I can remember how to talk, or swim. It's just there. It's only the personal stuff that's gone, somehow. Anyway, at least we know this is Alpha territory.'

'So we take as many apples as we can carry, and keep going.'

He nodded, but didn't move. In the village, a door opened, a woman's voice carried across the afternoon air.

I tugged at his arm. 'Kip? We need to keep moving.'

He turned to me. 'Can you ride a horse?'

I rolled my eyes. 'Omegas aren't allowed to ride.'

'What about before you and Zach were split?'

'There weren't horses in our village. There were some donkeys, but the others wouldn't let us ride.'

'But you've seen it done. Those men, by the river.'

'I know which end is forward, if that's what you mean.

I was carried on horseback, when Zach's men took me from the settlement, though that hardly counts. And you can't do it either, can you?'

'No. At least, I don't think so.' He smiled at me. 'But I wouldn't mind having a go.'

*

We waited until well after dark. From a perch in one of the apple trees at the farthest edge of the orchard, we watched as the children came out of the schoolhouse, perhaps ten of them, and played on the green around the well.

'Does it make you nostalgic?'

I shook my head. 'It wasn't like that for us. Not after we were very young. We weren't split; we couldn't go to school. The other kids kept their distance, mainly. So it was just Zach and me, together.'

'It's a wonder you didn't turn out odd. Apart from the whole fugitive seer thing, I mean.'

I smiled. 'And you – nostalgic?'

'By definition, you can't be nostalgic if you can't remember anything,' he said. 'I suppose amnesia has its advantages.' From across the orchard we could hear the children's shouts and laughter. 'Look at them: not a missing limb or flaw between them. Perfect little Alphas with their perfect little lives.'

'It's not their fault. They're just children.'

'I know. But it's a different world that they live in.'

'You sound like Zach.'

'I don't think he and I have much in common.'

'Maybe not. But what you said about a different world – that's his sort of talk. All that stuff about separation that the Alphas go on about.'

'It's a fact. Look down there – do you see any deformities, any brands? Each of those children has a twin, and their parents sent them away. And your Alpha family didn't have much time for you in their world, as I recall.'

I looked away. 'There's only one world.'

Kip gestured towards the village. 'You want to walk over there, introduce yourself, and try to explain that to them, be my guest.'

The men and women trailed back from the barn as the darkness mounted. A woman and a boy were hanging out clothes and sheets on a line by the well. Later a cart loaded with logs, pulled by two brown horses, approached from a road that led off to the east. Kip nudged me. A man sat at the front of the cart, and as it neared the village he jumped down and led the horses. A girl ran to greet him, and together they unhitched the wagon. I watched carefully, struck by how calmly they handled the huge animals. It was the girl, alone, who led both horses into the stable, the man giving the larger beast a gentle smack on the haunch as it was led away.

Some time later, the girl emerged and went into the house nearest the stable. The other children had dispersed too, now, and the noises of the village were muffled as the people retreated indoors. I felt vaguely guilty watching them, oblivious, go about their lives. Smoke began to unfurl from one or two chimneys.

Kip was impatient, but I made him wait until the dark was fully settled, the lamplights in the windows extinguished. Since we escaped we'd been grateful for the fine weather, but as we finally emerged from the shelter of the trees, I wished we had the cover of rain or fog.

On the way past the well we had to bend beneath the washing line, loaded with sheets and clothes. I felt a tug on my shirt, and turned to see Kip gesturing at the clothes.

'Steal them?' I mouthed.

'We're taking their horses. I don't think a pair of trousers is going to make a difference.' In the sleeping village, his whisper sounded loud to me.

I grimaced. 'We *need* the horses.'

'You're not the one who's been wearing a makeshift skirt for the last two weeks. I'll stick out, wherever we go.'

'Fine. But be quick.' I jerked my head towards the stables. 'Meet me in there.'

In the stable, it took time for my eyes to get used to the darkness, and when they did I was struck again by the sheer size of the horses, black masses in the dark. They were standing in two separate stalls, making noises that were alien to me: a snorting and shifting of weight. Bridles hung on the wall, and saddles were mounted on a low beam by the door, but the straps and buckles looked unfathomable, so instead I grabbed two decent lengths of rope that were looped on a nail by the door. I approached the smaller horse first. It moved backwards as I reached the front of its enclosure, and I winced at the clunk of its hoof on the back wall. Then it stepped forward and I was pushed to the left by its head, lowered over the stall door, rubbing against my side. I stifled a shout when the horse nipped at my hip, but when I stumbled back, my hand to where I'd been bitten, I felt the apples crammed in my pocket. I breathed out slowly. When I stepped forward again, a shrivelled apple in my outstretched hand, the horse took it with no hint of teeth. The softness of its lips on my palm was unexpected. While the horse chewed, I reached the rope slowly around its neck, looped it, and then, recalling the man with the cart, gave a firm pat on its shoulder, hoping to communicate an authority I didn't feel.

With the second horse, it was easier. By the time I'd got a second apple out of my pocket he was eager for it, and he submitted to having his neck stroked while he chewed noisily.

It took me a few seconds to work out how to open the stall doors, and to manage it while keeping hold of both ropes. I'd thought the horses might dash forwards, but they seemed unenthusiastic, and followed me only after much tugging, and another apple brandished beyond their reach. The larger horse sighed in a way that reminded me of Kip whenever I woke him at the start of a day.

Leading them from their stalls, I remembered the sound of hooves clattering on the shale of the cave when Kip and I escaped, and braced myself for noise, but the ground was soft and thickly scattered with hay, subduing the hoof-falls.

When I led the horses outside, the figure waiting in the darkness startled me for an instant, before I recognised Kip under unfamiliar clothes. He watched as both horses followed me obediently.

'Is that one of your seer things?' he asked. 'Can you communicate with them?'

'Don't be daft,' I snorted. 'I gave them each an apple.' I handed him the rope of the larger horse.

'Shouldn't we have saddles and things?'

I raised my eyebrows. 'There's no pleasing some people. Come on.'

'I even scored shoes,' he said, holding out a leg for me to admire his mud-encrusted boots. 'Left outside the door of the big house. Not the best fit, but I didn't feel like knocking on the door to ask if they had a bigger size.'

We were in the small green between the stables and the well. A low wall ran along one side, so I led my horse near it and stepped up onto the wall.

'You said you know which way is forward, right?' said Kip, watching me as his own horse busied itself happily with the grass.

'Shut up,' I said, hoisting myself up. I got my arms more or less around the horse's warm neck, and after a few ungainly swings managed to get my leg over the back. The horse gave a sulky whinny. The other horse snatched its head up and echoed the sound. Kip tried to tug it closer to the wall but it wrenched the rope from his hand, only to stop three feet away and resume its feast of grass.

Kip seemed a long way below me now. I watched him slowly approach his horse again, pick up the rope, tug more gently this time. The horse grunted, stamped a hoof, but wouldn't budge within reach of the wall. Kip tried to jump, but without the benefit of the wall's height he only clawed at the horse's back and slipped heavily down. The horse started backwards, bumping my mount, which started its own frantic dance, neighing loudly. In the house behind us a voice shouted, and a lamp was lit. A man rushed from the front door, his swinging lamp a slash of light in the darkness. From behind him, another man followed, with a flaming torch.

I'd been wondering how to get the horse moving, but the torch at least solved that problem, startling my horse off in a diagonal skitter across the green. I had to duck low, clinging to the horse's neck, as it charged under the washing line to take shelter on the far side of the well. But Kip, unmounted and clinging to the rope, was only a dozen feet from the men, now between him and the wall. His horse, like mine, started away from the flaming torch, and Kip was half running, half dragged, to keep up. He was hidden from me now by a huge white sheet on the line, through which the whole scene played out like a shadow play, lit by the torches behind. I saw the two men close in on Kip, heard the shouts of other people from the cottages. 'Thieves,' a woman yelled, and then, as more torches lit the scene and Kip became more visible, 'Omegas'. Even in silhouette, I could see that the growing crowd was armed: those without torches carried billhooks or sickles. One carried a long rope, looped at the end, and moved purposefully towards Kip. I tried to urge my horse back toward Kip but it only jittered on the spot. The man tossed the noose towards Kip's horse, but it darted backwards as the rope fell just short. As the horse passed close to the well, Kip jumped on to the circular surrounding wall, and from there made a dive at the horse's back. I heard a clatter from the well as some loosened stones tumbled into the deep. But there was no matching clatter of Kip hitting the ground, and through the white sheet I saw his silhouette, somehow astride the horse. Then the sheet itself was torn from the line and hurtling towards me as Kip raced forwards, shrouded in fabric and bent low over the horse's neck.

There was no way out, though. From every house, it seemed, figures had burst, and the edges of the green were ringed with lanterns and torches. The horses wheeled, backing into one another and skittering in panic. Kip was struggling to free himself of the sheet without releasing his grip on the horse's mane. The ring of flames tightened around us. A man with a torch darted close. He grabbed at my leg, his grip on my ankle a shackle that kicking could not shake. The heat from his torch scorched my knee.

Then he was enveloped in the sheet that Kip tossed at him. I kicked out at the grasping shroud of fabric, already aflame. My horse responded as if to a signal, and took off. As I careened toward the torches, the figures holding them were only black outlines, but I saw them loom closer, and then, at the last minute, dive aside, a blur of flame. Behind me, loud as my galloping heartbeat, I could hear the other horse.

I didn't dare to turn and check whether Kip was still mounted, could only shout his name. When he replied, over the pounding of hooves, I heard my body answer, a sound that was part sob, part laugh.

CHAPTER 12

In those first minutes of frantic galloping, I was afraid that we'd never be able to stop. We soon learned, however, that the horses were fundamentally lazy. After the initial panic had receded, and the lights of the village were no longer visible behind us, the horses slowed, and it was only with repeated kicks that they could be persuaded to move at anything faster than a walk. We rode most of the night in this fashion: bursts of reluctant speed, long periods of walking. I hadn't imagined how tiring it would be. I'd thought riding would be as simple as sitting, but the effort of just staying on, let alone cajoling the horse forward, made my hips and legs ache. My horse kept stopping to graze, and could only be dissuaded by sharp upward tugs on the rope round its neck. When I coaxed it to a faster pace, I was bounced around until I thought my teeth would loosen and fall out.

I knew, or sensed, that we were still heading south-west, though we'd left the road not long after the village. As the morning began to seep through the darkness, we saw that we'd reached a broad plain, disturbed only by tussocks of longer grass and small ponds. The horses slowed as they picked their way through the swampy ground. For once I didn't struggle against my horse as it began tearing grass from the soggy earth. Kip drew to a halt beside me and surveyed the flat expanse around us. 'If we get off here, we'll never be able to get back on again.'

'I've got a feeling it's easier without an angry mob,' I said. 'Either way, I don't think I can stay up much longer.'

'Do you know how to get down?'

I shrugged. 'Surely that's the easy bit. I've been struggling all night not to fall off.' I could make out a small coppice only a few hundred feet away. 'We could sleep there.'

'Right now, I could sleep anywhere.'

I swung one leg over to join the other and slid down, stumbling slightly when I landed. My legs protested as I straightened them. Next to me, the horse shook his neck happily. Kip dismounted too, landing evenly but wincing at his muscles' ache.

The horses took some convincing to move again, but after much tugging they swayed back into grudging motion, and before too long we reached the shelter of the small stand of trees. The horses drank from the swampy pond while I tethered their ropes to a branch. Within the huddle of the trees, where the ground rose slightly from the swamp-plain, Kip sat on the tufted grass. He gestured to himself with distaste. 'I finally get hold of some clothes, lovely clean clothes, and now they reek of horse.'

'I can't imagine we smell too great ourselves, these days,' I said. Sitting beside him, I fished out the last two apples from my pockets, passed one to him.

'How far do you think we've come?'

'A long way. Further than we would have made in days on foot, I think.' I knew we wouldn't be able to keep the horses all the way to the coast – Omegas on horseback would always be conspicuous – but every day of riding brought us closer to the island.

He spat out an apple pip. 'Far enough that Zach'll stop looking for us?'

I shook my head. 'It's not just him, anyway.' All through the night, even with the horse jolting beneath me, I'd felt The Confessor, felt that beam of thought trained on us. 'Not that I think he'll ever stop looking, but it's her I feel, mainly. The Confessor. And I don't know why she'd care so much. Why she'd be so concerned about protecting Zach.'

Beside me, Kip lay back. 'She works for him, right?'

'Sort of,' I said. 'I mean, she's an Omega, and he's on the Council, so yes. But it's hard to picture her working for anyone, really.' I thought of the imperious arch of The Confessor's eyebrows.

Kip sat up. 'I forgot – this is yours.' He took off the outer jumper, and then, beneath it, peeled off the jumper I'd lent him that first day. I put it over my shirt. It was filthy, and weirdly misshapen at the neck, from being stretched around his waist for these weeks. I looked down at myself and laughed.

'Sorry,' he said, pulling on his own jumper again. 'I guess I ruined it.'

'My clothes are the least of our worries at the moment, however ridiculous I look.'

'You don't look ridiculous. You look beautiful.' He spoke in a matter-of-fact way. I didn't know what to say, but he was already rolling over to sleep. 'Filthy, obviously. And you smell of horse. But beautiful.'

*

The horses were a mixed blessing. We could cover ground more quickly than before, but we also felt exposed. Two people on horseback were easier to spot and harder to hide, and two Omegas on horseback would draw attention from anyone we passed, not just the Council's soldiers. We agreed to keep the horses only for a few days, to cross the marshy plain, then ditch them when we started to encounter habitable land.

The riding got easier. I figured out that my horse responded better to squeezes from my legs than tugs on the rope around its neck. Mounting was still hard for Kip, with only one arm to haul himself up, but he took quickly to the riding. The unsteadiness that still plagued his movements was lessened on horseback, and he would show off, circling me, shifting smoothly between paces. We made good progress, drawn on always by the enticing sense that we were closer each day to the island. My visions of it were clearer than before, as though it were emerging from the fog of distance. When it came to me in dreams, I could see the black gloss of the mussels clinging to the rocks at the water's edge, and smell the salt-scoured air, soured with bird droppings.

My legs still ached from the riding, but I'd grown fond of my horse and often, in the evenings, would stand leaning against its neck, one hand on its shoulder, the other on the soft notch of its nose, between the huge, flaring nostrils. Despite my protestations, Kip could never quite rid himself of the idea that I was communicating psychically with the horses. In fact, it was the opposite that I warmed to, and that I'd found so disarming at first: the horses were so insistently present, in their sheer size and physicality, but not present in the sense that I was used to, that throbbing mental awareness that I felt around other people. When I stood with my face pressed to my horse's neck, I could close my eyes and imagine this might be what a non-seer would feel when with another person. A simple presence, a warm body. At night, when I slept close to Kip, I wondered if his lack of memories explained why I was able to feel so comfortable with him. Perhaps his mind felt so unobtrusive to mine because his lack of a past meant there was less clamour in his head.

He didn't talk often about what had happened to him, but I was surprised at how happy he seemed. The world appeared to hold a kind of novelty for him, and despite the hunger and exhaustion, he was largely cheerful. He tried to explain it to me, one night when we lay huddled close on the grass, the horses tethered nearby.

'When you broke the tank, it was like the blast. That's what it feels like. Not in a bad way, but in the way that everything split, right at that moment, into Before and After. The instant when you smashed the glass. That was the blast, for me, right down to the noise, rushing in. The crashing.'

I winced as I remembered it. The swing of the wrench; the explosion of sound in the tank room's hush.

He continued: 'Everything before then, it's lost to me. Of course it's sad. And of course I wish I knew. But everything since the smashing of the tank, that's the After. And I can't argue with it. It's what I've got. It's hard to explain, but it's exciting, in a way. Everything's new.'

I sighed. 'I could do with a little less excitement, myself.' But I knew what he meant. I also knew the responsibility that I had towards him. I was the tank-smasher, the blast-maker. I wasn't sure whether I was the apocalypse of his old world, or the prophet of his new world. Or both. Either way, I knew already that we were bound together, since the moment I swung the wrench into the tank. Perhaps from before then: from the moment his eyes met mine through the glass.

We passed only one settlement in the marshlands. We saw the hill from a distance, emerging from the swamp, the outline of buildings at its peak, its lower slopes planted with straggling crops. Its forsaken position marked it as an Omega settlement, but we nonetheless skirted widely as the sun set. There were no copses within sight, but half a mile west of the settlement we came across a patch where the reeds towered above the horses, giving good cover, so we stopped there for the night.

We'd planned to keep our distance and head off before dawn, but the music drew us in. As we were tethering the horses the sound of the pipes came slinking across the marsh. When the wind was low enough we could make out the twang of a guitar as well. It was the first time I'd heard music since my years in the settlement, where Sara the blacksmith used to play the pipes when we'd gather together after harvest, or for the midwinter bonfire. Omega bards, too, passed through our settlement sometimes, though in the last lean years few bards would stop there, when there were no coins to be given and the best they could hope for was a bed for the night and a meagre meal. On the marsh with Kip that evening, it had been so long since I'd heard music that the sounds reaching us seemed not just to come out of the darkness, but to come out of the past. Melodies half-heard and half-remembered.

The moon was slim, so it was hard work to pick our way through the marsh to the settlement, and several times one or both of us ended up knee-deep in water. Hunger had put paid to any qualms about stealing from Omegas, but as we drew closer the ramshackle buildings and the fetid smell of the sodden fields surrounding them suggested there'd be little to steal. But it was the music that I wanted to take. We crept through the patchy fields until the buildings began.

The noise was coming from the barn on the south side of the hill. It was brightly lit by hanging lanterns, and through the open door we could see figures, some seated on hay bales, others dancing to the tune.

Since this was an Omega settlement, at least we knew that there would be no dogs to reveal us as we crept around to the back of the barn. The music was loud there, and the rough beamed wall was generous with cracks through which we could peer inside. The lanterns seemed to flicker in time with the music. In the centre of the barn, on a makeshift stage of hay bales, two men played pipes while a woman played a guitar. They were travelling bards, by the look of them, their clothes both ornate and road-worn. Their visit was probably an excuse for this threadbare party. Around them milled the locals, thin but merry enough, and some of them drunk already, reeling to the music.

'Come away,' said Kip, pulling at my elbow.

'They won't be able to see us – not with the barn lit up like that,' I whispered, keeping my face pressed to the rough wood. Inside, a man was spinning a young girl by her arms, her single foot lifting from the ground as she orbited him, laughing loudly.

'It's not that.'

I turned. He stepped back, gave a half-bow, and held out his arm again.

'Dance?'

I stifled a laugh at the absurdity of it. But he met my grin with one of his own. 'Just for a few minutes, let's pretend we're not fugitives. Let's just be two people at a dance.'

He must have known, as much as I did, how impossible it was. At any minute we could be exposed. Even here, amongst our own kind, we dared not show ourselves. Word might have spread from Wyndham, if not from the village where we'd stolen the horses. There were soldiers after us, and a bounty, probably, which the bony faces inside the barn would find hard to resist. And somewhere The Confessor was out there too, her blade-mind rasping the night sky.

In the dark, though, with the music leaking through the gaps in the barn wall, and with the smell of smoke and ale, it was easy just to take his hand. The light from the barn painted bars on his face. Taking his arm, I rested my other hand on his side, and we swayed to the music. For a few moments, it was like a glimpse into another life: one in which we might be inside the barn, dancing with friends, instead of hiding outside in the dark. One in which our worries might be a poor harvest, or a leaky roof, instead of a chamber full of tanks, and a pursuing army. Where my sleep might be interrupted by dreams of a handsome boy I'd seen at market, instead of by visions of the blast.

We stayed there for several songs. A jig came on and we spun each other about, making up extravagant moves as we went. We didn't dare laugh, or even talk, but the dancers on the other side of the wall did it for us, their calls and giggles growing louder with the music.

A light rain began. It was warm enough not to matter, and we were part-soaked anyway from crossing the marsh, but it was a reminder that we were on the wrong side of the wall. That we were stealing time from a life that wasn't our own. Perhaps that was what I'd been doing for all those years, back in the village when Zach and I were children.

We didn't speak as we crept off into the night, followed by the music, and made our way back across the tussocked swamp.

*

144

As the days passed, we grew to envy the horses' constant feast of grass. On the marshes there was little for us to scavenge. The murky ponds yielded nothing but a few small shrimps, all fleshless shell. At least there was always water, and the inhospitable, swampy ground meant that we travelled for days without encountering a settlement. This was a relief, but it also meant there was no food to steal. Kip made fewer jokes. At night, as we sat together watching the horses chew, I caught myself mimicking their chewing motion with my own empty mouth.

'Don't you ever wonder why horses don't have twins?' I said, as we watched them graze nearby. 'Other animals either.'

'They do sometimes,' he said.

'Oh, they have multiple births sometimes, but not proper twins. Not linked.'

He shrugged. 'Animals don't talk or build houses either,' he pointed out. 'They're different from us. The blast, the radiation, it affected humans differently, that's all. It's not like it didn't affect animals too – you see deformed animals all the time. They just adapted in different ways.'

I nodded. That was the accepted explanation, though it was hard to think of twins as an adaptation, rather than as eternal. A world without twins seemed unnatural, impossible. Perhaps Kip was as close to such a thing as the After would allow. But even that was an illusion. He might not remember her, but his twin was out there, somewhere. They were like the two-headed snake we'd spotted by the river, a week before. Each head might imagine itself autonomous, but they had only one death to share.

The next day, I felt the swamp receding. Then the tangible signs began to show: the ground beneath the horses became less marshy, and we made better progress. To the west, we could make out a body of mountains. Then, toward the evening, smoke rose ahead.

When we'd slipped the ropes from the horses' necks, it took them some time to realise they were free. They began to graze where they stood. I laughed. 'Wouldn't that just be our luck, if we couldn't shake them now?' Still I didn't walk away, allowed myself one last pat of my horse's neck.

'Do you think they'll be all right?'

I nodded. 'They'll probably be caught again, eventually. And until then, it'll be like a holiday.' I stepped back. When the horse still didn't move, leaned forward again and gave it a firm smack on the side. It took a few experimental steps away. Kip's horse followed. Then, barely twenty feet away, they resumed their grazing.

'I sort of thought they'd gallop off into the distance.'

Kip shrugged. 'Too lazy. I haven't seen them gallop since that first night.' He held up the ropes. 'Do we need these?'

'I can't see why.' We left them where they fell.

Kip looked at me. 'You're going to miss the horses, aren't you?'

'Kind of. Some things, anyway.'

'Me too. I liked riding; liked having them around.' He began walking. 'If it's any consolation, we'll probably smell like them for a long time yet.'

*

We sat on a large boulder near the edge of the marsh, watching the network of roads visible in the distance, converging at a town. It was big, larger than anything I'd seen apart from Wyndham. The town seemed to spill down the hill, houses scattered further apart at the outskirts, with those higher up clustering tightly. From near the southern side of the town, a forest spread thickly into the distance, as far as we could see.

'Omega,' I said, eyes squinting against the sun setting low behind the city.

'How can you tell?'

'Just look at it.' I gestured to the makeshift buildings, the marshy land around. Some of the houses at the edge of town were barely shacks.

'There'll be some Alphas there too, though.'

'Perhaps a few patrols of soldiers. Some traders or travellers too, maybe. Shady types.'

'Will they be watching for us here?'

I sucked my top lip. 'I don't know. We've come a long way – probably further than Zach thought we'd get.'

'Further than I thought we'd get, to be honest.'

'Even so, he will have sent word out. I don't think we have a choice, though.' I looked down at my bony arms. On my hands, my knuckles stood out, sharp as fins. 'We can't keep going like this. Even if they're looking for us, the town's still got to be our best chance to find food.' I thought, too, of how I had hidden my doll, Scarlett, in full sight, amongst the other dolls in the toy-chest, when Zach had tried to take her. 'We might be safest in the town anyway. There, we'd be just two amongst thousands.'

Kip turned to me. 'And they're going to be looking for a seer and a one-armed boy, right?'

CHAPTER 13

On Kip's suggestion, we used my jumper to bind my left arm tightly around my body. After the weeks of hunger, and with Kip's jumper baggy over the top, the concealed arm was barely visible, folded across my stomach. Kip's appearance was harder to change. We tried stuffing his empty left sleeve with grass, thinking that he might fake a limp instead, but his scarecrow arm looked ridiculous. 'Anyway,' he said, 'there'll be hundreds of one-armed men in the city. You're the problem.'

'Thanks,' I said, but I knew what he meant. Seers were rare – The Confessor and the mad seer at Haven were the only others I'd seen in person, though I'd heard of others. Here, my body would be as anomalous as Kip's in an Alpha town.

Neither of us mentioned the other obvious precaution we should take, of separating. For me, off-balance and awkward with one arm bound, the idea of being alone in the town was too much. As we walked together towards the main road, I stumbled several times and Kip steadied me.

'You shouldn't use your real name, either,' he said.

'Good idea.' I thought for a moment. 'I'll be Alice. And you?'

He raised an eyebrow.

'Oh. Of course,' I said, laughing. In those few weeks I'd become so used to thinking of him as Kip that I'd forgotten I'd named him myself.

The city crept up on us. There were others on the road, mostly heading towards the town as the evening darkened. A man pulled a barrow loaded with pumpkins. A woman carried a bale of cloth over her shoulder. But nobody glanced at us – we were just part of the town's tide, being drawn back in with the night.

We reached the main part of town, where buildings crowded tightly over narrow streets. I'd thought the grime of the past few weeks would make us stand out, but many of the people jostling past were nearly as dirty as us.

I tugged at Kip's jumper. 'This way,' I said, gesturing up a side-street.

'Are you doing the magic geography thing again?'

I laughed. 'No – but I can smell food.' And the square that the street opened up to was indeed the market. At this hour, though, all that remained was the smell – a reminder of pastry, of overripe vegetables – and a scattering of cabbage leaves trodden into the mud. The last stallholders were sealing up their wares in barrows and leaving.

'Sorry – too late, I guess. Not that we have money, anyway.'

'We should have eaten one of the horses.' He was only partly joking.

'So we look for work.'

'Or steal, if we can,' he said, watching a stallholder wheel away a crate of pies.

'I don't know. We can't just gallop away on horseback

this time. And it feels worse, somehow, stealing from our own people.'

'What happened to *there's only one world*?' he teased. 'No – I know what you mean. I'd rather work. I just don't know what work we're fit for, that's all.'

Two men were crossing the market square towards us. One of them, a fat man leaning on a cane, paused by us, then bent in so close that I could smell his hot, sweet breath. He turned to Kip.

'A bronze coin for you, lad, if you'll let me take care of your pretty friend for an hour.'

Before Kip had a chance to reply, I struck the man across the face. The stubble on his chin was so coarse that it prickled the palm of my hand. I ran, looking back at Kip, who kicked the man's cane from under him before following me. But the fat man made no attempt to chase us. We could hear him give a loud curse, and then a whistle, his friend laughing noisily. I couldn't run well with my arm strapped across my torso, and as soon as we'd escaped the market square Kip pulled me into the cover of a doorway.

'I thought we were trying to be inconspicuous,' he hissed.

'You think I should have gone with him?'

'No – of course not. But we could just walk away. You don't need to start a fight, bring attention to us.'

I kicked the earth at my feet. 'He was disgusting.'

'Of course he was. But he won't be the last bad person we come across, and we need to stay out of trouble.' I said nothing. 'At least let him give me the money next time, before we make a run for it,' he said.

I had to turn my whole body to slap his shoulder with my free arm.

We continued up the alley, which made its way uphill. Behind shutters we could glimpse the light of fires and lamps. Where the alley joined a larger street we were again surrounded by people, but after our encounter at the marketplace, I was less comforted by the crowd. The man had been the first person to speak to us since our escape, I realised, unless you count the shouts of the Alpha villagers when we stole the horses. I hadn't thought much about how we would fit back into the world. Here, in the city's lively streets, we were still hungry, still pursued. The smells of food, drifting out from various houses, only made it harder. We saw no Council soldiers, at least, although on some of the walls, their posters were nailed: *Council Soldiers: Protecting Your Communities. Refuges: Your Council Caring for You. Tithe Dodging: Punishable by Imprisonment. Report Illegal Omega Schools (Reward Offered)*. This last one made us both grin, at the Council's use of written warnings in a town whose inhabitants they would claim were illiterate. We noticed, too, that some of the posters had been crudely defaced. Others had been torn down, leaving only wistful shreds of paper hanging from the nails.

A large building dominated the downhill side of the street, its window shutters thrown open and smoke rising from the chimney. From a bracket by the door a lamp swung, and below it a woman sat on an upturned bucket, smoking a pipe. I looked at Kip, who nodded, and followed me.

'Excuse me, please,' I said. The woman didn't speak, but replied with a puff of smoke from the pipe. 'Do you run the inn? And do you think we might work, in exchange for some food and lodging? Just for one night?'

The woman again seemed to signal her assent with a generous puff of smoke. I tried hard not to cough. Then she stood, removed her pipe, and stepped back on her awkwardly bowed legs, making room in the doorway for us to enter. 'It's not an inn,' she said, 'but I do run the place, and I reckon we can use you.'

We thanked her as we stepped inside. Despite her crooked legs, she moved quickly. The low-ceilinged hall was lit by candles, but almost immediately the woman kicked open a door into a side room, and ushered us in.

'Go on then. Get your kit off, both of you.'

This time it was Kip who stepped forward. 'Not that kind of work. I'm sorry, we misunderstood.'

The woman just laughed as he tried to shoulder past her, his hand in mine. 'Don't be daft. This isn't a knocking shop. But if you think you're going near my kitchen in that state, you've indeed misunderstood. Now get in there and my cook will bring you some water.'

The door swung shut behind her. Kip looked at me. 'It's not locked. We could leave?'

I shook my head. 'I think she's all right. It feels all right, I mean, this place.'

'But you don't know what it is?'

I shook my head. 'As long as they feed us, I almost don't care.'

We heard a shouted order beyond the door, and only minutes later a young woman in a red headscarf came in with a bucket and emptied it into the round wooden tub that stood by the fire. She made three more trips, throwing Kip a bar of soap the final time she entered. 'The boss said you'd be needing this, and by the looks of the two of you, she's right.'

The prospect of a proper clean was too enticing for us to wait for the water to warm fully. Kip gave me the soap and sat pointedly with his back to the tub while I undressed and stepped into the lukewarm water. It was deep enough that if I tucked my knees to my chest and lay back I could get my whole head underwater. Surfacing, I lay for a few moments, but my sharp bones were painful where they jabbed the tub, so I set about washing myself. The soap didn't lather well in the tepid water but I scrubbed until my skin, cleansed of its layers of grime, looked unfamiliar, and weirdly pink. I scrubbed my hair too, until it squeaked under my hands.

The door was pushed open again, and I banged my head as I curled low in the tub to hide myself, but the girl didn't enter this time, simply flung two towels and a bundle of clothes, and let the door slam.

'Can you pass me a towel?' I gave a stifled laugh at Kip as he politely sidestepped to the towel, then sidestepped back, keeping his back to me even as he tossed the towel my way.

'Oh for goodness' sake. You're not the one I have to hide my body from,' I said, stepping out and wrapping myself in the towel. 'You know I've got both arms. And I can't imagine the rest of me is any great surprise.'

'Sorry,' he muttered, but kept his eyes averted while I rifled through the clean clothes the girl had left us. When I had on a shirt and trousers I had to ask him for his help to bind my arm again, which we did with my old shirt, before concealing it with a thick jumper.

Kip picked up the second towel, stepped over and looked into the tub.

'I'm sorry it's so grotty,' I said, embarrassed. 'But at least it will have warmed up a bit more by now.'

Despite my earlier teasing, I did as he'd done and kept my back turned while he undressed and bathed. The sounds alone were oddly intimate, though. I could hear every splash, every reverberation of the tub against his elbow and shoulder-blades. Then the sounds of the towel rasping on his skin, of clothes being drawn over his body.

The woman with the pipe entered without knocking while we were putting on our shoes. She looked us over. 'That's more like it. Now come along to the kitchen. Leave your dirty clothes here. We'll get them washed. Best get rid of all that horse-hair, for one thing, before anybody starts asking questions.'

Kip and I shot each other a look as we followed her out of the room, down the long corridor, and into a room noisy with the sounds of cooking. Suspended above a huge fire, two pots steamed. Another fire, beneath a metal grill, kept a number of smaller pots bubbling, and the girl in the red headscarf was cutting carrots, her knife rapping a speedy beat on the chopping board.

The woman surveyed us unabashedly. 'Looks like between the two of you I'll get one good day's work. And you won't be good for that, I'm thinking, until you've eaten something. That's if you can remember how.' She seemed to view our thin state as a personal affront. As she spoke, she grabbed a cloth, lifted the lid of one of the larger pots, ladling the stew into two bowls, and jabbing a spoon into each. 'And when you're done with those,' she said, thrusting the bowls at us, 'you can wash those potatoes. Though there's not one of them as dirty as the two of you when you wandered in here.'

She left. Sitting on a low bench by the wall, we ate as fast as the scalding food would allow. Even though my stomach hurt at the onslaught of food, I devoured the chunks of vegetables, and scraped the bowl clean at the end. Next to me, bowl wedged between his knees, Kip did the same.

The young woman took our bowls. Below her red scarf she had a single eye, in the centre of her forehead. Her skin was dusky brown and she was plumper than the older woman. She introduced herself as Nina. Kip introduced himself too, and I gave my name as Alice. It didn't feel as unnatural as I'd thought it might. In the first month or two at the settlement I'd become used to hearing myself referred to as 'Alice's niece', and even at the end of my years there, everyone still called my home 'Alice's place'.

Nina showed us the potatoes, two bags half as big as me, slumped against the wall. Kneeling over the bucket of water, I was frustratingly clumsy with my left arm strapped tight against my stomach. I couldn't scrub the potatoes one-handed, so Kip and I ended up sharing the work: I'd hold each potato, turning it while Kip scrubbed with the small brush, then rinsing it in the bucket. We worked steadily, the pile of clean, white potatoes growing. The food, and the heat from the fires, made me sleepy, but I enjoyed the simplicity of the task, and the sense of working in tandem with Kip, as if we were two halves of a single body.

Nina got on with her work without chatter, so we were spared the questions we'd been dreading. The noises of the kitchen prevented the lack of conversation from seeming awkward.

It was Kip who finally asked what sort of place this was.

Nina raised an eyebrow. 'Do you not know?'

We shook our heads.

'You never thought all this food was for me and the boss?' Nina laughed.

Kip shook his head again. 'But there's nobody else around – it doesn't seem to be an inn.'

'Not a paying inn, no.' She wiped her hands on her apron. 'You'd better come and have a look.'

We followed her out of the kitchen and into a courtyard in the rear. As we crossed the yard, the night sounds of the city drifted in from above. At the side wall, Nina turned back to us and pressed her finger to her lips, before opening the door. At least three times as large as the kitchen, the room ran the whole length of the courtyard. Most of the candles in the brackets had burnt down, but two were still giving off the last of their light. All along one wall, neatly lined up, were beds and cots. With Kip beside me, I walked along the row of beds. All the sleepers were children, the oldest perhaps twelve, the younger ones only babies, all of them exposed in the absolute vulnerability of sleep. Some lay on their backs, mouths open like baby birds. In the bed closest to me, a small girl had kicked off her sheets and was curled tightly on her side, sucking her thumb. On every visible face I could see the brand.

CHAPTER 14

A door at the far end of the dormitory opened and the older woman entered, a sleeping child in her arms. She placed the child in a cot by the door, carefully tucking the blankets over the sleeping form. Then she joined Nina by the other door, indicating with a jerk of her head that we should follow. In the courtyard, she whispered some instructions to Nina, who returned to the dormitory, while the bow-legged woman led us back to the kitchen.

'Is it an orphanage, then?' asked Kip, as the woman busied herself with stirring the large pots on the fire. But it was me who answered.

'They're not orphans.'

The woman nodded. 'That's right. They're Omega kids, those whose parents can't find anywhere better for them. We're a holding house.'

'And how do they end up here?' asked Kip.

'Used to be that Omega kids would be taken straight into an Omega settlement. Just handed over to the settlement closest to the village. Or, often, the Alphas would stay in touch with their own twins, send them their Omega child to care for when the time came. So the kids would be raised by their aunt or uncle. But these days more and more Alphas won't go near a settlement, won't acknowledge their twin, let alone stay in touch with them. And the settlements have been driven further out too, to even poorer land. With that, and all the increases in tithes, Omegas can barely feed themselves, so they can hardly take on a kid. And no Alpha family will keep their Omega child long enough for it to be able to take care of itself, as some people used to.' She looked around at the kitchen, stacks of bowls piled high on the open shelves. 'So they come here.'

'The Alphas just dump them here?'

'It's not as bad as all that, lad. They can't risk any harm coming to the kids, of course, so they leave them with money, usually, enough to ensure we take care of them. It's just that the networks people used to rely on to take their Omega children – relatives, neighbours, even friends – they're weakening now. The drought years were the turning point – I've always said there's nothing like hunger to turn people against each other. Now, with all this stuff the Council goes on about – contamination, separation – Alphas can hardly bring themselves to speak to Omegas these days, so when it's time to hand over their Omega kids, there's nobody but us.'

'So the Omega children – do they stay here forever?' I asked.

'No. A few do – you'll see them tomorrow. Those who nobody else will take. But most, nearly all, we find a place for with an Omega family. We only do what the Alpha parents did themselves, once. Alphas have always banged on about contamination. It's just that this new lot in the Council seem dead set on acting on it.' She looked appraisingly at us. 'You'll be from the country then, maybe out east, if all this is new to you.'

I didn't want to say anything about our origins, so instead I said: 'I'm Alice. And this is Kip.' When the woman didn't respond, I added: 'And you? You haven't told us your name.'

'And I hope you've had the good sense not to tell me your real names. But I'm Elsa. Now, let's get the two of you to bed. I'll need your help in the kitchen early tomorrow.'

She lit a candle and passed me the holder, then led us back out to the courtyard and into a small room at the rear, where four empty beds were lined against the wall. 'The beds are small – they're kids' beds – but I reckon you've had worse lately.'

Kip thanked her as I placed the candle on the floor. As Elsa was closing the door she said quietly, 'The other thing about this room is that there's only a little drop from the window to the outhouse roof, and from there a person could get clean away down the back-streets. Just in case of a fire, say, or a visit from our Alpha friends.' The door was shut before we could react.

When I asked Kip to help me unbind my arm, he asked, 'What if she comes in, in the night?'

'She won't,' I said. 'And I don't think much would surprise her, even if she did. Anyway, I can't sleep trussed up like this – it's bad enough in the daytime.'

The knotted sleeves of the shirt, wrapped around my body, had drawn tight, and it took the two of us a minute to loosen the knot and free me. I stretched, enjoying the luxury of movement, then saw him watching me.

'What is it?' I climbed on the bed closest to the door, pulled the blankets up.

'Nothing.' He got into the next bed. 'It's just – your arm. Today, working in the kitchen together, it felt like we were the same. And I wouldn't wish it on you – you know that.

But seeing you untie your other arm now – it's just a reminder, that's all. That I can't do the same.'

The candlelight was enough for me to see him staring at the roof. Elsa had been right about the beds. I had to lie diagonally, and even then my feet were pressed against the bars at the end. Kip's feet stuck clear through the bars of his bed. But the soft mattress and the clean sheets were an almost forgotten extravagance. I licked my finger and thumb, reached down and snuffed the candle in between our beds.

The physical closeness that had gone unnoticed in our weeks on the run was suddenly conspicuous in these domestic surroundings. For the last fortnight we'd huddled close each night, sleeping in thickets and shallow caves and beneath fallen trees. Here in the tidy, unfamiliar room we lay staidly apart in our separate beds.

Finally I spoke. 'Can I come in with you?'

He sighed. 'Because my bed's not small enough already?' I heard him throw back the blanket. 'Come on.'

I climbed in next to him. He was on his back, and I lay on my side, where his left arm would have been. Facing him, I wrapped one arm over him, and his hand met mine, so that our clasped hands rested on his stomach. I could smell soap on both of us. Outside, a pigeon gave a small, somnolent coo, while on my forehead I felt the warm, rhythmic breath of Kip, already half-asleep.

*

The pigeons on the roof woke us, and we bound my arm quickly before heading across the courtyard to the kitchen. Nina greeted us with a distracted nod, set me to work stirring a pot of oats, and directed Kip to a pile of copper pots needing washing.

There was an eruption of noise in the courtyard when the children emerged. We could hear Elsa's voice, shushing and bossing, and then a rush of footsteps past the kitchen door. It took both Nina and me to carry the big porridge pot along the corridor and through to the dining room, where the children, perhaps thirty of them, were crowded on benches around two long tables, laid with spoons and tin bowls. The children were well fed and clean, but looked even younger in the daylight. Lined up on the benches, most of their legs swung well clear of the ground, and some of the bigger children held the littlest ones. A few looked barely awake. One girl sucked sleepily on her spoon as they waited for the porridge to be served.

Elsa took Kip to help her feed the babies, waiting back in the dormitory, so Nina and I were left to serve the porridge. The children didn't seem surprised by my appearance there – I supposed they must be used to people coming and going. They lined up in front of me and while I ladled the thick porridge into each proffered bowl, Nina walked down the line with a hairbrush, seeing to the children one by one. I noted how each child received a kiss on the forehead or a pat on the shoulder, along with a few sweeps of the brush through their hair. They were polite, too: they thanked me, if a little sleepily. Two seemed to be mute, but nodded to me as they took their bowls. One girl, without legs, sat in a small wheeled cart that was pulled along by one of the older boys, and another girl carried two bowls, one for the boy next to her who had no arms. A tall girl, without eyes, confidently navigated her way around the room by the walls. Which of these, I wondered, were the ones whom nobody would take in?

The pot was lighter now and I carried it back to the kitchen myself. As Nina had instructed, I filled a bowl for

163

myself and ate by the fire. The new regularity of food made me tired. When Kip returned to the kitchen I was asleep on the bench, head and shoulders leaning against the stone wall. I stirred as he joined me, feeling his warmth at my side and hearing the scrape of his spoon on his bowl while he ate, but it wasn't until Nina entered, with a clatter of bowls, that I woke properly.

We were kept busy in the kitchen all morning, but it was warm and Nina chatted easily with us. She didn't ask any questions; with the constant coming and going of different children she'd probably heard enough stories. As for us, we were greedy for news of the world. Nina's news was all linked to the children who came, and the families who'd delivered them. Babies dropped off before they'd even been weaned. A toddler left in the doorway in the night, and found near-strangled by the bag of silver coins in a pouch around his neck. The growing numbers, every year. 'Used to be Elsa would have ten, maybe fifteen kids here at any one time,' Nina said. 'But in the three years I've worked here, we're rarely under thirty. And we're not the only holding house in New Hobart – there's another by the western edge, not quite as big.'

The stories that she shared with us, however, also revealed glimpses of the wider world. Omega families were less able to take in children, she said, because of the pressure of ever-increasing tithes, and the restrictions on land, trading and travel that made it harder for Omegas to make a living. Edicts from the Council were intruding more and more into Omega life. Some of the names I recognised from before my imprisonment: The Judge, still ruling the Council, apparently, as he had since I was a child. I'd heard of The General before too, and Nina confirmed that she was still one of the more aggressive anti-Omega voices on the Council. The new laws to push Omegas to less fertile land, and outlawing settlements by any river or coast, she said, came from The General. 'We used to think The General was as bad as things could get,' she went on. 'But there are other young ones on the Council, in the last few years. The young ones are always the worst,' she said, scouring a pot viciously. 'This new lot are as bad as any: The Ringmaster, The Reformer.'

She didn't seem to have noticed that I dropped the dish-cloth when she spoke Zach's name. Why hadn't he abandoned that assumed name once he had me safe in the Keeping Rooms? Though I'd never heard of any Councillor going by their real name. It wasn't just to hide their real identities; it was part of the pageantry, the fear they inspired.

She went on, passing me another bowl to dry. 'Those two, together with The General, have done more damage than The Judge ever did. It's not just the rise in public whippings – it's all the other stuff. Registrations now for all Omegas: not just name, place of birth, and twin, but having to notify the Council if you travel, or even move house. Every time we find a home for a child we have to go through all that with the Council office. There's talk of curfews for Omegas in some areas, too. And there've been some Omega settlements sealed altogether: the Council soldiers won't let anyone in or out, they just take over.' She paused and looked at the door, before continuing in a lowered voice. 'There are other stories, too. People going missing – just taken in the night.'

I didn't trust myself to speak, nodding instead, but Kip dived in.

'What happens to them?'

Nina shook her head. 'Nobody knows. Anyway, it's only a rumour. Don't say anything about it, whatever you do.

You'll only scare the kids.' But it was she who looked frightened, and she changed the subject quickly.

We ate the midday meal with the children, and afterwards
Elsa called us into the dormitory, where she was finishing
bottle-feeding the youngest ones. A crying baby was hoisted
on her shoulder, and she patted its back with one hand
while looking us over.

'The two of you'll be wanting to have a rest in your room
for the afternoon, I'd imagine.'

I protested that we were happy to work, or just to play
with the children, but Elsa spoke over me. 'Afternoons we
open up for visitors – families come, to see about taking
the children, and Alphas come to drop them off. So I'm
thinking the two of you will be wanting to have a rest in
your room. With the courtyard shutters closed.'

I cleared my throat. 'Thank you. We – we don't want to
cause you any trouble, by being here.'

Elsa laughed loudly, setting off the baby again. 'I'm a
woman with crooked legs, a dead husband, thirty children
under my care, and more coming each day. You think I'm
not used to trouble? Now get going. I'll call you when
we've locked up after visitors.' She pulled a large pair of
scissors from her apron pocket. 'And take this with you, so
you can sort out each other's hair. I can't have you in this
house with your hair like that. It's a lice-trap. And people
could mistake you for a pair of horse thieves.'

Back in our room, my arm unbound, I sat Kip down,
wrapped a towel around his neck, and stood behind him.
His hair had been long in the tank, and was even longer
now, reaching below his shoulders. I lifted a lock straight
up, then cut it as close to his head as I could. He flinched
at the tug of the scissors' blunt blades.

'Do you even know how to do this?'

'I used to cut Zach's hair, my last few years in the village.'

'And he turned out just great.'

I laughed, but I could still picture the fear on Nina's face, when she'd mentioned the rumours about The Reformer. It was hard to reconcile my memories of Zach – my wary, watchful, twin – with this figure of fear. To know that he was responsible not only for what had happened to Kip in the tanks, but also for so many of the awful things Nina had mentioned. Hardest of all was to know that the responsibility for the damage he caused was partly mine. I could stop him right now, I thought, looking down at the scissors. All the Council soldiers in Wyndham couldn't help him, if I were to turn these blunted blades on my wrist. If I had the courage.

Kip turned and looked up at me.

'The long pause doesn't fill me with confidence. Are you sure you're not going to ruin my youthful good looks?'

I laughed, reached for the next strand of hair. It was warm in my hand from where it had lain against his neck. I held it for a few seconds before I began.

His hair was so long that it took a long time to cut, and wasn't perfectly tidy, but eventually there was a mass of brown hair on the floor, and his head was reduced to tufty stubble. It reminded me of the maize fields by the village, right after harvest.

I insisted on doing my own hair too, despite his protestations, though I let him help me with the back. I hadn't realised quite how long it had grown, and after I'd cut it to jaw length I kept shaking my head, unused to its weight-lessness. We swept up the cut hair and threw it out the back window, shaking the towel after it. Standing together at the window, we watched the tresses drift down into the street below.

Kip kept running his hand over his newly shorn head. 'It takes years, right? To grow hair that long?'

I leaned against him. 'Normally, yes. But there's a lot of things we don't know.'

He raised his eyebrows. 'That's an understatement, in my case.'

'I meant, lots we don't know about the tanks. How they worked – whether things even grew in there. Or how long your hair was when you went in, or if they ever cut it.'

'I know.' He continued rubbing his head. 'I know it's all just guesswork. And I know it probably won't get me anywhere. But it's hard to stop guessing.'

*

We'd meant to stay only a day or two, just long enough to regain some strength, but Elsa asked us no questions and seemed grateful for the extra help, so the days passed, and by the third week, we'd fallen into a comfortable routine. We worked each morning and each evening, and in the afternoons took shelter in our room, which gave me a chance to free my arm for a few hours. A few times our curiosity overcame our caution and I left my arm bound for an afternoon venture into the town itself. I still found it disorienting to be amongst so many people, after my long isolation in the Keeping Rooms. Kip, however, thrived on the crowds. Although we had no money to spend, he loved the crush of the market, the smell of the roasting nuts and mulled wine, the clatter of voices. For an hour at a time I could almost imagine we were normal people, that nobody was hunting us. But even in an Omega town there were occasional Alphas: tithe collectors, soldiers, merchants passing through. The few times we spotted an unbranded face, or the bright red of a Council uniform, we would turn swiftly, make for the nearest alley and take the back-streets all the way home.

As we approached the market square one morning we saw a crowd gathered by the central well. Two Council soldiers stood on a raised platform, so we hung back, but even from the back of the crowd, partly hidden by a barrow of melons, we could see what was happening. A man, perhaps ten years older than me, was tied to a stake, while one of the soldiers whipped his naked back. The beaten man was crying out with each stroke, but the noise of the whip itself was worse: the whistle as it sliced the air; the percussive smack as it hit his flesh. The second soldier stood a few feet away, reading aloud from a sheet of paper. He had to shout to make himself heard over the whip, and the cries of the prisoner:

'For that crime, ten strokes. Then, upon being apprehended for the illegal removal of a Council information poster, the Omega prisoner was also found not to have registered his change of address with the Council. For this crime, a further ten strokes, with an additional five strokes for failure to pay tithes during the three months in his new residence.'

The soldier finished his proclamation, but the whipping continued. The crowd was silent, but with each stroke the massed shoulders in front of us winced. Where the prisoner's back had earlier shown individual welts, some leaking red, now no distinct marks could be made out in the pulpy mass. The waistband of his trousers was darkened with blood.

I pulled Kip away, but even as we retreated down the alley we could hear the final strokes.

'But what about his Alpha?' Kip said, as we hurried back to the holding house. 'She'll feel that, for sure.'

'My guess is that the Council doesn't care,' I said. 'It's a price they're happy to pay – some woman miles away will scream for a few hours, but they get to make an example out of her twin for hundreds to see. And the Council's done such a good job of segregating twins from each other, she'll probably never even find out exactly what caused the pain. It's not going to bother the Council.'

'But if she did know – would Alphas stand for it? Wouldn't they be furious that their own Council was hurting innocent people?'

I stopped, turned to face him. 'That man – the man being whipped – do you really think he's any less innocent than his Alpha twin? Because he pulled down a poster, or couldn't afford to pay tithes?'

'Of course not. I know as well as you do that it's all trumped-up nonsense. But if they're beating people like that now, so badly their Alpha twins can feel it, won't it cause problems from their own side? Won't the Alphas be angry?'

'They will be – but not at the Council. I think if they found out, they'd be angry at the Omega twin, the so-called "criminal". If they swallow the Council line, they'll believe it's him bringing this on himself. The same way they think Omegas are going hungry because we're too lazy or stupid to farm properly, rather than because of tithes and blighted land.'

After that, we were more careful on the streets, venturing from the holding house only occasionally, usually in the early mornings on market days, when we could slip unnoticed amongst the busiest of the crowds. But it was easier to stay at home, in the cloistered courtyard world within Elsa's walls, where we could spend time with the children and try to forget that there lay a town beyond, with blood on the whipping post and Council soldiers in the streets.

We got to know all the children. Louisa, a sweet three-year-old dwarf, became devoted to me, and a slightly older boy called Alex took to following Kip around. Alex had been there for five years, Elsa told us, since he was a baby. He had no arms, and would sit on Kip's lap at meal times, Kip feeding him from his own bowl, alternating mouthfuls. Alex's head fitted neatly beneath Kip's chin, bobbing gently each time Kip chewed. Watching them, I noted how Kip's face had lost its starved look, his cheekbones less angular. I knew, too, that my own flesh was fuller, my bones less sharp. I was stronger, as well. Even with one arm bound, I could hoist the biggest pots up above the fire without assistance, or carry the toddlers on my hip for long stretches when they demanded to be cuddled.

I'd never thought much about children. Most Omegas didn't – what was the point? At best, you might hope to one day take care of an Omega child in need of a home. Since my branding I'd grown used to the taunts from the few Alphas who passed by the settlement: *dead-end, freak, monster*. Now, watching Kip with Alex, or seeing how little Louisa would reach her truncated arms up to me whenever I passed, the name *dead-end* seemed more painful than any of the other insults I'd been called. It was easy to reassure myself that we weren't freaks or monsters. The kindness of Elsa and Nina, or the ingenuity of the children as they negotiated the obstacles of their bodies, was proof enough of that. But I couldn't argue with *dead-end*. Whatever different deformations we Omegas had, that was the one we all shared: infertile. Dead-end.

Asking about the island had proved to be another dead-end. After a few weeks, I'd tried sounding out Elsa and Nina about the resistance. We were in the kitchen, the pots all washed, enjoying the brief lull before the preparations for lunch. Elsa stood at the window, watching Kip playing with the children in the courtyard, while Nina and I sat on the bench. We'd been teasing Nina about a young wine-seller at the market who'd been flirting with her for weeks. Nina had denied this, but it was true that she'd been volunteering to do the early-morning shopping lately, and had taken to doing so in her best dress.

'And where's he from, this loverboy?' I asked.

'He's not my lover,' she said, slapping at my leg. 'But he's from near the coast – further north.'

'Then how'd he end up here?'

She shrugged. 'You know how it is. It's harder by the coast – lots of Council raids, settlements being sealed.'

Elsa turned from the window, spoke a little too quickly. 'Good news for all of us that he came here, whatever the reason. Nina only complains half as much about work now she's in a good mood.'

I hesitated. 'The crackdowns along the coast – is that because of the island?'

Nina had been blushing, but now the colour dropped from her cheeks. She stood, knocking a basket of onions from the bench, and didn't pause to pick them up as she rushed from the kitchen.

Elsa spoke so quietly I could hardly hear her over the noise from the courtyard. 'We've got kids here. Be careful what you say.'

I knelt to pick up the scattered onions, avoiding looking at Elsa. 'But you know something about the island? What have you heard?'

She shook her head. 'My husband used to ask questions, Alice.'

'You never told me how he died.'

She didn't reply.

'Please. Tell me what you know about the island.'

'Enough to know it's dangerous.' She knelt beside me, helping with the onions. 'Even to talk about. I lost my husband already. I can't take those risks anymore – not with Nina and the kids to worry about.'

She stayed beside me until we'd gathered the last of the onions back into the basket. She didn't seem angry, but she never spoke of it again, and for three days Nina avoided me altogether.

*

In our room each night, Kip and I endlessly debated when to leave. I knew that he would have liked to stay, and I understood the temptation: in New Hobart, inside the holding house, we'd stumbled onto something that felt like normal life. But my dreams and visions were still dominated by two things: the island, and The Confessor. For all that I longed to succumb to the busy contentment of the holding house, the island still drew me to it, more urgently than ever now that I knew we were only a few weeks from the coast. And I could still feel The Confessor seeking me, her mind scraping at the layers of night in search of me. In my dreams, she reached out her hand and my secrets fell into her palm with as little resistance as overripe raspberries. When I woke, Kip said I'd been covering my face with my hands all night, like a hiding child.

I couldn't bear the idea that I could lead her to this place. To Elsa, Nina and the children.

'We can't stay,' I said to Kip for the hundredth time, as we went through the same argument again.

'We could explain to Elsa and Nina, about your arm. They'd understand. They wouldn't tell anyone.'

'It's not that. I do trust them. It's something else.' I couldn't explain the sensation. It was like a noose slowly tightening. It reminded me of the feeling I'd had for those last few months in the village, waiting for Zach to unmask me; or that frantic moment when Kip and I were stealing the horses and found ourselves trapped in that ever-shrinking circle of torches. Something was closing in around us.

When I tried to describe the feeling, he shrugged. 'I can't argue with you when you start on the seer stuff. It's your trump card. But it would help if you could be more specific.'

'I wish I could be. But it's only a vague feeling – like this is too good to last.'

'Maybe we've earned it. Maybe it's our turn to have something good for once.'

'Since when do people get what they deserve?' I paused, wishing I hadn't spoken so angrily. 'Sorry. I can't help it. I've just got a bad feeling.'

'Well, I've got a good feeling. And you know what it's from? From eating three meals a day and not sleeping under logs.'

I knew what he meant. But it was for him, above all, that I knew we had to leave. We weren't going to find the answers to his past here. And there were the others, too – those floating faces that still visited my dreams. Wasn't I betraying them, slipping into the comfort of this new life while they waited, silent, behind the glass of the tanks?

I tried again. 'You heard what Nina said about The Reformer. And you and I know even more about what Zach's doing.'

'And what makes you so sure that we'll be able to stop him if we somehow get to the island?'

I could understand his point. For me, the island remained a vivid reality. I saw it nightly. I knew the precise shape of its silhouette against the dawn sky, and through the fog of rainy evenings. I knew the texture of the black rocks that slashed the water at the base of the cliffs. More importantly, I knew what the island contained: an alternative. The Omega resistance. A place where we would no longer have to run or hide. For Kip, though, I could see how the island would seem abstract and uncertain, especially compared to the concrete reality of our daily lives since we'd arrived at Elsa's.

We could never resolve the argument. And despite my unease, I was happy to be persuaded by him, to have an excuse to stay longer. Just for one more day, I'd say to myself each evening. At night, curled next to Kip in the tiny bed, I did my best to ignore the images that crowded the periphery of my dreams. Above all, I tried to ignore the sense of The Confessor's seeking, as pervasive and inescapable as a ringing in my ears.

In the end Elsa resolved the argument for us, bursting into our room one afternoon with a sack in her hand. I'd been sitting on the bed with my arm unbound, so I lunged to hide under the blanket, but Elsa waved impatiently at me.

'Don't waste time with that. Think I don't know a skinny girl like you isn't bulky round the waist like that? And you're clumsy as hell with one arm. Not that he's much better,' she said, with a jab of her hand towards Kip.

I let the blanket drop. 'Then why not say something?'

'Because it wasn't a bad idea of yours. For the kids – we can't have them letting slip there's a seer here. Not just that it's rare, but you know what people are like, even Omegas, when it comes to seers.' I nodded, remembering the sniping comments of the others back at the settlement. 'The arm

stunt would work well enough on the street, at a glance,'
Elsa added.

I closed my eyes. 'I'm sorry we didn't tell you the truth.'

Again, Elsa brushed my words aside. 'Keeping your
secrets is a good habit for the two of you to get into. You've
done a decent job of that here. I hoped you might stay
longer. But you have to go, before tonight.' Even as she
talked, she was stuffing Kip's blanket into the sack.

He stood up. 'What's happened?'

'Council soldiers, in the market today. That's nothing
unusual. But there were more of them, and the word on
the street is that they're setting a watch on the town.
Building gates. They've told our mayor it's for our own
protection.' She laughed. 'Apparently there's a sudden
bandit problem, and the Alphas care so deeply for us that
they're guarding us themselves.'

'How long until they seal the town?' I asked.

She shrugged. 'I don't know. They've got guards already
on the main roads, but they won't be able to get a wall up
yet. Until then, they'll be trying to surround the place with
patrols – it depends how many soldiers they've brought.'

I stood up. 'They'll have come with hundreds. They're
trying to encircle the town. I should have known.'

Elsa nodded. 'That's what the baker said – men patrolling
the outskirts already, others putting up the wall. And that's
not all.' She pulled a crumpled sheet of paper from her
apron pocket, passed it to me. With Kip looking over my
shoulder, I smoothed the paper out on the bed, and saw
my own face, and his, take shape. Under the sketches, in
large lettering: *WANTED – HORSE THIEVES*. *Two bandits
(female seer; male missing left arm) guilty of midnight raid on
undefended Alpha village. If seen, contact Council authorities
immediately. Substantial reward offered.*

Elsa snorted. 'Amazing, isn't it – what good likenesses they were able to get from some villagers who glimpsed these horse thieves in the dark.'

I looked up at her. 'I'm sorry if we've brought trouble on you. On New Hobart.'

She grabbed back the piece of paper, screwed it up and shoved it into her apron. 'Don't flatter yourself. It's happening elsewhere, too – Alphas taking control of settlements, even big Omega towns like this. They're turning them into ghettos. It was always going to happen here eventually.'

'You weren't tempted to turn us in?' asked Kip.

Elsa laughed again. 'To be honest, I don't need the reward. If there's one thing Alphas are willing to pay money for it's to get rid of their Omega children. We'll be all right here, don't you worry.'

'And the horse thing,' I said. 'It's not what it seems.'

She shushed me. 'You think I took you in because I needed two starving, one-armed kitchen helpers? Listen. We lost some children once, a few years back, before Nina even worked here. The men came at night, with swords. They weren't in uniform, but I'd bet my life they were Council soldiers. They took five. Three were babies, two much older.' I heard an intake of breath from Kip as Elsa continued. 'And the only word we ever got about them was when three of their families came back two weeks later, set to wring my neck because their Alpha kids had died, suddenly, all three of them within a day of one another.' I thought of the skulls on the grotto floor when we'd escaped from Wyndham. Elsa went on. 'I don't know what they did to those kids, or what happened to the other two they'd taken. But I do know that there's lots of reasons to be on the run from the Alphas, and those reasons aren't about stealing horses either.' She passed the sack to Kip. 'There's enough food there for a few days, and water too. The blanket, a knife, and some other stuff that might be useful. You should stick to the small roads, which they might not have covered yet. You'd be safer splitting up, but I know you won't. Alice, you should hide your arm again.'

I tucked my arm beneath my jumper, but waved off Kip when he made to help me bind it. 'No – if I have to run, or fight, I'll need to be able to get it free.'

'Shouldn't we wait 'til dark?' he asked.

I shook my head at the same time as Elsa spoke. 'No – go now, while there're others about, and before they've sealed the city. Head to the southern edge of town, away from the market. I'm going back to the market now. There's a crowd gathering, not happy about what's happening. We can't fight the soldiers – we're not stupid – but we'll gather, and at sunset we're going to march, make a fuss. It'll be enough of a scene to draw some of the soldiers our way. Sunset – remember that. Now go.' She pointed us at the window, but I couldn't leave without asking one more time.

'Do you know anything about the island?'

She shook her head, but this time didn't avoid my eyes. 'Only the rumours – the same as what you've probably heard. I don't even know if it's true. But for your sake, I hope it is. The way the Council's treating us now – I don't understand it. Nobody does. It's getting so that the refuges won't be enough. It can't go on like this.'

I squeezed her hand before turning away. It was calloused from years of scrubbing pots, wielding brooms, lifting sleeping children.

'Will you say goodbye to Nina, and the children, for us? Especially Alex?' said Kip.

Elsa nodded. Kip hesitated at the window, where I was already crouched on the sill.

'Go on,' I said. 'Ask her.'

He looked back at her. 'You don't recognise me, do you? From the five children who were taken?'

Elsa reached out, rested her hand for a moment on his cheek. 'Sorry.'

He turned away, clambered onto the sill next to me.

'We can't thank you enough,' I said to Elsa.

She scoffed. 'Then what are you hanging around for? Get out of here, the two of you.'

CHAPTER 15

After Elsa's news, and the haste in which we'd left, it was a shock to find New Hobart largely unchanged. It was true that, from the direction of the market, we could hear the sounds of a massing crowd, and the occasional shout. There were many people heading in that direction, so much so that we felt conspicuous going the other way. But there were others, too, going about their ordinary business. At one point I jumped at a loud crack from above, only to look up and see a man shaking out a wet sheet from a balcony draped with washing.

Kip carried the sack, and although we didn't want to separate, we agreed that I'd walk twenty yards ahead, so that at a glance we wouldn't necessarily appear to be together. Sticking to the alleys, we skirted the main streets and their crowds. We passed several of the posters bearing our likeness. Each time, after checking we were alone, I ripped them down, shoved them in the sack. The sound from the market to the north grew louder, even as we moved further away. I concentrated, trying to distinguish between Kip's footsteps behind me and the city's noise.

181

The first Council soldiers we saw were on horseback, incongruous in the narrow streets. The hooves on cobbles announced them long before they came into sight, and we were crouching in a doorway by the time they rode past the end of the alley. We moved more cautiously after that, descending slowly through the streets until even the noise from the marketplace, on the far side of the town, no longer reached us.

When we drew close to the outskirts of the town, and saw how many soldiers there were, I felt a grim sense of recognition. The instinct that had plagued me for weeks, of something closing in, was now made tangible in front of us. From my vantage point behind a yew tree on a side-street, I could see patrols, groups of four at a time, passing every few minutes as they circled the town's straggling perimeter. From time to time more mounted soldiers would charge into view, riding so fast that the local residents had to leap out of their way as the horses careered through the winding streets. At the main road to the south the soldiers had already erected a gate, and from there the beginnings of a wall spanned out. They must have started building at dawn, or even overnight, given the expanse of posts already planted. At the town's new gate open wagons were arriving, loaded with more lengths of wood. Omegas were still being allowed to pass through the gate, in both directions, but only after careful inspection by the guards.

'It's worse than Elsa thought.' Kip had caught up with me now. He took a heavy breath as he peered over my shoulder. 'You wouldn't happen to know of any secret rivers or hidden tunnels around here, would you?'

I rolled my eyes.

For over an hour we tried to skirt the town's edges, but at the end of each alley the view was the same: the periodic passage of soldiers, and the ceaseless mallet-blows as the fence posts were planted.

It was late afternoon when we returned to the spot from where we'd first seen the main gate.

'Split up, and try bluffing our way through?' Even as I said it, we both knew it was a pointless suggestion.

'Somehow I don't think they're going to all this trouble just to be fooled by a fake name and a haircut.'

'I know.' I chewed my bottom lip. 'Make a run for it?'

He shook his head. 'Even if we could sneak past the patrol, it's too open – it must be nearly a mile to those woods.' He gestured at the thick woods further down the plain. 'They'd see us for sure. So do we go back to Elsa's?'

'What, and wait for them to finish the wall entirely? Wait for them to come searching, house by house?'

Below us, at the southernmost point of the spreading wall, there was a clatter as the last logs were emptied from a wagon. We watched the wagon being re-hitched to the four horses, and slowly hauled back through the gate and away towards the woods. Even at this distance, coming from the woods we could hear endless axe-falls, an interminable applause.

Kip nudged me. 'Look – the wagon.'

'You're not contemplating another horse-stealing venture, are you? Because that was bad enough the first time.'

'Not the horses,' he said. 'The wagons. Watch.' The road between the woods and New Hobart was a constellation of wagons, the ones coming toward the town loaded with felled wood, the others returning empty. Only a single soldier sat at the front of each.

We crept as close as we dared to the growing wall – close enough that when each patrol passed we could hear the thwack that their broadswords made against their boot-buckles with every step. We sheltered between two huge, empty crates that reeked of rotted vegetables. Peeking through the slats, we could see that a wagon, newly arrived, was being unloaded. It took another ten minutes for it to get close to empty. Four soldiers worked to unload the wood, throwing it down noisily into great piles, from which other men were constructing the wall. At some points the wall was barely a screen of rough branches, lashed together, while other sections were more solidly constructed, posts sunk decisively into the earth. And, all the time, the patrols passed, some mounted and some on foot, barely minutes between each one.

We didn't have to wait long for sunset, but the tightness in my stomach grew with each minute, as we watched the wall taking shape below us. We spoke from time to time, in whispers. After a while, Kip pulled out one of the posters scrunched in the sack, flattened it on to the paving-stones. 'Horse thieves. Really?'

I shrugged. 'What would you prefer?'

'I don't know. It's just – everything we've done, and that's what they put on the poster?'

'What do you expect them to put? "Escapees from the Keeping Rooms and our top-secret tanks"?'

He was about to fold the poster again when he paused. 'Unless they know something – about me, before the tank.' We were already crouching close together, but he clutched my knee. 'What I was.'

'A horse thief?'

His voice was racing now, chasing his ideas. 'And that's why they put me in the tanks.'

'Don't you think it would have to be more than that? They catch horse thieves all the time – you don't see them bundled off to secret experimental labs.'

'And it would explain the riding.'

I laughed, hushing myself quickly. 'You weren't *that* good.'

He returned the poster to the sack. 'I'm just saying there could be something to it.'

I watched him as he fumbled to tighten the drawstring. 'Look. I don't blame you for wanting to know something about your past. But I just can't see that this is the grand clue you want it to be. I'm down as a horse thief too, for one thing.'

He conceded a nod, passed the sack back to me and sank back into silence.

The sky to the west grew jaundiced. From the edge of the forest to the south, still ringing with axe-blows, came a glimmer of flame as the first torches were lit.

It happened quickly. The noise from the market didn't penetrate to this side of the town, but suddenly uniformed riders reeled from the east to the gate below us, conferred rapidly with the sentries there, and raced away, followed by others, hastily mounted. Men shouted along the wall, a cascade of sound and orders spreading east and west from the main southern gate. In minutes, the soldiers thinned. The patrols maintained the same route, but there were fewer of them, and many of the soldiers at work on unloading and building peeled away, following the main street up into the town. There was a swell of sound and movement. Kip's hand in mine, we slipped down towards the end of the street, the point at which the wall petered into a pile of wood and a wagon waited, the horses facing the gate that stood a few hundred yards further to the left. It was darkening rapidly now. At intervals along the wall, torches had been lit. From the shallow shelter of a doorway we watched as, to our left, the driver walked away from us, towards the four horses hitched to the wagon. His back was turned. I stretched my left arm out of hiding, back into my sleeve.

'You're sure?' Kip said.

'If they see us running for the wagon, it'll be too late for the arm to make any difference. More important that I can move quickly.'

We were just about to step into the open road, towards the emptied cart, when I pulled him back, nearly tumbling him down on top of me.

'What?' He wriggled free, looking out of the doorway where we crouched.

'Wait,' I whispered. Then, from our left, from the direction of the main gate, came the footfalls of a patrol. They were close – perhaps thirty feet away – but my eyes stayed fixed on the wagon. It didn't move. I heard the driver cursing, and a jangling of metal as he fiddled with the harness. A horse objected with a snort. Then the driver stepped back, and we saw him hoist himself up, calling out a greeting as the patrol met and passed him. The cart shifted into motion. But the patrol was still not clear, barely past us. I didn't realise I'd been holding my breath until I felt Kip release his with a suppressed shudder. The patrol was fifteen paces beyond us now, to the right, the wagon retreating further to the left with each instant. Kip turned back to me, eyebrows raised. I didn't speak, just nodded.

We were running, bent low as we crossed the road, chasing the retreating wagon. It was well underway, its progress jerky but fast. We were impossibly exposed as we ran further from cover but seemed to get no closer to the wagon. The patrol must surely turn, I thought, or another patrol would come around the corner ahead of them, or the gate sentries would spot the scurry of movement. We were losing ground, the wagon perpetually out of reach.

I tried to look behind me to see whether we had time to retreat, or whether the patrol had seen us. As I turned,

I stumbled. My knee and palms hit the ground, hard, and I wondered when the shout of discovery would come.

But Kip grabbed my hand, hauled me up. 'We won't get another chance,' he hissed, and kept hold of my hand as he took off again after the wagon. The cries of the sentries never came. I don't know whether the wagon was slowing slightly as it approached the turning to the gate, or whether Kip's hand in mine gave me the final impetus, but as we sprinted together the back of the wagon neared. I could see the sweat-patches spreading from the driver's armpits until they almost met in the centre of his hunched back. I could make out the rough weave of the hessian sacking covering the wagon's floor. Then we were diving onto it, throwing the sackcloth over ourselves. There was a sound, the scattering of smaller wood pieces shaken from the sacking, and I braced myself again for the shouts of discovery. But the cart's motion itself was loud: the creaking, the hooves, the driver's continuous shifting and his muttered admonitions to the horses. Through the sacking I could make out a vague image of passing flames above the wagon's low sides, as we jolted past the torches mounted at points along the wall.

We were definitely slowing now, turning to the gate, where I willed my body to total stillness, pressing my face hard against the wooden floor. I could hear Kip's breathing, and each breath of my own sounded obscenely loud. But the wagon didn't even pause at the gate. Another greeting was exchanged.

'Getting out of here before I grow a second head,' the driver called up to the sentries. Someone laughed, and the vibrations of the wheels changed as we left New Hobart's cobbled streets and began on the rutted dirt road towards the forest.

I hadn't imagined how painful the journey would be. The wagon lurched with each rut on the path, and at points I bounced, jarring my bones against the wooden tray of the wagon. My grazed hands and knee stung, but my greatest fear was that one of the jolts would dislodge the sackcloth coverings, exposing us to the view of the driver, or a watchful sentry back at the gate. I didn't dare to shift clear of the several small broken branches that jabbed me with each bump.

After five minutes' slow journey the din of the axes increased, heralding the forest. The road was more uneven, jolting me even more mercilessly, and squinting through the sacking I could see the darkness becoming denser. Voices, as well as axe-strokes, became audible, and the thick night in front of the wagon was ignited by the light of many torches, bright through the sacking. Kip had seen it too – when I reached out for him his hand met mine, squeezed it sharply, twice. At the third squeeze we moved, together, scrambling to our knees and then dropping heavily from the back of the cart. It was a short drop, but the ground was potholed and we landed half falling, half squatting in the wagon's wake, on a narrow road leading deeper into the forest. For an instant we froze, but the wagon didn't pause, and we could see the driver's oblivious back, silhouetted against the brightness of the scene he was approaching.

For a moment it looked familiar. Then I realised it evoked a lesser version of the blast itself, as I'd seen it so many times. The flames, the roar, the sound of trees falling. But this was a slowed, infinitely smaller version of the blast. Instead of the raw sheet of flame, there was a mass of torches. The axes, wielded by hundreds of soldiers, rose and fell in front of the flames like a dreadful machine.

We watched for only a second before running, almost

crawling, from the road into the deep scrub. Kip was carrying the sack that I had dropped on alighting. We stayed low, but in the discordant symphony of axe-blows, falling trees and shouts we didn't worry about noise, just pushed frantically through shrubs and clattered over fallen branches. I led, but my only thought was to get far away from the soldiers, the sound and the flames. It wasn't until we'd been running for ten minutes, and the noise and light had receded, that I slowed and tried to get a sense of our location. We'd had no choice but to drop our pace, as both the forest and the night had deepened. Away from the hellish glow of the torches it was too dark to see.

Standing close, neither of us spoke, both straining to catch the sounds of pursuit over our own panting breaths. Finally Kip whispered, 'Nothing?'

I nodded, and then remembered that he couldn't see me in the dark. 'Nothing. I don't feel a chase, either.'

He gave a heavy, shuddering exhalation. 'Do you know which way to go? Not that I care, as long as we get as far away from there as we can.'

'I think we should go back.'

He laughed. 'Sure. Because nothing promises a good time like hundreds of enemies with axes.'

'No – I'm serious.'

He snorted. 'Can I reiterate my point about the axes? And the flaming torches, too, which we've already done once, when we took the horses.'

'That's exactly what I meant – the torches.'

He sighed. I could hear him sitting down on a log. 'Please tell me this is a bona fide seer thing, and not just a really bad idea.'

I groped my way to the log, sat beside him. 'It's not always clear which is which. Do you still have the bag?'

I heard him kick it toward me. I opened it, and we didn't talk for a minute while I fumbled inside. Amongst the blanket's folds I felt a loaf of bread, the water flask, a knife in a sheath. Finally, a small box, wrapped in wax-paper, that rattled when I shook it.

'When did it last rain? It's been weeks, hasn't it?'

'You want to talk about the weather now?'

'Listen,' I said calmly. 'We need to start a fire. Burn down the forest.'

'No, we don't. We need to get as far away from here as we can, as quickly as we can. We're lucky we made it this far. And if we start burning things down, they'll know someone's out here. They'll come after us.'

'That's why we've got to go back to where the soldiers are. Start the fire there, so that they'll think it's their own torches.'

'We only just made it out of the town. Why go looking for trouble?'

'Because it's not just about us. You heard what Elsa said – they'll trap them all in there. Crack down even more. Check every single registration. This'll be a prison, not a town.'

'You think registrations are worth risking our lives for? It's just a way of keeping track of things.'

'Don't be so naïve. What do you think they're keeping track of? People like me, with powerful twins, so that they can lock us up. People like the kids taken from Elsa's, who they think are disposable, to experiment on. People they can put in the tanks, like you. Don't you get it?'

In the thick dark I could barely see his face. I waited, listening to my own breath, still slowing gradually after the running.

'It's nearly the end of summer,' he said finally. 'It's been dry, but not exactly bushfire weather.'

'I know. And it might not take off. But at worst, we'll distract them, slow them down. At best, we could seriously delay them. Get rid of their nice convenient wood supply, stall the building of the wall. Maybe give others a chance to get out of the town.'

'At worst, Cass, we get caught. Worst is me, back in the tank, and you locked up again. That's worst.'

I stood up. 'No it's not. Don't get me wrong – I don't plan on getting caught. And you know I don't want anything to happen to you. But it's not just about the two of us. We don't yet know everything that the Council's planning for Omegas, but we know it's not going to be pretty. And sealing New Hobart's just one more step in that direction.'

For a long time the only noise was the distant cacophony of axes. Kip was hunched low, chin on his hand. Eventually he looked up at me. 'Aren't you scared?'

'Of course I am.'

With his foot he stirred the mass of dried leaves and twigs on the ground. 'And we have to light the fire back there?'

'If we don't, they'll know it wasn't an accident. And the wind's going this way, away from New Hobart – if we don't get back to the town edge of the forest, the fire won't reach the axemen, won't slow them down, or burn up their immediate wood supplies.'

'That was my next question. No chance of us accidentally burning down the town?'

I shook my head. 'Not unless the wind changes.'

He stood up, heaved the bag to his shoulder, and began heading back the way we'd come. A few steps away he turned back to me. 'This time, you're carrying the sack.'

CHAPTER 16

The way back took much longer. The dark was now so absolute that I had to hold a hand in front of me to feel my way and to fend off the low branches. At times we had to crawl, or scramble. At least I didn't even have to think about navigating – we simply headed back towards the noise of the axemen, growing steadily louder.

'Do you think they'll keep going all night?' whispered Kip.

'No question. They might be working in shifts, I guess, but they'll keep at it for as long as it takes to get the wall up.'

Now the red glow was visible, and the forest before us became an outline, backlit by high torches planted at lengths in the ground. As we crept closer we could see, between the trees, the shapes of men and the ceaseless movement of the axes. Other soldiers were climbing the trees and hitching ropes, and whole teams of men were heaving at the weakened trees.

From the growing clearing the road led off to the left, to the forest's edge. Beyond, New Hobart was visible, ringed by dots of light, some moving as the patrols marched. Keeping always a few hundred feet from the torches, we went right, circling the clearing on the forest side, away from the town. I'd thought I'd get used to the noise, but the longer we were there the more violent and unending it seemed. Periodically a series of shouts and orders would herald the latest tree to succumb, and the men would scramble clear. There would be a long, wrenching wail as the trunk began its collapse, followed by the crash of the tree's landing, shuddering the earth.

As we reached the far side of the clearing, and began to sneak closer, I was grateful for the noise. Behind us the forest was already thinning, easing into the plain that led up to New Hobart. The noise felt as much like cover as the trees that shielded us. The very air within the clearing was churning with sound. Ahead of us, at the clearing's edge, the ring of torches flared. I told myself that, from the clearing itself, Kip and I would be shadows at most, behind the circle of flame. Opening the bag, I reached for the matches.

If anyone had been watching from within the clearing, they would have seen a small light flare briefly in the shadows as another flame caught on, closer to the ground than the ring of torches mounted on the posts. Then the flame split into two – two heads of light moving low and quick along the clearing's edge, pausing often. Where we paused, sometimes at ground level, sometimes at the height of the low-hanging branches, the flames left their mark, smouldering into more flames. The fire passed its whispered message along the northern edge of the clearing. The two bobbing torches carried on further, past the boundary of the clearing, to where the low scrub grasped at the flames without being persuaded, and the fire took off gleefully on its own.

That was when I realised that we'd become unnecessary: the trail we'd laid, perhaps five hundred yards long, was solidifying, the spots of flame reaching out to one another to form a line. The line grew higher, climbing up the low scrub and into the foliage itself. Kip and I, running at one end of the line, could spread the fire no quicker than it was spreading itself. The flames' whisper had become a rumour, and it was spreading fast. Igniting the northerly wind, it crept up to the orderly ring of torches at the clearing's edge, and then subsumed it.

I'd thought the noise of the clearing could not be beaten, but as the fire took hold it brought a noise of its own, a throaty, bass roar that silenced the axes. There were still shouts, but now they took on a new urgency, spreading and catching like the fire itself.

We didn't dare to wait any longer. When we ran, it felt like a repeat of our earlier, panicked dash through the forest, but this time the imagined pursuit was real, the hot wind behind us a constant reminder of the fire that it carried. The forest was both dark and light, now: the night thickened by the smoke, but reddened by the fire's advancing glow. Several times Kip fell behind, and I turned to look for him, reminded of how I'd talked him into this. But each time, when he caught up enough to emerge from silhouette, his face was flushed with a kind of glee.

I'd meant to head south, but as the trees began to thin I saw that we must have been blundering south-west, and so we found ourselves near the western edge of the forest. Behind us, to the east, the forest was a map of fire, and the distance and the smoke combined to block out any glimpse of New Hobart beyond. I didn't know if it had been my seer instincts, or blind luck, that had led us to the forest's western limit. Watching the fire consuming the horizon, it was clear that if we'd stayed in the forest we couldn't have outrun the flames much longer. On the plains though, which rapidly sunk to the marshy ground that we remembered from the east of the town, the fire kept its distance. Brief spot fires flared in the long grass close to the forest, but never took hold.

We stopped perhaps a mile from the forest's edge. Wading knee-deep into one of the marsh ponds, we drank, and splashed the water over our faces. Kip's face was tarnished with ash and smoke; when I looked down I saw the water running black down my own arms. When I stepped out of the pool onto the thick tussocks of grass, there was a tide-mark at my calves, above which my skin was ash-blackened. Even this far from the fire, the smoke tainted every breath. I rinsed my hands and knee, grazed from my fall, and dislodged a few stubborn pieces of gravel. Then I pulled the knife from the bag and cut two strips from the top of the sacking. Soaking them in the water, I tied mine around my face first, then turned to Kip and fastened his. Even with his mouth covered I could tell he was still grinning.

'Why so perky? You weren't so keen about this fire business beforehand.' My voice was indistinct, but breathing was easier through the wet cloth.

'I know,' he said, shouldering the bag as we headed off, parallel with the forest's smoking edge. 'But it felt good to be doing something.'

'We've not exactly been taking it easy for the last few months.'

'I know. But that's been different – being on the run, just trying to get clear of them. But this time, it's changed: we did something to them. Something decisive.'

I laughed. 'You weren't feeling so decisive a while ago when I was trying to persuade you.'

He laughed back. 'But that was before I became a hard-ened saboteur, you see.'

I shoved him lightly, toppling him from a tussock into the shallow water. He kicked through the water, splashing me. Against the backdrop of smoke and fire, our two small figures walked on, tracing a path amongst the marshy pools.

*

For three days, the fire was visible: at first the choking mass of smoke and a reddened glow in the air, and later as a black pall hanging over the horizon like a premature patch of night. When the rains swept through from the west, on the third night, I woke to find all trace of the fire gone, the smudge on the horizon wiped clean.

Ever since the fire, I could feel the island even more strongly. I was drawing closer to it. It was a splinter in me, working its way to the surface. But The Confessor's seeking was still present, too, a searching that made me distrust the very sky, and flinch at every insect that brushed my skin as we settled down to rest.

When I woke at dawn, screaming, Kip sleepily asked me: 'Which one was it tonight?'

'What do you mean?' I asked, sitting up.

'These days, it's always the island, The Confessor, or the blast. But as you were screaming, I'm guessing one of the second two.'

'It was her again,' I said. Whenever I dreamed of her, these days, her seeking was studded with rage. It lashed at the night sky like the whip we'd seen wielded in New Hobart.

Settling down again, closer to Kip, I was grateful for the wiry swamp-grass beneath me; for its itches and scuffs that steadied me back into my real body rather than my dreamscape.

'I should've known it was her,' said Kip, throwing over me the blanket that I'd cast off in my nightmare's thrashing. 'You scream loudest when it's her you're dreaming of.'

'Sorry. I know it's not exactly stealthy.'

I felt his shrug. 'Your visions have got us this far. The odd bout of screaming's a side-effect I'm happy to put up with.' Mosquitoes snagged at the edges of the silence. 'It does seem odd, though. I know The Confessor was no picnic, but how can those visions scare you more than the ones of the blast? Surely the end of the world has to trump her.'

I knew it would be hard to explain, even to Kip. The blast had its own brand of terror: its destruction was absolute, unanswerable. It took the world and turned it into fire. The Confessor was not worse than the blast – nothing could be. But whereas the terror of the blast was indiscriminate, The Confessor's hatred was specific, personal. She was seeking, sifting, scouring the land for me. The blast didn't hate – it was pure destruction. It turned hate into flames, along with everything else. But The Confessor's hatred was a pulsing thing. I felt it constantly, more than I'd ever felt it in the cell. Back then, her attitude to me had been one of disdain, or occasional frustration. When I'd dared to return her scrutiny, and had managed to see the wired chamber in her thoughts, she had been enraged, but even that anger hadn't matched the spite that now stained the air. Since I'd escaped from Wyndham, that spite was constant, as ever-present as the swamp-mosquitoes. I recognised it like an old companion: it was the same hatred that I used to see in Zach.

That day six riders came from the west. On the bland expanse of marsh, the white horses and red tunics of soldiers stood out from more than a mile away. When Kip saw them we dropped to the ground, then crawled on knees and elbows to the shelter of a reed-bed at the edge of a pond.

'They can't see us, surely – not from that distance?' Kip asked.

'Not if we don't move. And if we're lucky.'

We were lying waist-deep in a stagnant pool, its surface scummed with green.

'I don't know about you,' Kip said, wrinkling his nose as he looked down at the furred water, 'but I'm not feeling particularly lucky right now.'

The riders made slow progress on the marshy ground, so for most of the morning we were stuck, watching the horses pick their way across the horizon.

'They're not coming this way,' he said. It was as much a prayer as an observation.

'They're heading straight for the coast.'

But we discovered the next day that the soldiers had stopped off en route. We came across a settlement, a damp hollow where a handful of shacks propped up one another next to a small wood. We kept our distance, slinking past in the cover of the long reeds, but even from there we could see the gibbet. It looked new. The wood was freshly hewn, and it was the only vertical thing in the settlement, not yet having succumbed to the swampy, shifting land that had settled the older structures into lurching angles. An Alpha symbol was scorched into the top beam, from which a cage hung, suspended from a chain like a grotesquely oversized birdcage. Against the gibbet's rigid, perpendicular lines, the body slumped within the bars looked even more broken. She had only one leg, and even at a distance we could see that a whipping had shredded the back of her shirt and painted her with blood. The wind blowing off the marshland,

and the woman's occasional movements, twisted the cage back and forth, so that it looked like she was scanning the horizon with her closed eyes.

We alternated running with walking for the rest of the day, but even when the settlement had long passed from sight, and we had left the marsh behind us, I imagined I could hear the sound of the chain, sawing at the wind.

'We need to start walking at night,' I said. 'And taking turns to watch in the day.' It wasn't just the need for answers that drew me to the island, now. It was raw fear. There was nowhere else in this scorched world where we might be safe. Not New Hobart, not even the forsaken marsh.

'And on the island – what is it you think we'll find? What if it's not the resistance movement we're hoping for?'

'I don't know if they're militants or hermits on the island, or anything in between. But it's a place out of Alpha control, just for Omegas. That's enough to make it a threat to the Council. You saw the crowd in New Hobart, watching the whipping in the market and not daring to say anything. Because there's never been any alternative: Alpha rule is how it's always been. That's why the island frightens the Council: the idea that things could be different.'

'And if the Council hasn't been able to find it, after all this time, what makes you so sure that we can?'

I shrugged. 'The same thing that made me sure about the caves and tunnel under Wyndham.'

He looked at me carefully. 'I guess that's good enough for me.'

'Don't be too sure,' I said. 'I might know where we want to go, but getting there's another question. If a storm comes up, I wouldn't like our chances. It's a long way from the mainland, and weather's unpredictable, even for me. And I've never been in a boat.'

He sighed. 'Let's just hope it turns out that I was an expert sailor, before the tank.' But the laughter I was used to hearing in his voice was entirely absent. It had been left on the marsh, swinging from the gibbet.

*

From New Hobart, it took us nearly two weeks to reach the coast, travelling at night, and sometimes half the day too. We had a few provisions, at least, from Elsa, and the going was easier now that we were out of the marsh and amongst lightly wooded plains. The food lasted five days, though the bread was tough and ropey after two. After that, we foraged. A nest of eggs in a low tree branch was a feast that lasted us another two days, baked slowly on a reluctant fire. There were fewer mushrooms as we got further from the marshes, but those we did find were larger, and less dank. The landscape had become starker as we neared the coast, but after the soggy, circuitous marshes I welcomed the dryness of the rock-strewn hills. In the day we found cover beneath the edges of the white, hulking boulders, but took turns to keep watch. We saw nothing.

At dawn on the tenth day, when the grazes on my hands and knee had healed completely, came the smell of the sea. Only we didn't know it was the sea, just speculated that the new salt sharpness of the air was a hint of the coast to come. Then, rounding the peak of a hill, we saw it for the first time, close enough that we could make out bursts of spray at some of the lower cliffs.

'Do you think you've seen it before?' I asked, as we sat in the long grass and looked down to where the cliffs ended and the shifting blueness began.

He squinted at the horizon. 'I don't know.'

If he had seen it before, no familiarity remained – he was staring with the same wonder as me. If he'd seen the ocean in his past life, it was just another thing that had been taken from him. The tank had swallowed even the sea.

I leaned against his side. We sat there for at least an hour, watching the waves goad the shore. Somewhere out there, in the sea's massive blankness, was the island. And here we are, I thought, the two of us, tired and skinny, with no idea how to sail, going to seek out this island, the sea's secret.

*

We found the fishing village the next day. Cooler weather had begun to shift in, so smoking chimneys revealed the village from miles away. It was large, too – perhaps sixty houses clustered at the top of one of the cliffs. The herd of fat black-and-white cows grazing nearby was enough to declare it an Alpha village, even without the Alpha insignia on the wooden sign planted proudly by the main path. At the east, where the cliff dropped sharply to a small cove, a trail clung to the side of the cliff. For a day we watched, noting how early the villagers descended the path to the boats, and how they returned in the afternoon, met by the elderly and the children who helped them unload the nets slung with their catch. That was the worst – watching, from the ridge above, close enough to see the glint from the fish scales. By that point we hadn't eaten for a day and a half, the urgency of hunger nearly matching the sense of pursuit. We had to wait for night, when we made our way down to the harbour. It was just light enough to see without a flame, though we went slowly on the narrow path, wincing at each dislodged rock that clattered down to the shore.

By the edge of the jetty, a throng of gulls was jostling at

a huge cane container and picking at the discarded catch. When we approached, the birds set up such a squawking that I was convinced the whole village would be roused. But at that point I almost didn't care: the gulls, taking off, had revealed a mound of fish and offal, knee-deep. When we reached, grimacing, beneath the top layers on which the birds had feasted, we were able to grab intact fish. They were tiny, some the size of my smallest finger, but firm enough, and not rancid. We carried our hoard along the pebbled shore until we were out of sight of the harbour, and risked a small fire to cook them. I relished every bite. I even relished picking the sharp bones from my teeth, and licking my oily fingers. Kip's cheek had been anointed with a tiny flash of silver, where some scales had brushed off on his skin. The scales mirrored the firelight as we sat, looking out to sea, the small cairn of fish-bones between us.

'We could stay here, you know,' he said. 'It wouldn't be such a bad life.'

I ran my tongue along my teeth, scanning for fish bones. 'Sleeping under a rock, sneaking down here every night to fight the gulls for the Alphas' scraps?'

'It wouldn't have to be like that. We could go further along the coast. Catch fish ourselves. Build a little place.'

I shook my head. 'You really think they wouldn't come for us?' I thought of that presence that never left me, the appraising eyes of The Confessor. And the red riders on the marsh, and the whipped woman hanging in the cage. They were coming for us already. 'And even if they weren't hunting us, do you think Omegas would be allowed to live in a place like this, right on the coast, with all these fish for the taking? Even if Zach's men never came for us, we'd be driven out, sure as anything.'

He threw a small stone at the water. 'Maybe you're right.

I thought I at least remembered stuff like that – how the world worked, even if I didn't remember how I fitted into it. But I don't remember it being this hard.'

I shrugged. 'It's not your fault. Things have become harder, too – every year, lately. We don't know how long you were in that tank. It was only since the drought years that the tithes have crept up so much. The ban on Omega settlements on rivers and coasts, that's even more recent – since the General joined the Council, Nina said. And the registrations, and the sealing of the Omega cities – all that stuff's as new to me as you.'

He was rolling a pebble in his hand as if weighing it. 'What about Elsewhere?' he said.

'It's the same everywhere – even out east, these days, apparently.'

'Not elsewhere here. I meant Elsewhere – like in the stories. Another place, over the sea. Do you think it could be real? Somewhere where things might be different?'

Looking out over the infinite sea, it was hard to imagine anything beyond it.

I shrugged. 'Maybe there was, once,' I said. 'Right now the island itself seems far enough. And we need to get there – need to find the Omega resistance, tell them what we know.'

'What we know?' he said. 'Sometimes I feel like we haven't learned anything since we left Wyndham, except which mushrooms not to eat. We still haven't learned anything about me, or the tanks.'

I understood his frustration, but I shook my head. 'I think we've learned more than we realise. I've been thinking about Zach – the projects that he mentioned, the day I escaped. All the crackdowns on Omegas. And the registrations. The way they're trying to keep tabs on all Omegas now.'

'Sure, we've learned about all that stuff. But it still doesn't make any sense,' he said. 'Zach might be crazy, but he's not stupid. It doesn't make sense for them to push us to the point of starvation. Even with the refuges, it's not sustainable.' He rubbed the back of his hand over his tired eyes. 'They're stripping away everything, bit by bit. And now they're torturing people, whipping them, just to send a message.' He didn't need to say what we both feared. It was the weight we'd each carried since we saw the cage swinging from the gibbet: that the message was for us.

He tossed the stone into the sea. 'I can't make sense of the world anymore.'

I followed it with a stone of my own, not looking directly at him. 'Do you blame me for what Zach's doing?'

It was his turn to shrug. 'He put me in the tank, you got me out of it. So the two of you come out even.'

'Seriously.'

He looked at me. 'I blame Zach. I know you think that amounts to the same thing, but it's not. Whatever his plans are, they're his. You and your brother aren't the same.'

'He'd certainly agree with you about that.'

Below us, the sea inhaled and exhaled, wetting our shoes with spray.

I thought often about Zach: wondered what he was doing, where he was. More often, though, I thought about The Confessor. Even under tonight's broad moon, just waning from full, I was vividly aware of that other presence in the night sky, seeking me endlessly.

We took the boat that night. I'd been afraid of setting off in the dark, but the rising moon was bright, and growing brighter. We'd looked at several of the larger vessels, fishing reels and nets crowded on the decks, but in the end, the boat we stole was tiny. I'd thought a bigger one might be safer on the open sea but, as Kip said, with only three arms between us we couldn't deal with the web of ropes and pulleys on the larger crafts. 'You don't feel any stirrings of nautical knowledge?' I'd asked, half joking, and when Kip confessed that he was as baffled as me by the network of ropes and cleats, we settled on the smallest one there: a red dinghy, two long oars neatly stashed, a bucket by the tiller, and a small white sail wrapped around its mast.

'I'm guessing you won't accept this as an excuse to get out of rowing?' Kip asked, looking down at his empty left sleeve as he descended the ladder from the jetty to join me in the boat.

'You're guessing right,' I said, bracing the boat against the jetty while he clambered in, and taking from him the rope that he'd untied from the pier. 'By rights I should make you do it all, as I've got the job of navigating, but since we don't just want to go round in circles, I suppose I'll have to row too.' I threw the rope to the bottom of the boat, where it curled at Kip's feet. 'Anyway, if the wind picks up, and we can work out how, we'll use the sail.'

'Be careful what you wish for,' he said. 'The less wind the better, in this tiny tub, as far as I'm concerned.'

'Give it an hour of rowing and then see if you feel the same way.'

I'd always loved water, growing up by the river. This felt different, though: even on a calm night like this, the ocean's swelling beneath us was more insistent, more forceful, than the river's current had ever been.

The sound of our manoeuvring and scraping between the other boats seemed raucous to me, but no lights appeared on the path above, and after only a few minutes of rowing we found ourselves at the mouth of the harbour, where the swell was higher. I was reminded again of Zach, and the river. There was a game we used to play, dropping opened seed-pods into the river and watching from the bridge to see whose would win the race downstream. Now I felt as though Kip and I were setting out in one of those tiny seed-pods, lost in the enormity of water.

CHAPTER 17

The instinct that had pushed me to leave that night had been a good one: the weather held fine and the moon's light was so strong that we could see the land behind us even hours after setting off. Later, beyond the sight of land, the swell rose waist-height above the boat, but it was steady and regular. We found that if we kept the boat facing head-on to the swell, and didn't let ourselves turn sideways, we could negotiate the waves well enough. After some grappling we managed to raise the sail, and learned to steer a zigzag course to travel against the wind. Kip kept glancing back at the absent shore, but he seemed reassured by my certainty as I guided us. At one point, an hour or so before the first hint of dawn, I cautioned him to slow the boat. 'There's an outcrop of rock here, not far – we don't want to go aground on it.' I could feel it, like an eyelash in my eye, or a piece of gravel in my shoe: small but impossible to ignore.

Even by the moon's constant light we couldn't see anything, straining our necks in all directions while trying to keep the boat head-on to the mounting swell. Then I shouted at him to throw the tiller hard left, and dug my oar in too for added traction. As the boat shuddered to the right, we saw it, not two feet from the other side of the boat: the different shade of darkness amongst the black water. It was swallowed by the subsequent wave, but in the next trough we could see, again, the saw-bladed silhouette of rock.

After that, Kip stopped asking me how far I thought it would be, and left me to my squinting concentration. We endured the whole day, rationing the water in meagre sips. When night came it gave us respite, though the sea around us seemed to expand with the gathering darkness. The last dregs of the water were gone now, but the moon, at least, was bright enough to see by, just. When dawn had begun to break and the swell was lower, we tried to take shifts at sleeping. I went first, but couldn't manage even my allotted spell. I'd hoped that sleep might distract me from my thirst, but when I closed my eyes my mouth felt drier than ever, my tongue too large for my mouth.

When he took his turn, Kip fared no better, shifting awkwardly in the bottom of the boat where he'd tried to stretch out. 'Even the worst of the swamps and rocks we've slept on since we escaped didn't bounce about like this,' he said. 'I can hardly stay awake, but damned if I can sleep either. Move over.' So he resumed his spot next to me and we pushed onwards, the sun continuing to rise behind us.

It was well after noon on the second day, the salt spray making my lips raw, when we came to the reef. My visions had taught me to expect it, but I hadn't realised how daunting it would be: that vast expanse of water from which the rocks jutted unforgivingly. Some emerged six feet from the water; others lurked just beneath the surface, the sharpness visible only in the trough of each swell. The reef spread as far as I could see, reminding me of the boulder-strewn plain surrounding Alice's cottage and the settlement.

The wind had dropped, but still made precise steering difficult, and impossible with the sail up, so we lowered it and rowed haltingly amongst the rock-studded waves. Often the passage between outcrops was so narrow that we had to draw in the oars. If I lost concentration for an instant, the rocks clawed at the base of the boat. After two hours, the island itself became visible: as sharp as the outcrops of the reef, but towering conical and high. In some ways having the island in sight made the travel more frustrating, as we couldn't proceed straight towards it. Instead, we were forced to follow the painstaking paths of the reef, sketching an intricate route that seemed as often to take us away from the island as closer to it.

After hours of this, I lost my way. I could feel the rocks massing beneath the boat, but seemed to have lost the thread that had guided me this far. I lay at the front of the boat, one hand on the surface of the water, and groped through the shapes the water made in my mind. For almost an hour we just drifted, Kip nervously probing the water with an oar, fending off the outcrops of rock piercing the ocean's surface. The scraping of rock on the bottom of the boat was an interminable grinding of teeth. The boat's base, those few inches of wood, seemed now like such a fragile membrane, to keep at bay a world made of rock and dark water. I tried to drag my mind back into focus, but the demands of my body were distracting me. The sun had been doing its cruel work above, and my headache seemed to pulse in time with the waves. My lips were so parched that they split with each grimace, seeping blood that did nothing to assuage my thirst.

A larger wave sent us lurching to the side, where the

prow lodged on a barely-protruding rock. With the front of the boat raised, the back was forced downwards. Kip, standing quickly, was already calf-deep in water, and more was thrusting in with each wave. The boat groaned on its rock fulcrum as Kip scrambled to join me at the front. It took both of us, shoving our oars against an outcrop to our left, to dislodge us from the rock. When freed, however, the boat was still half-flooded and low in the water. Every wave pushed it again against the hungry rocks.

I tried to force my mind clear, ignoring the water massing at my ankles, the rasp of the hull on stone. Remembering how I'd mastered my thoughts in the Keeping Rooms, under The Confessor's interrogations, I pictured again the mussel-knife in my mother's hands, all those years ago. I made my mind the knife.

And there it was: the route once more opening up for me, meandering between the shards of the reef. As I took up my oar to direct us once again, I heard Kip exhale in relief as he grabbed the bucket and began bailing out the water.

Even when we'd penetrated to the heart of the reef, where the island loomed, it was hard to see how we could land. The island punctured the sea steeply, its walls sheer and black. There were no signs of habitation, no hint of a spot where we could safely draw close, let alone land. It took about an hour, straining my exhausted mind, for me to guide us around to the western side where, when we rowed close enough, we could make out a fissure in the steep sides, barely visible until we were twenty feet away. Yet when we rowed through, under a natural archway and into the shadow cast by the steep walls, the fracture in the stone widened into a small harbour. A fleet of boats, in a mismatched collection of colours, nodded in rows. A stony beach curved around the bay, where a blunt tower squatted.

On the pier, in the late-afternoon light, two children were playing.

Kip turned to me. His skin was mottled brown and white with sunburn and salt spray, his lips cracked. He barely looked like himself, until he grinned.

'It's real,' he said.

The journey had been hellish enough for me, and I'd known that the island awaited us. For him, I realised, it had been an act of faith. Faith in the island, or in me. As the harbour encircled us, I looked up at the peak jabbing defiantly at the sky. I matched Kip's smile, which turned to a laugh, and we were laughing together. The laughter was raspy, our voices scoured with salt, but they rang out unguarded. For the first time since our escape from Wyndham, we didn't care if we were overheard. The gulls on the masts of the moored ships took off, and the children turned to stare at us.

Something's wrong with the children, I thought, as we rowed up to the pier, where they had drawn closely together and were staring at us in silence. It wasn't the children's deformities that struck me. They were obvious, though not rare: the little boy was a dwarf, his limbs short in comparison to his strong torso. The girl's fingers, still holding her fishing-line, were webbed, and her bare toes too. I'd seen such things many times. Why then were these children so unsettling? It was only when we'd looped the rope around the pier and climbed the metal ladder, and the little girl raised one webbed hand to her face to swipe away a fly, that I realised the children were not branded. The rush of pleasure it gave me to recognise that unblemished skin made me forget my thirst. When I looked at Kip I saw that he'd noted it too: his own hand was unconsciously tracing his own brand, while he stared at the children.

'Are you strangers?' asked the boy.

Kip squatted next to him conspiratorially, and jerked his head at me: 'I am a bit strange, I suppose. But she's stranger.'

The girl laughed, but the boy kept his face stern. 'If you're strangers I should tell Owen.'

'That's a good idea,' I said. 'Why don't you take us to him?'

The children led us along a path that climbed steeply up from the beach, but we hadn't gone more than twenty feet when we saw three men in blue rushing down the path from the tower. Kip raised his arm in greeting, but the men were approaching rapidly and, I noted with alarm, bearing swords. Kip turned back to me.

'There's nowhere else to run,' I said. I was too exhausted even to cry. So we waited, Kip's arm still raised, but his gesture of greeting now a sign of surrender.

CHAPTER 18

The men were quickly upon us. I'd raised my arms too, but found myself, like Kip, forced to the ground, where one man held me down, his knee in my back. The tallest man turned my head to the side and quickly, efficiently, traced my brand with his finger as I coughed sand from my mouth. Next to me Kip was spared the same investigation, his empty sleeve speaking for itself. All of this took place in silence, with no noise other than the panting of the men. The man's kneecap was jammed against my spine, his hand still holding my face against the sandy ground.

The tallest of them now spoke, but he addressed himself to the children. 'How many times have you been warned about strangers? Any boat, any person you don't recognise, and you're to call the watchmen.'

'We were coming for you,' protested the boy. 'I knew they were strangers.'

'He's not stranger. She's stranger,' added the little girl helpfully.

The children's unconcerned manner seemed to calm the

man. 'We saw them from the lookout post,' he said to the girl. At last he turned to us. 'And we make it our business to greet strangers.' With a toss of his chin he gestured to Kip to stand, which he did, half hauled upright by the grasp of the other men. 'You came all the way from the mainland in that?' He shot a look at our dinghy. 'How did you get through the reef?'

Kip glanced down at me. My face was still pressed sideways against the ground, but I managed a slight nod.

'She knew where to go.'

'Who told you?' demanded the man. 'Who gave you a map?'

'Nobody,' I said.

One of the men emptied the sack that had fallen from my shoulder, using his foot to spread its sparse contents over the ground: the empty water flask, the knife and matches. The blanket, damp from the bottom of the boat.

The tall man bent to me, pulled me upright himself, and looked me over curiously as I brushed the sand from the side of my face. The men were all Omegas, all branded. One was a dwarf, like the boy; the dark-haired one held his sword in a malformed hand, fingers fused into a single broad digit. The tallest had a twisted foot, though it seemed hardly to slow him down. I could see him searching out my deformity.

'You're a seer,' he finally said. It wasn't a question.

'I've dreamed about the island,' I told him.

'Dreams are one thing, but to find your way through the reef – you dream maps?'

I couldn't explain to him how it had been. I remember when Mum had needed to put a nail in the kitchen wall to hang more pots, how she'd rapped along the white wall until the sound changed, the lack of reverberations revealing the wooden beam behind the plaster. My mind's probing of the water and the reef felt like that: a sounding out. But how could I, parched and shaking, explain that to these strangers as they stood over us, weapons drawn?

In the end, what put a stop to their questions was our evident exhaustion. I was stumbling over my words. Beside me, Kip was dazed and thick-tongued with tiredness and thirst. The dark-haired man nudged our interrogator, said quietly: 'We're not going to get anything more out of them tonight.'

The tall man looked at us for a moment, then spoke swiftly. 'All right. We'll lock them up for now, send word to the fort, and take them up at dawn. But I want extra watchmen out tonight, at all posts.'

We hadn't the energy even to object when we were locked in a low hut by the base of the tower. Our bag had been taken, but we were given food at least, and fresh water, which tasted sweet on our salt-parched tongues. When the candle was out and the gulls had settled down on the rooftop, we lay on the straw mat and pulled the single blanket over us, relishing the stillness of a world no longer rocked by the sea. Outside, in the harbour, the boats held their evening conversation: the creaking of bows, the straining at buoys.

'I really thought this would be a safe place for us,' I whispered. 'I'm sorry.'

'I'm just grateful to be off that damned boat.'

I smiled. Perhaps it was because I'd dreamed so often of the island that it didn't feel unfamiliar. Despite the locked door and the barred window, I was able to slip towards sleep.

'It's good, though, isn't it?' I said quietly. 'Seeing the unbranded children.'

'It might feel a bit more like the promised land if we

weren't locked up,' he pointed out. 'But it's very endearing that you can feel so warmly towards a place that greets us with armed men who promptly imprison us.'

I laughed. 'Zach used to call me naïve.'

'Far be it from me to agree with your brother.'

Both of us were giddy not just with exhaustion, but with a mixture of relief and fear. We'd made it: arrived at the island that had so far been no more than a rumour, a dream. But here we were again, imprisoned, interrogated. I was conscious that my lips were still cracked and dry, but when Kip rolled over to face me, swept my hair from my face and cupped the back of my head in his hand, I was too tired to deny myself the comfort. His lips, too, were parched, and his hand rough from the oar, but when we kissed I didn't feel it anymore. Or, rather, I did, but there was a kind of satisfaction and urgency, my cracked lips forceful against his, the good pain of it. And after all this time, kissing him felt the same as landing on the island had felt: the same sense of fear, and of arriving finally on a safe shore.

*

I first heard of Piper from the children. I woke to the sounds of them playing outside the hut, and arguing loudly over who got to play the part of Piper. I thought it was just another childhood game, like hide-and-seek – like any of the games and songs in which Zach and I had never been included back in the village. But the men who unlocked the door later that morning said it again: 'We're taking you to see Piper.'

'Who's the piper?' Kip asked.

'Not "the piper". Just Piper,' said the tall man who had

been there the night before. 'He'll decide what we should do with you; whether you can stay.'

He gave us back our bag, though I noticed that the knife had been taken. He and three others escorted us from the tower. The men carried swords, but were friendly enough. From the tower they led us up a narrow path towards the island's central peak. It was steep, and felt steeper in my tired state, but I was reassured to see that Kip's breath wasn't laboured by the steep march. In the months since our escape he'd changed a lot, his skin losing not just its pallor but also its waxy finish. While he would always be lean, he'd now taken on a wiry strength. He was still awkward, often, with tasks that called for two arms, but I assumed that would fade, just as I hoped the amnesia would.

The tall man had introduced himself: Owen. His earlier terseness was still present, but was outweighed by curiosity.

'What news of the Council now?' he asked. 'And any news from the settlements in the east?'

I turned to Kip, who shared my smile. Between us, we knew both too little and too much.

'Sorry,' I said, 'but we're the worst people to ask.'

'Been in hiding too long to follow the news? Or just out in the countryside?'

I cringed at how absurd the truth would sound. In the end I just said, 'We've been – underground. A long time. Me for years, and Kip maybe longer. Probably.'

Owen raised his eyebrows. 'You might want to get your story straight before you meet Piper. He's not one for messing around.'

'There's no story to get straight,' I said. 'Or, there is a story, but we don't know it. Not all of it.'

'Hardly any of it, in my case,' added Kip.

Owen stopped in front of us, and I thought he might

push the point, but instead he turned to the rock-face soaring above the path and swept aside the tumble of wisteria that hung to the ground. Behind it, carved straight into the rock, was a door, its rusted metal almost the same colour as the sandstone of the cliff face. Another of the men came forward with a key, and it took two of them to drag the door back. Inside was a narrow passage, steps leading steeply into darkness. My jaw clenched at the thought of entering that closed space, the walls narrow enough that they brushed Owen's shoulders on both sides as he entered. But Kip went in behind Owen, and I had no chance to hesitate. The men following me locked the door behind them before Owen had even finished lighting the torch he had taken from a wall-bracket. Following Owen's light upwards, at first I counted the steps, but lost count when Kip stumbled in front of me, his curse loud in the tight space. The tunnel was steep, and long enough that I had to concentrate to keep my breath even. Finally the shadows from the torch faded as the passage lightened, and I heard voices greeting Owen as his silhouette was framed by daylight ahead of us. He turned back to face us before stepping out.

'He's waiting for you. But think carefully, tell him what he needs to know. Piper's not like you,' he gestured to me, 'but he can still tell when someone's messing him about.'

I thought of The Confessor. The memory of those sessions in the cell frightened me in a way that this armed escort had not. Had it come to this – a different prison, a different Confessor?

We were out in the light now, and for several seconds I squinted against the glare. Behind us the sea was entirely hidden by the encircling edge of the crater that cupped the city. The stairs we'd climbed had cut through this natural battlement, depositing us halfway up the inside of the island's central caldera. When I stepped forward, I saw it. Or, rather, saw it again: the city, stacked upon itself within the steep hollow. It was so familiar, from the lake that pooled in the crater's base, to the houses massed on the far side. The pale grey fort that I'd seen so many times in dreams.

Owen and his men had already disappeared back down the stairs, and were replaced by three others, two women and a man, in the same blue uniforms. They didn't speak as they surrounded me and Kip and led us up the narrow central road that wound through the city. Kip kept looking about him. I had to remind myself that he'd never seen this place before. Several times I had to nudge him onwards as he stopped to gaze at the city around us. Above us, a man was hanging washing from a window, a third eye in the centre of his forehead; a woman with no arms or legs sat in a doorway, deftly rolling a cigarette with her lips. The adults were branded, but many of the children weren't. The crowd didn't return Kip's curiosity, though some people stared at me as we made our way up the hill. Our escort seemed unthreatened, and kept their swords sheathed. They moved so swiftly up the coiling road that we were almost jogging to keep up, and I was glad of the throng of people that sometimes slowed our progress.

We passed through several of the fort's outer walls, stopping at the inner perimeter, only a few hundred yards below the lip of the crater. A door, braced and studded with iron, barred the archway set in the base of the fort that loomed above us. Men on the inside, wearing the same blue uniforms as our escort, opened a smaller gate to the side, and we were ushered through. The sounds of the city were dulled here but still audible: the children playing, merchants shouting their wares, people calling from window to window across the narrow streets. The courtyard in which we stood was surrounded on three sides by the tall building, half-fortress, half-palace. The escort, now six strong but still silent, led us into the front entrance, up several flights of stairs, and up to a dark wooden door.

'He's waiting for you,' one of them said. It was the same phrase that Owen had used earlier. I glanced at Kip, who took a deep breath. I would have liked to take his hand, but I was on his left, where his sleeve hung empty, so I reached out and touched his shoulder, felt it lift slightly in response.

From the other side, the door was opened. Our escort stood back and Kip and I entered alone, passing the two watchmen who had opened the door. The room was brightly lit by a large window at its head, in front of which sat a high-backed chair on a platform. We approached together, stopping at the stairs that led up to the dais. I peered up into the light; it took several seconds to realise that the chair was empty. I turned back to the door, raised an eyebrow at the nearest of the watchmen, who had resumed their places by the door.

'We were brought to see Piper.'

The man grinned at me. He was, I realised, almost a boy, perhaps my own age or slightly older. 'He's a busy man. Why should he see you?'

He was tall, taller even than Owen, and though his right arm was strong, resting on the hilt of a long knife, his left arm was missing. The sleeve was not hanging empty, as many chose, but was simply cut off and stitched shut at the shoulder, no apology made for the missing arm. He moved with the same well-muscled vigour of the watchmen who had escorted us, and which I'd rarely seen in Omegas on the mainland.

'I have things to tell him. Important things, I think. And we'd like to stay here, for a while, at least.'

'And why should he let you? Or believe the news you bring?'

He stepped forward slightly, but the smile remained. Kip stepped towards him too, arm at his hip to match the watchman's, though Kip's was an empty gesture without a weapon.

'We'll answer to Piper, and not to you. He ordered us here.'

The man's grin broadened. 'Indeed he did. But you may find yourself answering to me after all.' He sat down at the low table beside the door, where a draughts board and two mugs of ale sat. 'Sit, and tell me what you've got to tell.'

He dismissed the other watchman with just a flick of the head. The man bowed casually and slipped out the door. We stood, stranded between the dais and the door. He glanced up at the dais, and the empty chair.

'The fancy chair? My predecessor had more taste for grandeur than me, I'm afraid. You can blame him for the ugly tapestries, too. I'm Piper.'

I looked at him, clad simply in the same blue uniform as the other guards. 'And the uniform?'

'I'm a watchman, just like all the guards here. Only difference is that I have a bigger jurisdiction. It's my job to watch out for all of us. For the island.' He leaned back, pushing a chair towards me with his foot as we approached. Whenever he moved, there was a jingling from the row of small throwing knives that hung at the back of his belt.

'I thought you'd be older. The way they spoke about you.' I scanned him again. He was entirely new to me, his wide mouth and dark skin unseen in my dreams. There was an easy confidence in his manner that I found hard to reconcile with the brand on his forehead. It wasn't just that he lacked the pinched cheeks of most mainland Omegas, the poorest so thin that their faces appeared to be stretched tightly over prominent skulls. It was also the way he sat: leaning back in his chair, legs wide, head thrown slightly back. On the mainland, Omegas had learned not to take up too much space. On the big roads near market towns, we walked close to the ditch, heads down, out of the way of the kicks and jeers of the mounted Alphas. When Council soldiers escorted the tithe collector to settlements, we queued mutely to hand over what they asked, avoiding the soldiers' gaze and the sting of whip that might accompany it. But here, in this grand chamber, Piper sat completely at ease, commanding the space. It seemed a small thing to notice: just one man's stance. But at the time it felt as dramatic a statement as the island itself. The cringing existence we led on the mainland seemed shameful in the face of this proud-jawed man, his broad smile etched into the wrinkles at the corners of his eyes. Even his body, so clearly strong, and well fed, seemed an audacious statement. On the mainland we were constantly told that we were broken, deformed, useless. So it was a joy to see Piper's beauty: the smooth skin of his arm and shoulder, muscled like a plaited loaf of bread. The wide-set, appraising eyes, bright in his burnished skin. The ease with which he wore his body would have been striking in an Alpha; in an Omega it was nothing short of shocking. And where most Omegas wore a fringe, or grew their hair long to cover their brands, Piper's thick black hair was cropped close to his head, the brand undisguised, unabashed. He wore it like a flag. I remembered examining my own brand, when it was new, and repeating to myself: *This is what I am.* That had been a mantra of resignation. But Piper bore his brand like a declaration, and a challenge.

'I don't see all new arrivals,' he said. 'I couldn't – we have so many now. But they're brought to the island. You're the first to find your own way. This worries me.'

'Brought here? How? It's not an easy journey.'

'That's an understatement. But we need newcomers – an island of Omegas can't exactly sustain its own population, after all. We have a network of contacts on the mainland. People seek us out. If we decide they can be trusted, we ship them out here. And sometimes, when we can manage it safely, we get into Alpha towns and take any Omega infants that haven't been branded yet. The Alphas call them raiding parties, but I prefer not to use that term. We call them rescues.'

'You take them away from their parents?'

Piper cocked his eyebrow. 'The parents who'd have them branded? Who'd send them away to scratch out a living with other outcasts on the scraps of land no Alpha would bother to farm? Those parents?' He leant forward, more serious now. 'But you two would ask that question. Your experience was rather different, I'm guessing.'

Kip and I looked at each other. I spoke first.

'You think I had it easy? I was sent away, a bit later than most, but sent away nonetheless. And I've had experience of raiding parties. Maybe not those that you organise, but I know what it's like to have them come for you, to be snatched away.'

'You don't agree with our methods. We'll have more time to talk about these things. But it's your story I need to know about for now. And yours,' he added, turning to Kip. 'Look.' He reached across the small table. With a single finger he lifted my hair from my forehead, traced my brand. 'You can say what you like about understanding the Omega experience, but your experience *was* different. The brand is made for infants, toddlers at the oldest. But your scar has hardly stretched, barely faded. You must have been nearly grown when this was done.'

I reached up and brushed his hand from my forehead, but his gaze remained fixed on my eyes.

'Thirteen. Then they sent me away.'

He smiled again. 'Thirteen? It's not unheard of for seers to conceal their nature for a while – years, even – but I've never heard of any lasting that long. Quite an achievement: the girl who had everyone fooled.'

'Not everyone,' I said, thinking of Zach, his watchfulness.

Piper turned suddenly to face Kip. 'And you – how did you manage it?'

'Manage what?'

Piper reached out, this time to touch Kip's brand.

'To avoid branding for so long. You're not a seer. It's a bit harder for you and me to hide.' He shrugged his left shoulder, glancing conspiratorially at Kip's own empty sleeve. 'So what I'm wondering is, how does somebody like you manage to avoid branding for half his life?'

My hand went to my own brand; next to me Kip mirrored my movement. I turned to him, giving a sound that was partly a laugh, partly a groan.

'All that time,' I said. 'All that time sitting there, every night, trying to dredge up some clue about your past. And it's there, in the middle of your head. We're idiots.'

'Speak for yourself. You're meant to be the seer, after all.' Despite his joking tone, his hand didn't shift from his forehead. I wondered if he was remembering the same moment I was: that night shortly after our escape from Wyndham, when I'd woken, frantic, from a dream of The Confessor, and Kip had grabbed me. *It's all right, shhhh, it's all right*, he'd said, and I'd pressed my forehead against his. I could still feel it, the neat match of his scar against mine. The same size.

226

'It's not much to go on,' Kip said, 'but it's not normal, right? So we should be able to work out something. Maybe they –'

Piper interrupted. 'It seems you know as little about your past as I do. Even less, possibly.'

Kip met Piper's eyes. 'My past began a few months ago, when I saw Cass.' Before Piper could finish the eye-roll he'd begun, Kip went on: 'I'm not being sentimental. That's literally when my memories begin. Before that – nothing, other than a few vague memories of the tanks themselves.'

It took us a long time to tell him: the Keeping Rooms, the tank room, our journey. I was eager to spread the word of what I'd seen in the tank rooms, but also hesitant about just how much to reveal of my past. Kip and I kept inter-rupting each other, then stumbling into silence whenever the conversation approached the identity of my twin. In the end I omitted all mention of Zach, but kept nothing else back. Piper asked us to draw maps, diagrams, of the chamber, the equipment, the light in my cell, the route we followed after our escape. I was worried that Kip would be uncomfortable as I described the wires and vats of the tank room, but he seemed excited to be telling someone his story, nodding confirmation as I described various details.

I told him about The Confessor, but it was clear that he'd already heard of her. 'She's a formidable character, by all accounts. I wish we could have got to her before the Council did.'

'Trust me,' I said. 'You wouldn't want her on your side.'

'Perhaps not. But I'm not sure I want her on theirs either – that's the problem.'

I told him about the moment I'd tried to fight back, and had snatched a glimpse inside her own mind. The huge chamber, bedecked with wires, that I'd seen there, and her furious response.

'It wasn't some other part of the tank room?'

'No. Completely different.' I pictured it again – the sinuous climbing of the wires around the metal casings and up the curved walls. It wasn't only that the chamber had looked unlike anything else I'd seen. It was the rage of her response, dagger-fast and sharp. Whatever it was that I'd seen, it was important to her.

When we reached our escape from New Hobart, and told him about the hanging cage outside the marsh settlement, he only nodded.

'You're not surprised?' Kip demanded.

'I wish I were. One of our own ships returned two days ago, with the same news.'

'They'd been to the same settlement?' It seemed an unlikely coincidence, given the vast expanse of marshland, where the only people we'd glimpsed had been the mounted soldiers.

Piper shook his head. 'No. Our scouts had been north of New Hobart.' Nausea blossomed in me as he paused. I knew what was coming. 'Two settlements there, and another closer to the coast. Soldiers rode through there as well. One person was whipped at each. They didn't even bother to trump up charges as they usually do – just checked their registration cards, to make sure they weren't twinned with anyone important. Then whipped them, and made sure they were displayed for all to see.'

He must have seen the horror in our faces.

'It might have been intended for you,' he said bluntly. 'I'm not going to offer you any false comfort. But reports reached us, too, of an uprising in New Hobart, after the Council began to seal the town.' I thought of Elsa, and

Nina. 'It didn't amount to much – nothing more than stones thrown, and marching and shouting – but even that kind of thing is unprecedented. There are lots of reasons why the Council might be trying to make an example of people right now.'

I pictured the small settlement where Kip and I had sneaked close to the barn and danced to the bards' music. Did a cage now swing from a gibbet there as well? I was too aware of the blood in my veins. It dragged like gravel. I wanted to reach for Kip's hand, but even the consolation of touch was more than I was able to grant myself. There was horror in Kip's face that I'd never seen before, not even as we sprinted from the fire, or battled the encroaching water of the reef.

Only after Piper prompted us were we able to continue. I could hardly hear my own words. I felt as though I were speaking over the sound of the gibbet's chain, creaking in my mind.

Piper was particularly attentive when we described our journey to the island. When we told him it had taken us two nights and two days, he'd nodded. 'Longer than usual, then, by a good twenty hours. But that's for experienced sailors, on the most direct route from the mainland and through the reef. And we'd never make the crossing in a boat so small.'

He asked me to try drawing a map, but after several false starts I pushed the paper away. 'I can't see it that way – it doesn't just come like that.'

'Try again. You made the journey recently, you must remember it.' Piper pushed the paper back across the table towards me.

Kip placed his hand firmly on the paper. 'Enough – give it a rest. You have maps, anyway – your people must have.'

'Of course,' said Piper. 'We have maps, though we guard them carefully. But no one ever made it here without one. Not even the seers. We've had two on the island, but they were brought here. Neither found their own way.'

'Lucky me,' I said. 'I made it all this way, only to be interrogated again.'

Piper didn't acknowledge the anger in my voice, though he did reach out and draw the paper back towards him. 'You two need to understand. Our location is the one thing that protects this island. They've known for a long time that we have a stronghold somewhere. Our rescues have been concentrated largely in the west, because that's what we can access most easily – so the Council must know we're off the west coast. But that's more than six hundred miles of coastline. What Cass has told me, about The Confessor, suggests they've narrowed it down. But the distance, the reef, the crater, they're our main defences. No one sets foot on this island who hasn't been brought here. Until you.'

Kip stood up. 'So you think we're a threat?'

Piper stood up too, but only to walk over to the cabinet on the side wall and retrieve a key that hung beneath the mirror.

'No. I think you're a gift. I think you may be the most powerful weapon we have.' He was looking at me now. 'I have to go, to talk to the Assembly, tell them what you've told me. We'll talk again soon. For now, take this.' He handed me the key. 'It's the gate to the fort. My guards will show you to your lodgings.' He turned to Kip, reached out his arm. They shook hands. Despite the difference in their sizes, I was struck by the symmetry of the movement.

On the way out, I paused at the door. 'Your predecessor – the fancy-chair guy. What happened to him?'

Piper looked straight at me. 'I killed him. He was a traitor – charging refugees money for safe harbour here. Planning to betray the island to Alphas.'

'And his twin?'

This time Piper didn't even lift his gaze from the maps laid out on the table before him. 'I killed her too, I suppose.'

CHAPTER 19

The next morning, as we finished the bread that had been brought to us for breakfast, a watchwoman leaned into the open door of our room. 'Piper wants you in the Assembly Hall.' But when Kip and I both headed for the door, she spoke again. 'Only her.'

The large hall, nearly empty the previous day, was busy now. Rumours of our arrival had obviously spread; as I made my way through the clusters of people, some pointed, while others just stared. I caught snatches of their not-quite-whispered conversations: *found us herself – seer – no map – so she claims.*

I found Piper at the same table as before. He waved away the woman he'd been speaking to, and ushered me to sit.

There were no preliminaries. 'The tanks,' he said. 'How could it work? How can the Council members keep their Omega twins unconscious, and keep functioning them-selves?'

'They're not unconscious. Not the way somebody is after a blow to the head.' I struggled to make words fit what I'd witnessed in the tank room. The liminal state that those people had occupied. 'Somehow the Council's found a way, using the machines, to keep them in a suspended state. Not sleep, but not death either. I think that's what was so awful about the place. Worse than death, because of the way they're still there in some way. Stuck.'

I couldn't explain it properly. A few times, diving for mussels in the river with Zach, I'd dived too deep, or stayed too long wrestling a stubborn mussel from a rock. That moment, swimming for the surface, when you realise you're almost out of air, and the light above seems impossibly far away, was where the tanked bodies were trapped. In the tanks, the limbo of that moment was drawn out forever. And I remembered what Zach had said to me, on one of the nights when Mum and Dad were arguing about us downstairs: *You're the problem, Cass. You're the reason we're stuck in this limbo*.

When Piper spoke again, I was glad to have my thoughts of Zach interrupted. It felt safer to keep Zach out of my mind, tucked away where our link could not be exposed. If Piper found out who my twin was, I knew it could be used against me.

'But apart from Kip, you didn't see any movements?' he asked. 'Any sign of consciousness?'

'A few had their eyes open,' I said. 'But he was the only one who was alert. His eyes moved. But I could feel the others – all of them.'

'If what you're saying is true –'

'It is.'

He leaned back in his chair. He didn't disguise the fact that he was appraising me, his brown eyes scanning my face intently. 'Yes,' he said eventually. 'I think it is. Then it confirms our worst fears about the Council, and what they're willing to do.'

'I'm sorry.'

He smiled, the lines at the outer edges of his eyes deepening. His face slipped easily into happiness, like a waterbird launching onto a lake. Even mid-smile, however, he was purposeful.

'Sorry because you bring bad news? Or sorry because your twin is involved?'

I looked away, but his gaze didn't budge. Eventually I turned back to face him.

'You still haven't asked me who he is.'

He raised an eyebrow. 'Would you tell me if I did?'

'No.'

'Exactly. I'm not in the habit of wasting my time.' He wasn't menacing, only matter-of-fact. He leaned forward, lowered his voice. 'We know he's in the Council. We know you're afraid to tell us who he is. We will find out.'

Where I might have expected anger, again I felt only exhaustion. Even here, on the island that had occupied my dreams for years, Zach could still jeopardise everything.

'We came here seeking shelter,' I said. 'Just like all the other Omegas who come here. Shouldn't this island be the one place where my twin can't be used against me?'

'I wish it could be,' said Piper. I looked at his face, and I believed him. 'But you changed the island, the moment you arrived. The way you came, and the news that you bring – those things have consequences, for every person on this island.'

Poison, I thought. It was just as Zach used to say, back in the village: *You're poison. Everything you touch is contaminated.*

*

'I'm beginning to feel like your maid.' Kip handed me a chunk of bread and resumed his perch on the windowsill, where he'd been waiting for me.

'You're too messy to be any good as a maid,' I said, pointing at his unmade bed as I joined him on the broad stone ledge. We sat facing each other, our backs against the sides of the window, our feet just touching.

'You know what I mean. You're off in council all day with Piper and the Assembly, I'm hanging around here like some kind of sidekick.' He leant his head back against the window. 'How was it?'

It had been three days since our first meeting with Piper, and I'd been summoned every day. Kip, however, was never sent for. The mornings we spent together, but every afternoon the guards found us and told me to go to the Hall. 'Just her,' they said, each time. On the third day he'd tried to accompany me, and the guards had turned him back at the door of the Assembly Hall. They weren't rough, just dismissive. 'You haven't been sent for,' the older guard had said, stepping in his path.

'I'd like him to come with me,' I said.

'Piper didn't send for him,' the guard repeated blandly, closing the door in Kip's face.

When I asked Piper why Kip couldn't join us, he'd just raised an eyebrow. 'He doesn't know his own name, Cass. What could he tell me?'

So while I was cloistered with Piper and the other Assembly members, Kip spent the afternoons exploring the island. When I returned each night he'd tell me of the things he'd seen. The old boat, carried up piece by piece from the harbour and reassembled on the western tip of the city, for the children to play at being sailors. The lookout posts concealed at the top of the crater, and manned night and day. The house at the outskirts of the city where an old woman had shown him the six beehives on her balcony, shimmering with noise. But though he told me what he'd seen each day, he was more eager to hear what I'd discussed with Piper and the Assembly.

'Don't get the impression that they're not interested in you,' I told him. 'Half the time that's what they ask about.'

'Then why don't they ask me? I feel like I'm begging for scraps, just hanging around all day and then getting leftover bits of news from you. If they want to know about me, why not ask me themselves?'

'What could you tell them?' I winced to hear myself echoing Piper's phrase.

'What can you tell them? If you've had any breakthroughs about my past, I'd love to hear about them.'

I kicked him lightly. 'Don't be a chump. They just want to know how I knew about you – you and the others. The visions I had, of the chamber. All that stuff I've already told you.'

'So you don't think it's just an excuse for him to spend time with you?'

I laughed. 'In the intimate, romantic setting of the Assembly Hall, with all his Assembly there too?'

'That's one way of making himself look impressive.'

'Come on.' Jumping back down into the room, I waited for him to follow. 'Let's go out – you still haven't shown me the western side. And there's a market there tonight, Piper said.'

'Did you point out that we haven't got any money?'

'I didn't need to.' I pulled a small purse of coins from my pocket. 'From Piper. For both of us.'

'*Now* I'm impressed,' said Kip.

I tossed him the bag. 'Doesn't take much to buy your loyalty.'

'For another few coins I'd even wear one of his fetching blue uniforms.'

From our quarters above the courtyard it was only a short walk to the market. The watchmen knew us now, nodded and held back the gate as we left the fort.

Watching Kip in the streets, I was reminded of how he'd always been eager for noise; how he'd thrown open the shutters at New Hobart and relished the busy street sounds. For the first days after I'd released him from the tank, I'd noticed him shaking his head to each side, probing his ears with his little finger, convinced that there were still traces of that viscous liquid trapped there. He seemed to associate silence with the tank, and with the greater silence of his past. Since we arrived on the island, I'd complained of the city's noise keeping me awake at night. Kip, however, relished it. He'd sit on the windowsill, eyes closed, absorbed in the noises of island life: the watchmen's footsteps in the gravel courtyard, and above, on the stone of the parapet. The pigeons that clustered and heckled on the windowsill. The clatter of donkeys on the flagstones, and the chants of children.

Watching him grinning as we made our way to the market, I couldn't begrudge him the din. We followed the noise: the cries of the stallholders trading cloth, cantaloupes, onions. The children shouting as they ran amongst the legs of the crowd. Even the sounds of livestock: pigs corralled into flimsy pens, chickens in cages hanging from pegs on the stone walls. In the city, because of the steep walls of the crater, dawn came late and sunset came early. For all but the middle of the day, when the sun was directly over-head, the streets were shielded from the heat. Now, in the early evening, the darkening sky was warmed by the lambent glow of the torches in brackets, and candles in windows. A goat was tethered in a tiny patch of grass between two houses, chewing mournfully.

'Piper says the animals are a nightmare,' I told Kip. 'Getting them out here on the boats is tough. And they're less efficient for food than just growing crops, especially in such a tight space. But people really want them here, just because we're not allowed to have animals on the mainland.'

'I'm not sure that secret goat-farming is the most effective show of defiance.'

'He said a goat got loose on a boat once, on the way out here, and they just about capsized trying to rescue it.'

'I thought all these private meetings with you every day were high-level strategy, not a chance for him to impress you with his amusing goat anecdotes.'

'Yes, because the man who runs this island, and the whole Omega resistance, needs to rely on his goat anecdotes to impress me.'

He rolled his eyes as he took my arm in his.

All along the street the market flaunted its wares. We bought two plums, their skin such a deep purple that it was tinted black. 'I've never tasted one of these before,' I said, biting into the fat flesh.

Kip grinned. 'Welcome to my world.'

'But it can't really be new to you, can it? You know most stuff, really. What things are, how to read, how to tie your shoelaces. It's not like a child, actually seeing things for the first time.'

He paused to examine a table displaying small wooden boxes. Removing a lid, he admired how neatly it fitted when he put it back on. 'Yeah – but that makes it weirder, in a way, not easier. That I know how to aim for the pisspot, but don't know my own name.'

'You have a name now.'

'Sure,' he said. 'And it's a nice name. But you know what I mean.'

We'd reached the end of the market now and sat on a stone bench that looked back along the bustling square.

'When I remember my past,' I said, 'it's mainly Zach I remember. I can almost imagine not remembering other things, but I can't imagine not remembering your twin. Because they're part of you, really.'

'The Alphas don't exactly see it that way.'

'They must, I think. They wouldn't be so afraid of us if they didn't know, really, how much like them we are.'

'Afraid of us? You've got to be joking. That's why we're hiding here? And all these people too?' He gestured back towards the market's throng. 'The Alphas must be cowering in terror, with their big army, their forts, their Council.'

'They wouldn't be so desperate to find the island if they weren't afraid of it.' I remembered once more The Confessor's insistence on asking me, again and again, about the island. The jabbing of her finger on the maps; the probing of her mind.

Kip looked around. 'Why, though? For all his posturing and his uniformed watchmen, Piper's hardly a threat to the Council. What's he going to do: march on Wyndham with his gang of one-armed soldiers?'

'He doesn't need to. It's enough that the island's here. I'm sure the Council's got practical concerns, like getting no tithes or registrations from those who make it out here. But that's not the real issue – it never will be. What really worries them is the fact that this place is beyond their control.' I remembered what Alice had said to me, before she died. 'It's the idea of the island, as much as the actual island.'

'The actual island is enough for me,' he said, leaning

back and grinning as he looked up at the soaring crater's edge, cupping the horizon.

I looked up too, mirroring the angle of his head. 'I know. Even though I'd seen it so many times in visions, it's different really being here. Feeling part of it.'

'You do, then? Feel part of it, I mean.'

'Don't you?'

'I want to believe that I am.' He spat out his plum-stone, watched it settle in a gap between cobbles. 'To believe we could stay here.'

'But you're not sure?'

'I find it hard to be sure of anything. And the way Piper ignores me isn't exactly reassuring. It's like they all think that after what happened to me, I'm nothing. Like I don't count.'

I surveyed his face. The straight, narrow nose, tilting slightly up at the end; the cheekbones and jaw sharply defined. Every angle of his face had become so intimately known to me. It was easy to forget how unfamiliar he must be to himself, without the anchoring of his past or, above all, his twin.

'I can't get my head around how strange it must be for you – the twin thing most of all. How lonely.'

'More lonely than having a twin like yours? Who'd expose you, hurt you, have you locked up? Seems to me it's a pretty lucky kind of loneliness to have.'

'But you must think about her,' I said. 'You must wonder who she is.'

'Not knowing about my twin is probably the only normal thing about me. Your experience is the unusual one. These days, now people are split so young, all most people have of their twins is a name, the place they were born.' He was silent for a while, gazing at the crowded street, each passing

241

body bearing its own deformity. I waited for him to speak again. 'But I do wonder about her, sometimes. Mainly just about the obvious stuff, to be honest. You know the sort of thing: is she about to tumble off a cliff somewhere and take me with her? So I hope she has a safe, boring life; a safe, boring job, with no ploughs to get caught in, or fights to get involved with.'

'Lots of healthy food, and early nights,' I joined in.

'Keeping chickens for a living. Or – weaving rugs.'

'By hand, though. No dangerous looms.'

'Now you're talking,' he said, turning to plant a kiss on my forehead as we walked on together through the crowd.

*

The next day the sun's glare persuaded me to skip our planned walk up to the crater's edge. Kip left straight after breakfast, with a water flask and a pocket full of fresh figs, but I made my way to a small terrace that we'd found the day before, halfway up the tower. From decades of footsteps, the stone stairs of the tower were worn down, rounded at the edges like softened pats of butter. It was still a few hours short of noon, but out on the terrace the paving stones were already hot. When I lay down in the sun, the stones scorched the skin where my shirt had ridden up at my waist. I basked in the brightness. Since the Keeping Rooms, the sun and the open sky retained their novelty – even the hellish boat journey hadn't destroyed the pleasure of sun on my skin. It was a pleasure, too, just to concentrate on simple bodily sensations. To step back from all the machinations and complications and to focus instead on sun on skin, skin on stone. In the Keeping Rooms, I'd had to resort to pain to keep my mind from the nightscape of my visions and fears. Now, pleasure did the same thing.

It was the island, too, that permitted these simple joys. Even in New Hobart, where the streets had thronged with Omegas, the cringe of fear and shame was still present. At any moment a Council soldier might ride through the street, or the tithe collectors might come to remind us of our subservience. I'd seen, in Kip, how our very movements were different on the island. He had shrugged off the furtiveness, and the tentativeness, of our months on the run. I thought again of Piper himself, the unbowed cock of his head and the breadth of his shoulders. I was beginning to realise that some of the joy of being with Kip came from the island itself, and the unabashed Omega bodies that it permitted. Of all that the island had given us, this was perhaps the most unexpected: the gift of our own bodies.

The day before, I'd found a bruise-like mark on my neck from where one of Kip's playful bites had turned into a kiss, and then back into a bite. He'd been apologetic when the morning's light had revealed the mark on my skin, but I'd felt oddly jubilant. My body had borne too many marks that I hadn't chosen. The brand. The pallor of the Keeping Rooms. The scrapes, blisters, and sharpened bones of our long journey. Instead, this mark on my neck had been made in joy. Now, lying on the warmed stones, I ran my fingers over it and smiled.

I don't know how long I dozed there. When I felt the shadow pass across my closed eyelids, I sat up with a jerk. I was fully dressed, but there was an intimacy in the abandon with which I'd given myself over to the warmth.

Even when backlit by the harsh sun above, Piper's silhouette was unmistakable.

'Sorry,' he said, stepping further out on to the terrace. 'I didn't mean to startle you.'

'You didn't,' I said, and began to stand.

'Don't get up.' He squatted to my level. 'They told me you were up here, but I didn't know you were sleeping.'

'Not sleeping properly,' I said. 'I don't do much of that, anyway.'

'The visions?'

I nodded. He settled down beside me, cross-legged, and turned his face up to the sun.

'I'm sleeping less, since you and Kip arrived, if that's any consolation. The whole Assembly's been shaken by it.'

'Us? It's not as if we invaded the place. We're just two more hungry Omegas. The only difference is that we happened to find our own way out here.'

'"We" didn't find the way here – you did. Not Kip.'

'We did it together.'

'That seems to be the way with you two.' He glanced at the bruise on my neck, then changed the subject. 'You have to understand – arriving unescorted, unannounced, like you did. It scares people, when this whole place is built on secrecy.'

'It's not me and Kip you should be worried about,' I said, 'with The Confessor searching for you.' The memory of her stole the heat from the stones beneath me.

'If only there were a limit to what I should worry about.' He sighed. 'You don't know how bad things have become, on the mainland, even in the years you were locked away.'

'I got some idea, at New Hobart.'

'What they did there – that's in line with what we've been seeing everywhere. More restrictions targeting Omegas; higher tithes; Omega settlements sealed off. The reports we're getting – beatings, whole settlements nearing starvation – none of it makes sense. The Council's expanding the refuges, at least, but it's still nonsensical. Why drive us to dependence on them? If they lowered the tithes and the

244

unreasonable controls, we wouldn't need the refuges, and they wouldn't need to provide them.'

For a moment, he looked tired.

'So you can see why the Assembly's nervous about your arrival. People are suspicious of seers at the best of times. And now more than ever, we need to know the island's secure.'

'Kip and I are hardly a threat.'

'I've told you that I don't think you are.'

'And Kip? You don't trust him?'

He shrugged. 'I don't know anything about him. He doesn't know anything about himself.'

'That's not his fault.'

'I know. But it doesn't make him useful to me.'

'Is that really how you see people? Useful or not useful?'

He didn't deny it, as some people might have done. 'That's how I have to see things. It's my job.'

'But what about you – outside of your job?'

He laughed. 'Maybe once there was a place where the job stopped, and I began. Now, I don't know.'

'But you wanted this – you chose to run for leader.'

'I knew I could do it better than the others. I was right, too.' He rested his elbow on his raised knee, dropped his head forward to let the sun warm the skin on the back of his neck. 'Once I knew that, it wasn't really a choice.'

We sat in silence for a while. I was so used to being alone with Kip, I'd thought it would be strange to find myself so often spending time with Piper. Whenever we were together I was sharply aware of the one great silence between us: my twin's name. That silence sat in the centre of all our conversations. It was like the crater in the island itself: everything else was constructed around it. But when we avoided that topic, it was easy to be near him. Easy to bask in his grin, and to feel safe under his commanding gaze. But as we sat there, in the companionable sun, I reminded myself of Zach, my shadow half. Of Piper's dead predecessor. Of the knives that glinted from his belt.

He turned to me. 'And you – being a seer. Is there a place outside of it, where the visions end and you begin?'

'It's not a job, or a choice. Being a seer isn't something you do. It's who I am.'

'Maybe it's the same for me, now. Taking care of the island.'

'And if it were a choice – would you choose it again?'

'Would you choose to be a seer?'

I didn't have an answer to give him.

*

Our quarters had separate beds, but I perched on the end of Kip's as we talked into the night.

'He was asking again today about my visions – what I'd seen about the island, before I came here. He didn't ask about Zach, not directly.'

'It doesn't mean he's not trying to work it out. You know that. He knows we haven't told him everything.'

'If he didn't trust us, do you really think we'd have a key to the fort, be free to wander all over the island?'

'Seems like the perfect way of keeping an eye on us,' said Kip. 'This place is crawling with his guards.' I thought of what Piper had said that morning, on the terrace: *They told me you were up here.* Kip went on. 'Plus, I'd bet my life that if we went anywhere near a boat we'd find we didn't have such free rein after all. He likes to have you right on call for his little interrogations.'

'You could hardly call them interrogations. We talk. He

tells me things, too. If he didn't trust us we'd be in a dungeon somewhere.'

'Nothing we wouldn't be used to, at least.' He reached over for the jug of wine on the table, and I held out the cups while he poured. 'What does he tell you, then?'

'Stuff about the island. The situation on the mainland, too.'

'Anything you didn't know already, from your visions?'

'Loads. It's not like that, anyway, the visions – I've told you already. It's vaguer than that. It's not like there's a neat narrative.' I sipped the wine, sucked my top lip to clear the dark red tannin that clung to it.

'He's going to find out about Zach. He must already know that your twin's important. Who else would have access to the Keeping Rooms?'

'I know. But that still leaves hundreds, maybe more, that it could be. He doesn't know what Zach is, exactly, what he does.' I paused. 'Even I don't know what Zach is, or what he does.'

'You have a pretty good idea. But how long do you think you can keep it from Piper? He'll figure it out. Council members might go by different names – but he'll work it out. He's not stupid.'

'Most of the time you're trying to convince me what a dumb thug Piper is.'

'Don't mess around, Cass. I may not like him, but it doesn't mean he's not smart. He's going to figure it out, if he hasn't already. Sooner or later he's going to realise your twin's behind all of it – the stuff they did to me, and the others in the tanks. Then what?'

'You want me to walk up there and tell Piper I'm Zach's twin, and let him get rid of us both? Will that make you feel better about what happened to you?'

'I don't even *know* what happened to me.' He realised he was shouting, reverted to a whisper. 'I just don't want Piper to have that over you. They'll use you to get at Zach. You know that.'

'I don't know that, and nor do you.'

'So why haven't you told him, then?'

I slumped back against the wall, staring fixedly at my feet hanging over the side of the bed. He leant back next to me, but not touching. I lolled my head to the side to look at him.

'Don't you get exhausted by it – never trusting people?'

'It doesn't matter whether I trust Piper or not,' he said. 'Zach's your twin, it's your decision. I just worry for you. You always want to believe the best of people. Look what happened with Zach, even after your mum warned you.'

'If I hadn't trusted Zach, and ended up in the Keeping Rooms, I'd never have found the tanks. I'd never have got you out.'

He laughed. 'Only you could see four years in a cell as an endorsement of your trusting attitude.' He took my hand. I pulled our clasped hands closer to me, slowly kissed each of his long fingers.

'So what are you going to do?' he said.

'I don't know. I get the feeling it might not even be up to me.' I sighed. 'I think you're right about Piper. Not that we can't trust him, necessarily, but that he's smart.'

CHAPTER 20

The next day Piper sent for us both. 'About time,' Kip grumbled, but I could tell he was glad not to be left behind. It was early afternoon, and the Assembly Hall was busy: watchmen came and left, sometimes reporting to the members of the Assembly gathered around the foot of the dais with the empty chair. As was often the case, Piper stood slightly apart from the main group. He was deep in conversation with Simon, one of the Assemblymen. He was twice Piper's age, and grey hair had settled in around his temples. A third arm hung beneath his right arm, something that contributed to his reputation as a fearsome fighter. He shared the same vitality as Piper. Many times when I'd been summoned, I'd arrived to find them talking, the older man not hesitating to debate forcefully with him. I guessed that this was why Piper preferred Simon's company to that of the more deferential members of the Assembly. Once or twice I'd found the two men in a heated exchange, gesticulating and interrupting each other as they bent over maps or papers, but they always parted amicably, Simon gathering his papers and leaving with a polite nod to me.

This time, when Simon stepped aside, Piper ushered us to a table on the far side of the Hall, beneath the stained-glass windows, where we couldn't be overheard. He poured us each a small glass of wine, invited us to sit.

'You've been patient with us, all these summonses, all these questions,' he said. 'The Assembly and I wouldn't keep bothering you, if it weren't crucial.'

'Not crucial enough to bother me for, evidently,' said Kip.

Piper ignored him. 'Things have been changing. The information you brought was new to us, but it seems to confirm what we'd already observed. A new mood, originating from the Council. It started with the drought years – when people are hungry, desperate, they're quicker to turn on each other, and the Council exploited that, playing up anti-Omega sentiment. Things have been getting steadily worse for us, since then, but in the last few years, it's been dramatic. Tithe increases, and other reforms led by The General: more and more Omega settlements being moved from fertile land, or cast out from Alpha areas. Villages out east, where Omegas had stayed till five, six, or even longer, now sending them off to settlements as toddlers. Raids on settlements, crops stolen or burnt. What seems to be a concerted effort to drive Omegas to the refuges. Of course, I've already told Cass this.'

'And she's told me,' Kip said pointedly.

Piper continued. 'Then we started hearing rumours of something more: our people being taken, being used strategically by their twins, or their twins' enemies.'

'The Keeping Rooms,' I murmured.

'Yes. And not only being used by the Councillors themselves. There were several reports of wealthy Alphas, unconnected to the Council, paying to have their twin imprisoned there, for "safekeeping".'

How many were still there, I wondered, still stuck in cells like my own?

'Then it got worse,' Piper said. 'About five years ago, the Council started getting serious about registrations – insisting on keeping track of us at all times.'

'There's a reason they're enforcing the registrations so strictly,' I said, remembering the man being whipped at New Hobart. 'It's all part of using the link between twins to manipulate us – they use that information to decide who's disposable, and who they can use. I don't know how they keep track of it all, but it underlies a lot of what they do.'

Piper nodded. 'I agree. But the registrations were only the start. Other reports started coming in, from all over: that Omegas who went to the refuges never came out. And we started to pick up rumours of missing children. Experiments. Even the settlements and the Keeping Rooms weren't enough, it seems.'

Kip pushed his chair back loudly. 'We already told you this – gave you all the details, not just rumours.'

I placed a hand on Kip's arm as Piper replied.

'You did. The details you've brought have been invaluable. And it's confirmed our suspicions about the shift in attitude in the Alpha Council, the shift that we'd seen coming.'

'You saw it coming?' said Kip. 'Thanks for the warning.'

'We didn't know exactly what was going on. But we did know about a new power in the Council chamber, rivalling even The General. A young Alpha. Started young, but rose quickly. Went by the name The Reformer.'

My hand on Kip's arm tightened momentarily.

Piper went on: 'Right from the start of his ascent, he's been pushing this radical anti-Omega agenda. More and more restrictions on our people. Policies to drive us out into settlements, and into the refuges. Then more.'

'Is he ruling the Council now?' I was amazed at how calm I'd managed to keep my voice.

Piper shook his head. 'No. He's too young, too extreme.' From the sheaf of maps and papers on the desk he pulled a huge sheet that looked at first glance like a family tree. It was a list of names, more than sixty, each one illustrated with a sketch, all connected by a series of arrows. He looked up at Kip. 'You can read?' Kip nodded impatiently.

Piper placed a finger at the head of the page.

'The Judge,' I read, looking at the sketch accompanying it: an old face with a distinctive thicket of white hair.

Piper nodded. 'He's ruled for over a decade now; was hugely powerful, at first. But we've long suspected that he's a figurehead. They need him – he's trusted, well-enough liked, even by some of our people. But he's always been a moderate. In his early days he was against tithes, and permissive about cohabitation in the eastern regions. This new stuff isn't coming from him.'

'So is he just outnumbered, now, on the Council?' asked Kip.

'Or they've got hold of his twin,' I said, matter-of-factly.

Piper agreed. 'We think that's probable. A man of The Judge's convictions is unlikely to use the Keeping Rooms for his own protection. We think they're holding his twin, manipulating him that way.'

'And who's "they"?' I asked, though I knew the answer. Piper's finger moved down the chart now, to a cluster of names.

'Here: the real power base, for the last few years at least. The General, The Ringmaster, The Reformer. All young, all radical.'

I leaned in to examine the sketches next to each name.

The Ringmaster's face looked incongruously warm. Beneath his mass of curly, dark hair his eyes were welcoming, his lips carving a smile. In the sketch to the right, The General's long, pale hair was pulled back from her slim face. Her features looked exaggerated: brows arched, cheekbones sharp. Her eyes lacked the animation of The Ringmaster's. Instead, her expression was appraising, controlled.

Piper saw my scrutiny of the picture. 'You've heard of her?' he asked.

I nodded. 'Everyone has.'

'I wish I never had,' he said. 'She's as ruthless as they come. Makes The Ringmaster look like an Omega supporter in comparison.'

Then I saw Zach's face: The Reformer. The sketch was basic, but the artist had done a good job with Zach's eyes: their intentness; their defensiveness.

'Do you recognise any of these faces? Or the names – do they mean anything to either of you?'

He shoved the paper closer to me. I was reminded of the sessions with The Confessor, with her map.

I was careful to examine the other faces with equal care, but my mind, and my eyes, kept returning to The Reformer. How awful, I thought, to have to hide like that, to construct a persona and maintain it always.

'I've heard of these two,' I said, carefully keeping my voice even. 'The Ringmaster and The Reformer. We were told about them in New Hobart.'

Then I saw it. This sketch wasn't linked to the tree-like hierarchy of the others. The name and image floated to the left of the page, blank parchment around it. Piper followed my gaze to the sketch, the grinning, calm visage.

'I wondered when you'd notice her. The Confessor. Your old friend.'

253

'Not exactly,' I said. I couldn't look away from the sketch. It was remarkable how those few skilful lines of ink could bring it back: the terrible intimacy of those sessions in the Keeping Rooms. The probing of my mind.

Piper continued. 'She came on the scene about six years ago, recruited by The Reformer, we think.'

'Why does she work for them?' asked Kip.

'I know it seems perverse, that she'd work for those who'd rid themselves entirely of people like her. People like us,' Piper said. 'But she works with them, I think, rather than for them. She's powerful – they recognise that, I think, by using her as they do. She's no pawn.'

I watched his finger lingering by The Confessor's sketched face, and remembered the current of fear in Zach's voice when he spoke of her. 'I can see why they need her. I've seen her power,' I said. 'But what does she need from them? Like Kip said, why does she do it?'

Piper laughed. 'You think all Omegas are good? That they all work for the improvement of humanity? That no Omega can be bought, for the price of gold, or power, or security?'

I met his gaze. 'What about Alphas then? Do you think they're all evil?'

He ignored me, looked back at the sheet, then jabbed once again at the sketch of Zach, so forcefully that I had to suppress the impulse to wince.

'All our sources bring us the same news – The Reformer's the key. The General's scary, in her own way, and The Ringmaster's always been anti-Omega, but The Reformer's the one driving this new agenda. We don't know for sure that it's him holding The Judge's twin, but it's him calling the shots.'

While I did my best to avert my gaze from the sketch

of Zach, I saw Kip's eyes straying back there, squinting attentively. Piper noticed too.

'He's the one, Kip. Just over five years ago, after his position on the Council was consolidated and he had The Confessor working with him, our people began to disappear. Not just the twins of Councillors, but in huge numbers. People like you.'

Kip looked up sharply. 'Insignificant people, you mean?'

'I mean people who don't have a direct link to the Council. There's a chance, of course, that your twin could be related to the Council. But that doesn't narrow it down as much as you'd think. There are several hundred Councillors, almost half of them women. Then factor in other Alpha women the Councillors might value enough to protect: wives, daughters, advisors, friends. Any of those might ultimately have their Omegas tanked. But it's more likely that you have no link to the Council. That you're one of the many they've taken for their experiments: Omegas of no perceived value.'

'No perceived value,' repeated Kip.

'From the Council's perspective, that's exactly what it is,' said Piper impatiently. 'Experimental subjects, usually young, who pose no risk to the Council if it goes wrong.'

'If they're killed, you mean. You don't need to sugar-coat it for us,' I said. 'I've seen the tanks, and Kip's been in them. We've seen the bones in the grotto below.'

Piper nodded. 'It's hard to keep track, given the thousands they've taken, but we've had hundreds of confirmed accounts of deaths. Of the Omegas taken for the experiments, so many of their Alpha twins have died suddenly that even the Alphas are starting to ask questions.' He looked at Kip. 'You survived. You might be luckier than you realise.'

'I can't think why I haven't been more grateful,' said Kip.

'But none of this answers the big question,' I pointed out. 'All this stuff about how the Council's treating us – it still doesn't make sense. What do they gain from treating us like that, driving us to the point of starvation? Their lives depend on us. It's the one unchangeable thing.'

'That's the blessing and the curse,' Piper said. 'The link is our only protection, but it's also what makes Omegas complacent. It's why we struggle to recruit people to the resistance: they know the Council could never really let us come to any serious harm. Even when things have got so much worse, these last few years, we've always known that the Alphas depended on us too much to see us starve to death. The refuges are seen as testament to that. Much as people hate to hand themselves in, to relinquish control over their own lives, the refuges are a safety net – and the recent expansions have reassured people. Nobody's stupid enough to swallow the Council line that the refuges are an act of charity. But even though they're clearly driven by Alpha self-interest, the refuges are an acknowledgment that there has to be a limit to what they can do to us. A line they can't cross.'

'Seems to me they're crossing that line pretty emphatically now,' said Kip.

'But why?' I said. 'Why now? What's changed?'

'For a while we thought they might be trying to break the link between twins,' Piper said. 'There've been rumours about that for as long as I can remember: breeding programmes, experiments, anything to try to produce children that weren't linked. But nobody's ever succeeded. For the Councillors, at least, tanking their twins offers the next best thing.'

I nodded, but I was distracted. 'What did you say before – about the expansions of the refuges? You said something about it the other day, too. On the terrace.'

'It's not enough to account for the numbers needing them,' said Piper dismissively. 'Nowhere near. See for yourself.' He flicked through the sheaf of papers on the table, finally laying a map on top of the others. It was on a much larger scale than the coastal maps he'd shown me previously. This one showed a cluster of buildings and fields, all enclosed by a double fence.

'This is Refuge One, just south of Wyndham.' His hand hovered above the right-hand side of the map, where a mass of buildings surrounded one huge rectangular building half as big as the rest of the camp itself. 'That whole complex there, it's all new – they started building it last year. Same thing reported at all the refuges we've been able to monitor. But the new buildings are still nowhere near enough to accommodate the increase in people turning themselves in. We're talking about thousands of people. These new barracks are big, but not enough for thousands of people to live in.'

'Why would they want to take on responsibility for so many of us?' said Kip. 'It'd be simpler, and probably cheaper, for the Council just to make it easier for us to survive outside of the refuges.'

'Unquestionably. But there's something to be said for a captive population, in terms of control.'

'No,' I interrupted Piper. 'I mean, you're right, but it goes beyond that.' I thought of what Mum had said about Zach when she came to warn me at the settlement: *he's ambitious*. And I heard Zach's words to me on the ramparts: *I've started something, and I need to finish it*. I remembered, too, his words to me all those years ago, when Alice and Dad were dying: *Why can't you do something?* I saw it, now: Zach's attempt, in his own sick way, to 'do something' about the fatal bond between twins. I looked down again at the map of the refuge, and that huge new building.

'You said the new buildings aren't big enough for thousands of people to live in. But they don't want us living. They just want us alive.'

'Is there a difference?' said Piper.

'Now there is – thanks to the tanks.' When I closed my eyes it played out before me. First a single tank, like the ones I'd seen so many times before. But then my vision drew back, and the further away from the tank I was, the more I saw: row upon row of tanks, dwarfing the tank room where I'd found Kip. They were all empty. They were all waiting.

I took a long breath, wondering if my idea would sound ridiculous once I'd committed it to syllables.

'They want us all in the tanks, eventually. Every Omega.'

The easy smile that was Piper's habitual expression was entirely gone. He stood up. 'You're sure?'

'They're going to push it as far as they can,' I said. 'You said it yourself: they've been trying to break the link between twins. If they can't do that, this is their next best option. Think about it: a world of Alphas, physically perfect, living their unblemished lives, until they die of old age on a feather bed.'

'They couldn't,' said Kip.

'I'm not saying it'd be easy,' I said. 'Or that they're capable of it yet. But what if that's their goal? A population of Omegas all neatly classified, documented, and ultimately tanked.'

'And the refuges,' Piper said. 'They're not even workhouses now – just collection centres for the tanks.'

I nodded. 'If they're not yet, they will be.'

'All Omegas?' said Kip. 'Could they really be aiming for that?'

I felt ashamed for Zach, even admitting it to myself, let

alone voicing it. But I also knew it was true. 'It's the only thing that makes sense of how they're treating us. They'll tank us from birth, if they can. Imagine it – just getting rid of us from the start. An Alpha world.'

Kip grimaced. I knew that we were remembering the same thing: the tiny skull on the floor of the grotto, picked clean by water and years. And the babies taken from Elsa.

'They've already started trying,' I said.

Piper swept the papers to the floor.

'If you're right, it changes everything. All this time, we've had a false sense of security. Even with all these creeping "reforms", we thought they could never let it get to the point that we were actually endangered. But what you've told us – it removes the whole idea of co-dependence. Any sense of mutual obligation is erased. There's no limit to the Council now. If their goal is all of us in tanks, I don't think they're even concerned that some of us are dying under the current regime. Before, it would have been a disaster, unsustainable. Now, they'll just see that as a short-term side-effect of the plan: oppress us, and even if a few die in the process it's only a short-term problem.'

I nodded. 'But it's not just a side-effect, the way they're treating Omegas now. It's part of the plan: the more oppressed we are – the more starved, weakened, dispirited, the more who turn themselves in to the refuges – the easier it is for them to tank us.'

*

Piper sent for me the next day, but the watchman bearing the message told me to go to the tower instead of the Assembly Room. When I reached the top of the winding stairs, he was standing at the low battlement that ringed the huge, circular space, looking down over the city. He didn't turn, but must have heard my footsteps.

'It's a nice view from up here, but it's pointless, defensively,' he said. 'It looks over the city, not the ocean. By the time any invader reaches the city, it's already over. Whoever built this place knew that secrecy was the best defence. Even from within the reef, there're no signs of habitation, not until they penetrate the harbour. I don't know why they bothered with a tower at all, let alone battlements, other than to make themselves feel important.'

'But you seem to like it up here.'

He shrugged, still with his back to me. 'It's quiet. And I like seeing the city itself – everything we've achieved.'

I was reluctant to step away from the stairs and join him – the memory of those precarious minutes on the ramparts at Wyndham was still too raw. But he turned and ushered me forward, so I came to stand by him. We looked down together at the steep city, diligent with movement. His hand on the wall, close to where my hands rested, was broad, the fingers strong. My skin had browned in the months since the Keeping Rooms, but was still nowhere near as richly burnished as Piper's.

I broke the silence. 'Why did you send for me? Is it about what I told you yesterday?'

He nodded. 'In part. The Assembly met for most of the night to discuss it. Some don't believe it; others are convinced.'

'And you?'

'I wish I didn't believe it,' he said. 'It's so huge that it seems implausible. But the way they've been treating us, these last few years – that's even more implausible. Until you told us about the tanks. If that's their endgame, then it all makes sense.

'It's perfect, in a way. They just keep raising the tithes, which drive us to starvation, and eventually to the refuges, but it also pays for what they're doing. The new buildings at the refuges, and the development of the tanks – Omegas paid for all that, with the same tithes that will eventually drive them to the tanks themselves. We're paying for the tanks, and eventually we'll even hand ourselves in.'

I could admire it, the same way I could admire Zach's cunning when he exposed me back in the village. There was a horrible simplicity to it.

'What's your Assembly going to do about it?'

'That's what we were trying to decide last night,' he said. 'Spread word to avoid the refuges, at any cost. That'll be the first step. But even that's easier said than done. People don't go to the refuges lightly. And if people are starving enough, desperate enough, it'll be hard to warn them away, unless we can offer them an alternative.'

'And can you?'

'We can offer them this.' He gestured at the island below us. 'Barely big enough to support our current numbers. It's only in the last few years that we've been self-sufficient enough to stop shipping food in. And now this place is under threat, if The Confessor's focusing on us as you say. I can't stop thinking about her, what it would mean for us if she finds the island.'

'Then you know how I feel most of the time,' I said. 'I can never stop thinking about her, ever since we got away. She's looking for me.'

'You can feel it?'

I nodded. Even here, standing beside him in the island's clear light, I could feel her hunting. The scrutiny of her mind, insidious as unwanted hands on flesh. 'All the time. It's worse even than when she used to interrogate me.'

'And you don't know why?'

'Isn't it obvious? I got away.'

He smiled, shook his head as he turned to face me. 'You think she's after you just because you got away? You think if anyone else escaped from the Keeping Rooms that it would be such a problem for them? You have no idea what you're worth.'

'Worth? I'm not for sale at market. And if you think I'm worth so much, stop patronising me.'

He looked at me carefully. 'You're right, of course. It's just that I'm always slightly taken aback by you – by how much you underestimate your own powers. Think of The Confessor's value to the Council, the threat she poses to us. They've been hunting us ever since the first Omegas discovered the island – over a century ago. But they can't trawl every inch of ocean. Now, though, with her, they don't need to. She'll find us, eventually, just like you did.'

'I'm not like her.'

'You keep saying that. And I do understand what you mean. But if you recognised what you're capable of, you could be the one real threat to them. Think of everything you've achieved already.'

'Achieved? All we've done is manage not to get caught yet.'

He had a way of looking directly in my eyes that was disconcerting. 'You resisted the interrogations of The Confessor, for four years. You escaped from the Keeping Rooms. You found out about the tanks and, even more, found them yourself and got somebody out alive. You escaped the sealing of New Hobart, and delayed it by burning down half the forest. You found your way to a place that has depended on complete secrecy and the impenetrable reef for the last hundred years, and warned us of the

Council's master plan to tank us all.' He cocked an eyebrow at me. 'Seems to me you've done quite enough to keep them on their toes.'

'But all that stuff just happened. I didn't plan it, as part of some strike against the Council. I wasn't thinking about the resistance. Until I got here, I didn't even know for sure that there was a real Omega resistance.'

'But now you do know. So the question is what you can do for the resistance. Starting with telling me who your twin is.'

I didn't speak for a while. The sounds of the city wafted up to us. Below the city's sprawl, in the hollow at the base of the crater, the lake nestled. Around the lake, and on the side of the crater opposite the city, the fields of wheat and maize had been harvested and were humped with bales of hay. In the city itself, even on the busiest streets, the roofs, windowsills and tiny, steeply terraced gardens were clustered with pumpkins, tomatoes, spinach.

'Are there any other seers here, now?' I asked.

'Not now. We've had two. Both useful in different ways. One we got to before he was split, before branding. That's made him invaluable for undercover work on the mainland. There are a few other Omegas who can pass for Alpha at a glance: the less visible mutations, which can be hidden by clothing. But none as convincing as seers.

'The other was branded, so she couldn't go undercover. Her powers weren't quite like yours, I think – she could never have found her own way out here. But she was handy in planning the rescue trips. She helped with locating newborns, or others in need of refuge, or warning us of Council patrols near the coast. But, for the last year or so, she was half-mad.' Most people avoided this topic around me, or retreated into euphemisms: *not quite stable*, they'd say, or *you know how it can be, with some seers.* But Piper was as direct as ever. 'The visions were too much for her. She didn't know what was real anymore, I think.'

I remembered those final months in the Keeping Rooms, taunted by my visions of the tanks, and by The Confessor's probings. How I'd felt my mind giving up on me.

'You talk about her in the past tense,' I said. 'Did the Council get hold of her?'

He shook his head. 'No. A ship went down, in heavy seas, on the way back from the mainland. We lost ten people that day.'

'I'm sorry.'

'It happens. It's the price we pay for this location.'

'There you go again: price, worth. Like we can calculate the value of lives.'

'Can't we?' Again, that penetrating stare. 'It's my job. To do whatever will benefit the most of our people.'

I stepped back, away from the battlement, and from him. 'That's the problem with you: "our people". That's why I can't tell you who my twin is. You don't get it, any more than the Council does.' At the top of the stairs, I turned back to him. 'Twenty people died, when that ship went down, not ten.'

As I began to descend, I was hoping to hear the sounds of him following, or calling after me. But I was followed only by the sound of my own footsteps.

*

In the week that followed, Piper continued to summon me daily. He made no mention of the argument on the tower. His questions were specific, detailed: the layout of the Keeping Rooms. The secret caves and tunnels under

Wyndham. He got me to draw the tanks, every feature I could remember. He asked about the bones I'd seen at the bottom of the grotto pool. Often we were joined by members of his Assembly, with their own questions. The maps The Confessor showed me: how detailed were they, and which areas had they covered? The soldiers I'd seen at New Hobart: their numbers, their weapons, the proportion that were mounted. I answered all the questions except the one Piper returned to most often: my twin.

About ten days after our arrival he sent for us both again.

'Good news,' he said, when we were ushered into the huge Assembly Hall, empty for once except for Piper. 'I thought you'd both want to know.' There were papers in front of him on the table. He swept them aside, pushed his chair back slightly as we sat down. 'We can take him out. The Reformer. We have a source in the Council Halls, watching him for a long time now.'

'One of us?'

'One like you,' replied Piper, turning to me. 'The seer I told you about – the unbranded one. He's seventeen, now, has been working to infiltrate the Council since he left here two years ago. His seer abilities have helped, of course, though at times he's feared The Confessor might sense him.'

'How close has he got?' I asked, working hard to suppress the tremble in my voice.

'He's a serving boy, in the private household of The General. It's not just access to her though – he has access to many in the Council, waits on privy meetings with The Ringmaster, The Judge, others too.' He looked clearly at me now. 'The ship that came in late last night brought a message from him. He's starting to get access to The Reformer, too. He's been alone with him several times now.

He's in a position to make a hit. I just have to give the word and we can have The Reformer killed.'

Even as Piper reached for the bell at the table's edge and rang it, even as the two guards entered, he kept his eyes fixed on me. Kip, too, was watching for my reaction. I said nothing. I felt suddenly exhausted, a physical surge of tiredness like I hadn't felt since our arrival on the island.

With one of his characteristically careless jerks of the head, Piper indicated the watchmen waiting attentively, just out of earshot.

'So what do you say?' he asked me. 'Do I give the order?'

Kip turned to him. 'Why ask us? You don't care what we say.'

Piper answered Kip, but kept his gaze on me. 'I wouldn't count on that.'

CHAPTER 21

I slammed the door to our quarters before Kip had even reached the stairs that led up to it. He got there in time to hear the key turn on the other side.

'I had to, Cass,' he called through the door.

'It's not your choice to make,' I shouted from inside. From where he stood, against the door, he would have heard the crash of the wine bottle, cups and mirror. I threw the lamp against the door; its metal base bounced towards me while the glass shattered.

'What was I supposed to do?'

He was answered by another crash, as I kicked over the small table between the beds.

'You think you're a big hero?' I yelled. 'Jumping in and telling him Zach's my twin? That's not your decision.'

'You think *you're* a big hero? Keeping quiet, letting him kill Zach, kill you?'

I stepped over the broken glass, unlocking the door and wrenching it inwards so quickly that he almost stumbled onto me.

'Don't you get it?' I said. 'He doesn't have a seer at Wyndham. The Confessor's too good. And even if they got past her, I'd have felt it – a threat to Zach, to me. I'd have felt something coming. He was calling our bluff. Why do you think he asked you to come along?'

'Did it occur to you that he might actually value my opinion? That as the only one here who's actually been in one of your twin's science experiments, I might have the right to know what's happening?'

I just raised an eyebrow and waited.

'Oh crap.' Kip slumped down on the bed. 'He knew I'd try to stop him.' He closed his eyes. 'He wasn't really able to have Zach killed. But now –'

Quieter now, I sat down next to him. 'Yep.'

'And he wouldn't need spies, sources, assassins.'

'No. Just me.'

He tipped his head back against the wall. I did the same.

'I can see a cup that you missed, on the windowsill,' he said. 'Want to smash it?'

'Maybe later.' I gave a tired smile, closed my eyes.

He waited a long time for me to say something.

Afterwards, when we'd swept up the fragments of glass and pottery, we lay in silence in our separate beds. Under the door we could see the patient shadow of a watchman who'd been posted there immediately after our return from the Hall. At the window a ribbon of smoke was visible, from the pipe of another guard stationed on the rampart below.

Kip looked across at me. 'I don't mean to bring down the mood or anything' (I snorted at this), 'but why haven't they killed you yet?'

'I've been wondering the same thing.'

'But it's good, right?'

I laughed outright at this. 'Well, I'm glad I'm not dead yet.'

'You know what I mean. It's a good sign – that he didn't kill you right away.'

I rolled over to face him across the small room. 'When did we become grateful for such small mercies?' I watched his face, his anxious, tired eyes. 'But you're right, I think. He must think we're useful.'

'You don't have to patronise me, you know. It's you he can use. What good am I to him?' He paused. 'Or to you.'

'You don't have to keep apologising.'

'Really? Because on the scale of things to apologise for, surely condemning someone to near-certain death has to be up there.'

I was silent.

'Sorry,' he said. 'I shouldn't have said that.'

I sat up. 'Can I come over there?'

'Sure – though I don't know what I've done to deserve it.'

He shifted over to make room. I lay on my back, so he rolled on his back too, but we were pressed tightly against each other.

'I like it when you lie on that side of me,' he said. 'When I feel your arm, next to me like that, it sort of feels like having an arm on that side.'

'I picked this side because it stops you getting handsy.' We both laughed.

'Why aren't you angrier at me?' he said, after a while.

'Because he was right.'

'Piper? You're defending him now, after how he played us?'

'Oh, he's not right about everything. But he was right about you.'

'Yeah. That I'm an idiot.'

'No. That you'd do whatever it took to protect me.'

*

The next day the door remained locked. The sentry outside ignored our shouted requests for information. In the afternoon, a watchman opened the door and stood guard while another stepped inside. Kip jumped to his feet, rushed in front of me.

'Don't bother,' I said. 'Piper's not going to send someone else to do it.'

The watchman placed a tray on the table by the door and left without speaking.

'He'll do it himself,' I said.

'How can you be so sure?' said Kip, picking up the tray and bringing it to my bed.

'He's not a coward.'

'Yes, because nothing would show courage like killing an unarmed prisoner.'

After two more days locked up, I demanded that the sentry pass on a message to Piper asking that we at least be allowed out for air. No answering message came, but in the late afternoon four watchmen came and escorted us both up to the tower, and stood waiting in the stairs below.

I stood at the battlement, looking down. The city looked the same as it had a few days before, when I'd stood there with Piper. But now it was a prison rather than a haven.

'Maybe it would be for the best,' I said. 'They get rid of me, they get rid of Zach. Rationally, I can't argue with it.'

'Don't be so stupid. It's not irrational, or selfish, to not want to be killed.'

'I'm not being stupid. It seems like quite an obvious answer, actually: he's behind all this stuff. The things they did to you, and others. We don't know how many – maybe hundreds, thousands. So if you do the maths, it seems like an easy answer: my life against theirs.'

'It's not a maths problem, Cass. It's not that simple.'

'That's what I was saying to Piper, not so long ago. But what if it does come down to calculation? What if I'm only making it more complicated because that gets me off the hook?'

Kip sighed. 'Sometimes I can't believe that you're meant to be this crash-hot seer.'

'What do you mean?'

'I mean, since when have you worried about getting yourself off the hook? You've never worried about that. You smashed me out of that tank instead of just getting out of there – that could've landed you back in the Keeping Rooms. The same goes for all the times since then that I've slowed you down.'

'But when it comes to the core issue – the problem the island's facing, the problem that put you in the tank in the first place – I could solve it right now.'

I gestured at the drop in front of us. One hundred feet below us, the city was going about its business.

'You won't do it,' Kip said, getting up and walking back towards the stairs. 'You think Piper would let us up here if he thought there was a chance you'd jump? He's right about that, although he's got the reasoning wrong. He thinks you're protecting yourself. Thinks that's why you tried to keep Zach's identity secret.'

'And you think he's wrong?'

'Of course I do.' He didn't even turn around as he replied. 'You're not protecting yourself. You're protecting Zach.'

I called after him. 'Isn't that just a different kind of self-ishness? A different kind of cowardice?'

He looked back at me from the top step. 'You've always imagined a world where twins don't have to hate each other. An unsplit world, where we wouldn't even need a place like the island. Maybe it's cowardice. Or maybe it's a kind of courage.'

*

My nights had always been broken by visions, but that night each time the sentry shifted outside our door, I pictured the small knives at Piper's belt. Kip couldn't sleep either; I could feel him tensing at each sound from the door or window. When we kissed it wasn't the same delirious haze of that first kiss, or the gentle explorations of the following weeks, as we'd settled into this new intimacy. Now there was a sense of urgency: that at any moment it could be over. The key in the lock, the knife blade. And the idea of my own death was crueller to me, now, because Kip and I had only just discovered each other. Because there were parts of his neck I hadn't yet kissed, and because the feeling of my fingers clutching his hair was still a novelty. Such little things to grieve for, I told myself, in the face of all the years I'd lived, and everything I stood to lose. But in the bed that night they didn't feel trivial, and when I cried it wasn't for the imminent knife blade, but for the loss of his hand on my skin, the tender abrasiveness of his stubble on my shoulder.

Piper sent for me in the morning. The watchman took me without speaking, leading me swiftly from the room before Kip and I could exchange anything more than a glance.

I was led into the Assembly Hall, where a number of the Assembly were gathered. Simon was there, and I recognised several of the other men and women. Over the last couple of weeks, they'd questioned me at length, but not aggressively or without sympathy. Now, instead of greeting me, they fell silent when I entered. Even Simon stood quietly, all three arms crossed against his chest. Piper wasn't in his usual seat at the table near the door. The watchman guided me through to an antechamber at the other end of the Hall. It was a tiny room, not much more than a cupboard, but I saw by the maps pinned on the walls and the comfortable clutter that Piper had made it his base. In the corner a sleeping mat was clumsily rolled, a blanket shoved beside it.

'This is where you sleep?'

'Sometimes.' When the door had opened, Piper had risen quickly from the stool. He waved the watchman away, stepped across the small room himself to shut the door behind me. He stood with his back to the door, pointed me towards the stool. The knives still hung from his belt.

'Surely you, of all people, would have proper quarters?' I sat, glancing over at the sleeping mat in the corner. There was something touching about his hurried attempt to tidy it away. 'A proper bed, at least?'

He shrugged. 'I have quarters upstairs. But I like to be here, closer to the barracks, closer to all this.' He gestured at the mess. Some of the maps were held to the wall not by tacks but by throwing knives, jabbed into the rich tapestries that upholstered the room. 'Anyway,' he went on, 'it's not important.'

'OK,' I said.

He leaned his head against the back of the door. For the first time, I sensed he was nervous. I knew, then, that he hadn't brought me here to kill me.

'You didn't send for me to talk about your sleeping arrangements.'

'No,' he replied, but said nothing further.

'We could talk about my sleeping arrangements, then. About the fact that Kip and I are still locked in, a guard at the door.'

'And the window,' he said calmly.

'I should be flattered that you think we need so many.'

He raised a dark eyebrow. 'You think you could take on one of those men? You and Kip?' He laughed.

'We got this far,' I pointed out.

He exhaled impatiently. 'The guards aren't there to stop you getting out.'

It took me a few seconds to understand. I remembered the stares of the Assembly in the Hall outside. I knew now what it reminded me of: the expression on the faces of the children I encountered on the day I left my parents' village.

'How many know who my twin is?'

'Only the Assembly, so far,' he said. 'But how long it can stay that way, I don't know.'

'They want me dead.'

'You've got to understand.' There was only one stool, so he sat down on the bed roll opposite me, and leaned in close. 'Lewis, my oldest advisor –'

'I know Lewis,' I said. I remembered the impressive, grey-bearded man, perhaps fifty, who had questioned me many times.

'His niece – his twin's Omega child who Lewis has cared for since her birth – she's one of the ones who was taken. Why do you think he pressed you so hard for details of what you saw in the tanks where you found Kip?'

'I only saw a handful of people,' I said, angry at the weight of this unsuspected responsibility. 'He couldn't expect me to have seen them all – there were so many.'

'Exactly,' Piper whispered urgently. 'There are so many. Branded, taken, killed. Everyone out there has lost someone because of The Reformer. Everyone on this island knows he's looking for us. Have you heard the games the children play? *Come out and play, come out and play –*'

'*He's coming to take you away.*' Without thinking, I completed the chant, familiar from the cries that had drifted up from the city to our window every morning and evening when the children played in the streets.

Piper nodded. 'It's him they're playing at – The Reformer. There are other Councillors with aggressively anti-Omega policies – The General in particular. But none like The Reformer. When the children on the island wake up at night, shouting from a nightmare, it's him they're thinking of.'

I almost laughed at the impossibility of reconciling Zach with that nightmarish figure. Zach, who had burned his finger on a griddle and cried. Zach who had sidled behind Dad's legs when a bull was led through the market square. But my laugh never formed. I knew, somehow, that they were the same thing: Zach's fear, as a child, and the fear I recognised in the children's chant. One was the source of the other. All the things that I knew about Zach – the memory of how gently he had cleaned my burn after the branding; his body shaking with tears when our father was dying – were deeply buried now. I believed in them – the same way I had believed in the sky during my years in the cell. But I knew what he'd done – I'd seen it myself, manifested in the unanswerable glass and steel of the tank rooms. In the bones that lay in the grotto. I couldn't expect that anybody else would understand the tenderness and fear that lay beneath The Reformer. And I knew that nobody would deny it more ferociously than Zach himself. The Reformer was his creation. What remained of the boy who had reached for my hand, outside the shed where Alice lay dying, and begged for my help? I'd kept my faith with the sky in the Keeping Rooms, and I'd emerged from the cell to find the sky waiting, unchanged. But did that frightened boy, my brother, still exist somewhere within The Reformer? And could I keep my faith with him, without betraying Piper, and the island?

I met Piper's eyes. 'Are you trying to justify why you're going to have to kill me?'

He leant forward, his voice an urgent, whispered hiss. 'I need you to justify why I shouldn't. Give me a reason that I can take to the Assembly, to Simon and Lewis and the others, to explain why I haven't done it already.'

Again the weight of exhaustion settled on me. I felt as though I were being eroded, worn away like the stone of the island itself, where it met the sea. 'This island is meant to be the one place where we don't have to justify our right to exist.'

'Don't lecture me about this island. I'm trying to protect it – it's my job.'

'But when you kill me, or lock me away, this won't even be the island anymore. It'll just be the Keeping Rooms with a sea view. The Assembly will just be a Council, by another name. And you'll have become just like Zach.'

'I have a responsibility to the people here.' He looked away from me.

'But not to me.'

'You're one person. I'm responsible for all these people.'

'That's what I said to Kip. And he said it wasn't that simple: that it's not a question of numbers.'

'Of course he said that. He doesn't have my job.'

276

I looked past him at the maps on the walls. All of them were heavily annotated in black ink, to show the Council garrisons and refuges, as well as the villages, the settlements, the safehouses. The whole network that the resistance relied on to get people out to the island. All those people relying on him.

'If that's your job, then why haven't you killed me already?'

'I need you to change the numbers. Give me a reason not to do it.'

My voice was calm. 'I've told you everything I know about Wyndham. About The Confessor. I was the one who warned you about Zach's plans for tanking more Omegas.'

'There has to be more. About the search for the island.'

I shook my head. 'That's not news to you. You know they're looking. You know they'll find it, eventually. It's only a matter of when.'

He grabbed my arm. 'Then tell me when. Give me details.'

I wrenched my arm from his grip. 'I don't have anything more to tell you. It doesn't work like that – I don't get dates, maps. My visions aren't something you can pin to your wall. They're inconsistent – sometimes I can tell what's going to happen, sometimes I don't have a clue.'

'But you found us – you found the island.' He paused, lowered his voice further. 'What about what lies beyond here?'

I shook my head. 'What do you mean? There's nothing beyond here. Everything's back east.'

'Everything we know about. But it wasn't always that way. What if there are other places, further west? Or even east, past the deadlands.'

'You mean Elsewhere? That's just old stories. Nobody's ever found it – there's nothing to find.'

'Most people on the mainland think the island's just a story, just a rumour.' His face was absolutely serious.

'You know something about Elsewhere? You've found it?'

'No. I was hoping you might be able to help us.' He pulled a map from the wall. Much of what I saw, as he lay it in front of me on the floor, was familiar. The coastline I recognised from The Confessor's maps, and from others I'd seen on the island. And I recognised the island itself, barely a speck, adrift a few inches from the western coast. But this map was different: it left out the mainland itself, which was cut off by the right-hand edge of the paper. Except for the stain of coast down that margin, the map showed only sea. But it was scrawled with pencil marks: currents, reefs, a tracery of pencil markings emanating from the island and reaching far out west.

I looked up at him. 'You're sending ships out. You're looking for Elsewhere.'

'Not me. At least, not just me – it started before I was in charge. But yes – we've been searching. Maybe five years now. There are two ships out there as we speak – our two biggest. They'll be gone a month next full moon.'

'And you really think there's something to be found?'

He kept his voice low, but I could feel his anger. 'There are some ships that haven't come back. You think I'd take those risks if I didn't think there was something out there?'

I looked down at the map, avoiding his gaze.

'Help us, Cass. If you can sense something – anything at all – it could change everything.'

I realised I'd pressed my palm to the map, as if it would help me scan those miles of ocean with my mind. I closed my eyes, tried to probe the unmapped space. I concentrated until I could feel the blood straining in the vein at my left temple, but all I could see was the stubborn ocean, the grey miles of sea that spread in all directions.

'It's too far,' I said, lifting my hand from the map as I slumped back.

'Not in the Before it wasn't. They had bigger ships, faster.' He grabbed my hand and pressed it on to the map again, hard. 'Try again.'

I did try. I forced my mind as I'd done when I was on the boat, in the clutches of the reef. I visualised the reef, then the open sea beyond, and I probed westwards. My whole body tensed; when Piper finally released his hand, my own palm had left a clammy print on the map. But I could see nothing, feel nothing.

'I'm sorry,' I said. 'If it's out there, it's too far for me – I've never sensed anything about it.'

'I'm sorry too,' said Piper. Although his hand had been on mine until a moment ago, he suddenly seemed very distant. 'It would have simplified things if you could have helped.'

He glanced in the direction of the door, behind which I could hear voices, raised and abrasive. 'They want you dead. They want to take out The Reformer and you're the price they're happy to pay. It's an easy decision for them.'

'Not for you?'

'I think your death might be too high a price. I think we need you. You, your visions, could change the whole picture.'

'But you won't let us go.' It wasn't a question.

'I can't. But I can keep you safe.'

'And I'm supposed to be grateful, while you use me as a hostage to stop Zach from attacking?'

'I thought of that,' he said evenly. 'But if we let him know we have you, try to use you to rein him in, there's every chance his own people will take him out. He's not running the Council – not yet, anyway. Any hint that he might be under our sway, and they'd kill him themselves. We'd be rid of him, but there're others who'd still hunt us down. And you'd be dead too.'

'Which seems like a shame.'

He looked at me. 'Yes. It would be a shame.'

He escorted me back through the Hall where the Assembly, suddenly silent, turned to watch our progress. He put his arm on my shoulder as he guided me through the gathered men and women, but I shrugged him off.

One of the men leaned close to me. It was Simon, Piper's most trusted advisor. 'I wouldn't be so quick to brush him off, if I were you,' he said. 'Seems to me he's the one thing keeping you alive.'

Another man laughed at that. I turned to face him. He was stocky, with a dark beard, a crutch under one arm. 'That's right,' he said. 'If I had my way, you'd have been finished off by now. You and your twin.'

I replied only quietly. 'My twin shut me in the Keeping Rooms to stop me being used against him. If you kill me, you confirm everything the Alphas think: that we're a liability, a risk to them. That we need to be locked away, to protect them.' There was no response, but they were all watching me. 'You want to kill me? Why don't you go even further and get rid of every Alpha that way? Sure, you'll kill all of us by doing it, but it's worth it, right?' I was shouting now, as Piper dragged me from the Hall.

CHAPTER 22

When Piper came to our quarters early the next morning, I wasn't sleeping, but my eyes were still closed. Something had woken me a few moments before, a dream or a vision, and I was concentrating on it, eyes clasped shut as I tried to prolong the state of half-sleep to clarify what it was that I'd seen.

I heard Kip jump up from his bed as the key turned in the lock, and move between me and the door.

'Relax,' said Piper. 'I'm not here to hurt her.'

'Quiet,' Kip whispered. 'She doesn't sleep much at nights – often mornings are the only sleep she gets.'

'How much sleep do you get, if you're watching her all night?' asked Piper. He'd dropped his voice, but I could picture the way his eyebrow would have arched.

'Just don't wake her.'

'Actually, it's you I want to see.'

'There's a first,' muttered Kip. I heard them move away from my bed. I dared to peek between my half-closed eyelids. They stood at the window, their backs to me. Outside, the crater's encircling walls blocked the rising sun from view, though the dawn light was suffused with red.

Kip looked down at the guard who leaned against the wall on the balustrade beneath our window. 'He's not getting much sleep either, I suppose.'

'You'd rather take your chances?'

'I don't know.' Kip's answer was calm. 'I'm not crazy about the idea of your mates from upstairs coming to get us, to be honest.' He glanced down at the knives lining Piper's belt. 'But Cass and I have spent enough time locked up, before we got here. We didn't expect more of it, here of all places.'

'You don't know how long you were in that tank,' Piper pointed out.

'True. Imagine if I found out it was only twenty minutes. Embarrassing, really, after all this fuss.'

Piper laughed with him, but only briefly. 'The Assembly – my "mates from upstairs" – you don't concern them, I think.'

'I guessed as much, during one of the many times I've been left here while you and they consult Cass.'

'I'm not trying to diminish your importance,' said Piper. 'You're the only one we've found who's been in the tanks. We all want to find out what goes on in that place. But I'm trying to reassure you: I don't think you're in any danger.'

'Not from your lot, maybe. But I'm guessing there're some Alphas on the mainland who're pretty keen to re-acquaint themselves with me.'

'You'd rather stay here, under guard?'

'You say it like we have a choice.'

'You do.' Piper reached to his belt. I was about to spring up, thinking he was going for one of his knives, but then I saw he was proffering Kip a key. I scrunched my eyes closed again as Kip turned to look at me.

'No,' said Piper. 'You know she's too valuable for me to let her go. But there's no reason for you to be kept here.'

'And your reason for letting me go – it's entirely altruistic, is it, and nothing to do with getting me out of the way and having Cass to yourself?'

'If I needed to get rid of you, you'd be gone by now.'

'So this doesn't have anything to do with how you feel about her?'

Piper sounded unconcerned. 'There's a boat leaving in an hour. There's room on it for you. It doesn't matter what you believe my motives are.'

'You're right,' said Kip calmly. 'It doesn't matter. You really think I'd leave, either way? Or that she'd be grateful to you, for letting me go?'

'Not really.'

I peered again through one eye. Piper had turned away from Kip to face the window once more. Through the window, above the crater's edge, a flock of geese trailed its V on the lightening sky.

'Have you ever seen a bird hatch?' asked Piper, as the cries of the geese drew further away.

I could hear the frustration in Kip's voice. 'Sure. It's the one thing I remember. Not my name, or my twin. Just really vivid memories of birdwatching.'

'If you take an egg away from the mother before it hatches, when the chick comes out it attaches itself to the first thing it sees. Follows it round like its mother. When we were kids, we had a duckling my twin watched hatching. After that, it followed her everywhere.'

'So I'm the duckling in your little allegory, yeah? Hatched from the tank and latching blindly on to Cass?'

Piper met Kip's gaze unapologetically. 'I think maybe that's part of it, yes. But I can't figure out if it's a bad thing.'

283

'Not for you. You've already used me to get to her –
counting on me to expose who her twin is.'

'You're right. I was testing you, and you acted how I
thought you would. But I don't know that necessarily means
you failed.'

'And you're testing me again now.' Kip looked back down
at the key, which Piper had placed on the thick stone sill.
'Any surprises?'

'No.' Piper took the key again, pocketed it. 'I didn't think
you'd leave, though I hoped you would. I still can't work
out if you're a liability. For her, I mean.'

'Sure,' said Kip, rolling his eyes. 'Your reasons were
entirely selfless.'

'Of course not. Why do you think I gave you separate
beds?' Piper grinned wryly, and looked over at me. I hoped
he didn't make out the flicker of movement as I shut my
right eye again. 'But I'm beginning to think you should stay
with her. I think you have to.'

'I'm not a liability anymore, then?' goaded Kip.

'You might well be. But the reason you're a liability is
also the reason you should stay.'

'This is all very magnanimous of you both, deciding who
I need, what's best for me,' I said, throwing back the blanket
and swinging my feet down to the floor with a thump. 'But
did it occur to you that I might have an opinion about that
as well?' I rubbed the right side of my face, creased from
the pillow.

Kip spoke first: 'Don't think it hadn't occurred to me.'

'Or me,' added Piper hastily.

'Don't you talk to me,' I said to him. 'Sneaking in here,
trying to play with us like the pins on your stupid maps
upstairs.'

'That's what I said to him,' said Kip.

284

I turned on him. 'Don't you talk to me either. You're no better. Why wouldn't you go?'

He looked uncertainly at Piper, who grinned.

'Don't start smirking,' I said to Piper. 'Ducklings? Seriously? For crying out loud. Of course Kip should go, but you're an idiot to think he ever would.'

'So you do want me to go?' Kip ventured.

'Yes, of course, for your sake. No, of course, for mine. But what I want, more than anything, is for the two of you to just stop all this nonsense. I'm trying so hard to keep my head clear, to stay alive, to see what's coming, and you two are behaving as if I'm a prize to be won at a fair. As if nothing's up to me.'

Piper spoke first. 'I'm sorry. Mainly for being foolish – I knew Kip wouldn't leave.'

'Shut up,' I said.

'I'm being sincere.'

'No, shut up. I need to think clearly. For all your blathering about ducklings, something else had me half-awake just before you came in. Something important.'

'This isn't important to you?' asked Kip.

'You know what I mean. I'd had a vision, something urgent.' I closed my eyes again, trying to coax the vision back from the haze of sleep. 'A man – he was crying – and he put a knife in his boot.' I looked up quickly. 'Someone's coming.'

Piper had moved to the window and slammed the shutters before I'd finished speaking, but it was the door that shook as something crashed against it. The key turned, the latch lifted and, with almost comical slowness, the door scraped open, pushed by the weight of the guard who had died against it. Kip was halfway to the door when the intruder stepped over the dead guard and rushed at me, a bloodied knife still in his hand.

He'd reached me when Piper's knife landed in his throat, so that as he fell he dragged me down with him. Clutched to the man's front, I felt him quiver as another of the throwing-knives hit him in his back as we went down. The back of my head hit the stone floor when I landed beneath him, and for an instant the room around me became blurred. It took a few seconds for Piper and Kip to drag the man off me and lay him on his back, eyes still fixed on me. As my vision steadied, I saw that it was Lewis, Piper's advisor. The small knife in his neck twitched with each of his heart-beats, but he hardly bled until Piper bent down and calmly retrieved his knife, unleashing a rhythmic spurting of blood.

I lurched forward and pressed my hand across the wound, looking frantically up at Piper. 'Stop. I know what he came here for.'

Kip snorted. 'I think that's pretty clear.'

I shook my head. 'No, but why he did it. It's about his niece, the girl they took.'

'He already asked about her, when you were questioned by the Assembly,' said Piper, watching with distaste as I crouched over Lewis.

Between my fingers the blood continued to pulse, and I was shocked at how hot it felt. Lewis's beard, sticky with blood, was no longer grey.

'Lewis. Can you hear me?'

He was pale. His unfocused eyes blinked with deliberate slowness.

'I'll do everything I can to find her, if she's alive. To stop what my twin's done. I promise. Can you hear me?'

His head had dropped to the side. Piper slid his boot beneath it and gently levered it up; when he removed his foot the head lolled back. Piper turned away. 'He's gone.'

I looked down at my hands, and at Lewis's wound, which

no longer bled. I was crying, and when I wiped my face I smeared it with blood.

'He would have killed you,' Kip pointed out.

'He betrayed me; betrayed the Assembly,' added Piper.

'I know.' I wrapped my arms around my knees, pulled them tightly to me.

'You're not hurt?' said Kip. I looked down at myself, my hands coated in blood, black around my fingernails.

'It's all his,' I said. The blood had soaked up my white sleeve, past the elbow.

'Are you going to make a habit of making deathbed promises to everyone who tries to kill you?' asked Kip. 'I only ask because that could be quite a lot of promises.'

Piper turned from where he was bending over the dead guard. 'Two men just died, Kip. One of my Assemblymen, and a good watchman. It's not a time to joke.'

'Four,' I said.

Kip and Piper looked at me.

'Not two. Four people just died.'

*

From then on, we were even more closely guarded. When I woke up screaming, three days later, two watchmen were in the room before Kip could even get across to my bed. One of them knocked him to the ground, and it wasn't until several torches had been lit that the guards could be persuaded to retreat. Kip, rubbing his cheek where the guards had pressed him against the flagstones, sat on the edge of my bed.

'I need to see Piper,' I said to the last guard before he locked the door. 'Send him now.'

'You can't tell me?' Kip asked quietly.

I shook my head, angry. 'This isn't about me choosing which one of you gets to hold my hand. This isn't just a bad dream. It's important.' I couldn't keep still. My eyes were racing from side to side, as if trying to memorise the script of my dream.

'I suppose it'd be too much to hope that you might have seen something good for a change?' he said, moving closer to me. My nightshirt had the faint tang of sweat, and my lips were dry. 'Like a really good breakfast,' he continued. 'Or a brilliant apricot harvest this year – that kind of thing.'

My laugh was only one quick exhalation, but my body relaxed a little and leant into his. He kissed my shoulder, but I shook my head. 'I need to concentrate.' I closed my eyes, my lips moved rapidly but in silence.

'You can't tell me?'

I shook my head. 'I need to concentrate,' I said again.

We stayed like that until Piper burst in, barely minutes later.

I stood before he could even speak. 'They're coming. The Alphas. And I know when, and how.'

Without looking behind him, Piper aimed a forceful kick at the open door at his back, slamming it closed. His hand was pressed to his lips.

In a whisper, he said, 'I thought you said it wasn't like that. Not dates and details.'

I shook my head, eyes still jerky and unfocused.

'I saw it. I could see the moon, and how full –'

'Then don't speak. Don't say it – don't tell me.'

'You don't understand. I saw everything.' I rubbed at my eyes. I felt as though I could hardly see Piper and Kip, peering as I was through the haze of smoke and blood that had filled my dream.

This time it was Kip who hushed me. 'What are you doing?'

'Exactly.' Piper was whispering, fervent. 'This is your bargaining chip – don't give it away.'

Kip looked warily at Piper, then back to me. 'He's right – you need to use this. Tell the Assembly you'll give them what you've seen, if they let you go. That you'll send word back when we're off the island.'

I dropped my voice but it was more of a hiss than a whisper. 'Listen to me. This is too important to play games. You need to tell the Assembly now. You need to start planning how to evacuate. They'll be coming, on –'

Piper pressed his hand to my mouth, looking pleadingly at Kip. 'Stop her. If she tells me I have to act.'

'Look at me,' Kip said. He brushed aside Piper's hand, and placed his own on the side of my face. He bent down so his own face was close to mine. 'They'll never let you go.'

I shook off his hand, jerking backwards. 'It doesn't matter.' I was no longer whispering. 'Piper, listen to me. Get these people off the island. Do it now. They're coming at the full moon.'

All three of us turned to the window, where a pregnant moon loomed.

'Two nights. Maybe three,' said Piper.

'Two,' I said.

'Our defences?'

I shook my head distractedly. 'No good. The crater hides you from the coast, but once they've found the island, it's just a trap. You've always known that. They'll come from the north at first, with so many men. You can't stop them.'

'Tell me what else you see.'

I closed my eyes, concentrating on translating the noise

and blur of the visions into words. 'Fire in the streets, people trapped in the windows. Blood on the stones.'

'So they're coming to kill, not just take prisoners?'

'That doesn't make any sense,' said Kip. 'They'll have Alphas dropping dead all over the place. There'll be resistance from their own people.'

I screwed my eyes more tightly shut. The images refused to slow down, refused to submit to sense or order. 'They'll take some people away, on boats,' I said. 'The others, they'll kill.' I looked up at Piper. 'Kip's right – it's crazy. You can't have been expecting that?'

'I wish I could say I wasn't. But if they find us, they'll be coming to make a statement. They want to put an end to Omega resistance, even if it costs them Alpha lives.'

I nodded. 'That's what it's like, in the vision. These people – they're so angry. They know they're killing Alphas too, but they don't care. Or, they do care, but they blame us, as if it's one more burden we place on them.'

Piper strode to the window. 'Ring the bells,' he shouted down to the guard below. 'Now.'

At Haven, a huge bell in the tower used to sound before the opening and closing of the city's gates. And in Wyndham, the few times I'd been on the ramparts, sounds of bells had drifted up from the city below from time to time. But this was nothing like those melodic sounds I remembered. First there was a single bell, the huge one in the tower. It didn't just disturb the dawn silence, it shattered it. A catastrophe of noise, so deep that my lungs reverberated with each bass strike. It was answered by other bells, all through the fort. Then, in the city below, people responded with shouts from house to house, and the banging of pots and pans. A metallic thrash and clatter, urgent and tuneless. It was like the time at New Hobart when one of the children had run through the kitchen and upset a stack of pans. But this went on for minutes, until the whole crater was a bowl of sound.

'They'll start evacuating right away,' Piper shouted over the noise. 'I have to go – to explain to the Assembly. And to prepare the guards.'

'We can't fight them.'

Piper nodded. 'They'll come with double the soldiers we could ever muster. Better trained, better fed. Better armed, in every sense.' He glanced at his left shoulder with a quick grin. 'But our guards know the territory. We'll be able to hold them off a while.'

'That's not what I meant,' I said. 'Not that we can't fight them because they'll win. We can't fight them because there isn't any winning. Each of them you kill means one of us, somewhere, drops dead too.'

'But it's the same for them. All we can concern ourselves with now is this island. What happens here, when they come for us.'

'Then you're only ever looking at half the story.'

He shook his head. 'This is the story I'm responsible for. These people, here. If the Council's found us, we can't hope to defend the island. All of that's over now. But we can buy time to get as many people off as possible.'

'Do you have enough boats for them all?' asked Kip.

'Nowhere near. You're talking about arrivals over decades and decades. Our fleet's small as it is, and two of the largest ships are still out west. If we load the boats as fully as we dare, it'll still take two sailings, just to evacuate those who can't fight.'

'How long will that take?'

He was already looking out the window, reading the wind in the trees silhouetted at the crater's edge. 'If we're lucky, we could have the second load off the island in two days.

But the same wind that helps us on the way back will help the Council's fleet too. And even if we evacuate those who can't fight, that leaves hundreds more.'

Again I saw what my dream had shown me. The blood. They were coming for me, and the island would bleed.

Piper left without saying anything else to me. Just before he pulled the door shut, he turned back to Kip.

'You,' he said to Kip. 'Watch her. Don't let her do anything stupid.'

From our locked room we watched the island mobilise. By the time the sun was fully risen, the ringing of the bells had been replaced by chimes and clashes from the armoury and the blacksmith, as swords and axes were gathered, sharpened, distributed. Blue-clad guards carried beams to reinforce the gates, and the sound of hammers pounded the morning air as shutters on the lower levels were nailed closed. And through all this activity, the city drained of people. First went the children and the elderly, and those whose mutations left them unable to fight. Some were carried, others leaned on canes or crutches. There was no time, nor space, for belongings, only hastily bundled parcels of food and water flasks. No time, either, for crying – even the youngest children moved quickly and quietly, hurried along by the guards who marshalled the crowds. Those who had to wait for the second sailing were led into the fort, which would shelter them if the Council's fleet arrived before ours returned.

It was an intricate choreography in which Kip and I had no role. We stood for hours, hand in hand, watching the exodus. Our sense of helplessness was only compounded by what I'd seen in my vision. It was hard to imagine that all the diligent preparations unfolding beneath us could change what I had already witnessed, and what I kept seeing when

I closed my eyes. Flames reflected on a blood-pooled floor. The thickening of smoke in tunnels and narrow streets.

We watched as three guards erected a crude flagpole at the crater's rim.

'Hardly compatible with the whole "secret refuge" thing,' Kip pointed out.

'That doesn't matter now. They're coming. They know how to find us.'

I thought of the tapestries in the Assembly Hall. In other battles, perhaps people had fought beneath embroidered flags, made of rich fabrics. This attempt was tatty in comparison: a bedsheet with the Omega symbol emblazoned on it with the same tar the sailors used to mend their hulls. It was lashed at two corners to an old ship's mast. The guards were struggling to plant the pole firmly in the high wind.

'In the face of imminent invasion, Piper's got them spending time redecorating?'

'It's not a waste of time,' I said. 'It'll be the first thing the Council fleet sees, when they come into sight. It sends them a message.'

'More effective than the subversive goats, at least,' said Kip.

The guards had wedged the pole into a crack in the rocks and were piling stones high about the base.

'It won't last more than a couple of days in these winds,' said Kip.

There was no answer, just the sound of the makeshift flag slapping at the wind. Neither of us needed to say what we both knew: in a couple of days, it would be over.

CHAPTER 23

There were footsteps on the stairs, and the sound of Piper conferring with the guard, before the door was unlocked.

'They're gone,' he said. 'The first fleet. The youngest of the children, and the most incapacitated. Plus a handful of adults, to help them on the mainland.'

'And now?'

'We wait.'

I'd never before listened as carefully to the wind as I did in the night that followed. For those waiting hours, with each gust I pictured the mismatched fleet racing its way to the mainland. Somewhere, too, was the Council's fleet, with its cargo of death. I was afraid to sleep, but afraid not to, in case a dream might reveal something useful. It didn't matter, in the end: the vision came to me while I lay on the brink of sleep, Kip's whole body cupping mine. The fleet of ships cutting resolutely across the horizon. They were bigger than any ship I'd seen – many times bigger than the largest of the island's fleet. On their decks were lashed clusters of smaller boats, hulls upward, like unhatched eggs. It wasn't the size that was terrifying, though. It was the contents of the first boat.

I shouted for the guard to bring Piper. Although it was still long before dawn, he came within minutes.

'Their boats – they're too big to get through the reef. But they have smaller boats on board, to launch.'

'Landing craft.' Piper nodded. 'That will slow them down, at least for the last few miles. And the reef itself – how will they know the way through?'

'I'd thought maybe they'd have a map – that they'd managed to bribe someone, or torture them. But they won't need one.' I closed my eyes, remembering the presence I'd sensed. 'She's there – The Confessor. On one of the ships, guiding them.'

'She can find us without a map, like you did?' said Kip.

I nodded, though it felt strange to compare our own dinghy's haphazard journey with the decisive advance of that fleet. It wasn't simply the fact that she would guide the fleet to the island. It was the knowledge that she would be here herself. I hated the thought of her setting foot on this place. Piper had said to me, once, that our arrival had changed the island. But her arrival would surely be the end of it.

I heard my voice quaking. 'How much longer until our ships get back?'

'Not before noon,' he said, 'for the fastest of them, and that's if all's gone well. It's not just getting to the mainland and back again – they have to find a safe landing spot, out of view, and unload the evacuees. We're talking about hundreds of children, and the most crippled and slowest of us.'

'And the two ships out west, looking for Elsewhere? You said they were our fastest.'

'If I could call them back, don't you think I would've done?' He looked down. For a moment I saw him as he might look when alone, in his tiny makeshift room, away from expectant eyes: deflated, tired. He rubbed his forehead with his palm, and spoke quietly. 'They've been gone for a month. We don't even know if they're still out there.'

I closed my eyes, scanning the sea for the island's returning fleet, or for those ships that had gone west. Nothing. Only the knowledge that the Council fleet was drawing closer. The prospect of that was imposing enough, but The Confessor's presence made it incalculably worse. If she arrived before our own fleet returned, the island would be no more than a trap. The remaining children, all those who couldn't fight, would stand no chance at all. Were there tanks enough yet, I wondered, for all of them?

At noon the wind brought me a vision, but the ships I saw felt distant, and irregular. Trying to see them was like squinting into the sun – all I could make out were silhouettes and glare. They were ships, all right, but whose? It was another hour or two before details became apparent. A fishing net lying tangled on the floor of a boat. A hull painted in yellow and blue stripes. A sail so full of patches that it looked like a quilt.

'It's our fleet,' I said to Kip. 'They're close.'

We called the guard to send for Piper. 'Get them down to the harbour,' I told him while he was still shutting the door behind him. 'Our ships have come back. They've unloaded the first evacuees. They're almost here.'

He shook his head. 'I've had the lookout posts sending word every half hour. Still nothing.'

'They might not be in sight yet,' said Kip, 'but if she can sense them, they're coming.'

'There's time,' I said. 'If you act now, you can get the next load of people off the island. Get them down there and ready to board as soon as the ships arrive.'

He shook his head again. 'If the Council fleet arrives first, we'll have our most vulnerable completely undefended at the harbour. There's no shelter down there – we might as well tie them up with a bow for your brother's soldiers. Think of who we're talking about. Some of them can't walk, let alone scramble back through the tunnels quickly. They'd never make it back inside the crater, let alone the fort.'

'That's why you've got to get them down there and ready to board now. It'll take time. If you wait until our ships are in sight, it'll be too late. They won't get away.'

'At least they'd have the shelter of the fort.'

'You know as well as I do that the fort's a trap. The whole island is, once the Council fleet arrives.'

'We can defend the fort, at least for a while,' he said. 'Until I know for sure our fleet will be here before theirs, I can't take the risk.'

'She does know for sure,' said Kip, but Piper was already halfway out the door.

'Wait,' I called after him. 'Is there a ship with blue and yellow stripes?'

He halted in the doorway.

'The *Juliet*,' he said. He dared the start of a smile. 'You saw it, in the vision? It was that specific?'

I nodded. 'Get them down to the harbour.'

He didn't say anything, but only minutes after he'd locked the door, we saw the remaining civilians begin to file from the fort. They were the older children, and more of those unable to fight. They moved more hesitantly than the first evacuees. The children were holding hands, and the adults had bowed heads. No fleet awaited them yet in the harbour – only the hope of one, and the fear of another. I watched them go, and wondered whether I was sending them to a slaughter.

An hour later, the bells rang again. For a moment, my heart rang in my chest as loudly as the bells themselves. But this time the noise from the tower was different: not the cascade of clanging that had sounded the day before, but three single chimes, clear and high. From the courtyard, we could hear the soldiers whooping. Cries were passed down from the sentry posts: *Nearing the reef now. All of them, in full sail.* Kip and I didn't join the cheering, but I turned my head to his shoulder and let out a breath that shook my whole body.

Piper returned, an hour or two later.

'I'm moving you,' he said with no preliminaries. 'This room's too close to the outer perimeter.'

'The second load – they're away?' I asked.

'The last of them should be clear of the reef shortly.' There was relief in his voice, but his eyes were grave. We were on our own now: there was no chance of a third sailing. The full moon was already rising in the late-afternoon sky. It gleamed above the Omega flag on the crater's edge.

'Are there any boats left?'

'Nothing big enough to make the crossing,' he said. 'We've stashed them all in the caves east of the harbour – but it's only the rafts and wherries, and a few of the smallest dinghies. The boats the children learn to sail in.'

There were no children on the island now. Would children's voices ever be heard again in the hidden city?

'Pack up your things,' he went on. 'If they penetrate the fort, I need you secure.' He gave us only a minute to bundle our few belongings into a rucksack, then tossed us a pair of hooded cloaks, like those worn by the watchmen. 'Wear these. After what happened with Lewis, it's not safe for you to be seen.'

He escorted us himself, pausing for a whispered exchange

with the guard at our door. With the cloak's hood up, my view was a series of curtailed glimpses. A blacksmith with a load of axes hoisted on his shoulder clattered past. Guards rushed along the corridors. When one young watchman stopped to salute Piper, he growled, 'No time for that nonsense – get to your post.' It was dark in the lower levels of the fort, where the windows had been boarded shut. Only the arrow-slits allowed slants of light in. At one, we passed an archer with no legs, sharpening arrows as he waited on an upturned crate.

The room Piper finally showed us into was small – a compact chamber part-way up the tower, with a narrow window mounted high in the curved stone wall.

Piper saw me eyeing the room's thick-beamed door.

'Don't even think about it,' said Piper. 'See those?' He gestured at the barrels stacked high against one wall. 'This is where we store the watchmen's wine rations. It's got the solidest lock in the whole fort.'

Remembering Lewis, I didn't know whether I should feel secure or trapped.

'If the fort falls, I'll come for you. If anyone else tries to get in the door, even one of the Assembly, signal from the window. Wave one of the cloaks.'

'You'll be down there?' I looked out at the courtyard below. 'Not in the Assembly Hall?'

'Up there, giving orders, while I can't even see what's going on? No. I'll be at the gate with the other guards.'

I stood on tiptoes to peer out the window, which looked over the courtyard and the main gate, and the streets beyond. Guards were already waiting at their posts. On the parapet encircling the courtyard, some squatted, rocking slightly on their haunches. Near the reinforced gate, others paced. One woman tossed her sword lightly from hand to hand.

'We can fight,' Kip said. 'Let us out, and we can help.'

Piper cocked his head. 'My guards are trained. Skilled. You think you could just pick up a sword for the first time and be a hero? This isn't some bard's story – you'd be a liability out there. Anyway, I can't risk Cass. It's not just the Council soldiers who might attack you.'

Again I pictured Lewis. The blood running off the handle of Piper's knife, as it juddered with Lewis's blood.

Kip was about to speak, but the bells sounded again, the clashing warning alarm of two days prior. From this high in the tower, the very stones seemed to throb with the sound. My teeth felt loosened in their gums, vibrating with the clamour of the bells.

'They're here,' said Piper. Within seconds the slamming of the door was added to the bells' din. When he'd locked the door, the tiny room felt overstuffed, bursting with the smell of wine and the clashing of the bells.

We dragged one of the wine barrels to beneath the window, knelt on it together, heads pressed close so that we could both peer out into the lowering night.

We'd waited two days for the Council fleet's arrival, but the few hours between the bells and the first Council soldier cresting the top of the crater felt even longer. As we waited, I tried to picture what would be going on outside the caldera: the fleet drawing near, the landing craft being launched and navigating the reef. The first encounters with the island's guards, down at the harbour. But through the double-darkness of night and distance, I couldn't get any clear visions, only fragments. A black sail being furled. Oars slicing water. A torch held at the prow of a boat, its flame reflected in the waves.

The first news we had of the skirmishes at the harbour was when the injured guards began to emerge from the tunnel opposite the city. By the light of torches we saw them, bloodied and limping, being helped back to the fort. Shortly afterwards there was a mass retreat from the harbour, several hundred of our guards pouring from the tunnel and falling back to posts in the city itself. Then, perhaps twelve hours after bells had foretold the island's doom, Kip and I caught our first glimpse of the Council soldiers. It was early morning. Movement on the crater's southern edge drew our attention: a few of our guards struggling to hold back a phalanx of red-clad soldiers. At the same time, the first tunnel must have fallen, and the Council soldiers penetrated the crater itself.

Piper had said, *This isn't some bard's tale*, and what unfolded on the island that day made it clear. When bards sang of battles, they made it sound like a kind of dance. As if there would be a beauty to the combat, a musical clashing of swords while soldiers parried to and fro, and individual fighters distinguished themselves with feats of skill and daring. But what I saw allowed no room for such things. It was all too cramped, too quick. Jabs with elbows and knees. Sword-butts shattering cheek-bones. Teeth rolling like dice on the stones. No battle-cries or slogans – just grunts, swearing, and shouts of pain. Knife handles slippery with blood. The arrows were the worst. They were not light, airy things. They were thick, and fired so fast that I saw a Council soldier pinned through his shoulder to a wooden door. Each arrow made a tearing noise as it flew over the courtyard wall, as if ripping open the very sky. We were perhaps forty feet above the courtyard, but the smell of blood reached the window, seeping into air already thick with the scent of wine. I wondered if I would ever be able to lift a cup of wine to my mouth again without tasting blood.

Our guards were fighting to kill. I saw one plant her axe so deeply in the neck of a Council soldier that she had to brace her foot against his fallen body and heave at the handle three times to free the blade. A dwarf guard reached up to slice open the stomach of a soldier, his insides unspooling into his hands as he clutched at them. Arrows found their way into chests, stomachs, eyes. For me, each was a twofold dying. With each Alpha soldier killed, I felt, and sometimes saw, an Omega on the mainland fall. A soldier beneath me took a sword blow that left his face shattered like a broken plate. I closed my eyes and saw a woman with blonde hair fall down on a gravel path, dropping a bucket of water. A Council soldier climbing one of the fort's outer walls took an arrow in her chest, but when I flinched and closed my eyes I saw a man in a bath slip wordlessly beneath the water. Each of the deaths had its echo, and I saw them all, until only Kip's hand, clutching mine on the windowsill, could keep me from screaming.

Despite our guards' willingness to kill, the Council soldiers had numbers on their side, as well as the physical strength of their unhampered bodies. Our one-armed guards could handle a sword or shield, but not both; the legless or lame archers could kill unerringly from a distance, but when the Council soldiers gained the outer wall and came upon them, they couldn't flee in time. When pressed in close combat, the Council soldiers were killing too, but it quickly became clear that they were taking prisoners whenever possible. Already ten or more of our guards had been dragged, injured, back to the Council lines. Where one bleeding guard had been hauled by her legs, a serrated smear of blood marked the road. High on the crater's lip we could see the silhouettes of longbows, but the Council archers were holding back, avoiding the indiscriminate killing dealt at a distance. All the arrows came from within the fort.

'I can't watch,' said Kip, stepping back from the window. I envied him that. I knew that if I turned aside, the images would be there anyway, some of them already familiar from my earlier visions.

'Can you see her?' he asked.

'The Confessor? They won't risk her in the fighting – she's much too valuable. But she's out there – maybe on the fleet still. I can feel her.' Her presence was as thick in the air as the scent of blood and wine. But she was holding back – her malignant presence felt like a storm about to break over the island. 'She's waiting.' The worst of it was the calm of her anticipation. I could feel no nervousness in her – only a deadly patience. She had probably seen the same outcome that I had. So she waited for the island to fall, observing it with all the detachment of someone listening to a bard's tale that they've heard before.

In the chaos of the fighting at the city's edge I couldn't distinguish Piper, but periodically I saw him disentangle himself from the battle, and drop back to the courtyard where he consulted with the senior guards and Assembly members gathered there. Over the messy sounds of the fighting, his voice could be heard, shouting orders. *More archers to the south side, to cover the tunnel entrance. Water to the West Gate – now.* As the hours passed, one phrase reached us more than any other: *Draw back.* Again and again we heard it, Piper's voice increasingly hoarse as the hours of fighting devoured the day. *Draw back from the west tunnel. Draw back from the market square. Draw back to the third wall.*

The steep crater meant that sunset in the city was always rapid. First the horizon above the crater's western edge was tinged pink, as if the blood on the streets was staining the sky. Then, quickly, it was dark, the fighting only illuminated by the patches of fire that were spreading upwards from the city. The battle line had moved close to the fort itself now. The red-clad figures had overrun the eastern half of the city, and most of our guards were mustered within the fort's outer perimeter, although there was still intermittent fighting in the street beyond.

In the growing darkness, the figures outside had been reduced to flame-backed silhouettes. I had no chance of making out Piper, and hadn't heard his voice for some time. I'd almost convinced myself that he'd been taken, when he unlocked our door, shutting it quickly behind him.

He seemed uninjured, though his face was spattered with blood, a fine spray across one cheek that reminded me of the freckles that Zach used to have.

'I have to hand you over to the Assembly,' he said.

'You're taking orders from them?' said Kip. 'Aren't you in charge?'

'That's not how it works.' Piper and I had spoken in unison. He looked at me for a moment, then turned back to Kip. 'I might be the leader, but I work for them. Even if I wanted to, I can't counteract their decision.'

Kip stepped between me and Piper. 'But it's too late. Even if the Assembly kills her, and gets rid of Zach, it won't stop the Council. It won't stop what's happening out there.'

'The Assembly doesn't want to kill you.'

To anyone else, those might have been words of comfort. To me and Kip, having seen the tanks, and the cells, Piper's words snatched the air from the room.

'Kip's right, though,' I said. 'Even if you hand us over, they still won't spare the island. You know they've been looking for you for years – since long before we arrived.'

'You can't give her to the Council, after all she's done.' Kip was shouting. 'Without her, you'd have had no warning. You wouldn't have had the chance to get anyone away from here, let alone two sailings.'

I couldn't hear his words without thinking of what else I might be responsible for. Had I drawn The Confessor here? Had I brought this upon the island? None of us spoke it, but the thought rang in the room, as strident as the island's warning bells.

'Would you?' I said to Piper. 'If you could choose. Would you still hand us over?'

The city below us was burning, and he had come straight from battle, but this was the first time I'd seen him look nervous.

'I've already asked too much of these people. They've stood back while the children, the old, and the sick have been sent away. They're witnessing the end of everything we've built here, over decades. You could be our only bargaining chip. How can I refuse to hand you over?'

'This island is a place of refuge for Omegas,' I said quietly. 'That includes me and Kip. If you hand us over, today won't just be the end of the island. It'll be the end of what it stood for.'

'Look out the window, Cass,' said Piper. 'Can you tell me to stand on principles while my people are bleeding?'

It wasn't the shouting that frightened me, but the phrase 'my people'. It was like the night when Kip and I had watched the dance through the wall of the barn. Here we were again, on the wrong side of the wall. Pursued by the Alphas, rejected by the Omegas.

Slowly, Piper pulled from his belt a long knife, three times the size of the nimble throwing knives that always hung at his back. It glinted sharply in the torchlight, though

I flinched when I saw the blood clotted around the base of the blade.

'The Assembly must know you had us guarded, to protect us from them. Why would they trust you to take us to them now?'

He was still weighing the knife in his hand.

'They don't. They sent six men to collect you.' His smile seemed incongruous on his bloodied face. 'But I didn't tell them that I'd moved you. They've sent the guards to your old room.'

With one flick of his arm, Piper spun the knife so that the handle was proffered to me.

'It'll buy us a few minutes, at most. But I can't spare anyone to escort you. And even if I could, there's no one I can trust at this point. Can you find your way to the coast without being seen?'

I nodded. 'I think so.'

'She can,' said Kip.

'The Council's taken the two largest tunnels, and Simon's brigade is only just holding them off at the entrance to the north tunnel. That's bad news for the city, but good for you – they're pouring through the tunnels rather than scaling the outside. If you go over the top of the crater, while it's dark, it's your best chance.'

'And then?'

'The children's boats, in the caves east of the harbour. We've never made the crossing in anything so small, but they're not much worse than the bathtub you arrived in. If the weather stays fair, it gives you a chance.'

I took the knife silently, and the scabbard that he unhooked from his belt. As I slid the bloodied knife into its sheath, I said, 'You'll never rule the island once they know you've let me go.'

Piper laughed soberly. 'What island?'

I passed Kip the knife. He threw it into the rucksack, along with the few possessions we'd brought with us from the other room: a water flask, some leftover food and a blanket.

I faced Piper by the door. Even as I was pulling my jumper over my head I didn't stop talking. 'The north tunnel will fall not long after midnight. Don't rely on it. And watch out for the fire – it'll spread fast.' He reached for my arm, straightened my bunched sleeve, left his hand there. I continued. 'Their archers will use flaming arrows soon, on the fort itself. That's how they get the main gate down in the end.'

He squeezed my shoulder. 'I'll get the rest of these people off the island.'

I shook my head. 'You don't need to lie to me,' I said quietly. 'I've seen it already.'

He met my gaze, nodded. 'Once you're through the reef, don't sail south-east, the way you came. Sail north-east, to make landfall where the Miller River reaches the coast. Then head east, directly inland, towards the Spine Mountains. You won't see the mountains from the coast, but you'll feel it, right? It's the biggest river in the area, the only one to reach the sea on that stretch of coast.' I nodded. 'We have people in that region,' he said. 'We'll find you. If we make it off the island, if there's still a resistance, then we'll need you.'

I took his hand from my shoulder, but held it in my own for a moment before turning away.

We wore the cloaks again, but getting through the fort itself was straightforward. The upper levels were nearly empty except for archers at the arrow slits, who didn't even turn as we ran past. As we neared the courtyard level the corridors were crowded with the injured and those caring for them, but nobody looked twice at two more blue cloaks making their way through the crowd. When we emerged into the courtyard, we saw the Council's burning arrows, painting streaks of flame on the night, and we stuck close to the wall. The main fighting had almost reached the courtyard gate – only the fort's outer walls remained defended, and already the arrows had done their work, and several fires were glowing within the walls. We made it out of the courtyard just in time, in the wake of a brigade of reinforcements rushing out the side gate. Only when we reached the last checkpoint in the outer perimeter did anyone query us, and even that was just a shout from one of the guards manning the gate. 'To the north tunnel?' he asked, leaning towards us, his flaming torch held high. We kept our heads down.

'Yes,' Kip replied. 'Reinforcements to Simon's brigade.'

The guard grunted. 'Two of you? It'll take more than that. They're saying it's about to fall.' He spat on the ground, his spittle blackened with smoke, before lifting the bolt and bar and waving us through.

Beyond the fort, we could hear the sounds of battle from our right, where the fighting was concentrated at the mouth of the north tunnel. We headed uphill, skirting the fort's outer perimeter and sticking to the narrow streets. At one point we had to turn back when the way ahead ended in flames; another time we slipped into a doorway, mercifully unlocked, and squatted for a breathless minute while a skirmish passed us, two retreating guards harried by three Council soldiers. As we crouched against the inside of a stranger's door we could hear the clash of sword on sword, each strike followed by an involuntary grunt. The street was so narrow that the sword swings thudded against the wooden houses on either side. The scuffle passed in moments, the shouts chasing one another downhill. When we creaked open the door, the moonlight showed a fresh slash in the wood, inches deep, and a bloodied handprint on the white-painted doorframe.

It must have been almost midnight when we reached the crater's edge, and the encircled night sky opened to the sea's expansive horizon. To the east, the moon was fully fattened now, but dulled by the smoke rising from the city. Occasional cries from the battle still reached us, and I wondered if Piper's voice was amongst them. Below us, tucked into the island's western edge, the harbour was crammed with the sleek, dark landing craft of the Council's fleet – so thickly packed in the tiny harbour that it looked possible to walk across it by stepping from boat to boat. To the east, beyond the mile or two of sea churned by the reef, we could see the fleet moored, the huge sails furled.

The scramble down the outside of the island would have been impossible without the full moon. There were several paths that zigzagged their way down to the coast, but the islanders relied on the tunnels rather than those narrow, circuitous trails, deliberately kept small so they couldn't be seen from the water. We avoided them too, for fear of encountering soldiers from either side, and instead took our chances on the steep, jagged rock. In places it was so sharp that to grab at it for balance was like grasping at blades; at others it was so thickly coated with bird droppings that any purchase was impossible. All my concentration couldn't steer us entirely clear of the fissures and crevasses that opened in the slick stone. We were climbing more often than walking, pressed so tightly against the rock that my cheek was grazed, and the straps of the rucksack that I wore kept snagging on the claws of the rockface. Even when we could walk, the way was so sheer that twice I fell, catching hold just in time to stop myself skidding down to the unforgiving rocks below. It would almost have been comical, to have escaped the battle and died from something as mundane as a fall. But the prospect felt too real to be amusing, as we crept our way down the island's carapace.

By the time we were close to the sea, a light wind had picked up, and dawn was beginning to threaten the darkness to the east. I had no trouble finding the caves, half a mile east of the harbour, though they weren't easy to reach. They weren't caves, strictly, but a series of shallow clefts in the rock, easily visible from above but concealed from the sea itself by the way the broken sheets of rock jutted from below. They were only twenty yards above the water, so close that seaspray made the rock even more treacherous, and with the dawn coming we felt exposed as we scuttled down to them. Each moment the light grew, we became more careless with our bodies – we moved so quickly we might have been fleeing the light itself. From here we couldn't see the harbour packed with Council boats, but the large ships were still indistinct at the distant reef's edge, and knowing that The Confessor was nearby added to the sense of exposure.

The boats not deemed safe for the crossing had been hurriedly stashed out of sight there, some stacked atop one another, others jammed on their sides into narrowing crevices. A few tiny, rickety dinghies, but mainly the children's rafts and wherries, or the canoes used for fishing within the reef itself. We opted for the smallest craft with a sail we could find – a narrow-hulled dinghy with flaking grey paint and a mud-coloured sail.

One of the island's defences was the difficulty of landing anywhere other than the concealed harbour, and we quickly learned that launching from anywhere else wasn't much easier. We had no hope of carrying the boat down those twenty yards of near-vertical rock. We tried lowering it by the rope fastened to its front, but it was too heavy and, after a few scraping yards, it skidded down the slickened stone so fast that the rope scorched our hands. Kip managed, at least, to hang on to the tail of the rope, and the boat landed the right way up, and wasn't impaled on one of the rocks that stabbed from the waves below. We tied the rope around Kip's waist and followed, clinging to the glass-slick rock. After the first few yards, the rock was colonised by mussels. The sharp shells shredded our fingers but at least gave us purchase. There wasn't enough slack in the rope, so each time the small waves moved the boat, Kip was jerked outwards and downwards, towards the waiting rocks. He managed it, though, finally getting close enough to jump into the boat. It was me who slipped the final few feet and ended up in the pulsing water.

Before the splash had even subsided, the pack on my back was lugging me down with the weight of the soaked blanket and the water flask, and when I kicked out to try to regain the surface, the rocks answered with their teeth. Kelp insinuated itself around my bleeding legs, and all I could think of was The Confessor's interrogations, the tentacles of her mind wrapping themselves around my thoughts and dragging me down. It was that memory, as much as the water closing above me, that sent me into panic.

Kip's hand found me, hauling me upwards by one of the rucksack's shoulder straps and holding me up until I'd calmed myself enough to peel off the bag and pass it up to him. The boat was so tiny that he had to lean against the far side to counterbalance my wet weight as I hauled myself over the side.

Kip slid the oars into the oarlocks and shoved the rucksack under the seat. For a minute I stood, balancing, the salt water making my wounds stream pink, and looked up at the island. From here it looked huge and empty. But smoke was still rising from the crater, the island's cupped hands full of blood and fire.

Kip reached over and steadied me as I stepped back to join him on the central seat.

We moved out quickly, in the opposite direction to the Council's massed fleet, and into the sharp embrace of the reef.

CHAPTER 24

I didn't bother to hide my crying from Kip. He'd witnessed me crying from nightmare visions; grimacing as I ate raw marsh-shrimps; shouting with fury on the island. But this, the sobs convulsing me as I rowed, was new. At least he didn't say anything, or try to comfort me. He just rowed, following my directions even when my crying rendered them barely intelligible. We made our way north through the lacework of half-submerged rocks, putting as much distance as possible between us and the fleet at anchor at the reef's eastern edge. The intricacies of the reef were easier to negotiate in the relatively calm sea, but finding our way still required all my focus, and put an end to the crying. Once we'd emerged into open sea we put up the small sail, with less fumbling than on the first journey. The wind was mild but steady enough to snap the sail taut. I retreated to the front of the boat and let the wind take us.

It wasn't for several hours that I felt able to speak.

'You know what the worst thing is?' I said. 'It's not even the people left on the island that I'm upset about. I mean, of course I'm thinking about them, and terrified for them.

For Piper too. But that wasn't why I was crying. It was for me – for us. Because we thought we'd found a place where we'd be safe. Where we could stop running.'

'And here we are again,' he said, nodding at the surrounding sea. 'I know.'

'And I'm not much of a seer, as things turn out. I should have seen it.'

'You did see it. If it weren't for you, those people wouldn't have had any warning at all. They'd all have been wiped out.'

'Not that. I meant from the start, when we were heading for the island: I should have seen that it wasn't the refuge I thought it would be. That I'd bring trouble to the island. That it wasn't going to be some kind of happy ending for us.'

'There isn't going to be a happy ending. Not for you, while Zach's still out there, making the rules. When are you going to realise that it's him who's the problem?'

I was staring down over the boat's front, into the grey-black water. 'And you? What about a happy ending for you?'

He shrugged. 'Not for me either. Not while Zach's pulling the strings.'

'Because you won't leave me? Or because Zach and his people must be looking for you too?'

Another shrug. 'Does it make any difference? Neither of those things is going to change.'

For a long time we were silent. The day swayed onwards with the monotony of the swell. Although it was autumn now, the sun was still hot enough to drive us under the blanket's shade for the midday hours. The wind at least was with us, bearing us, unresisting, north-east. When the dark settled, I moved back to the rear of the boat with Kip, and we spent the night huddled there, slipping between sleep and wakefulness.

The next day, watching the blank expanse of water, Kip and I hardly spoke. The sea ignored our silence, and the smack of the wooden base as it dropped into each trough was unrelenting. The boat was too small for swell this size, and even with the calm weather, the larger waves splashed over the sides and we took turns to bail. By the afternoon we were sunburnt and thirsty, the water flask empty. We couldn't complain, though, knowing what was facing those we had left on the island.

'It's not even the fighting that sickens me most. It's the thought that she's there – The Confessor.'

'Worse than what we saw from the window?' Kip was grimacing at the memory. 'Hard to imagine.'

I knew what he meant. But if I had a choice, I would take my chances against fire and swords rather than The Confessor's calm disassembling of my mind.

'That's what Piper was on about,' said Kip, when I tried to explain.

'The Confessor?'

'No,' replied Kip, tightening the sail, holding the rope with his teeth between pulls. 'You. About what you could do.'

I took the rope that he passed me and began wrapping it around the cleat. 'It's not like you to be echoing Piper.'

'It's not just him. It's this.' He looked around at the ocean surrounding us. 'Us being on the run again. And feeling like we'll always be on the run. But you could change the game. Not just react to Zach, but take the fight to him – do something to change the rules. You've got all this power –'

My snorted laughter interrupted him, as I gestured around us at the flaking boat, at the two of us, red-eyed and sunburnt. 'Oh yeah; look at me. I'm just brimming with power.'

'You're wrong. You're terrified of The Confessor, but that's what you could be for the Omegas, if you weren't so scared of fighting back against Zach. You think you're being self-effacing, or modest, but you're not. You're protecting him.'

'Don't ever say I could be like her.' I dropped the rope-end into the bottom of the boat.

'Of course not. You'd never do what she does. But you could do something. Why do you think she's coming after you? It's not just Zach securing his own safety. He probably couldn't justify all this manpower, just for that. It's you. They know what a risk you could be to them – a seer like you, on the loose.'

Kip leaned on the tiller, and the canvas caught the wind.

'That doesn't make me feel much better. The idea that they're all after me, rather than just Zach.'

He had to squint into the lowering sun to meet my gaze, but he did. 'I'm not trying to make you feel better. I'm trying to show you what you're capable of being.'

'There you go again, sounding like Piper.'

'Good. At least you've always taken him seriously.'

'What do you expect me to do?' I hated the sound of my own voice, shouting against the wind at Kip, but I couldn't stop myself. 'I thought I *was* being useful, doing something to stop Zach. It was me who dragged us to the island, because I thought I could help. And instead, I drew the Alphas to the island. I did that.'

I turned away, let the wind blow my hair over my face so he couldn't see me crying again.

'You still don't get it,' Kip said. 'The reason you're a threat to them. The real reason you could change everything. The Council, even Piper – they've got it wrong. They think you're dangerous because you're a seer, and because of your link to Zach. But they're all wrong. There are other seers, other Omegas with powerful twins. That's not it.'

He was shouting, his voice ragged in the gusting wind.

'It's because of how you see the world. How you don't see Alphas and Omegas as opposed. I tried to tell you back on the island – in the tower. That's what makes you different. They've been chasing you for all the wrong reasons, and Piper's been protecting you for the wrong reasons too. And they all think it's a weakness that you care about Zach – that you don't see it as us against them. But that's your strength – that's what makes you different.'

I didn't even look at him. 'I don't need another reason to feel different.'

*

The second night on the boat was worse than the first. Even this far from the island, the thought of The Confessor, and Kip's words, contaminated the salt-tinted air. I stayed awake, afraid that if I succumbed to sleep I'd have to revisit my dreams of the attack. When the light began flirting with the eastern edge of the night sky, I could hear from Kip's breathing that he was awake too, but we still didn't speak. For all of that day we were silent, except for my occasional muttered directions: *More that way. Straight on.* By noon we'd passed a few isolated outcrops, occupied only by the odd gull. The first glimpse of shore came a few hours later – not the high cliff country we'd embarked from weeks ago, but a more gradual, cove-moulded coast, slipping down to meet the sea.

I directed him along the coast for a while, until a wide cove mouth opened, dunes dense with reeds on each side. We dropped the sail and rowed for the final few hundred yards, and then right up into the cove itself, into which a broad river opened. Rather than row upstream, we pulled towards the bank, wading in to drag the boat clear of the river's current and up onto the sand. I knelt down and splashed water onto my face. It still had a salty tang, but was half-fresh and felt unspeakably soft after days of salt wind and sun.

'Do you think they're still holding the fort?' he asked.

Still kneeling at the water's edge, I shook my head. 'I think so,' I said. 'But they can't last much longer.'

'Will you know, when it falls?'

'I don't know,' I said, but we found out that night. We'd dragged the boat into the dune where the long pampas grass covered it from view. Then we headed upstream, beside the river, just far enough for the dunes to give way to forest and for the river water to be drinkable. As soon as there was enough cover we retreated into the trees to sleep. It was still light but we'd barely slept during the days on the boat and both of us were stumbling. We had no way to light a fire, so we just ate some of the ever-drier bread, drank the river water and lay down in the cover of a scrubby bush.

After midnight I woke with one short, strangled scream. Kip held me until my shaking had stopped.

'The island?' he asked.

I couldn't answer, but he knew. When he tried to kiss me I pushed him away. It wasn't that I didn't want to. More than anything I would have liked to bury myself in his embrace and let the comfort of our bodies distract me from my visions. But I couldn't bring myself to touch him. I didn't want to contaminate him, tainted as I was by what I'd seen. By what I'd done, leading The Confessor to the island.

Through each moment of that broken night I saw what was happening on the island. I saw the fort's huge gate succumb to flames. I saw the kicking in of doors, and the flaring of fires in the courtyard itself. I heard the metallic rasp of swords being drawn, and then striking. I saw the market square, where Kip and I had sat and eaten plums. I saw the cobbles slick with blood.

CHAPTER 25

The next morning I could still hardly speak. We sat on the riverbank chewing on the stub of the bread that we'd taken from the island. Its crust was now so hard it cut my gum. I kept watching downstream, where the river broadened out to the sea. The only remaining food was a few pieces of jerky we'd grabbed when we left our quarters, but Kip remembered the length of fishing-line in the boat, so before continuing upstream we headed back down to the dunes to collect it. It wasn't far, and soon Kip was kneeling in the sharp grass beside the boat, groping under the seat to unsnag the line where it had caught on something, while I turned again to watch the rivermouth and the widening sea beyond. That huge, calm expanse, the island not even a hint on the horizon, betrayed nothing of what I'd witnessed in my vision last night. I couldn't stop scanning the sea.

Perhaps that's why I never saw the man coming, though I sensed him just before I heard the sand slipping beneath his feet. I turned in time to see him racing at Kip from above, charging down the dune so fast that Kip had no chance to heed my warning shout. The man not so much tackled Kip as crashed into him, knocking them both to the ground. By the time I'd got within a few feet of them, the man had the fishing-line tight around Kip's neck from behind. From where I stood I could see how sharply the line cut into his flesh, the skin whitening around it. I stopped, raised my arms, but the man shouted at me anyway.

'I'll have his head off. You know I will.'

Kip didn't cry out. I didn't know if he could; already his neck above the fishing-line was bulging, his blood straining at the skin. On the left of his neck a swelling vein pulsed, fluttering madly, a moth against a window.

'Stop. We'll do whatever you want. Just stop.' I heard my own voice before I knew I was speaking.

'Damn right you'll do what I want.' The man stood behind Kip, who was still on his knees. He was bearded, a heavily built Alpha, with thick blond hair, and more hair tufting from the neck of his shirt. When he loosened the cord Kip gave an animal gasp. The line was still around his neck, but loose enough that I could see the indentation it had left on his skin. Hand at his throat, Kip stood slowly. He was still facing me, so he couldn't see the knife the man had drawn and was raising behind Kip's neck. I tried to keep my face calm so Kip wouldn't see what was coming. But the knife stayed raised, and the man spoke.

'You'll both come with me, and if either of you makes a move I don't like, he'll be slit like a fish.'

I nodded fast. The man waved me forward with his knife, his other hand still wrapped around the twisted fishing-line at the back of Kip's neck. 'Get forward where I can see you. Up the dune, that way, but if I see you taking off I'll have his blood in the sand before you've gone five steps.'

I nodded again and took a few steps up the dune, the loose sand slipping away underfoot, sending me stumbling.

I turned back, but could barely glance at Kip before the man shouted at me again. 'No need for you to be checking on your little mate, unless you want me to have his other arm off.' I turned away and scrambled further up the dune. I thought of my own knife, in the side pocket of the rucksack slung over my shoulder. But even as I tried to work my hand inconspicuously backwards into the bag's opening to grope for the knife, I sensed the futility of it. The man wasn't alone. I could feel someone else, in the long grass nearby, watching us.

The Alpha girl stepped out as we neared the top of the dune. She had her arms crossed at her chest, but the morning sun picked up the glint of sharp steel in both her hands. I was about ten feet beneath her, could hear Kip and the man stumble to a stop a few feet behind.

'You won't get them both back to town alive. Not like that.' The girl's tone was casual, conversational. She was tall, muscles visible under her dark skin, and wore a pack on her back. Her curly hair was pulled loosely back and twisted into a thick, high bun. She stood very still but seemed somehow relaxed, as if unconcerned with the tableau below her.

The man grunted and moved forward so that I could hear his breathing, and Kip's, behind me. I concentrated on my right hand, moving with awful slowness into the pocket of the bag. I could feel the knife handle, just, and tried to grasp it with the very tip of my fingers, without reaching backwards too obviously.

'I'm not sharing the reward with any stranger,' the man shouted up at the girl. 'You find your own freaks. Soldiers said there might be any number coming in.'

'So they did. But you won't be getting those two back alone.'

The man shouted again. 'I told you, I'm not sharing the reward, least of all with some cocky girl. I got no problems here. You move along now.'

While he was distracted I dared to reach deeper into the bag. I had the knife now, its steel handle cool in my shaking fist.

The girl turned away. 'I'll leave you to it.' She began moving across the ridge, calling out over her shoulder: 'Just as long as you don't mind that the one in front's already got a knife halfway out of that bag you didn't see fit to take off her.'

I felt the jolt before I'd even registered that the girl had turned. By the time I looked down at my hand, my knife was in the sand. Beside it, buried hilt-deep, was the knife the girl had thrown. A little of my blood was splashed on the sand where the throwing knife had knocked my own blade from my hand, but I didn't pause, just spun around to see Kip.

The man had jerked Kip back by the fishing-line noose. The knife-tip was lodged at Kip's throat, where his neck was once again bulging above the line's wire-tight embrace. I screamed, but the man didn't even look at me, keeping his eyes fixed on the girl on the ridge.

She spoke, still unruffled. 'You can slit his throat if you like, and I suppose there's a chance you could catch the other one, and pocket the payment for her at least. Soldiers won't be too happy, though, when they hear you killed one – you know the warnings about bringing them in alive. Or we can take them in together and score the reward for both of them, plus the bonus if the questioning turns up anything juicy.'

He grunted, but I saw the knife at Kip's neck recede slightly. I was watching so intently that I could see the pale hairs on the back of the man's hand, the dirtied leather wrapped around the handle of his knife. 'Minus your cut, I suppose?'

She shrugged. 'I'm not doing this for charity. You would've lost one or both if I hadn't shown up. I'll take half – but you can keep the bonus, if there is one. I won't be sticking around long enough for the questioning to be done.'

The man released the fishing-line and shoved Kip to the ground in front, where he landed on his knees, retching slightly. I ran to him and helped him free his neck from the tangled line. By the time I turned back, the man had picked up both knives from the sand and was examining the throwing knife carefully. 'That's a cute trick,' he said finally, stepping up to hand the knives to the Alpha girl.

He turned back to me and Kip, now standing up. 'I'm guessing you two won't be trying any more funny stuff with her around.' The girl didn't acknowledge him, just stood, tapping her knife against the knuckles of her left hand.

'Throw me the bag,' she said to me. I slipped it from my shoulder and tossed it on the ground where the knives had lain. The blood there reminded me to check my hand, but the bleeding had already slowed: just a small slice along my knuckle where her blade had nudged me as it dislodged my tenuous grasp on my knife.

The girl upended the rucksack, shook its contents loose: the blanket, the water flask that we'd refilled at the river that morning. I winced as the last of our jerky was dumped in the sand, then chastised myself: food was hardly our most pressing problem now. The girl scanned the items, then tossed me the empty bag. 'Pack it up and bring it along.'

'Why give it back to her?' grunted the man.

'I'm not throwing away useful stuff. You want to carry it?'

327

He turned and spat in the sand, and the girl nodded at me to continue bundling the things back into the rucksack. When I stood again, the girl pushed Kip forward to join me. 'You two stay in front, just like that. Keep it steady, and no talking, unless you want to catch a knife in the back of the neck.'

I tried to look at Kip without turning my head too obviously. There was still a raw mark encircling his neck, and his eyes were speckled with red where blood vessels had burst. I took his hand, felt him return my squeeze.

'Cute,' snorted the man from behind us.

Once we were over the top of the dune we could see the road below us. To the left it traced the back of the dunes, running parallel with the coast. To our right it led away from the sea to the higher country, lightly wooded. Descending the dune was easy, compared to climbing it, and twice the girl cautioned us to slow down, but when we reached the road, and the man shouted at us to go left, I reckoned our captors were at least ten steps behind us.

I kept looking straight ahead as I whispered to Kip. 'There's something about her. Something's not right.'

'You don't need to be a seer to tell that. Bright ideas?'

'I thought maybe I could fight him. But she's another story.'

Kip touched his throat. 'I wasn't that crazy about him either, to be honest.' He paused. 'Where are they taking us?'

'There's a big town, not far along here.'

'You can feel it?'

Aware of the scrutiny from behind us, I had to resist shaking my head. 'Sort of. But mainly it's the road – look at it. You don't get huge roads like this in the middle of nowhere – there's a decent-sized town around, and not too far away.'

He squinted at the road ahead. 'We could make a run for it, past that bend, when there are more trees about.'

'You've seen her do her thing with the knives. We'd be dead before we left the road.'

'If they get us back to the town, it's finished,' he said. 'Worse than dead, and you know it.'

'There's something else going on though. Something strange about her.'

'Apart from the whole bounty-hunter psycho thing?'

'It's something to do with Piper.'

Kip let go of my hand. 'Piper's not going to help us now. He's got his own problems.'

'Stop talking, I need to think.' I could feel Piper's presence – it was a certainty, as certain as the knowledge that he was still on the island. The road was smooth enough that I could close my eyes as I walked, to concentrate on what I was feeling. The moment I did, I realised what it was about the girl.

CHAPTER 26

I'd turned to tell Kip, so when I heard the man's shout I
thought for a moment he was yelling at me. But the sound
was cut short, and by the time we'd looked back, the man's
body was on the road, a dark patch spreading in the dust
beneath his neck.

The girl still had her knife in her hand. Looking down
with distaste, she knelt and wiped it, twice, on the back of
the dead man's shirt.

'Did you have to kill him?' I asked.

She tucked the knife back into her belt. 'You want him
spreading the word about who he's seen?'

'Couldn't we have tied him up or something?'

'He'd have been found. Or died slow, from thirst. I only
did exactly what you were planning to do when you were
going for your knife back there in the dunes. You should
be grateful.'

Kip looked from me to the girl and back again. 'Oh yeah,
really grateful. You only did it so you can claim the reward
yourself.'

'No.' I put a hand on his arm, addressed the girl. 'You're

331

Piper's twin.' I turned back to Kip. 'Remember the throwing knife?'

'The knife she was throwing at you five minutes ago? Hard to forget.'

The girl interrupted us. 'You two can argue later. For now you have to help me hide the body.' She grabbed one of the feet, began walking backwards, hauling the dead burden towards the road's edge. 'But you're right about my brother,' she said to me, without looking up.

I nodded, and bent to pick up the other leg. As the girl turned to look behind her, I saw several small knives hanging from her belt.

'What are you doing?' Kip shouted. 'It doesn't make any difference whose twin she is. She's an Alpha. Hasn't Zach taught you anything?'

The girl looked up. 'You'd better learn to keep your mouth shut about Cass's twin, if you want to keep the two of you safe.'

'Because you're all about our safety, you are. Cass – she threw a knife at you, for crying out loud.'

'I know.' I dropped the dead leg and held up my hand, showing him the neat slice on the knuckle, already clotted. 'I should have realised then – she could have put it right through my hand. But she barely scraped me – just knocked my knife out.'

'Why do it at all, if she's on our side?'

She laughed. 'I didn't like her chances of taking him on.' She glanced down at the body. 'And I didn't want to tackle him while he had a knife to your throat. So if you're done bitching, give us a hand to get this done.'

Kip looked at me, but I'd already picked up the man's leg again and, with the girl, was dragging him clear of the road. Kip called after us: 'What's your name, at least?'

'Zoe,' the girl said. 'And I know who you are. Now kick some dirt over that blood trail. They'll find it if they come with dogs, but it might buy us some time.'

We didn't dig a grave, just found a hollow by a fallen tree, the best we could manage in the sparse cover. Before we covered him with branches, Zoe checked his pockets and, with a flick of her knife, slit the cord holding a small leather purse around his neck.

'It wasn't enough to kill him – you have to rob him too?' asked Kip.

'If I hadn't killed him, you'd be in a Council cell by the end of today. And when they find him, we want it to look like a robbery.'

'You think they will? Find him, I mean?' I asked.

Zoe emptied the purse, pocketed the few coins, and threw the purse down next to the man. Crouching again, she freed the knife still clutched in his hand. 'Bound to. We're not half a day from the town. But with everything that's going on around here at the moment, they might not come looking right away.' She passed the knife to Kip, who grimaced, but tucked it into his belt.

'Everything that's going on?' he asked.

Zoe kicked some fallen brush over the body. 'Council soldiers came through yesterday. Put word out all along the coast that there might be Omegas landing by boat. Offered a bounty. Most of the Alphas for fifty miles are out there now looking for you.'

'Us in particular?'

Zoe shook her head. 'No – the bounty was for any Omegas on the move near the coast. This idiot' – she threw a final branch over the body – 'didn't know he'd struck it lucky. But Piper had told me about you, so I knew what to look for. Then, if I wasn't sure enough already, I recognised

Piper's knife,' she said, taking from her belt the one she'd knocked from my hand earlier. 'Wear it on your belt from now on,' she said, thrusting it back at me. 'If things are kicking off, you don't have time to fish it out of your bag.' She surveyed the partly concealed body a final time. 'Now we move.'

'Why didn't Piper tell us about you?' I asked as we followed her.

'Did you ever ask?'

'No. I don't know why.'

'I do. Because you'd assume an Alpha wouldn't have anything to do with him. With what he stands for.'

I didn't argue with her. 'But why didn't he tell me anyway?'

'From what I hear, you weren't exactly forthcoming about your twin, either.'

'It was too dangerous,' said Kip.

'Exactly. That's why we don't spread the word around. I'm only useful as long as people don't know who I am, what I do. You think the Alphas are hard on the Omegas? They'd be even less generous if they caught one of their own kind working with the resistance. And even those few on the island who know aren't crazy about it.'

For the rest of the day we walked, virtually jogging whenever the scrubby terrain allowed. We tracked our way back towards the river near where we'd landed, then headed upstream, into rapidly thickening forest. When the sun was high we ate the jerky while we walked, brushing off the sand as best we could. I could still feel it crunch between my teeth. We hardly spoke, barring hurried consultations between me and Zoe about direction. Only when it was reaching full-dark, and the forest was thick around us, did we stop to rest.

Zoe left the small clearing to fill the water flasks at the river, which was still audible to our right. Kip and I sank down into the loamy dirt and leaves.

'Would you have killed that guy?' he asked me. 'If you'd got your knife out?'

I shrugged. 'I would have tried. I hate the thought of it – killing him and his twin. And I don't know if I could have managed. But I would have tried.'

We sat in silence for a while longer, before he spoke again. 'How do you know we can trust her?'

'You'd be dead by now if you couldn't, for one thing,' said Zoe, stepping back into the clearing. She crouched opposite us and tossed us a heavy flask. 'And how do I know I can trust the two of you?'

Kip rolled his eyes. 'You're the one with the fancy knife-skills.'

I leaned gently into him. 'She gave us knives too, Kip.'

'Perhaps, but we both know she could fillet us if it came to a fight.'

'Look at it from my perspective,' Zoe said. 'I get messages from Piper, once a week, from the courier ship. A few weeks ago he sends word that they've had a surprise arrival on the island.' She leaned back against a tree, absently fingering one of the knives at her belt. 'And that's big news in itself, because nobody's done it without a map before.' With a movement that managed to be both speedy and casual, she flicked the knife forward, burying it into the tree behind me and Kip, a foot above our heads. 'Then I hear from him again, all excited because one of the arrivals is this big-time seer, the greatest thing that's ever happened to the Omegas.'

Kip snorted. 'I got the impression Piper thinks that's his own role.'

Zoe ignored him. 'Then he sends word that he's identified your twin: our old friend The Reformer. But this week, no message, no boat at the usual place.' Another blade thrummed into the tree, directly beneath the first. 'Then, a few days ago, evacuees start landing. First around here, and then another load further south – the whole damn fleet, if the rumours are right. And Council soldiers swarming the coast and offering a bounty for catching any of them. So what I want to know is this.' A third blade quivered above us, so close now that I felt a tiny yank as some strands of my hair were pinned to the tree trunk. 'Was my brother wrong to be excited about you? It seems a big coincidence that the Council just happened to find the island right after your arrival. And how is it that the two of you are safely ashore while my brother and the rest of the islanders are probably being slaughtered?'

'If you're who you say you are, then Piper's fine,' said Kip.

She interrupted him. 'Alive. He's alive, but there's a difference between being alive and being fine. You should know that. Piper told me about the tanks she found you in.'

I jerked my head to the side, flinching as I pulled free the pinned strands of hair.

'We warned them,' I said. 'I felt the attack coming, told them to get off the island. Piper sent us away.'

'He could have used you as a hostage. If you're who you say you are,' said Zoe.

'He could have,' I said. 'A lot of people on the Assembly would have wanted him to. And in the end they wanted to hand us over. But Piper didn't. So really it's not a question of whether you trust us. It's a question of whether you trust him.'

Zoe stared hard at both of us, then darted forward. By the time Kip had got his hand to his knife, she'd already snatched her three knives from the tree trunk, and stepped back.

'If you're a seer, you'll already know the answer to that question.' She slipped the knives back into her belt. 'Time to sleep,' she said, turning her back to us as she stretched out on the ground.

*

I woke early but Zoe was already up, sitting on a log and using one of her knives to flick the dirt from a handful of large mushrooms. When I sat up, Zoe tossed two of the mushrooms to me. 'I got a rabbit too, but we're still too near the coast to risk a fire. Tonight, maybe.'

She reminded me so much of Piper that I was ashamed not to have realised earlier who she was. It wasn't just the sheen of their dark skin, or the thick black hair – these were common. It was more about the way they held themselves. The defiant set of the jaw. The way that each movement managed somehow to be both decisive and languid. The bond between the two of them was self-evident, even when they were apart. Watching her made me understand why I'd felt so comfortable with Piper, despite the many good reasons to fear him. I didn't know how they'd managed it, but somehow he and Zoe had stayed close. The similarities in their manner and movements spoke of years of intimacy, of a bond that is as much habit as choice. I recalled what Piper had said to Kip, in passing, when I'd eavesdropped on their conversation on the island.

It also explained, perhaps, why he'd chosen to believe in me. For all his utilitarian approach, and the demands of his role on the island, if he'd worked closely with Zoe for all this time, then he must know what it was to see your twin as something other than an opposite. I'd thought that I was almost unique in that experience.

Seeing Zoe made Piper seem closer and, at the same time, further away. He was so present in Zoe's every movement that his absence seemed starker. When I saw Zoe's hands, busy with the knife, I thought again of Piper's hand on my shoulder when we'd last seen him.

Kip yawned, rolled over. Zoe stared at him. 'Piper told me about him too, you know.'

'The courier ship?' I asked.

She nodded. 'The island couldn't work without some kind of communication: news of planned rescues, warnings of coastal patrols. New Omegas needing transport out there – more and more over the past few years. Supplies, too, though for the last year or two they've been close to self-sufficient. They grow most of their stuff themselves.'

The present tense hung in the clearing. I thought of the neatly ploughed fields around the lake below the city, and the terraced garden plots clustered on the steep sides of the caldera. The goats in the market square.

'Then,' she continued, 'ever since you got there, all the news has been about you two. How you arrived the way you did, without any contact with any of the safehouses or the network. What that means for the island's security.'

'I think that's how they found the island too,' I said. 'The Alphas, I mean. They have a seer too – she was on the raiding ships.'

'The Confessor,' said Zoe, and I nodded.

Kip was surfacing from sleep. He sat up, caught the mushroom Zoe tossed him. 'The network you mentioned, here on the mainland,' he asked through a mouthful. 'Are there other Alphas?'

'Does it matter?' asked Zoe.

'It seems to, to every other Alpha we've met.'

'I'm not like every other Alpha you've met,' she said, throwing him another mushroom.

'No kidding,' he said.

'Anyway, The Confessor working for the Council,' Zoe said. 'She proves it doesn't always come down to Alpha or Omega.'

'It's not like that,' I said.

Zoe stood. 'You're going to defend her?'

'No. I meant, it's not like you said: that she's working for the Council. She's more powerful than that. She's calling the shots. Maybe not obviously, but a lot of the new stuff that's happening – it's coming from her.'

She gestured for us to get up. 'She's not the only one, the way I hear it.'

We stood slowly and I hoisted the bag to my shoulder. 'You can't think I agree with what my twin does.'

'Then we have that in common,' said Zoe. 'I wouldn't have let you go from the island, like Piper did.' She nodded towards the river. 'Five minutes to fill your flasks and clean up, then we move.'

That night Zoe reckoned we'd travelled far enough from the coast to risk a fire. Used to the pace and rhythms of travelling with Kip, I'd found Zoe's pace unrelenting. In the unsteady light of the fire I could see that Kip, too, looked tired, though all day neither of us had asked to pause or slow down. On the other side of the fire, Zoe was skinning the rabbit. I was grateful for the meat, but couldn't help looking away as she peeled back the fur. I thought again of the dead bounty hunter, his open eyes and the slack wound at his neck.

Later, hands greasy with rabbit meat, we watched the fire settle to ashes. Zoe was cleaning her fingernails with one of her tiny knives. Kip watched her carefully.

'The whole knife thing,' he said. 'You and Piper had to learn that together, right?'

'It's not a coincidence, if that's what you mean,' said Zoe, not looking up.

'So you were never split?' Kip continued.

'Sure we were. You've seen his brand.'

Kip and I nodded together. I pictured Piper's face as it had looked that last night on the island, flecks of blood across his brand.

'I thought maybe you were raised out east,' I ventured. 'I heard things used to be better there. That they didn't always send Omegas away. Or not so early, anyway.'

'It used to be that way,' said Zoe. 'Not these days. We've got contacts there, get word from time to time. Seems the Council's brought the east into line, last decade or so. Even the farthest settlements, on the edge of the dead-lands.'

'But you and Piper?'

'Yeah – we were from out that way. Got split late, like you said. He was ten when our parents sent him away.'

I looked at her. 'You were the lucky one.'

'Sure, nobody drove me out.' She looked up at us and grinned across the subsiding fire. 'But I left the next day anyway.'

Kip matched her grin. 'Two ten-year-olds – how did you live?'

Zoe shrugged. 'We learned fast – hunting, stealing. Some people helped, along the way.' She stretched her arms, yawning unapologetically, and looked at me. 'Still think I'm the lucky one?'

'Yes.' There was a pause. 'You got to stay with your twin.'

Zoe snorted, lay down. 'Doesn't sound to me like your twin would be great company.'

340

'Trust me,' said Kip. 'I've tried making that point to her before.'

I rolled my eyes. 'And I get it. I do. But if things were different – if he hadn't grown up being terrified of the split – he wouldn't be like he is. This whole system – it's what made him. It's what makes Alphas turn on us.'

Kip cleared his throat. 'Not all Alphas – obviously.'

'Don't speak too soon,' said Zoe. Again, that flash of teeth, the broad grin that reminded me so much of Piper.

Later that night, when the darkness was almost complete, Kip asked where we were running to. 'Don't get me wrong – it's not that I'm not enjoying spending all day madly scrambling through the forest. But I was wondering what the end-point was.'

'This whole area's crawling with soldiers looking to kill you, or worse,' said Zoe. 'And now they've put word out to local Alphas too, we need to get you away from the coast – there's nowhere within fifty miles of here that you'd be safe.'

'So we head away from the coast – I get that. But then?'

'It depends. Piper and I have meeting spots. Usually we meet on the coast, but when that's unsafe there's another place, on the far side of the mountains, where he'll come, or send word, if he can. After that, it's up to you.'

'We'll keep moving. Safer that way,' I said. 'Maybe try to head east.'

'So that's it then?' Zoe asked. 'You just keep running?'

'We tried staying put – at the island. That didn't work out so well,' Kip said.

'It worked out pretty well – for you,' she said quietly.

For a few minutes the only sound was the fire's lazy sputtering. I spoke first. 'We couldn't have saved the island.'

'Maybe. Maybe not. Piper could have used you.'

'To kill her, you mean?' said Kip. 'And kill Zach?'

'Not necessarily. But threatened it, at least. To make them stop.'

'Piper let us leave the island,' I said. 'If we get caught now, that's it – there'll be no point to what he did.'

'And if you just keep running, what's the point then? He let you leave because he thought you'd be valuable – thought you could help us.'

My voice was unsteady. 'I tried to help, and all I did was get locked up by the Assembly, and draw The Confessor to the island. I don't know what everyone thinks I'm supposed to be able to do now.'

'Nor do I. So far, to be honest, I'm not seeing what all the fuss is about. But Piper saw something in you. And the Alphas sure as hell found a use for their seer. So it seems to me that running away is just throwing away the sacrifice that he made. That all those people on the island made.'

'She gave them warning,' said Kip. 'Two days' notice, which they wouldn't have had without her. All of those who got away, that's thanks to her.'

'Is that it, though? Is that all you're good for, the secret weapon that Piper believed in enough to throw away the island's last chance?'

I closed my eyes. 'I didn't choose this. I didn't choose to be some kind of secret weapon.'

'I know that,' said Zoe. 'But maybe you should.'

We were lying close enough to the fire that I could hear the shifting of the ash as it settled into new configurations. Beside me, Kip's breathing was starting to assume the light, even sounds of sleep. Across the fire, Zoe's body was an indistinct shape, but I could tell she was still awake. I whispered, trying not to wake Kip.

'Everyone on the Assembly except for Piper wanted me

dead. If I get involved with the resistance again, why would it be different? The minute they know who I am, that's it for me: I'm most useful to them dead. The one thing I could do for them – kill myself, and Zach – is the one thing I can't do. I can't do it to Zach. You of all people should understand what it's like to care about your twin.'

Zoe propped her head on an elbow. 'Right now, I'm waiting to see whether your twin is going to succeed in killing mine, and me. You really expect me to see your twin as some kind of poster-boy for reconciliation?'

'But you and Piper stuck together. You can't really want a world in which twins are split up.'

Zoe laughed quietly. 'What makes you think the world has anything to do with what I want, or what you want? The world is how it is. If Alphas are going to treat Omegas like they do, then Omegas need somewhere separate. It's safer that way. That was the whole idea of the island.'

'So now we just find another island? And then another, when the Alphas raid that one?'

'I don't see you coming up with any better solutions.'

I closed my eyes, remembered what Kip had said to me on the tower: *an unsplit world, where we wouldn't even need a place like the island.* 'I don't have any solutions. I just think that when you run out of islands you're going to realise that the real problem's still there.'

'Don't preach to me,' she hissed. 'You can talk as much as you like about bringing Alphas and Omegas together. But for the last few years, while you've been safely locked up, Piper and I have been seeing exactly what your twin and his kind can do. And we've been fighting to do something about it. You really think you can change people's minds, people who've seen children taken away, locked up, killed in experiments?'

There was a silence. 'I saw the experiments. Not all of them, I mean. But you know I saw the tanks.' Another pause. 'And Kip understands. He doesn't always agree, but he gets what I mean, even after what he's been through.'

Zoe grunted. 'What he's been through? The whole problem with him is he doesn't remember what he's been through. Piper told me – he's a blank slate. You could convince him of anything.'

I didn't even feel myself scramble up, or cross the fire. I just launched myself at Zoe, pinning her down and striking wildly at her.

As soon as she got free of her blanket she caught one of my wrists and wrestled me to the side, but it was Kip's shout that stopped me.

'What the hell's going on?' He was standing, peering blearily across the fire at our struggling figures.

Zoe released me with a shove.

'Did she attack you?' he asked me as I retreated to our side of the fire.

Zoe rolled her eyes. 'Yeah. I rescued the two of you just so I could attack you in your sleep.' She pulled our blanket from the edge of the fire, where it had fallen, and stamped the smouldering corner before throwing it back at us. 'Don't worry. She was just defending your honour.' She rolled away as if nothing had happened.

Kip looked from me to Zoe, and back again. I shook out the blanket, wrinkling my nose at the smell of burnt wool, and settled back down.

'Sweet of you to bother,' he said, as he lay down next to me, 'but next time, I'd rather you just let me sleep.'

CHAPTER 27

It was raining again in the morning. We didn't relight the fire, but crouched in the shelter of the trees at the clearing's edge and ate the cold scraps of rabbit, the fat congealed and clammily white. When we set off, Kip made to continue following the river, but Zoe shook her head.

'We leave the river here. There's a big town less than a day's walk upstream – we can't risk getting any closer. And I reckon they'll be watching the valley. If I were on my own, I'd take the valley road, but with the two of you, it's too risky.'

I looked around, staring up above the trees. Behind us the valley widened as the river traced its way towards the sea. Ahead, the valley carved an ever-narrowing path between the mountains. On either side, those mountains imposed themselves on the sky. The trees faded out less than halfway up, exposing cliff faces and collapsed sections of scree.

Kip sighed and looked to me. 'Don't suppose you're getting a feel for any secret tunnels that are going to save us the climb?'

I smiled. 'Not this time – sorry. But Zoe's right – there's a big town upstream. And people on the move all around it.'

She nodded. 'It's a market town – there'll be people from all over making their way to it for the end of the week. If we've got to cross the mountains, the easiest pass is this side of the river.' She gestured at a dip in the peak to our left. 'But they'll be watching it, for sure. So we should cross the river here and take the high pass beyond that peak.'

Following her pointing finger, I looked up at the peak to our right, across the river. I shook my head. 'There's a big town there – bigger than the one in the valley. Are you out of your mind?'

'One of us is.' She was already moving down, towards the river.

'You don't know what you're talking about,' Kip shouted. 'She can sense stuff like that.'

'I know she can,' Zoe called back. 'And she's even better than I thought, if she can sense that town.'

'She's never been wrong,' said Kip, following her so he didn't have to shout.

'I'm not saying she's wrong.' Zoe turned to face us. 'But her timing's a bit off. There was a town there – a huge one, bigger even than Wyndham. But that was in the Before.'

I shook my head again. 'I could have sworn. I can feel it so strongly.'

'Thousands of people – hundreds of thousands – lived there, for hundreds of years.' She shrugged. 'Wouldn't that leave a trace?'

'It doesn't make any difference,' said Kip. 'It's taboo. I'm not going anywhere near a town from the Before.'

'If you're worried about breaking the Council's laws, I'm fairly sure that ship has sailed,' she said.

'This is different. It's not about the law. You know that – it's about the Before. You can't go near any of that stuff.'

'That's why Zoe's right,' I acknowledged. 'Nobody will go near it. If the pass goes through the town, it's our best chance of getting through the mountains without getting caught.'

'There's a reason nobody will go there. It's contaminated. Deadly. You've seen the posters.'

'Yeah,' I said. 'But I've also seen the posters about how we're dangerous horse thieves.'

'And don't forget all those posters about how Omegas are worthless, dangerous, a burden on the Alphas,' added Zoe.

I nodded. 'Even if the taboo were there for a reason, it couldn't be more dangerous than our other options.'

He sighed as he headed off towards the river. 'I wouldn't mind so much if the town weren't on top of a damned mountain.'

*

None of us talked much the rest of the day. The climb was steep, and we were often clambering through scratchy, dense undergrowth. After lunch, a handful of stringy mushrooms that Zoe had found, she left us for nearly an hour, coming back with a rabbit and two small birds hanging from her belt. 'I'd normally have got more, but there're people around, coming up the valley. One patrol of Council soldiers, and a lot of local Alphas, still after that bounty.'

'Do you think they caught many of those who got away from the island?' I stretched my legs as I stood.

'Some, probably,' she threw on her pack. 'The evacuees will have split up, spread out, tried to make it to safehouses.

But there's a lot of Alphas looking for them. The good news is they're so damned noisy they had no chance of catching me, and they seem to be sticking to the lower slopes, not far above the river. The bad news is they've scared off half the game on the slopes, and there's not much hunting higher up.'

'How long to the pass, do you reckon?' Kip asked.

She wrinkled her nose. 'With the two of you slowing me down, three days, I'd say. Maybe more if the searchers come higher and we have to play it safe.'

For the rest of the afternoon we kept quiet but made steady progress, stopping for the night not far below the tree-line. We didn't risk a fire, and although Kip and I swore we couldn't face the raw meat Zoe offered us, we both ended up forcing down a little. Water was more of a problem: we'd filled the flasks at the river, but hadn't passed a spring since then, and were limiting ourselves to occasional sips. I sat leaning against a tree trunk, too narrow to provide any comfortable support, and wincing as I picked tiny thorns from my legs, cross-hatched with scratches. I kept running my tongue over my teeth, slightly tacky from the heat and lack of water. I tried not to think about the meat, its gluey texture and the strings of uncooked fat that had snagged between my teeth.

Zoe, sitting opposite, spoke suddenly. 'Do you think it's over?'

'The fighting on the island?' I closed my eyes for a moment. 'I can't tell. I haven't felt anything more, not since the night before you found us, when I had a vision of the fort's gate being breached. But I don't know if it's over, or if it's just that we're too far away now for me to sense anything.'

She was picking at her nails with a knife, in the now-familiar movement. 'Too far away? I hate to break it to you, but with you two tagging along, we don't move all that fast. Anyway, I didn't think distance was a big deal for you. You could feel them coming before they'd even launched the boats. That's what you said.'

I looked down at my hands. 'I did. But the seeing depends on a lot of things, and distance is one of them. Along with a kind of –' I paused, '– intensity. Like with The Confessor, looking for me – she's so focused on me, so intent, that I can feel that all the time, no matter where I am.'

For a while the only sound was the impatient clicking of Zoe's knife on her nails. Eventually Kip spoke. 'It's not Cass's fault that it doesn't work the way we want it to.'

She looked at him. 'You say that because she hasn't found your twin?'

'I'm not even sure I want to know. But the whole seer thing – it's not straightforward. You've seen how she wakes up every night. It's not easy for her.'

'Her waking up in the night isn't easy for any of us,' she said, turning back to me. 'And if you're going to do it again tonight, try to cut out the whole shouting bit. There are still people looking for you.'

I smiled sheepishly. 'Sorry. And I'm sorry I can't tell you more about the island, or Piper. But I think he wouldn't have been taken alive.'

Zoe shrugged. 'You don't need to be a seer to figure that out.'

'But it's still good news, isn't it? We know he's not dead. And if that means he isn't caught either, then there's a chance he's OK.'

'Guess we'll find out in a few days. If he's OK he'll come to the meeting place.'

I settled down next to Kip, wrapping the blanket tighter

around us both. 'I don't believe you, you know,' I said quietly. 'About not wanting to know who your twin is.'

Zoe, lying down a few feet away, joined in. 'It's not like me to agree with Cass, but I don't believe you either. How could you not want to know?'

'It's not as weird as you think,' he said. Lying behind me, when he spoke I felt his breath warming my hair. 'People lived for thousands of years without twins, in the Before.'

Zoe snorted. 'And look how well that turned out.'

*

It rained lightly in the night, and a thick mist squatted over the valley as we packed up and set off in the morning. 'It's good news,' Zoe pointed out, when I complained of the weight of the wet blanket. 'We'll be clear of the trees by noon, but the mist will give us cover if it stays.'

'It'll stay,' I said.

We could see only a few feet ahead, and all sound was muffled. When I slipped and grabbed a narrow treetrunk for support, the bark was loamy and damp, coming away on my hand. After an hour or so I was able to lead us to a small stream, a trickle really, but boosted by the night's rain. We filled our flasks, drank furiously, and filled them again before continuing to climb through the gradually thinning trees. Within a few hours the trees had given up altogether, leaving a landscape of scree and boulders. Here we had to proceed more carefully, as the slopes of the lower mountainside were replaced by rifts and loose rocks. Twice we had to backtrack to find a passable route, before Zoe grudgingly let me navigate. The scree slopes were the worst, slipping out from underfoot and sometimes threatening to give way and carry us down the mountain. Several times we recoiled as a small cascade of stones hurtled beneath us, the noise loud even in the muffling fog. We tried to stick to the bouldered areas, but the progress was slow, and we found ourselves climbing as much as walking. Although Kip never complained, his single arm made the climbing hard for him, and even Zoe helped him from time to time, reaching back down to let him grasp her arm.

In the treacherous conditions, we had to stop as soon as the light became bad. It wasn't raining anymore, but the mist had left a pervasive damp over everything. We agreed to risk a fire, but it was hard to find unsoaked wood, as only a few scrappy shrubs risked existence above the tree line. The wood took us half an hour to collect and lasted only long enough to barely cook the rabbit, over a spitting, petulant flame that gave out more smoke than heat. My body was so tired that there was a kind of satisfaction in the weariness, as I lay by the fire stretching my legs and probing the countless aches of my muscles. It was cold, and when I nestled down close to Kip the wet-wool smell of the blankets reminded me of the horses, their musty, organic scent, and those first days on the road together. So many days and weeks, now, with Kip; at least three months, I estimated. The years before – the village, then the settlement, then the Keeping Rooms – felt very distant.

For him, I reminded myself, these recent months were all there was, apart from those indistinct and ghastly memories of the tank. And not only was he unanchored by his past but, strangest of all, he was adrift without a twin. He was a question without an answer. I knew it was strange, like Zoe had said, that he claimed he didn't want to know about his twin. I wondered whether our bond had gone any way to filling that void. The symmetry that linked us, ever since his eyes had caught mine through the curved glass of the tank.

351

But it wasn't symmetry. I rolled away from him, pulling the blanket higher. Because it wasn't only the pair of us. His twin might be unknown, but mine was always there, as pressing and vivid as Kip, Kip who lay next to me, breathing the endearingly noisy breath of sleep.

*

The next day was still wet, but by noon we broke through the mist and found ourselves looking down on a valley entirely hidden by the sulky grey clouds. It was steep, still, but the going was more certain. The boulders and scree were below us, only bare, stark sheets of rock remaining.

I was used to seeing the world as being shaped by the blast: craters wide enough to form their own horizon; piles of rubble; cliffs, even mountains, crumbled like sand-banks. There were places, however, where you could still get a glimpse of the world formed by other, earlier forces. The island had been like that: its crater predated the blast, I was sure. Here, too, the slabs of stone showed the layers formed over many centuries, heaved out of the earth in a way that spoke of long, inexorable shifting.

I felt exposed, the three of us moving across the naked mountain-face, but Zoe pointed out that we would be invisible to anyone below the cloud line. 'There would have been a road up here, once,' she said. 'The climb would have been straightforward, in the Before.'

'There would have been a lot of things,' Kip said.

Within an hour, as the ground plateaued, we began to see signs of it: three metal poles, each leaning nearly parallel to the ground, at precisely the same angle, their melted bases showing where the blast had wrenched them. The foundations of a wall, barely visible along a section of the plateau. And then the city itself, tucked in the hammock of the mountain pass.

Except it wasn't a city at all. It was more negative space than anything else. The metal rods of building foundations were exposed, bowed like the ribs of dead cattle on the roadside in the drought years. There were some walls and some concrete slabs partly intact, but only ever enough to hint at the shape of a larger structure, now gone.

I'd seen a machine from the Before, years ago at the settlement. I'd known it was risky even to pay the bronze coin to see the travelling show that promised to display a real artefact. But when the exhibit had arrived on its grimy wagon, I lined up and paid, like almost everyone else in the settlement. It was a cool morning, long past harvest. When I reached the front of the queue and the crier's son ushered me inside the tent, there was a rough plinth in the centre, its base showing where the red cloth draped over it failed to meet the tent floor. The crier in the morning had said it was a machine scavenged from a taboo town to the west. At first I thought the machine must be inside the bruised metal box that sat on the plinth. Then the crier ceremoniously opened the lid, and I realised that the machine was the box itself. Inside, the top half contained fragments of what looked like tarnished glass. The bottom half was splintered, a mass of melted blackness. A cord, in parts withered away to a single thread of wire, hung from the box, ending partway down the red cloth. 'For the Electric,' the man whispered, confidentially. I'd heard about that too: how, when the Electric broke in the blast, the Before was stranded. Houses, whole cities, full of forsaken, useless machines, each with its own wistful cord.

Nothing in this mountain town looked as well preserved as that box had been. The strangest thing about the place was the disjunction between the town itself – the desolate, vacant space – and the crowd of impressions that surrounded it. To me, it was almost a roar, the sheer volume of lives that had shared this space. Their absence was as vivid as their presence. It didn't feel like my visions – not even my visions of the blast. It was more like a residue. It was the resonance of a bell, echoing long after the bell itself has stopped.

I was surprised to look up and see Zoe and Kip unaffected. Both were moving warily amongst the rubble, and Kip kept looking over his shoulder, but it was evident that neither of them felt the same silent cacophony that was besieging me. Kip noticed me, though, and the way my hands had moved, instinctively and uselessly, to cover my ears. He moved to my side, stepping over a twisted metal beam.

'I guess if you could feel the city from the valley, it must be pretty strong up here?'

I nodded, but didn't speak.

'It's all a long time ago, you know.' He took my arm.

I nodded again. 'I know. But they don't. It's like –' I checked Zoe was too far away to hear me – 'like nobody told them they were dead.'

He looked down, turned over a small chunk of concrete with his foot, watched the grey dust rise and settle. 'We don't have to go this way. We can backtrack – go around.'

I shook my head. 'It's OK. I just didn't expect it to be this strong.'

I kept hold of his arm as we caught up with Zoe and followed her through the wreckage. Some of the time it was clear where the old roads had lain, and the going was easy. Often, however, the road disappeared under rubble, and we had to pick our way through. A number of the buildings had collapsed into their cellars, leaving sink-holes crammed with debris. We were heading more or less through the town's centre. I kept expecting the ruins to come to an end, but the town seemed infinite, and after more than an hour we stopped for a drink, perching on the few remaining stones of a low wall.

'Weird to think that there're more places like this,' said Kip.

'Heaps more,' Zoe said. 'I've been to a few.'

'As big as this?'

'Bigger. There's one, on the south coast, must have been ten times this size. Most of it's underwater now, but you can still see stuff, if you take a boat out. And some of the tall buildings still poke out of the sea, at low tide.' She passed me the flask, the water warm and barely refreshing.

'So do you think there's anything in it? The taboo, I mean,' he said.

'All the ruins are just like this.' Zoe waved her arm at the rubble surrounding us. 'Useless, rather than scary. There's not much to be salvaged. The stuff people warn about – the radiation, the dangerous stuff – it might have been true once, but not now.' She tossed a stone against a sheet of iron, half-buried in dust. It gave an apathetic clang. 'Now it's just a heap of junk. But people are scared of it because of what it stands for: the Before, the blast. All of that.'

'And the machines?'

'None of them work anyway. Even if you could piece some of them together, they'd still need the Electric.'

'They have it, you know,' I said. 'The Alphas, in Wyndham. Not just in the tank rooms, but in my cell. The other cells too, and some of the corridors.'

I told her what I'd told Piper, about the glass ball hanging from the ceiling of my cell. Its unwavering, cold light.

She nodded. 'I thought as much. There'd be an uproar if people ever found out, but I'm sure they've been dabbling in that stuff for years. I'm just surprised they haven't done more of it. People say that in the Before there were travelling machines, flying machines, a whole lot of stuff I bet some on the Council would love to build again, if the people would stand for it. But the fear runs too deep, after the blast. The Council knows better than to risk another purge.'

We both turned at the same time, at the strangled shriek of metal as Kip heaved open what was left of a door, leading into a concrete structure largely submerged in the earth. Zoe's hand went straight to her knives, but nothing followed the sound but a haze of dust, rising briefly then settling, anointing Kip's hair, eyebrows and shoulders with a chalky white.

She sighed, turning back to me. 'He could make more noise, but only if I gave him a drum and a trumpet.'

But I was still watching Kip. I saw how he had frozen. How his hand, powder-dusted and taut, still gripped the door. When I reached him he still hadn't moved. It took me a while to make out what he was staring at, particularly as Zoe, joining us, blocked out the last of the light from the doorway. When I did see what was inside, for a moment I didn't understand why Kip had reacted like that. It looked innocuous at first: a cabinet mounted on the wall, its cover blasted or fallen off. From inside it, snaking out into the darkened room, was a mass of wires, their colours faded but still distinct: red, blue, yellow. Some were bundled together, others hung loose. It wasn't a dramatic sight: just another piece of detritus from the unfamiliar world of the Before.

That's when I realised it wasn't entirely unfamiliar. I remembered the wires snaking along the wall above the tanks. Bundled together in places, elsewhere branching out like ungainly ivy. The wires, the cords, the tubes. And the scar in Kip's wrist, perfectly round and still visible, where one of the tubes had entered his body.

When I tried to pull him away from the door, his whole body was stiff. I had to wrap both arms around him and haul him back into the light, as Zoe moved out of our way. When I manoeuvred around to face him, still in my arms, his eyes remained fixed on the doorway. He was completely silent, his face expressionless.

'Shut it. Shut the damned door,' I said.

Zoe responded quickly. From behind me, I could hear the squeal and thump of the door as it closed. I didn't move, didn't take my eyes from Kip's face. I remembered the first time I'd seen it. His eyes, back then, meeting mine through the tank's glass, had been more animated than they were now as he stared blankly over my shoulder. For the minutes that we stood there, he didn't speak or move.

Zoe broke the silence. 'We've been in the open too long. If he's going to have a breakdown, he'll have to wait until we find some cover.'

I was thankful that she asked no questions. Between us, we half steered, half dragged Kip through the debris, taking shelter finally in an alcove between two collapsed concrete slabs. Around us, as in much of the city, small plants had taken root. Big trees wouldn't grow at this height, but vines and creepers had infiltrated the cracks of the concrete.

'You want to explain what that was about?' Her question was addressed to me, but Kip replied.

'It was the same as the tank room. The wires and stuff.' He looked up apologetically. 'I guess I never expected to see something like that again.'

Zoe raised an eyebrow. 'It was the same?'

357

'Not the same,' I said. 'Not the tanks, or anything like that. But the wires – there were wires like that all over the room, when I found him.'

She wrinkled her nose. 'Piper saw a team of Council soldiers, once, in a taboo town out west. Shifting stuff out, taking it away by the cartload.'

'But the tanks, where you found me,' Kip said. 'I never heard about anything like that, from the Before.'

'I'm not saying they had machines just like those ones. But the technology the Alphas are building on – look around you,' Zoe said. 'It's from the Before. All that stuff Cass told Piper about – the tanks, the tubes, the machines – you really think The Reformer and his Council mates just knocked that up with an anvil and a bit of thatch? Come on. They might not dare to go public with any of it, but they've been perfecting this stuff for years – it's all from the Before.'

'But they're the ones who enforce the taboo,' he said. 'If the Council wanted to use things from the Before, wouldn't they just change the law?'

I shook my head. 'Think about what you were saying before, about why you didn't want to come into a taboo town. It's not about the law. People hate this stuff – anything to do with the Before. They'll never embrace it, or anything to do with it. The Council couldn't let people know they're using it.'

'Or,' added Zoe, 'they want to make sure they're the only ones using it.'

'Both, probably,' I said.

Kip was still looking pale, but Zoe was insistent that we'd halted too long already. As we moved off through the outskirts of the vanished city, the light was leaching from the sky, and the ruins were casting long, jagged shadows in the dust.

'How long to the meeting place?' Kip asked.

'We can reach it tonight, if there's enough moonlight to see by.'

He nodded. I knew he was longing to rest, to close his eyes against the world that had ambushed him with the memory of the tank rooms. But it was equally clear that Zoe wouldn't pause. Moonlight or not, I knew we'd be walking tonight until we reached the meeting place. I tried to make my mind grope ahead for some hint of whether Piper would be there, but my thoughts were still too muddied by the clamorous dead, and by my awareness of Kip's clenched hand in my own.

There was something else, too: the wires and cables that had set Kip off had resonated in my mind as well. They'd reminded both of us of the tank room. But for me they'd also evoked that other room, the one I'd snatched a glimpse of from within The Confessor's mind, on my last day in the Keeping Rooms. When Kip had frozen at the sight of those wires, I'd seen that room again, only this time I recognised it. Not the wires that clambered up the walls, but the walls themselves: the precise curve of them. I'd never been inside the room before, I was certain. But I was equally certain that I knew the place from outside. The old silos that Zach and I used to go to as children.

CHAPTER 28

If the climb had been exhausting, the descent had its own challenges. The moon did its best, but once we reached the tree line we were walking mainly in darkness, stumbling often. Zoe was sure of the way, or reckless with anticipation, leading us with unhesitating speed. I'd been worried about whether Kip could keep going so long, but he seemed to welcome the frantic pace, the distraction necessitated by keeping up, scrambling through trees and amongst boulders. Several times I heard him stumble or skid, heard the scatter of stones and the grunt of breath as he grazed the ground, or struck out and clutched at something to hold him upright.

Zoe froze. In the darkness we didn't know she'd paused until Kip and I almost stumbled over her. She didn't need to hush us; the sudden and total stillness of her body was warning enough. In the silence that followed I was acutely aware of how noisy our progress had been before.

Worse, I realised at the same time that we weren't the only ones waiting in the darkness. To our left, deep in the condensed black of night, something amongst the trees shifted, paused, shifted again. The day had been such a concatenation of terrors that I couldn't even tell what I feared most: Alpha pursuers, or the taboo town's unquiet dead, somehow revived by darkness. Beside me, Kip held his breath. I felt, as much as saw, Zoe slowly raise an arm and jerk her thumb backwards. I ventured a step in retreat, and felt Kip doing the same beside me. But I was still staring at Zoe's hand. Backlit by moonlight I could see the silhouette of her knife, poised to throw.

'Stop.' My voice shocked me as much as the others. The realisation had come so suddenly, and so certainly, that I didn't pause to think. 'It's Piper.'

He stepped forward, barely twenty feet from us, a shape emerging from the darkness and only recognisable by his voice.

'I like to think she would have checked before she let that knife fly,' he said.

'Don't count on it,' said Zoe. 'You'll get us both killed, sneaking around at night like that.' She moved towards him. They didn't embrace, or even touch, but even in the nearly total darkness, I felt that I should look away.

It lasted only a few moments. As I stood, my face turned to Kip's shoulder, I heard Piper move towards us. He reached out, cupped my face with his hand, turned it to him. It was too dark to see his face clearly, but I could feel him inspecting me. He searched my face with the intentness of a lover. Or of a buyer at market, checking for flaws. He swept his thumb along the top of my cheekbone, pressing firmly, as if reassuring himself even of my bones. When he finally exhaled, his breath was warm on my cheek, even while my hand was still in Kip's.

Piper didn't take his eyes off my face. 'Thank you for keeping her safe.'

'I didn't, really,' said Kip.

'I was talking to my sister.' He dropped his hand, turned to Kip. 'You made it too, I see.'

'I never thought I'd come to see you as the charming one of the family,' Kip said to Zoe, who had joined us.

'Tell us what happened on the island,' she said.

Piper shook his head. 'Not now. We need to keep moving. I'm not the only one who could have found you.'

She nodded. 'We're almost at the meeting spot anyway. We'll get settled there for the night.' They moved off in unison.

Kip and I followed. 'It's the first time I've ever seen it,' he whispered to me.

'Seen what?'

'Twins together.'

I knew what he meant. I, too, had been mesmerised by the pair ahead: the symmetry of their movements, the perfect match of pace. They could be each other's shadow.

After less than half an hour, as the descent was becoming steeper and rockier, Zoe and Piper led us sharply south, following a rock ridge that mounted higher to our right. The cave itself was well hidden by ivy and low scrub. When Zoe had wrenched back the ivy and we'd squeezed inside, Piper and Zoe couldn't stand without hunching, but there was space for the four of us to lie.

The darkness in there was complete, and it seemed to make every noise more acute. As Kip and I were getting settled, brushing loose rocks from beneath us and shaking out the blanket, I could hear each movement as Zoe and Piper did the same. In the small space, our blanket's reek of wet and burnt wool was noticeable. I feared my own smell would be just as obvious. I couldn't remember the last time I'd washed properly. Even the hasty rinse in the river was days ago now. I knew that Kip's face, by daylight, had taken on a veneer of dirt, darker in the creases around his eyes and on his neck.

The others were quickly settled, clearly used to the place. I could understand, now, Piper's preference for the tiny antechamber on the island, the thin, rolled-up mattress.

'Tell us what happened,' I said.

He spoke quietly, sounding exhausted. 'Wouldn't you rather sleep than hear the details?'

'If I sleep, I'll only dream about it anyway.'

Zoe sighed. 'You'd better tell us now then. If she's seeing stuff in her sleep again, none of us will get any rest at all.'

'OK.' There was a long pause. 'Well, it was better than you'd predicted, in some ways. Numbers-wise, I mean – because we'd managed to get the second sailing safely away.'

'And in other ways?' I asked.

'Worse, obviously. Because of what they did with those they'd caught.'

'But when we were on the island they were taking prisoners, mainly, from what we could see. They were holding back.'

'I know.' Piper shifted on the stone floor. 'They weren't killing – not at first. They had all the prisoners herded together in the courtyard, after they'd taken the fort's outer walls. We'd had to draw back to the upper levels. I was on the ramparts. I could see everything. They had them all tied up, even the injured. They kept checking them against a list, one by one. Looking for certain features. Some they took aside, then down to the ships. The others they just killed there and then. Slit their throats, in a row, with the other prisoners waiting, while the woman with the list moved down the line. Checking.'

I could see it, as he described it. I'd seen glimpses already, on the first night back on the mainland, when I'd woken Kip with my screaming. But, like most of my visions, that had been a series of indistinct impressions. Now, Piper's words were solidifying what I had seen, and painting in colour what had been a blurred and grey sequence of moments.

'How could they possibly know who was who? And who their twins were?' said Zoe. 'It's not as if you had registration papers on the island.'

'Don't underestimate how much information they have,' he said. 'We've long thought that they'd be building a list of who they suspected of being on the island – the way they're keeping tabs on Omegas these days, it's harder and harder just to disappear. But that's not how they knew who to kill,' he said. 'Or not all of it.'

'The woman with the list,' I said, watching it unfold from behind my closed eyelids. 'It was her.'

'I couldn't see her brand from the ramparts,' he said, 'but it had to be The Confessor. You could see it in the way the soldiers kept their distance from her – she wasn't an Alpha. But they followed her orders all right. She was checking the prisoners against a list, but often she'd also lean over them, or put her hand on their head, with her eyes shut. Once she had what she needed, a nod from her was all it took, and the soldiers would step in, cut the throat.'

I saw it all. Her nods were somehow more brutal than the soldiers' blades on flesh. She was so casual about it – giving a nearly imperceptible jerk of the head to the waiting soldiers, as she already turned to move on to the next prisoner.

Zoe spoke first. 'How many got off the island?'

'More than two-thirds got away clean, on the boats. All the children, and nearly all the civilians. But the second sailing was in too much of a rush, and overloaded too. One of the ships foundered in the reef. We managed to save three of them, in the children's dinghies, before we hid them in the caves.' He laughed, bleakly. 'Much good it did those three – they were on the island when the Alphas arrived that night.'

In the silence, my memories of the battle replayed in my mind, so vividly that I could again smell blood and wine. I knew that Kip and Piper would be revisiting it too.

'You saw how the battle started,' he said. 'After you left, it went a lot like you'd warned. The north tunnel fell after midnight, like you'd said, but we'd set up barricades beyond it. They'd overrun the whole caldera. A lot of the fighting was done in the streets – at close quarters. But they were so cautious – the Alphas, I mean. They were killing, but not indiscriminately. A lot of the time they used fire, to flush people out.'

'And in the end?' Zoe was insistent.

'We were just overrun. And after a while, it was clear there was nothing left to defend. They'd burnt the city, blocked the tunnels. They'd breached the main gate into the fort, we were only just holding the upper levels. After they'd slaughtered most of the prisoners in the courtyard, there must have been ninety of us left, alive and uncaptured, against maybe six hundred of them. We'd never have got out of the fort alive, if they weren't holding back from killing. I'd never have thought I'd be grateful for The Confessor.' He spat her name. 'But they didn't kill anyone if they could help it, not until they'd got them tied up and checked by her. So when we made that final break out of the fort, in the dark, they were holding back. The smoke helped too – they'd burnt half the city by then. But they thought they had us trapped, anyway. They didn't know about the boats in the caves, so when we made it over the lip of the crater, they regrouped to protect the harbour. When we headed for the eastern side, they must've thought we were going to swim for it.' Again, that bleak laugh. 'They're not sailors, that's for sure. Once we'd launched the rafts and canoes into the reef, their big ships couldn't get near us, and quite a few of their landing craft foundered when they tried coming after us. They couldn't catch us, even in our ridiculous boats. We were the raggediest fleet you ever saw, and we'd never have made it to the mainland. But we know the reef backwards, and they couldn't make any headway in the dark. And out past the reef, at anchor, their own fleet was hardly manned, except for the ship with the prisoners. We boarded two of their ships before they knew what was going on. The others hadn't even enough crew on board to come after us. But I think they'd figured, by then, that they weren't going to find what they were looking for.'

'How could they know?' asked Kip.

'The Confessor would know,' I said. 'She'd feel it, I'm sure.'

'Maybe. But they didn't even need her. They just asked.'

'I didn't realise you were on such chummy terms.'

Piper ignored Kip's interruption. 'It was when they'd rounded up all the prisoners, before they started to kill them. The soldiers shouted up from the courtyard.'

In the silence that followed, I knew what he would say next.

'They said they'd spare them, if we handed you both over.'

I felt Kip's rushed exhalation on my shoulder. I closed my eyes, but in the darkness it made no difference.

*

I woke early, surprised that I'd managed to sleep at all. I didn't want to face the others, so was relieved to hear nothing but sleeping breaths in the cave. But when I'd forced my way through the vines at the entrance, wet with dew, I saw Piper was already out, methodically sharpening one of his knives against the rock on which he sat.

I hadn't seen him by daylight since the island. The sky was now only hinting at dawn, but there was enough light to make out his wounds: one eye two-thirds closed under a fat swelling, and a long gash on his arm.

'It's not as bad as it looks. Zoe hardly felt it,' he said. 'And the eye was just an accident – I copped an oar in the face when we were scrambling to get the little boats down from the caves.'

'You don't have to lie to me,' I said.

He looked at me, gave a half-smile. 'Not much point trying to, it seems.' He touched the edge of the swelling around the eye. 'We both knew it was a risk, letting you go. When I told the Assembly what I'd done, a few of them let me know how they felt about it. I have Simon to thank for the black eye.'

'I'm sorry,' I said. 'That's it for you, then, isn't it – with the resistance?'

He shrugged. 'That's it for me as leader. But that doesn't matter. I'll keep working – if there's any resistance left to work for.'

'But that one,' I said, gesturing at the wound on his arm. 'That one wasn't from your own Assembly.' I bent closer to it. I could see it had been stitched, though clumsily.

'No, that one was a Council soldier.' He followed my gaze. 'I know it's not pretty. To be fair, it was stitched up by a one-armed woman in a rocking boat.'

I laughed, as he moved to make space for me on the

rock's flat top. 'Sorry – I shouldn't be laughing,' I said. 'Me of all people.'

He looked at me carefully. I was embarrassed at how close his face was to my own. I could see the hairs of his stubble. When I looked down, I saw the skin around his arm wound, and how it puckered at each stitch.

'You didn't sleep much last night?' he asked.

I shook my head. 'But I don't sleep much at the best of times.' A long pause. 'The others – the ones who got off the island with you, like the woman who stitched you up – where did they go?'

'We split up; didn't even land the two ships together. The others from my ship are heading east. But the network'll be stretched, with all the ones who fled earlier. If they landed safely and found their way inland, the safehouses will be inundated. I can guarantee I'm not the only islander who slept rough last night.'

I asked the question, dreading the answer. 'And the others – how many?'

'Killed? Maybe four hundred, on the island – some in the fighting, but mainly in the courtyard. A few more taken prisoner – maybe ten, fifteen. For the rest, it depends if they landed safely. We lost thirty in the boat that sank on the reef, and we won't account for all the other boats for weeks yet.'

I could feel him looking at me again. 'It was my decision, Cass. Not yours. I didn't have to let you go.'

I nodded, but still didn't look up.

'You think I shouldn't have?'

I couldn't speak. All I could manage was breathing; words had given up on me altogether.

'I think I made the right decision,' he went on. 'Though maybe for the wrong reasons. I do believe that we need you – that you could be a powerful weapon for the resistance. But that wasn't it, or it wasn't all of it.' He paused.

'Do you remember, on the terrace on the island, how I said I didn't know if there was a place where my role on the island ended, and I began?'

I nodded.

'I learned the answer, when the Assembly decided to hand you over. What I did, it was the right thing to do, but I didn't do it for the island. And people bled for my decision.' When he spoke of it, I could see that he was seeing it again: the blood congealing on the cobbles. He looked straight at me, without any embarrassment. He knew that I was seeing what he saw – that my visions had shown me The Confessor directing the massacre. It made us closer, and also further apart. Whatever he'd thought of, or hoped for, when he made that decision, the blood in the courtyard would never be unseen. Whatever his feelings were, the blood made them at once too weighty, and too trivial.

'It's done now,' he said.

In the trees above us, the day's first birds were summoning the sun. I remembered a story I'd heard at the settlement: that when the blast came, all the birds in flight that weren't killed instantly were blinded. I tried to imagine it. Those that couldn't land, that flew until they dropped. I pictured the blind, inexorable descent.

'Zoe thinks you're running scared,' he said.

'I am,' I said. 'Scared, I mean.'

'But not running?'

'No.' There was no point now. There was no distance that would spare me the knowledge of what had happened on the island. And there was no safety to be gained anymore.

370

CHAPTER 29

When the others emerged, we lit a small fire and ate.

'Now what?' Zoe asked. I was surprised that the question was addressed to me, not Piper.

'We have to go back towards Wyndham. It's time to strike back at them.'

Kip sighed. 'We haven't been very efficient about this. We've spent the last few months running away from that place. I never thought I'd be going back to see those tanks again.'

I spoke quickly. 'You won't be.'

'You're not going without me.' A statement, not a question, though his eyes shifted quickly from me to Piper and back.

'Of course not. Maybe I ought to be trying some heroic solo mission, but it didn't even occur to me. But we're not going back to the tanks.'

'That's not your plan?' Piper and Zoe looked as nonplussed as Kip.

'Think about it,' I said to Kip. 'You were the only one, in all those tanks, who was alert, conscious. We got you out of there, but it was luck – or being a seer – that let me find you. The others, though, we don't know what kind of state they're in. And we only just got out of there – they'll have tightened up security since then. We can't go back.'

'You're leaving them there, then – all those others?'

I shook my head. 'You've told me before – about being conscious, in the tank. Seeing the others, in the tanks nearby. You were looking out of there for who knows how long. Years, maybe. But you never said anything about anyone looking back.'

He looked down. 'I was in and out of consciousness. I could have missed it.'

One of Zoe's knives twanged impatiently as she flicked it under her nails. I ignored her.

'You made a promise to that guy on the island,' Kip said. 'You promised you'd do all you could to help those people.'

'To Lewis. I know. And you told me at the time it was stupid. Look, I want to get them out – all of them. But even if we could get in, we don't know if we could get them out alive. They might not be as strong as you.' A simultaneous snort from Piper and Zoe. 'It could kill them – and their twins. And even if they could survive getting out of the tanks, how would we get them out of there, from the middle of Wyndham, with armed guards everywhere? I can't pull a secret escape route out of the hat every time we need one, let alone with hundreds of half-dead amnesiacs in tow.'

'They mightn't be amnesiacs.'

'Exactly. They mightn't react to the tanks the same way as you. That's my whole point. I can't risk it if I don't even know that I can get them out alive.'

Piper interrupted. 'And keep them that way. In the past, we might have been able to use our network of safehouses, keep them in hiding, maybe even smuggle them as far as the island. But that's not an option now. The island's gone, the network's in chaos.'

Kip didn't even look at Piper, just kept his gaze on my face. 'So we leave them there?'

'We have to. For now, anyway.'

'That's your big plan?' said Zoe. '*Not* attacking the tanks complex?'

'If only it were that easy,' I said. 'But I think there's another target, just as important, and with less chance of people being killed.'

Piper interrupted: 'Killing people isn't a deal-breaker. It isn't for them, so it can't be for us.'

'That's the whole problem right there,' I snapped. 'Them and us. Why can't you see that it makes no difference who you kill? You still wipe out both. It's just that you only have to stick your little knife into one of them.'

'Our "little knives" have saved your bacon more than once,' said Zoe. 'Don't blame us for doing what you can't bring yourself to do.'

Shaking my head, I tried again. 'But there's a target that's not guarded. Or hardly at all. It was the wires that Kip stumbled onto, in the taboo town, that made me realise. It reminded me of the glimpse I had, from The Confessor. It was important to her – so important that she freaked out when I saw it.'

'A weapon? Like a bomb?'

'Worse, in a way. It's where they're keeping all the names – the pairing up.'

'The registrations?' Piper lifted his head.

'So? People know who their twins are anyway. Even those who were split young. He's the only person I've ever met who doesn't,' Zoe said, gesturing at Kip. 'And he's not exactly normal.'

'Most people know, sure,' I said. 'Though many don't know what becomes of their twin, after they're split. All most of them have is what's on their registration papers: their twin's name, the place they were born. But even if people knew every detail about their twin – that's not the same as the Council knowing.' I turned to Kip. 'You saw what they did to that man in New Hobart, just for not being registered. Why do you think it's so important to them?'

'The last few years, we've had more and more reports of that,' Piper said. 'They're ruthless in enforcing the rules on registrations – more strictly even than tithe payments.'

'I still don't see how a few pieces of paper can be more of a threat to us than the tanks,' Kip said.

'It's not just a few pieces of paper,' I replied. 'It's millions of them, and it's the source of all the other stuff. How do you think they pick who goes in the tanks? Or track down people like me, with powerful twins?'

'And the list from the island,' added Piper, 'that The Confessor was using to decide who to kill, who to take away?'

'By the sounds of it, that was The Confessor rather than the list,' said Zoe.

'She's a big part of it,' I conceded. 'She's right at the heart of it, somehow – that's why she was so shocked when I saw that chamber. It's close to her – dear to her, even. Her, the registrations, the list, and that chamber I saw in her mind. It's all part of the same thing. They've got all that information; they're using it to manipulate everything. Everything about you – what you've done, who you are, who your twin is – it's all there to be used in any way they see fit.'

'But how can they use it?' said Zoe. 'Like you said, there

must be millions of registrations. How could they keep track of it all?'

'The machines. That's what I saw in the chamber – the wires, the metal boxes. They're using the machines to keep track of it all. They could do it with paper – they managed like that for years and years. But with the technology, they're infinitely more efficient. More information, more quickly. It's deadly. All this time everyone's been so paranoid that if people started using machines from the Before again, it'd end in another blast. And it turns out it's much simpler than that: just the information. That's all they need.'

'No it's not. What about the technology in the tank room? All that stuff. You think that's not important?'

'Of course it is.' I took Kip's hand. 'But where do you think they get the information about who to put in the tanks, who to experiment on? The information's the first stage. Everything else is built on it. Even if they didn't have the tanks, they'd just have locked you all up in cells somewhere.'

'That's not the same.'

'It's not. I know. And one day, if we don't stop them in time, they'll be able to tank us all, indiscriminately. But they're not there yet – nowhere near. And until they are, this information is what they're relying on. It's what they use, every time they choose who lives or dies. Who walks free and who gets whipped, or locked away, or tanked.' I was leaning in close to his face, close enough to see the tiny flecks of darker brown in his irises, the flared pupils pulsing. 'If they didn't have the names, the pairings, they wouldn't know who they were after, or where to find them. That's the source of it all.'

'I thought your twin was the source of it all,' said Zoe.

'He is. I'm not denying that. Him and The Confessor.

Others too, like The General. But the information is the thing that's allowed him to do all these things. And I know where to find it.'

*

It took two weeks' hard travelling to make it back to the outskirts of Wyndham. When Kip and I had escaped, we'd headed south-west for weeks, avoiding the Spine Mountains that bisected the land, extending north to south until they petered out above the marshy lands towards New Hobart. Now, after landing from the island much higher up the west coast, with Zoe we'd cut straight across the Spine Mountains, so that from the cave we were heading almost directly east towards Wyndham.

We travelled mainly at night, though in the empty plains east of the mountains we risked the daylight too, sleeping only for a few hours a day, when shelter presented itself. Even then we took shifts. Kip and I would never have managed to maintain the relentless pace, except that unlike when we were travelling alone, this time we were never hungry. Zoe and Piper caught birds, rabbits, and, one morning, a snake that only Piper dared to eat, though he swore it was delicious. But even with full stomachs it was exhausting, and in the scorched plains thirst was the problem. Zoe and Piper took turns to scout ahead, while I guided us to the few sparse springs that I could sense, where we filled our flasks. We talked little, even when settling down for sleep. It felt like the delirium of those first few days of my escape with Kip, in the tunnel through the mountain: wake, walk, sleep, wake, walk. I saw how tired Kip was. At night, when I curled back-to-back with him, his spine was sharp against my own. Neither of us wished to slow, though. There was a momentum to our journey now, a sense of purpose that had been lacking in the past. I remembered Kip's comment, months earlier: *away isn't really a destination.* We have a destination now, I thought, though who knows what will come of it.

Despite this new purposefulness, Kip himself was edgy. He spoke less, even at night when the two of us curled together, away from Piper and Zoe. I thought his new silences might just be the result of exhaustion. But we'd been exhausted before – he and I had been pursued across the country and back, and he'd never been so hushed. This new silence, which he carried with him like a weight, had been with him only since the taboo town on the mountaintop. The wires there had taken him back to the tanks, and he hadn't fully emerged. Perhaps I'd underestimated, over our months together, what the tanks had done to him. It was easy to forget, amongst his quips and his lopsided smile, what he had lived through. His physical recovery had been so quick. His body was strong now, despite his leanness, and his movements had little of the initial clumsiness the tanks had left him with. But his raw panic in that mountaintop ruin, snaked with wires, had reminded me that something was still broken. Something that all the days we'd spent together, and all the nights, couldn't even begin to heal.

One morning he whispered to me, so quietly that in my half-sleep I could hardly hear it.

'What if it comes back to me, and I don't like what I remember?'

I rolled closer to him. Under my hand, his heart was beating too quickly, a trapped thing. 'What if I'm not a good person?' he went on. 'What if I remember, and the person I was isn't someone I want to be?'

'Do you remember something?'

I felt him shake his head. 'No. But we've always assumed that remembering my past would be a good thing. What if it's not?'

I patted his chest slowly, coaxing his pulse to keep time with my hand. So many times, when I'd woken screaming from visions, he'd patted my back the same way. What had I offered him? What had I given him to fill his hollow memory, except the burden of my own horror-filled nights, and the new horrors of pursuit, and battle?

'You choose who you are,' I said.

'You believe that?'

I nodded into his shoulder.

'I know you, Kip.'

*

As the dry plains receded and the network of rivers began to spread its grasp, there were more signs of habitation. At first, just a few settlements in the dry but still arable land. These were meagre Omega outposts, some consisting of only a few shacks, but we still kept a safe distance, skirting each settlement widely and not lighting fires at night. Then, as the land grew richer, the Alpha habitations appeared: groomed fields and orchards surrounding large buildings. We saw people at work in the fields, or riding on the roads. But the country remained open enough for us to make our nocturnal way, unseen, avoiding the busiest roads even at night.

Two nights from Wyndham, there was a safehouse, Piper and Zoe said. A lone Omega house in a damp valley, owned by a couple sympathetic to the resistance. Somewhere we could sleep indoors, wash, take shelter from the scrutiny of the open spaces. All through that night's journey I imagined the feeling of lying in a soft bed again. The luxury of being oblivious to weather. But when we crested the valley, just before dawn, we were greeted by nothing but charred beams, some still smoking, and a puddle, black with ash.

'Somebody got careless,' Piper said, as we crouched just below the crest of the hill. 'I was afraid this would happen, after the raid on the island: too many refugees, getting desperate, seeking shelter. The Alphas must have spotted something, found them out.'

'Or somebody gave them up,' said Zoe. 'The hostages they took, maybe, from the island.'

'Maybe.' Piper peered down at the wreckage. 'I don't think we can risk getting any closer; it could be watched.' He turned to me. 'Is there anyone alive down there?'

I shook my head. No feeling emanated from the valley, only the smoke. 'I can't sense anyone. But that doesn't mean they've been killed. They might have been taken.' Since the discovery of the tanks, that idea was hardly comforting.

'We need to move on,' said Piper. 'Find cover. But it's looking more and more like what I feared. The whole network might have been cracked open.'

Two days later we drew within sight of Wyndham. I realised that I'd never seen it from the outside. My hooded, night arrival had shown me nothing, and my only subsequent impressions had been from the ramparts of the fort, above the city. Now, approaching from the west, with the sun beginning to rise ahead of us, the city reared up, buildings clinging to the hill like mussels on a rock, right up to the fort. Beneath the fort, the river emerged from the hillside and meandered its way downstream to the north. Just a day or so's journey downstream, the silos waited for us. Further downstream was my childhood village, and my mother. Our mother. And on the southern side of the mountain, hidden from sight now, wound the other river, which I couldn't think of without gratitude: the river that Kip and I had followed in those first days of escape, months before.

Zoe looked appraisingly at the city's peak. 'That fort's full of soldiers, and the three of you are on top of their wanted list. The city's crawling with them, too.'

'What about you?' I asked.

She shrugged. 'It depends how much they've penetrated the network, since the attack. We've done our best, but you can't do what I've done for years without some people getting word of it. For years I've been escorting refugees to the pick-up points, helping with rescues, meeting and sending messengers. With the hostages the Council took, chances are that somebody will have squealed by now. They might not know about me being Piper's twin, but my guess is that they've got some idea of who I am, what I do.'

'But they won't be expecting us to have come back here, of all places,' said Piper.

'Don't underestimate The Confessor,' I warned. 'But I think you're right: they know we were on the island only recently. I don't think they'd expect us to have headed back here, let alone so quickly.'

For most of the day we rested, under cover of a scrubby copse, and when we set off in the afternoon we avoided the roads. By the time darkness was sloping into the valley, we'd skirted north of the city to join the river, me leading the way.

'How far downstream do you think?' Piper asked.

'A day's walk, I'd guess. The silos were half a day upstream from our village, and Wyndham about a day further upstream – far enough away that we never went there.'

It must have been a few hours past midnight when we

passed the small, slumbering outpost where the gorge left the river. It wasn't much more than a stable block and a single, long barracks, topped by an Alpha flag hanging slackly in the still night air. The garrison hadn't been there when I was a child.

'Room there for fifty soldiers, maybe more,' said Piper. 'These kinds of outposts are springing up more and more, these days.'

An hour beyond that, having made our way up the rock-strewn gorge, we came within sight of the three silos. Round, flat-roofed and huge, they blocked the stars behind them. They were still windowless, as I'd remembered them, but were now connected to one another by walkways near the top. Where the doorways used to gape open, now a closed door was visible at the base of each silo: an oblong of dark metal against the pale, moonwashed concrete of the buildings.

'They're from the Before?' Kip asked.

I nodded. 'The doors are new, and the walkways at the top. But otherwise it looks the same as when we used to come here.'

'Why aren't they guarded?' Zoe spoke quietly.

'The same reason they're hidden all the way out here, miles from Wyndham. They don't want anyone to know about it. Plus it's taboo, so it's not as if they need to worry about random visitors wandering in. There're the barracks nearby, but this is Zach and The Confessor's pet project. They don't trust anyone.'

'Even if we don't have guards to worry about, what about the doors?'

Zoe grinned. 'I already told you how Piper and I got by, as kids. I've been picking locks since I was ten. I can get us in there.'

'You can let me and Kip in,' I said, 'but you're not coming with us.'

She rolled her eyes. 'First you didn't want to get involved in the resistance, and now you're going to do the whole martyr thing?'

'It's not a martyr thing. If it were, I wouldn't drag Kip into it. This isn't going to be a battle. It's a machine, not an army base. I told you, Zach's too paranoid to trust soldiers here.'

Piper shook his head. 'But he's not stupid. You shouldn't go in alone.'

'I won't be alone – I'll have Kip. That's our best chance: keeping it small, keeping it quick. I'll know where to go, what to do.'

'It makes sense,' Zoe turned to Piper. 'Think about it: if they get taken out, we'll still be able to carry on with our work.'

'Nice to know you care,' said Kip.

'But she's right,' I said. 'The resistance is falling apart since the attack. There are refugees from the island being chased by bounty hunters and soldiers; the network of safehouses is collapsing. What Kip and I are going to do here, it matters. But it's not the only thing that matters. You and Zoe need to get things back on track.'

He looked at me appraisingly. 'You don't need to make up for what happened on the island.'

'Just get us in there.'

'Then what?'

'When we get out, we're going to need to get away, as far from here as we can. And quickly, too, before the dawn. Do you think you could make it back to the Council outpost, get hold of some horses, without raising an alarm?'

Zoe nodded. 'We could be back within the hour, meet

382

you at the neck of the gorge, where there's some cover. But we can't hang around – not so close to the barracks. If we take horses, the alarm will be raised as soon as the soldiers are up. If you're not back by dawn, we'll have to leave.'

'Ever the sentimentalist,' said Kip.

'It goes both ways,' said Piper. 'If we're not there, go on without us. Head east. As far as the deadlands if necessary.'

I murmured my assent as I tightened the straps of the rucksack. Piper checked I still had his knife at my belt. Kip's hand, too, kept returning to the knife at his own belt. We approached the silos slowly. For the last fifty yards there was no cover; even the sparse bushes that lined much of the gorge had thinned out. But there were no windows in the silos to overlook our approach. Only the same sense of surveillance that I always felt: the unrelenting scrutiny of The Confessor, seeking me.

I led us to the door of the largest silo. There was no handle in the studded steel, just the lock. Piper pressed his ear to the door, waited several moments, then nodded at Zoe. She knelt, pulled from amongst the knives on her belt a tiny metal tool, and fiddled for a few seconds with the lock. Her tongue emerged from the corner of her mouth, and she closed her eyes. Her hand moved swiftly and jerkily. It reminded me of Kip when he slept: how his body alternated between twitches and stillness. Two seconds later, there was the satisfying click of the lock giving way.

Zoe stood. There were no big farewells, just the meeting of eyes in the darkness.

'Neck of the gorge, before dawn,' Piper said, briefly brushing my arm.

'Before dawn,' I repeated, like an incantation. Then Piper and Zoe stepped back into the night, and I turned to the unlocked door.

CHAPTER 30

I remembered the noise in the tank rooms, how it had surprised me. The silo was the same, though louder. Inside, it was one huge room, a spiral staircase running up one side, leading to a small platform near the roof. Banked five feet thick all around the walls were the machines. Hundreds, I thought at first. But when I arched my neck back to trace their climb up to the ceiling, I saw that there were thousands. Around the edge of the floor huge black boxes hummed, each one disgorging hundreds of cables that then spread their way like cobwebs up the machine-stacked walls. Electric lights were suspended from the ceiling, but not much light penetrated to the floor two hundred feet below, where we stood. The little light that did reach us fell in intricate, trellised patterns from the cables that criss-crossed the hollow room. After the coolness outside, the heat in the silo was pressing and static. When my arm brushed against one of the machines, the metal casing was hot.

Kip already had his knife in his hand. 'So we just start cutting wires?'

'No.' I looked around. 'I mean, it couldn't hurt, but it

won't be enough – they'll be able to fix that kind of damage. We need to get at the heart of it – into the system.'

'Where would you start?' He began to spin around, slowly, head back, scanning the immense mass of metal, punctuated by the occasional blip of a flashing light. But I hadn't moved, my eyes still fixed on the highest point, the platform at the top of the stairs. The wires emanating from it were in such thick clusters that they'd been bound together, forming muscular boughs of cable.

He followed my gaze up the precipitous stairs, and sighed. 'Once. Just once, couldn't it be easy?' I smiled ruefully. 'But we can do some damage while we're down here, at least,' he added. He took an experimental swipe at a nearby cable, leaping back and dropping the knife when a blue arc sparked. 'It couldn't hurt, you said?'

'I wasn't speaking literally.' I looked nervously at my own knife. 'Maybe if we just pull the cables out?'

'No,' he said, picking up the knife. 'It startled me, but I'm fine. We'll do more damage this way.' He sliced at a cable stretched above him. The severed ends leaped apart with a jealous hiss.

We made a rapid circuit of the huge space, slicing and unplugging as we went. Whenever I tugged on a cord, and felt the resistance shift to release, I was reminded of the tube I'd unwittingly pulled out when I'd discovered Kip.

Next to me, he used his knife to lever open the casing of one of the machines. The side landed on the floor with a clash of metal on concrete. Inside was a miniature version of the room itself: units connected by wires in a sequence that seemed chaotic at first but was in fact precisely choreographed. When Kip and I took to it with knives and hands, it protested with smoke. The lights along its base blinked urgently, then stopped altogether.

When nobody came, despite the clangs and sparks, we grew bolder. Kip wielded a narrow strip of metal casing like a crowbar, swinging it into the control panels of the machines. Now our footsteps were amplified by broken glass. Even though smoke was beginning to claw in my throat, I was shocked at how much I enjoyed the destruction: tearing the casings from the machines, ripping out their tender, wired insides.

When we'd completed a loop of the chamber, we began climbing the spiral stairs, slicing as we went at the cables within reach on the wall. The heavier cords clanged satisfyingly as they dropped, severed, against the machines on the opposite side. The smoke from the damage on the ground level was thinner here, though still enough to blur the floor, further and further below us, and to make my breath rasp.

As we neared the top I paused and held my hand out to halt Kip behind me. I squinted slightly, then closed my eyes. Above us the platform loomed, extending almost twenty feet from the wall, blocking a third of the roof. Beneath its base, all the room's cables culminated. I looked up at the point where the staircase penetrated the platform's floor, right by the wall. From below, all I could make out was the square opening, brightly backlit by the lights above.

'Somebody's up there.'

He raised an eyebrow. 'If they've let us do this much already, I'm guessing they're not looking for a fight.'

I shook my head. 'It's not always that simple.' I noticed we were whispering and thought how absurd it was, given the cacophony we'd created in the last ten minutes. 'I can't tell. I've felt her so strongly, for so long – and this place reeks of her and Zach anyway. But I think it could be her.'

'The Confessor?'

I nodded.

'So now what?' He was one step below me. His hand came up the rail to reach mine, gave it a squeeze.

'I don't think we can finish this without going up and facing her.'

'I never thought I'd long for Piper and Zoe, but shouldn't we come back with them?'

I shook my head.

'Cass, I'm sure you're a hellcat in a fight, but when you say "finish this", don't you think it would be better if there were more, you know, deadly, knife-throwing rebels involved?'

'No. We've brought enough on them – we can't put them at risk like that. Too much of the resistance depends on them. Anyway, with The Confessor, it's a mind-game; I don't think she could fight any more than the two of us. When I said "finish this", I didn't mean it had to come to blood. I just meant –' I paused, struggling to explain it to him. 'I meant that this started with us. And the whole time, it's been her I've felt, tracking me. More even than Zach. We can't keep running away from her. All of this' – I gestured at the machine-encased chamber below us – 'she's the core of it. We can't finish it without facing her.' I slipped my knife back into its sheath at my belt.

He kept his knife out, but stepped up next to me. The spiral steps were so narrow that the two of us were crammed close and off-balance, but I was glad to feel him beside me as we climbed the final few stairs and stepped onto the platform.

Set against the wall, next to a closed steel door, was a huge control panel at which The Confessor sat in a wheeled chair. Her eyes were closed, but I could see them moving busily beneath the twitching lids as her hands roamed the console, pressing buttons, caressing dials. Around her fore-head sat a metal band, a steel halo, from which a single wire draped to meet the central console.

'It's her?' Kip whispered at my side.

I nodded.

Unhurried, The Confessor spun in her chair to face us. 'I wondered when I'd be seeing you again.'

I opened my mouth to answer, but saw that The Confessor hadn't even glanced at me. Still staring at Kip, she stood, lifted off the metal band, narrowed her eyes, then smiled slowly. 'We'd guessed there'd be damage, but it's strange to see in person. And it's worse than I'd realised. You really are a blank slate, aren't you? Remarkable.'

'What do you know about Kip?' I said. My voice echoed back at us from the roof of the silo.

'Kip – is that what they're calling you now?' She stepped closer to him until there were only a few feet between them. 'I had another name once, too. It's been so long now, I can hardly remember it. I'm very much like you, you see.'

'You're nothing like him.' I darted forward, snatched the metal band from her hands, tore it from its cable and hurled it from the platform. The noise was obscene. The contraption hit the far side of the chamber before ricocheting its way down to the floor with a final, resounding clang.

The Confessor hadn't moved, just raised her hands and shrugged. 'You let off steam as much as you like. I cut off the high-voltage power when you started your little frolic downstairs. Slashing at live wires with knives and bare hands – you're lucky you didn't kill yourselves. So I've been running on the auxiliary generators.' Her words meant nothing to us, but she ignored our baffled expressions. 'Just enough voltage to give you a nice fireworks show, keep you busy. And, of course, for me to get on the intercom, call your brother, to let him know the prodigal twin is back.' She peered beyond the edge of the platform at the smoke-strewn wreckage beneath. 'Much of the damage will be superficial, by the way. The computers are a huge asset, of course, but most of the crucial stuff goes on in here.' She tapped her head, then looked at me. 'But you knew that already, of course.'

'You don't need to give us another incentive to kill you,' said Kip.

She laughed. 'Believe me, you don't want to do that.'

I waved a hand at the console, the machines massed below. 'How can you do this, to your own kind?'

'It's no stranger than an Alpha running about with the Omega resistance.'

'We're telling you nothing about them,' said Kip.

'Oh, you mean your friend Zoe – Piper's twin. Yes, we know all about her. And I'm sure her whereabouts, and his, will be one of the things the interrogators will be asking you about shortly. But I wasn't talking about her.'

Kip and I exchanged blank looks.

'And as for "my own kind",' she went on, 'you of all people should know it's not that straightforward for a seer. The Omegas resent us, because we're not deformed like them. And the Alphas are scared of us: we're like them, only better. We don't belong anywhere.'

'I do,' I said.

'Where? With your parents, who were so keen to get rid of you? Or how about that bleak little settlement you scraped by in, after your folks had kicked you out? Or maybe on the island? Though if you belonged so well there, it seems odd that you'd leave them to be slaughtered.'

'With me,' said Kip. 'She belongs with me. And Piper and Zoe.'

The Confessor laughed gently. 'How very sweet. But you're not quite one of them, are you, Cass? You're worth more than any of them. This Piper, at least, must have realised what you could be worth to them, or he'd have killed you as soon as he got hold of you, to be rid of Zach.' She cocked her head slightly as she stared at me. 'Though I'm beginning to wonder whether I didn't overestimate you. Whether we all didn't. I'm sure you have your moments. I'm guessing we have you to thank for the evacuation of most of the islanders; probably the fire at New Hobart too. But I'm surprised at your blind spots. You still haven't harnessed what you're capable of, it seems.'

She'd drawn even closer to us, but as always it was her mental presence that was most confronting. The calculation behind her still eyes; the probing that made me want to wince.

'You're disappointing, Cass. Like these machines. It turns out they're not everything we might have hoped. Oh, they're great for storing the information. It's all in there.' She waved vaguely at the stacks of machines below. 'You should have seen the record chambers at Wyndham, before Zach and I had it moved into the computers here. They had the information, but it was so unwieldy. Now, if I need to find something straightforward, it's phenomenally good. Think of the thousands of clerks we'd need, all scuttling about with millions of files, just to keep track of the basic details. With the computer, it's all synthesized, in one system. Like a live thing. So I can tap into it, interact with it, use the information as fluently as thinking. If we'd stayed with paper records, we'd never have been able to do what we've done.'

'And what a tragic loss that would be.'

The Confessor ignored Kip entirely. 'But the computers are still – how can I put this? – limited. For complex things

– predictions, deductions – they don't match the human brain. They will, one day – and perhaps they did, Before. Though I doubt they'd ever eclipse what a seer is capable of. But what they'd achieved, back then – you wouldn't believe it.'

'Oh, I'm pretty sure we've all seen what they achieved,' I said.

Again, the interruption didn't even seem to register. 'In the Before, all of this information, all this power, would have existed in a single machine, no bigger than one of those generators. We're not there yet, and it's doubly hard, under the pressure of secrecy. People still aren't ready to embrace the benefits. Our fault, perhaps – we've preserved the taboo, maybe too zealously, for too long. So, for now, we work with what we've got. Quietly. And for the really complex stuff: that's where I come in.

'We could have used you, too, if you'd worked with me. You could have been a part of it. Already, with just me, and access to all that information, there's not much I can't do. It's so much more than what I did on the island. Think about it. Some Omega rabble-rouser out east, giving the Council a hard time about tithes, and with his own body-guard of resistance fighters? We can track down his Alpha twin, going under a different name and working on the south coast, in half an hour, and have a knife at his throat in half a day. An Alpha from Wyndham running for election against your brother? You'd be amazed how fast he'll retire to his country estate once we've got his twin in custody. Better still, we can predict hot spots. We've got algorithms that monitor everything, day by day, in a way we never could before. We can keep tabs on which towns have low registration rates, patchy tithe collections. Move in early, wipe out the whole place before we have an uprising on our hands. Zach's been focused on the tanks, but none of that's possible without this.'

'Why so unprotected, then? Why could the two of us just waltz in here?'

'There's a lack of curiosity, and we're not particularly keen to change that. Councillors and soldiers aren't above being terrified of the taboo, either. Nobody wants to know about this installation. Oh, they know, but not the whole story.' She gestured to the floor below. 'The generators down there, and in the other silos, provide the electricity for half of Wyndham – most of the Council buildings are wired now, in some form, and the Council knows about the tanks. They're hypocrites: happy enough to have Electric lights in their private chambers, even to have their own twins tanked, but they won't resist the taboo in public. They don't dare. And they don't see the potential to take it further.

'Your brother and I had more of a vision, though. Plans to take it to its logical conclusion. That's why we've kept this quiet: it's ours. If we start drafting in a security detail, everyone's going to want to know.'

'The logical conclusion,' I echoed. 'All of us in tanks, you mean. And you and your Alpha friends, living as if we never existed.'

'She's melodramatic, isn't she?' The Confessor said to Kip. 'It's more complicated than that. Think of the logistics: millions of Omegas to be dealt with. Even with our recent experiments with mass tanks, you're still looking at a whole lot of infrastructure. It's not going to happen overnight, despite what Zach might want. That's why we've been focusing on this database, and on strategic tanking, for now – just key targets. And, of course, at the other end of the scale, low-value targets in the experimental stages. It took us three years of solid work just to get the first tanks viable. We suffered quite heavy losses in the development process.'

'*You* suffered heavy losses?' Kip had been edging closer the whole time. His knife was in his hand.

'She has a twin, Kip,' I whispered, grabbing the back of his shirt.

'So do all the people she's killed. She's the system. If we take her out, we shut it down. Think of what we'd achieve. That was the plan when we came here.'

'No. When we came here, we didn't know the system was a person.'

'She hardly counts as a person.'

'That's how the Alphas feel about us,' I said. 'We can't be like that.'

'We have to.'

He rushed forward. I followed, without thinking. I could hear my own pulse, urgent, competing with the crashing sounds as Kip brought The Confessor down hard against the floor, the chair skidding into the consoles. He was on top of her, one knee on her chest, but she grabbed at his hand, and with both arms was twisting his wrist, forcing the knife back towards him. His single arm couldn't withstand the force and he had to roll to avoid the knife, until she was on top of him. I looked around. The knife in my belt was too deadly. On the whole platform, starkly glass and steel, the chair was the only alternative. I grunted involuntarily as I picked it up, then swung it back and launched it at The Confessor's head.

At first I thought I must accidentally have hit Kip too. The Confessor slumped heavily sideways, her head bouncing as it hit the floor. Kip did the same: his shoulders dropped to the floor, teeth snapping shut as the back of his head hit the metal surface. But it didn't fit. The chair hadn't touched him. I'd seen it clip The Confessor on the side of the head on its way to the far edge of the platform where it now rested on its side against the door, wheels spinning.

In the silence of Kip and The Confessor's dual unconsciousness, I realised what I'd missed. It came sharply into focus, like Kip's face emerging from the blur of the tank months ago. I wondered whether, as with my mother's warning about the Keeping Rooms, I'd known all along.

CHAPTER 31

The Confessor was the first to come to. She blinked several times, shook her head, grimaced. When she opened her eyes properly, her first look wasn't at me, standing over her, but at Kip, still unconscious.

'All this time,' I said. 'I felt you searching for me. Ever since I escaped.'

'Since he escaped,' corrected The Confessor.

'All that time, I thought it was me you were looking for. But I still don't see how it's possible. You can't both be Omegas.'

'We had to take off the arm. Just branding him wasn't enough,' she said, sitting up further. 'The arm was Zach's bright idea. There'd be resistance to the idea of tanking Alphas, even amongst those working on the tank project. And we couldn't have him traceable to me – too much of a liability. So we had to make him look like an Omega. The amnesia is an added bonus, though I can't take credit for it. It's not something we anticipated. They've never brought anyone out of suspension before – the effects were unknown.'

'And you didn't care what it would do to him.'

'I cared that it didn't kill him.' She touched the side of her head, looked with distaste at the smear of blood on her hand. 'Now you know why I wasn't scared of the two of you finding me here. I knew you'd stuck together. If you'd grown close to him, you'd never harm me. But I underestimated the effects of the tank. I could sense that he'd been damaged, but not that he'd completely forgotten everything. And I overestimated you. I assumed you would have worked it out.'

'I've been so blind.'

Wincing, The Confessor pressed her swollen temple again. 'We both have. I should have told you immediately. It was rash.' She turned back to Kip, now shifting groggily on the floor. 'But he's changed. The coward I knew would never have attacked like that.'

'You don't know him. He might be your twin, but he's nothing like you.'

'Perhaps not. Any more than you're like Zach. Zach and I were both burdened with twins who lacked our ambition.'

I knelt over Kip, lifted his head just enough to slide my arm beneath it and raise him, slowly, until his shoulders and head rested on my knees. He clenched his eyes more tightly shut, then opened them, flinching at the light.

'Her?' he said. 'It's impossible.'

I shook my head. 'They cut off your arm, Kip, to disguise you. I'm so sorry.'

He closed his eyes again, for a long time. Several times his lips began moving, as if he were about to speak. When his eyes opened again he looked straight at me. 'Is it true?'

I nodded. There was another long silence.

'Guess this means I can't hold your twin against you anymore,' he murmured to me, staring beyond me at The Confessor as she stood. 'Looks like both of us really hit the sibling jackpot.'

He was searching her face, his expression more intent than I'd ever seen it. As if he might recognise himself in it. As if he would see, written on her pale skin, all the secrets of his lost past.

Her eyes, usually so implacable, were surveying him curiously. 'Even now, you really remember nothing?'

He shook his head. 'Why? You want to start reminiscing about our childhood?'

'There wasn't an "our",' she said. 'I was sent away at eight, as soon as I couldn't hide my visions anymore. But that wasn't enough for you, of course. Nor was this.' She swept her hand over her branded forehead. 'Not enough to have me branded, scraping by at a settlement while you took over Mum and Dad's farm, lived the good life. Nothing was ever enough for you, when it came to hating me. So three years back, you wanted to make sure I wasn't a liability. Approached the local Councilman, asked for help to track me down. Told him you'd heard rumours that a wealthy person might pay to have his twin "taken care of" in the Keeping Rooms.'

Piper had mentioned this on the island. But I couldn't imagine it of Kip. I could come to terms with the idea of him as an Alpha. But this person she described – spiteful, cruel – I couldn't recognise at all.

'That wasn't me,' he shouted, sitting up. 'I don't even know who I was then. I don't have any memories at all, because of what you did to me.' I'd never seen him cry before, but now tears streaked the dirt on his cheeks. 'I don't even care about the arm,' he said, shrugging the stub of his shoulder. 'It's everything else. You took away everything.'

'I took away everything?' Her laughter was a curved blade. 'What about me, sent away at eight? You never cared about me. You would have done to me what I did to you.' There it was: the hatred that had pursued us ever since we escaped. It had nothing to do with me. 'I knew you'd come after me, eventually,' she said. 'Someone as spiteful as you – I knew you were never going to forgive me for those first eight years.' Her voice was still quiet, but her eyes were narrowed, her jaw so tight that her words had a staccato quality. 'I had to find a way to protect myself. That's one of the reasons I sought out Zach, started working with him. Maybe that's why he and I work so well together – he has his own axe to grind when it comes to being split late. I've always known what drove Zach, because I saw the same fear and spite in you, even if you were never ambitious like he is, or smart like he is.'

Was that how she made sense of the world, I wondered? Not Alpha against Omega, but the ambitious, pitted against all who weren't willing to match them in ruthlessness?

'I can't argue about our past with you.' Kip's voice was so low I could hardly hear it. Each word dropped into the silo below us like a stone down a well. 'I don't have anything left of it. It's all gone. You did this to me.'

'No.' She shook her head. 'You did this to me. You made me what I am.'

'You don't know Kip,' I said.

'He's my twin,' she said. 'I know him better than you ever will.'

I was about to retort, but Kip spoke first. 'Cass is right. You don't know me. We have nothing to talk about.' He turned back to me.

She was standing between us and the stairs. A wary stillness connected the three of us. I looked at the steel door set in the wall, but knew it was hopeless even before The Confessor spoke.

'Don't bother. It's locked.' She was still focused intently on Kip. 'I used to go and look at you, sometimes, you know,' she said. 'When you were in the tank. It was peaceful, seeing you like that. Like keeping a pet frog.'

'That's sick,' I said, remembering Kip floating in the tank, and the automated, muted terror of that scene.

'He would have done it to me,' she said. 'He tried to pay to have me put in a cell.' She turned back to him. 'When I used to watch you, you were livelier than the others. Sometimes I could have sworn you looked back at me. The technicians reported it too: signs of possible alertness from you. They didn't know why, of course – didn't know you weren't an Omega like the others.'

I tried to shut her out, and to focus only on Kip as I bent low over him. 'The stuff she says about your past,' I told him. 'I know it's not you. I know it's not the person that you are.'

'I'm sorry,' he said again.

'No,' I shook my head. 'Don't say that. It's not you.' I remembered what he'd said a few nights earlier: *What if the person I was isn't someone I want to be?*

He guessed what I was thinking, of course. 'I didn't know,' he said quickly. 'But since the taboo town, and all those wires, I started to have some flashbacks. Nothing specific, and nothing about her, or about being an Alpha. It was just like being in someone else's skin. And I didn't like that person. I'd thought not knowing was the worst thing. But this was worse. The person I could feel – he was full of disgust. And fear.' He looked down. 'I'm sorry.'

'That's not you.' I spoke loudly enough for The Confessor to hear. I wanted her to know. 'Don't be sorry. I know you,' I said.

I followed the curves of his brand with my finger. 'It

doesn't make a difference that you're an Alpha.' I dropped my voice again, trying to carve out a moment of privacy between the two of us, even under The Confessor's gaze. 'Though I'd started to think there might have been a touch of seer in you, too.'

He shook his head. 'Then you'd think I would have seen *this* coming.'

But I did, I thought. I felt it the whole time. I was just too stupid, too self-obsessed, to realise what it meant.

'Maybe you didn't sense that,' I said. 'But there was other stuff, just little things. The way you know what I'm thinking or feeling. How you butt in and say what I'm about to say.'

'I think maybe there's another word for that,' he said, with the crooked smile that had become so familiar.

'So your little escapade is over,' interrupted The Confessor. 'Now we wait. You can't fight me.' She picked up the knife from where it had fallen from Kip's hand. I stood to face her as she approached, the knife held out in front of her. She ran it up my neck, then down again, stopping at the hollow between my collarbones. I thought of the many nights when Kip and I had huddled close, his nose buried in the same notch where the knife blade now rested. 'That door's locked. Zach's not far away – he was working in another facility nearby. The soldiers won't be far behind him. It'll be up to him to decide what he wants to do with you, but I'd imagine, after this, you'll both be heading for the tanks.'

'I'm not going back.' Kip stood up, a little unsteadily.

'Oh, they'll keep you out for a while – you in particular. Once we're done interrogating you both, we'll want to run tests on you. You'll be quite the medical curiosity. We've never tanked an Alpha before, you see. And we don't ever bring people out of suspension, let alone after as long as that. It's a one-way ticket. But after we've satisfied our curiosity, you'll go back in, eventually.'

The knife sank a little further. I wasn't aware of any pain, only the warmth of the blood that trickled from the wound, the slight tickle as it traced between my breasts.

'What's his name?' I said. 'His real name, I mean.'

The Confessor went to speak, but Kip interrupted her. 'It doesn't matter.'

'You're not curious? Not at all?' she asked.

With the knife at my throat, I couldn't turn my head, but I strained my eyes to the right, where I could just see Kip.

'I was,' he said. 'A few months ago I would've given anything to know who I was. But it doesn't matter anymore.' He was sidling further into my line of sight, towards the steps at the far edge of the platform. 'I know who I am now.'

The Confessor turned, keeping the knife at my throat as she manoeuvred behind me. 'Take one step down those stairs and you know I'll kill her.'

'I know,' he said, edging closer to the staircase.

The Confessor tightened her arm further around my neck. 'This I hadn't expected – and that's saying something, coming from me.' The blood was soaking into the front of my shirt now. 'How about you, Cass? You ever think he'd betray you this way?'

I looked straight at Kip. I knew, then, what he was doing, with the same sudden certainty that I'd felt earlier when I'd realised his link to The Confessor.

'Don't do it,' I said.

When he stepped backwards my eyes were still fixed on his. I barely registered his half shrug, the final leap over the low railing behind him. As he dropped I refused to blink or look away, as if my gaze were somehow holding him to me, as if it were a lifeline that would arrest his fall. The Confessor screamed, but I made no noise. I reached the platform's edge without even realising, so I could trace his fall all the way down, until the silo's cement floor shattered my gaze.

When I opened my eyes again, I was huddled on the ground, the platform's metal floor cold against my cheek. Only three feet away, staring blindly at me, was The Confessor's motionless face.

CHAPTER 32

It might have been only seconds before Zach arrived; it might have been minutes. I heard noises, not from below but from the next silo: running footsteps, a key in the metal door. I ought to have been startled at his presence, after so long, but I never could be. It was his absence that had always felt strange.

He did look different, though: older, and thinner, and his eyes frantic with motion. He looked first over the railing, down to where Kip lay. Then he came to bend over me. He kept glancing from The Confessor to me, and back again. His hands and his lips were never still, angular fingers twitching as if working out some complex calculation. Periodically, his hand would move to his neck, pressing against the place where the knife had pierced me.

I didn't move. Where my face rested against the floor the metal was warming slowly. My stillness matched that of The Confessor. It came to me again, the moment I'd first seen Kip, his face drifting into sight through the glass of the tank. To move away now, to break this symmetry with his twin, would be to move one step further away from that moment. To move into a world in which he was gone.

'Get up.' Zach's voice hadn't changed, though it echoed strangely in the round chamber.

'No.' I closed my eyes. Below us, the silo door opened; shouts and footsteps echoed up to us. 'That's your men down there, no doubt. They can drag me if they have to. But I won't move.'

'They're coming now, you idiot. You have to go.'

That made me look up. 'What are you talking about?'

'If they find out you were involved, that'll be it for me. Even if I locked you up myself, they'd get to you, or take me out directly. You've blown it now. She was our biggest asset.' He gestured at The Confessor's body. 'If they link her death to me, it's the end of both of us.'

'It doesn't matter now,' I said. 'Not to me.'

'You don't get it.' The noises below grew closer. The soldiers were on the stairs now. 'If you disappear, I can blame it on him. I can contain it: tell them it was just her twin, gone mad, out for revenge. The two of you haven't been seen together since the island. But you have to go, now.' He fumbled at his belt, thrust me a small leather loop threaded with two keys. 'Take these. Go out the way I came – the big key gets you out on to the walkway between silos. Then the smaller key for a red door, into my private offices in the next silo. Get down to the base, then it's the same key for the outside door. It's unguarded. You can be away in minutes. They'll never know you were here.'

I sat up, looked at him. 'You could come with me. Get away from all this.'

'Why?' I wasn't sure if he was asking why I would offer, or why he would accept. But before I could answer he shook his head again. 'I can't. It's all gone too far. There are things I need to do.'

His hand was shaking so violently now that he dropped the proffered keys. I watched them land, settling between me and The Confessor's body. Another shout from below, the footsteps clanging steadily closer on the steel stairs. It all felt very slow, as if Kip's fall had broken time once and for all.

'Please.' It burst out with Zach's exhalation, more a raw sound than a word.

I looked up at him as I took the keys. 'I'm not doing this for you.'

'Faster.' He shouted loud enough for the soldiers on the stairs to hear him, but it was really me he addressed.

I stood. I knew that if I looked down, if I saw Kip's body again, I would never be able to stop looking. So I ran, as much away from that sight, crumpled at the base of the silo, as from the soldiers' shouts that were nearing the top of the stairs.

Once I'd locked the door behind me, it was just as Zach had said: the narrow steel passage between the silos; the red door; his chambers, occupying the top floors of the silo, the plush carpets weirdly opulent within the industrial stark-ness of the walls. A spiral staircase like the one next door, but this time in a bare expanse, just a concrete tube below the chambers at the top, lit by sparse Electric lights. At the base, the outer door, which released me into the night. A hundred feet to my left, where the larger silo rose into the darkness, I could hear voices, even the familiar sounds of horses. But I was shielded from sight by the silo from which I'd emerged. I locked the door behind me, watching my hand turn the key with a kind of disbelief: that I could still function, still move, after what had happened. As I moved up the gorge, away from the cluster of silos, I was surprised by my own breath and my footsteps, abrasive on the gravel.

That my body was still capable of making such ordinary sounds.

When I heard the riders approaching me rapidly from behind, I sped up, my body reacting even when my numbed mind could not. I was still a mile from the meeting place. And even if I could reach it, I couldn't risk leading the pursuing soldiers to Piper and Zoe. I dived from the path, through the brambled ditch that snagged at my skin, then scrambled up again into the cover of the longer grass. But the riders leapt the ditch too. Before I had time to look for more cover, they were upon me. Then, just like all those years ago, I was scooped up and thrown across the saddle.

'We were halfway through getting the horses when an alarm sounded at the barracks,' shouted Zoe, holding on to me tightly. 'We only just beat them here, but I don't think they saw us. Where's Kip?'

It wasn't the shock or relief that silenced me, but his name. I didn't answer.

I couldn't see Zoe, though I could feel her leaning over my back. I could just make out Piper, his dark horse drawing beside us as we slowed slightly. Zoe hauled me upright. I felt my body obey, my leg manoeuvre over the horse's back.

'Did you do it?' Piper said. 'The machine?'

'It's gone,' I said. 'Finished.'

'What about Kip?' I could feel Zoe's breath on my neck as she spoke.

I met Piper's eyes, shook my head.

He didn't hesitate. 'Go,' he said to Zoe. I closed my eyes, felt my body slump back and surrender to the momentum, the horse's syncopated strides carrying me forward over the twice-broken world.

CHAPTER 33

For a long time after that, I couldn't speak. It was as if all my words had been left back there, on the floor of the silo. What happened there had shattered language. Even when Zoe shook me, or when Piper splashed water on my face and tried to coax words from me, I couldn't form a syllable.

We rode for three days and nights, stopping only for a snatched half-hour once or twice a day. The horses were ragged with tiredness, stumbling heavy-legged. Froth gathered at their lips like soap-scum lathering in dirty water.

After the second day, the landscape began to change. I'd never been that far east – we were approaching the deadlands. The skin of the earth had been peeled back. There were no trees, no soil. Only flinty stone, on which the horses' hoofs clattered and slipped, and drifts of grey ash shifting endlessly in the hot wind. The colour had been stripped from the world; everything was shades of black and grey. Our own clothes and skin were the sole flashes of colour, but the ash-heavy wind soon blackened these too. Black dust clung to the edges of the horses' eyes, and rimmed their lips and nostrils. The only water was to be found in greasy, shallow pools, their surface slick with ash. By the edges of these ponds lurked patches of ashen grass, so sparse that our two horses stripped them bare each time we stopped. As for food for us, Zoe and Piper didn't even bother hunting – nothing lived out here.

We made it to the black river just in time. The horses were stumbling and we were drunk with tiredness. It took both Zoe and Piper to help me dismount. The river moved sluggishly, but its shallow valley heralded a respite in the landscape: grass, shrubs, and even one or two bony trees littered the banks.

'It's safe to drink,' Piper assured me when we bent over the dark water. 'Just shut your eyes and ignore the ash.' But by that stage I would have drunk anything. And when Zoe came back from an hour's hunt bearing a bony lizard, we didn't hesitate, snatching the strips of pale flesh from the fire still half-raw.

That night, as it grew dark, I found my way back into language – haltingly, at first, but then with urgency. Perhaps it was the food and drink, or the softening light of the fire. And I wanted to tell them what had happened; what Kip had done for me. I told them, too, about Zach's plan to blame the destruction on Kip, and to pretend I'd never been in the silo. 'It explains why we weren't pursued, at least at first,' I said. 'But you took two horses. Even if they believed Zach initially, they'll know by now that Kip wasn't alone.'

Zoe shook her head. 'No – we opened up the stables and let out as many horses as we could – almost all of them. It must have slowed the soldiers down, after the alarm was raised – we were round the back of the silos before the first ones arrived. They never saw us.'

'And with half the horses missing, they won't be able to confirm that more than one was stolen,' added Piper. 'If Zach keeps to his story, there's nothing to disprove it.'

'Weren't there sentries, at the stable?'

Piper nodded, but didn't meet my eyes. 'Only two.'

He looked relieved when I asked nothing further, but Zoe jumped in. 'We didn't leave any of our knives in the bodies, if that's what you're worried about. Nothing that could be linked to us.'

Piper shook his head at her, and she took the hint.

'Kip's missing arm,' he said. 'I never saw a scar. There wasn't one, was there? Not even – up close?' He'd suddenly become oddly attentive to the fire.

'Nothing.' I remembered kissing Kip's truncated shoulder; the firm skin; the contours of muscle and bone beneath my lips. If there was any scar, it must have been perfectly concealed; perhaps in the crease of his armpit. I couldn't reconcile the painstaking, delicate attention required to heal a wound so immaculately, with the brutality of taking off his arm and tanking him.

'Doubtless that's more technology they're keeping under wraps, then. Who knows what advances they've made, medically, if they're at the stage that they can keep people alive in tanks.'

Zoe spat into the fire, which hissed back at her. 'Think of what they could do for Omegas – for anyone sick, or injured – if they put that sort of stuff to a better use.'

Piper nodded. 'But however flawlessly they stitched it up, The Confessor still must have felt it. She'd still have felt the pain.'

'It wouldn't have put her off,' I said. 'She was tougher

than you could imagine.' I hated using the past tense for
The Confessor. That single word – *was* – wiped out Kip
too.

*

'Are there any safehouses this far east?' I asked.

Zoe laughed. 'Safehouses? There're no houses, safe or
otherwise. This valley's the last strip of life before the
deadlands, Cass. There's nothing here.'

That suited me well enough. We stayed for nearly a week,
camping by the blackened river. There was enough grass
for the horses, and Zoe and Piper managed to keep the three
of us fed, albeit mainly on lizard-flesh, grey-tinged and oily.
When they weren't hunting, they made plans. Huddled
together at the water's edge, they had long, detailed conversations about the island, about establishing a new sanctuary,
rebuilding the resistance. They sketched maps in the dust,
and tallied numbers: safehouses, allies, weapons, ships.

I stayed out of it. A heaviness had taken over me. I was
as listless as the ash-clogged river, at which I spent whole
days staring. Zoe and Piper knew better than to bother me.
The two of them had a kind of self-sufficiency, the self-
containment of their twinship, that let me feel alone, even
in the cool nights when the three of us slept close for
warmth.

I'd told them everything that happened, except for what
The Confessor had told me about Kip's behaviour in the
past. I could hardly shape that into thoughts, let alone
words. After what Kip had done in the silo, Piper and Zoe
were, at last, no longer being dismissive about him. I couldn't
bear to tell them what The Confessor had said, and to
expose him once again to their judgment. More than that:

if I told them, it would become real, and I would have to make my own judgment. I had already lost him in the silo. I couldn't let The Confessor's revelations take him from me twice over. The news of his past was a jagged reef I knew I couldn't negotiate, not at the moment. So I skirted The Confessor's words, not admitting them even to myself.

Instead, while Piper and Zoe talked each day, I thought about the island, and what had happened there. I remembered what Alice had said to me, just before she died: that even if the island was just an idea, maybe that was enough. I thought about the two ships that were still out west, searching the oceans for Elsewhere. I thought about the promise I'd made to Lewis, to help those who still floated in the tanks. I recalled, again and again, what Zach had said in the silo: 'There are things I need to do.'

Mostly, though, I thought about what Kip had said to me, on the island and again on the boat: about my weakness being my strength. About how I viewed the world differently, in not seeing Alphas and Omegas as opposed. I thought of what my different perspective had cost him, and whether anything could ever make that worthwhile. And whether I could still see the world that way, after what Zach and The Confessor had done. Kip had been the only one who had begun to understand how I felt about my twin. But his broken body on the silo floor had changed everything.

The knife-wound at my neck wouldn't heal. By the end of the week it was inflamed, and I could feel my pulse in it, each heartbeat a jab in the reddened flesh. Piper went off for an hour and returned with some murky green moss that he chewed into a paste. Kneeling in front of me, he pressed the sharp-smelling gum into the gap where the unravelled edges of my skin refused to knit.

Zoe was watching from across the fire. 'Don't bother,' she said to him. 'It won't heal until she stops fiddling with it.'

I hadn't realised she'd noticed, but it was true. Whenever I'd thought myself unobserved, I couldn't stop myself from tracing the wound. My fingers scrabbled at its scabbed edges, prodding the reliable pain of the exposed flesh. It was The Confessor's last touch, and I couldn't let it go.

Piper pulled my right hand towards him and turned it over. It was dirty – we all were – but two of my fingernails were crusted with tell-tale blood, from where I'd picked at the wound.

I thought he might shout at me, but he only exhaled heavily. 'We can't afford for it to get infected. Not out here, not now.'

He didn't say it, but I knew what he meant: not after all these people have died to keep you safe. As if I didn't think of them all the time already. Not just Kip, but the dead islanders too. Their blood weighed on me until the blood in my own veins was heavy. I'd hardly moved since we arrived at the river.

He picked up the dampened cloth that he had been dabbing at my neck. Gently, he wiped my hands clean.

'Tell her,' said Zoe from behind him.

He nodded, without turning around, but paused before he spoke. 'We're leaving.'

I didn't reply. These days, even my words felt heavy – the few times I spoke, I half expected my words to drop at my feet, gathering in the ash.

'If we're going to stop Zach, we need to move now. Destroying the silo machine was a huge step. They'll try to rebuild it, but from what The Confessor told you, she was the key to the whole thing. And she was central to so much of what they did. It was The Confessor who led them

414

to the island. Getting rid of her has been the biggest strike you could've made against the Council.'

'I didn't do that,' I said. 'Kip did that.'

Piper nodded. 'And it's huge. The Council will be reeling from losing her and the machines. The fact that Zach was afraid, that he had to cover up your involvement to protect himself – that shows what a blow it is to them.'

'But it's not enough,' Zoe said. 'We need to do more, while they're still dealing with it.'

'She's right,' said Piper. 'We need to head west, join up with the resistance –'

'What's left of it,' she added.

He went on. 'We need to act. It'll be risky, but we can't stay here, hiding. The Omega Assembly will be gathering again, trying to see what's left after the island.'

I was still silent.

'We can't make you come with us,' he said.

Zoe shifted impatiently. Behind her, the sun was beginning to lower. Through the ash-clouds the sunset was like a blaze of light on a darkened mirror. It was beautiful and terrible. I wished Kip could see it.

I looked up at Piper. 'We should leave tonight. We need to get back to the coast, try to find word from the missing ships.'

'They can't be the priority,' said Zoe. 'We don't even know if there's anything out there to be found. But right here, now, there are safehouses burning, people in tanks.'

'I know,' I said. 'And I'll do everything I can to help with the resistance, and the tanks. But if we're going to fight back, and rebuild the resistance after the island, we need to give people something to hope for. An alternative. We have to be able to offer them something more than this.' I gestured at the charred valley.

'Have you sensed something? Had a vision about Elsewhere?' said Piper.

I shook my head. 'No. It's got nothing to do with being a seer. I don't have any guarantees. Elsewhere's still just an idea. But once, a long time ago, the island was just an idea. Before it ever got started.'

Zoe started flicking her knife in her nails again. Piper, though, was still kneeling in front of me, his face close to mine.

'You know I want to believe in Elsewhere,' he said. 'I'm the one who's sent the ships. But it's a leap of faith – you know that.'

I remembered how Kip had taken a leap of faith, following me to the island before he knew it was real. And how his final leap, too, was a leap of faith: how he believed that saving me would be worth something.

'What if the ships never come back?' Piper went on. 'What if we never find Elsewhere?'

I stood up. 'Then we'll have to make our own.'

*

We rode off before midnight. We were so close to the deadlands that the darkness seemed only an extension of the blackness that had already coated the landscape. After the listlessness of the last week, it felt good to be moving again. Zoe's tall back was warm in front of me, and I could hear, but not see, Piper's horse ahead. We were heading west again, closer to the island, where blood still flaked from the cobbles of the empty streets. Closer to Wyndham, where Zach waited. And closer to the indifferent sea, where two of the island's boats still sailed in search of a place that might not exist.

Acknowledgements

It's a delight to acknowledge the readers whose advice and enthusiasm helped to shape this novel. For invaluable feedback, sincere thanks to Andrew North; Sally, Alan, and Peter Haig; Clara Haig-White; Sharyn Pearce; and Lucy Carson. I've also benefited from the insightful suggestions of my editors, Emma Coode and Natasha Bardon at Harper*Voyager* (UK), and Emilia Pisani and Adam Wilson at Gallery Books (USA).

Special thanks to my brilliant agent, Juliet Mushens, a passionate advocate and an astute reader. Thanks also to Sasha Raskin, for skilfully representing the novel in the US, and to Rich Green, for handling the film rights with panache.

I'm extremely grateful for the award in 2010 of a Hawthornden Fellowship, during which I worked on this novel. I was also fortunate to receive funding from the Faculty of Humanities and the Department of English at the University of Chester, which provided me with writing time at the wonderful Gladstone's Library.